THE ELGIN CONSPIRACY

JULIA GOLDING

One More Chapter
a division of HarperCollins*Publishers* Ltd
1 London Bridge Street
London SE1 9GF
www.harpercollins.co.uk
HarperCollins*Publishers*
Macken House, 39/40 Mayor Street Upper,
Dublin 1, D01 C9W8, Ireland

This paperback edition 2024

1

First published in Great Britain in ebook format
by HarperCollins*Publishers* 2024
Copyright © Julia Golding 2024
Julia Golding asserts the moral right to
be identified as the author of this work

A catalogue record of this book is available from the British Library

ISBN: 978-0-00-863689-0

This novel is a work of fiction. Any references to real people, places and events are used fictitiously. All other names, characters and incidents portrayed are a work of the author's imagination and any resemblance to actual persons, living or dead, events or localities is entirely coincidental.

Printed and bound in the UK using 100% Renewable Electricity
by CPI Group (UK) Ltd

All rights reserved. No part of this publication may be reproduced, stored in a retrieval system, or transmitted, in any form or by any means, electronic, mechanical, photocopying, recording or otherwise, without the prior permission of the publishers.

To Joe Gallagher, with thanks for your enthusiasm for my writing and for your Hollywood hospitality.

Chapter One

Stonehenge, Salisbury Plain

Dawn approached. Three members of the Society of Roman Knights stood in their druidic robes and waited for the sun to edge above the horizon. Half buried in the mist that clung to their knees, they seemed pale ghosts of the ancestors who had raised the Sarcen stones into this circle.

A fiery edge appeared on the north-east horizon.

'Approach, Brother Quintus,' said the eldest, face hidden in his hood. The three men turned to the shadows where he waited.

Dressed in the black robe of an applicant, Quintus walked into the ring from the west. The sun dazzled him as it rose, framed by the Heel Stone. The drama of the dawn was breathtaking. He relished his moment entering centre stage, thanks to the stone proscenium arch erected by the druids to worship the sun. His presence here might be questionable, but Quintus wondered if at least half of his battered heart was not sincere when it leapt in response to such sights.

'Brother Quintus, you have chosen your Roman name and put

aside your old identity. You have passed our initiation rite. By your oaths, you have sworn adherence to our sacred principles. Do you hold firm to your intention to become a Roman Knight?'

Quintus hid a wry smile, thinking that turning up in this desolate spot before dawn should be proof enough. 'I do.'

'Then kneel.'

Quintus knelt on the grass and bowed his head, feeling a thrill of excitement. He was so close now. The cold steel of a naked sword kissed the back of his neck, and he barely contained a shudder. He was not a man to give his trust easily. Only absolute necessity made him endure anyone getting so close with a deadly weapon.

'Do you agree from this day on that you will comport yourself with the honour of a legionary?' asked the elder.

What was honour? Quintus had never been sure. One person's honour was another's treason. Still, these knights were not men to appreciate the quibbles and queries in which he took delight. He had a part to play. 'I do.'

'Now receive your ring, sign of your allegiance to our cause.'

Quintus raised his face to see the man to the right offer him a bronze ring on a velvet cushion. The ring bore an engraving of a two-headed eagle and the motto – *Temporis Vtrivsqve Vindex*.

Champion of each era.

I am certainly that, he thought, slipping the ring onto his finger. His life was dedicated to championing what remained of the past. In a modern world of small people fighting foolish wars, it was the one thing that made everything else worthwhile, all the lies, the subterfuge, the killing.

'By taking this ring, you join us in the noble fight to rescue our history from foreign perversions.'

The elder continued with his speech. Quintus mused that, for all these fine words, there was only one champion who stood a chance of achieving victory in the rush to preserve the past, only one truly great man. That was the commander he had chosen to serve – and he did not stand among the men before him.

The elder concluded his speech.

'Welcome, Knight Quintus,' intoned the ring-giver.

The third man was silent. Unease crept up Quintus's spine.

When nothing more happened for a moment, Quintus made to get up. He allowed himself a little self-congratulation. After months of work, he had been given entry into one of society's most secretive associations, the Guy Fawkes allowed into their parliament. What havoc he could make from within!

The sword touched his shoulder.

'Stay down, Quintus,' said the elder. 'Now you are a full member of our society and put yourself under our authority, there is one more piece of business to be done before we leave this hallowed place.'

Quintus's heart began to race. He recognised this feeling from the brink of past battles. Think, man! This was outside the usual protocol as his informant had described it. Had they realised that he was not what he claimed? He should run. But where could he go? They were in the middle of Salisbury Plain. It wasn't likely he would get far – three against one. He was foolish to have left his most effective weapons behind when he'd donned this pocketless robe in the carriage. Still, he had a stiletto in his boot. He could take at least one of them with him.

'What business is that, sir?' He was proud his voice remained steady and affable.

'You will address me as Sir Knight,' corrected the elder.

'Sir Knight,' echoed Quintus.

The elder threw back his hood and basked in the arrival of morning, no longer hiding his identity. Meeting the senior knight face-to-face had been one of Quintus's goals coming here. He didn't recognise the gentleman. Maybe not a London man? The rising sun flushed the elder's face and hands with a bloody light. He had the craggy face that would've suited a Roman centurion.

'Some objected to your application, but my colleague argued it was better to turn you from a weapon used against us to one we can employ in our service.'

He didn't like the sound of that. No one should think he had any sharp edges at all.

'We have been watching you, as we watch all applicants,' the elder continued.

That couldn't be good. 'I hope you were not bored. I live a very quiet life.'

There was a snort of derision from the ring-giver.

'We need to talk about blackmail,' said the man on the left, speaking for the first time. When he pushed back his hood, Quintus recognised him immediately and swore under his breath. A client – here? That was a nasty surprise and could spell disaster. He must be the colleague the elder mentioned.

The man produced a book from his robes and dropped it on the ground before him. It flopped open to a particularly vivid page. Quintus knew that volume of illustrations all too well. They were incendiary stuff.

'Consider your answers carefully or you will not leave here alive,' said the man who Quintus had thought of as one of his best customers. 'Tell us what you were planning to do with this.'

Chapter Two

1812

18 May, Newgate Prison, London

The crowd was strangely quiet for the execution of John Bellingham, the assassin who had shot Prime Minster Spencer Perceval but a week before. Dora Fitz-Pennington had expected them to be celebrating and jeering, yet the mood in the prison yard was respectful.

She tipped the doorman to let her into the packed yard despite her late arrival. Having by unhappy chance witnessed the deed in the Houses of Parliament and then attended the trial, she had felt obligated to be present for his punishment. She was already regretting that decision as it would be a sad business. However, she had an appointment to keep and could not back out now.

Weaving her way through the crowd, she joined Dr Jacob Sandys under the prison-yard clock as they had agreed. Tall, suitably sober in his black jacket, trousers and top hat, Jacob was easy to spot in the throng. At least, her eye was always drawn to him, no matter the company, like a compass needle to the north. He had most recently been her partner in the Hellfire investigation, had become her lover, though she was no longer sure what he was to her. It had become a pressing question that needed an answer, but not one to be settled right this moment. There was a death to witness.

Jacob brushed his fingers over the back of her hand as they were jostled together by the spectators.

'Are you well?' he asked.

She looked up and caught his concern. She hadn't been to a public execution before. By contrast, Jacob's time in the army had made him an old friend of death on battlefields, in hospitals and as the result of military discipline.

'I can bear it. I'm no coward.'

'That's the last word I'd apply to you, Dora.' His pale blue eyes, so cold to others, warmed when they looked at her. She felt a little flip in her stomach, the connection between them still strong. He wore his dark hair a little longer than fashion dictated, brushing his collar, but she liked that about him. It helped her remember, when his upper-class status daunted her, how close he was to his wilder side. How, beneath the buttoned-up demeanour of the gentleman that he showed the world, was a passionate artist.

That thought was interrupted by a shove. Served her right for wool-gathering. She righted her bonnet, knocked askew by a man behind her. Jacob scowled at the offender, earning her a muttered 'Sorry, miss' and a little more space.

'*Is* Bellingham mad, do you think?' she asked Jacob. That defence had been argued in the trial at the Old Bailey, but the judge had dismissed the plea.

He shook his head. 'Not under any medical definition. Many

merchants suffer ill fortune. He should've blamed the Tsar for his imprisonment and losses, not Spencer Perceval.'

His answer revealed anew the gap between them, her a lowly actress and Jacob, the son of an aristocratic family. He'd never known the grind of hunger or homelessness. A merchant's woes were far separated from his world; even gentlemen of imagination like Jacob struggled to understand those on the lower rungs.

'Poverty can drive a man to take extreme action. He was facing ruin.'

Jacob grimaced. 'My sympathy for Bellingham has its limits. Others suffer and they don't murder to lessen their own pain. He became obsessed that Perceval was behind it all.'

'Obsession can be a kind of madness,' she suggested.

Any reply he might make was cut off as the clock struck noon and the door onto the gallows opened. It felt horribly like curtain-up – the same feverish expectation.

Bellingham, a square-jawed man with long sideburns and a prominent nose, stepped out, accompanied by a warder and a priest. The scene felt unreal – that man was going to die. Why was he so calm? If she were up there, she'd be making a last-ditch attempt to escape, because what was there to lose? His shackles had been removed but his hands were tied behind his back. A few words passed between priest and the condemned to which Bellingham nodded. His head was held high. Mad or sane, he was going to his death having believed he'd made his point.

The executioner did not linger. He put a blindfold on Bellingham, slipped the noose over his neck, gave the rope a tug to check it was secure, then stepped back. Without further ado, he pulled the lever to release the trap and Bellingham fell sharply, the jolt on the rope indicating his neck had snapped. Dora released her held breath.

'It's over,' said Jacob, squeezing her hand.

She pressed his fingers in return. 'I'm glad. Anthony told me they often botch hangings.'

'Unfortunately, your brother would've witnessed ones in the army done by amateurs, but they don't usually make mistakes at Newgate.'

'Yes, it's all very professional here, isn't it?' Her tone was bitter. Many a thief of a pocket watch had had their life stolen by Jack Ketch – hardly a fair exchange. She shivered and wrapped her arms around herself.

Noting her misery, Jacob frowned, but he attributed it to the wrong cause. 'Your brother, God rest his soul, enjoyed scaring you rather too much.'

Anger flared. 'And now he will no longer have the chance to do so, will he?' Her eyes glistened with tears. She told herself it was the dust in the air and swiped them away. There had been too much death in her life of late. Anthony had been murdered but a month ago. 'I would give anything to have him back, even with his gruesome stories.'

'Of course, you would. I didn't mean to add to your distress.' His tone gentle, he drew her away through the people massed within the walls of the prison. Some surged closer to the scaffold, believing it lucky to touch the hand of a dead man. They were unlikely to succeed as Bellingham was now the property of the anatomists and they were jealous of their prize.

Jacob guided her past a seller of penny pamphlets already immortalising the story of the only man to assassinate a British prime minister. They emerged through a side gate and onto Newgate Street. Carriages waited to collect the notables who came to witness the death on behalf of the Crown, while the commoners clustered, squeezed into too small a space.

'Lord Byron! It's him!' So ran the whispers through the crowd like a burning fuse leading to a powder keg. Dora looked up in time to see the poet withdraw with a wave from the window where he had been watching proceedings, breaking the spell over his admirers who had come to watch it with him. Even Dora felt the thrill of glimpsing the famous writer.

'Did you see him?' she asked Jacob.

'Who?'

'Byron is here.'

Jacob gave a huff. 'He's everywhere – drawing rooms, balls, in the newspapers. Doubtless, he's rushing off to write a sonnet on Bellingham and feed the public appetite for his jaded wisdom.' From his scornful tone, Jacob was not an admirer of London's latest celebrity. He frowned down at her, doubtful. 'You don't like him, do you?'

'Me? I haven't spared him much thought.'

'Good.' He sounded jealous and, for some reason, that lightened her mood.

An elbow in her back recalled her to their predicament. There were too many people in this street and the mood was impatient, voices rising in protest. The crowd surged, someone stepping on the heel of her boot, making her stumble. If she hadn't been holding on to Jacob, she might have gone down and been trampled. Unease stirred in her chest, a tightness of breath as awareness of the danger grew. The slightest alarm could turn it into a stampede.

'Dr Sandys!' A man hailed Jacob from inside a carriage. No ordinary conveyance, it had a coat of arms on the door. A nobleman's coach. 'Fearful crowd today, is it not? Might I offer you a ride?'

To her chagrin, Jacob hesitated. Did he not want to get into the carriage with her? Was he ashamed to be seen in her company? However, he must have seen the danger and chose the lesser evil.

'Thank you, my lord. My companion and I would be much obliged.' Rescuing her from the sea of people, he handed Dora into the lifeboat of the carriage. 'Lord Elgin, this is Miss Dora Fitz-Pennington.'

An earl, no less! This might be normal life for Jacob but for Dora she thought this might be the first time she had ever met so elevated a personage. No wonder Jacob hadn't wanted to introduce her lowly self to him.

Lord Elgin nodded to her. 'Miss Fitz-Pennington, a pleasure to meet you.'

It was a relief to get out of the press of people even if meant cosying up with nobility. The carriage was a cocoon of calm after the storm outside.

'My lord,' she said warily. She had expected a nobleman of his rank to balk at meeting a humble actress, so his politeness surprised her.

'News of what you did to protect the nation's secrets from those Hellfire Club lunatics are circulating among those who know,' Elgin continued, explaining his warm reception of her presence in his carriage. 'We are all very grateful to you.' He tapped the roof with his cane, signalling the coachman to drive on. Dora wondered how many common toes would get crushed by the aristocratic wheels of the carriage. 'I'm returning to the Lords to report that justice has been served. Where would you like to be taken, Sandys? I can ask the driver to convey you where you want to go afterwards.'

'Albemarle Street, if you please,' said Jacob. 'I'm staying at Grillon's Hotel. I'll escort Miss Fitz-Pennington home from there.'

She agreed silently that it wouldn't do for an earl's carriage to take her to her modest lodgings in Camden. Her neighbours' tongues would wag. They already thought she was Jacob's mistress, an impression she hated from the bottom of her heart. If an earl was added to the gossip, she'd get no peace.

The carriage finally escaped from the crush in front of the prison and joined the traffic on Fleet Street.

The Elgin Conspiracy

'I take it as a sign that our paths crossed this morning,' said Elgin. 'A storm has blown up in my private life and I believe you can assist me in settling the matter.'

Dora settled back in the corner of the carriage, casting herself as an interested observer to their exchange of news. There was also something about the earl and Greek statues, wasn't there? Some recent diatribe from Byron (Jacob was right – he was everywhere) which had got everyone talking about Elgin's collection.

'I thought you were in calmer waters, my lord,' said Jacob. 'Congratulations on your marriage by the way.'

'Thank you. I will pass on your good wishes to the new Lady Elgin. We have a son now. James. George and the girls are delighted by their half-brother.'

Dora studied the lord's reflection in the glass. Elgin had an oddly blunt nose and the pale complexion of someone who had long been ill, though traces of handsomeness remained in his proud expression and dark-arched brows. He'd make a decent Julius Caesar if he could act – inflexible and confident he was born to rule.

'Double congratulations, then,' said Jacob.

Elgin nodded and gazed out at the view, his thoughts far away for a moment. They were passing around St Paul's, the soot-smudged walls rising out of the city like a nest with a great white egg inside.

'Sandys, you're a man of discretion,' said Elgin, evidently having reached a decision.

Jacob could hardly disagree with that. He bowed.

'And you, Miss Fitz-Pennington.' The earl smiled wryly. 'I mean, a woman of discretion, naturally.'

But not a lady. She nodded coolly.

'Then I'll lay it out bluntly. I am being threatened.'

That was forthright. Who could threaten a lord and get away with it?

'You don't mean Lord Byron's sniping, do you, sir?' asked Jacob.

Elgin waved that suggestion away. 'Attacks from that rhyming cub? I'm not worried about him. He may be lionised now, but the problem for lions is that hunters like to shoot them and turn their skins into rugs.'

Dora had to allow that his was an accurate analysis of the cyclical nature of fame, the wheel of fortune that had you up with the gods at one moment, then down in the gutter the next.

'Public attacks in print I can weather,' continued Elgin. 'The threat I'm talking about is personal. Someone wants to destroy me.'

'Destroy you? In what way?' Jacob asked.

Elgin's eyes glittered with anger. 'At first, I thought it was an attempt to force me to retire from public life. But now one of my archaeologists has turned up dead, and I really think they are intending to kill me, too.'

Chapter Three

Jacob's thoughts went immediately to the one archaeologist he knew in Elgin's circle: an old school friend, Harold Fisher. He had been one of Elgin's classicists assisting with the work to rescue the marbles and was the reason Jacob had met the earl in 1802. A vivid recollection came to Jacob of joining Fisher in Athens on his way to Egypt. In those days, Fisher was bright-eyed and eager, fresh from university. He remembered him crouched over the torso of a fallen goddess, gently brushing away the earth with a lover's care. The Aegean Sea sparkled in the distance as the sun beat down on the Acropolis. It would be a painful loss to hear he had died.

'Who is dead, my lord?'

'Richard Brooking.'

Relief flooded Jacob. 'I'm not familiar with him.'

'One of the Brookings from Wiltshire. His father is a canon in Salisbury Cathedral – a good sort. Brooking was skilled at identifying genuine artefacts from fakes and had a good eye for detail so I had him working on the catalogue of the marbles.'

'I'm sorry to hear of your loss. How did he die?' interjected Dora.

Elgin seemed a little uncomfortable that she inferred this was a personal loss. 'His family are naturally distraught. He was an only son.'

'That's doubly sad.'

Dora was commendably compassionate, thought Jacob, but it was the wrong note to strike with the earl. He hadn't wanted to bring her into the carriage; Elgin wouldn't have the life experience to appreciate a woman like Dora, who defied usual social boundaries. Thankfully, so far, the earl had offered her no insult. He must want something from them.

Elgin ran his finger around his collar and gave it a tug to loosen it. 'Yes, well, the landlady discovered Brooking in a shabby tenement in Soho two days ago, stabbed in the throat.'

'Did he live there?' Jacob wondered what Brooking was doing in a tenement. Scholars, though poor, could usually do better than that.

'No, it was the kind of room let for a few hours. The Runners jumped to the conclusion that he must've been with a...' the earl glanced at Dora, 'a lady of ill repute. I apologise for raising an indelicate subject, Miss Fitz-Pennington.'

Dora nodded. 'Please, go on.'

'The Bow Street Runner investigating the death said he was likely killed for his money, but why then did she not take this?' He dug in his pocket and held out a bronze ring between finger and thumb. 'They gave it to me to return to his parents, but I thought it might provide an indication as to whom he had really been meeting.'

Jacob took the ring from Elgin, read the inscription, then passed it to Dora. 'Champion of all times – or maybe "eras" is a better translation. It looks like a fraternity ring, but not one I recognise.'

'Nor do I,' said Elgin. 'I thought you might be able to find out more about it. Bow Street always seizes on the most obvious conclusion and shows no interest in pursuing this.'

'Perhaps the thief thought this was too identifiable to be fenced?' suggested Dora.

'Brooking was also found fully clothed, though his pockets were empty.'

'I see what you mean,' said Dora thoughtfully. 'Good quality clothes and boots have a value and are not easy to trace. Did you tell the Runners that you were being threatened – that there might be a connection?'

Jacob winced. It was a question that shouldn't have been asked, showing a certain naïvety.

Elgin turned frosty. 'I would not discuss such sensitive matters with a Runner. It would be bandied about Fleet Street by the next morning.'

Dora wouldn't understand this from her position in society, but Jacob and Elgin both knew that going to Bow Street would've been a disaster. The Runners were some of the best informants for journalists looking for sensational stories and Elgin was a favourite subject thanks to his famous collection and acrimonious divorce. Jacob studied the peer, weighing the matter. Elgin did not strike him as a man to take alarm without cause, and his recent history would have taught him to expect enemies around every turn. This did sound intriguing. A mysterious ring. Threats. Danger.

Jacob groaned inwardly. Puzzles such as this were like catnip to him. It was impossible for him to walk away once his brain had begun untangling a mystery, no more than he could put down a novel without reading to the end.

Shaking his head at himself for giving into his impulse – and for not even asking Dora if she agreed with him to begin a new investigation – Jacob heard himself ask, 'We are very interested in this case, my lord. The threats – when did they begin?'

Dora stiffened beside him, obviously noting he had included her in his reply. He would have to apologise later, but he could hardly ask an earl to stop his carriage so they could talk it through.

'The threats?' Elgin gazed out of the window again to gather his thoughts – a habitual gesture, Jacob surmised. Did Elgin wish he were somewhere else, away from London gossipers? They were passing along the Strand, rattling by the Inns of Court and Somerset House. Civil servants, naval and law officers rubbed shoulders, passing in and out of the same coffee houses and taverns, exchanging news and scandal.

'Do you remember how we first met in Athens ten years ago?' asked Elgin.

'I do.' Jacob had been on his way to his post as a surgeon with the army in Egypt. The day at the excavations on the Parthenon had been seared into his memory – blue skies, white stone, the sun grilling him through the columns that still stood on the hilltop. 'It was the day you uncovered the torso of the goddess.'

Elgin's wintry features warmed. 'A wonderful piece. I had to buy the whole house from the janissary before I could get permission to pull it down and dig her out of the foundations.'

'What is a janissary?' asked Dora. Jacob wished she would save her questions until later so he could explain without Elgin seeing her ignorance exposed.

'An officer in the Ottoman army,' said Jacob quickly. 'The Turks have made the Parthenon into a garrison.'

She wrinkled her brow. 'I thought it was a temple to Athena?'

'History does not stop with the Ancient Greeks, Miss Fitz-Pennington,' said Elgin magisterially. 'First, it was a temple, then it became a Byzantine cathedral, latterly a mosque. The Parthenon had seen many tenants over the centuries.'

'That is why Lord Elgin brought the marbles back to London,' added Jacob, hoping that would end the questions. He pressed her thigh discreetly with his, wishing she would get the hint. Not that he blamed her for asking, he himself had been full of questions ten years ago. It had been disorientating to visit Athens after seeing illustrations in his father's books on classical architecture. The city had been nothing like the pictures, a diminished place of only a few thousand people. A minaret stood where the great statue of Athena had once daunted her worshippers. Barracks housing the army of the Ottoman overlords crowded the hilltop, goats grazed and chickens pecked, lowly successors to the priests who had performed rites for the faithful. You could pick up body parts of heroes and deities all over the hill, thanks to the explosion in 1687 that had taken off the roof and scattered the statuary. If Elgin hadn't stepped in, it was debatable how much of it would survive long into the new century.

'The day we met was the last golden day. I've not known a peaceful moment since then,' said Elgin. 'My run of bad luck was extreme. Shipwrecks and imprisonment followed. But recent events have made me wonder if it was not so much ill fortune as an enemy seeking to undermine me.'

'Why think that now?' asked Jacob. With his thigh still pressing hers, Dora glowered beside him but kept silent.

'Because I received this the day after Brooking was murdered.'

Elgin passed Jacob a folded paper. On it was a sentence written in Greek.

'*The heavy rains of blood will crush the house,*' murmured Jacob. 'It is a quotation from *The Oresteia.*'

'The play about a vengeful wife stabbing her husband on his return from the wars,' Elgin said pointedly.

'I know what *The Oresteia* is,' muttered Dora.

But that hadn't been Elgin's meaning. 'You can't suspect your former wife surely, sir?'

'Oh, but I can. If not her, then that ingrate she married.'

'But why would either of them do this?'

'I have my theories, but I do not want to prejudice your investigation.'

The carriage rolled to a stop and a footman opened the door.

Elgin called up to the carriage driver:

'Take Dr Sandys and his companion to Grillon's.' Stepping down to the pavement, Elgin turned to them. 'I will leave the matter in your capable hands. Find me proof as to who is sending threats and killing my people and I will see you are well rewarded.

Chapter Four

'Did you mean to humiliate me?' Dora seethed with fury. Jacob had shut down her questions in the carriage, meaning she had scant idea as to what they had agreed to investigate. They had both been engaged, hadn't they? Or did Elgin mean only Jacob was required? Oh, yes how like men to take her presence for granted!

'Humiliate you?' Jacob scrambled to catch up as she stalked off up Albemarle Street towards her lodgings in Camden. 'How did I do that?'

And that was the problem, wasn't it? He didn't even see what he'd done.

'How am I to investigate a case if you don't let me ask simple questions?'

'Exactly – they were simple questions to which I had the answers. I wanted you to save them until we could discuss the case together.'

A street preacher, a scruffy fellow with a mad-eyed look, approached them. He waved a banner in their face. 'The end is nigh!'

'You're right about that,' Dora shot back, to the man's shock. It was high time she went back to her own people. The theatre troupe should be in Lancaster by now.

'Dora, please!' Jacob caught her arm and steered her away from the preacher into a doorway. 'I apologise. I'm sorry.'

She looked up into his beloved face and took a calming breath. She breathed out, letting the two of them become the still point in the world turning around them. Even the cries of the hawkers and rumble of carriages seemed to drop away. She sighed. 'What are we doing together, Jacob?'

A look of panic crossed his features. 'We are working together. Aren't we?'

'But we're worlds apart. There's no future.' She tugged his lapel. 'It was a dream, spun in the aftermath of that night in the Hellfire Caves.' She had wanted that dream, but life had taught her to expect cold-hearted reality.

His eyes showed his hurt. 'I'm sorry I let you down. The opium … it won't happen again.'

'This isn't about your weak moment.'

'Isn't it?'

Jacob was so preoccupied by his attempts to put the drug behind him that he didn't see the far bigger obstacles between them. He'd gone from being fixated on getting his dose of opium to being obsessed with conquering his habit.

'Jacob, our problem is that you don't really respect me.'

His face registered his outrage at that suggestion. 'I do! I adore you. If you'd let me tell you, I'd say I—'

She cut him off. 'I won't allow that word. We've only known each other a month.'

'But what a month it has been, Dora.'

Well, he was right about that. Having seen him in good and bad times, she knew more about Jacob than she did many of her friends in the theatre. Her feelings for him, which were already strong, would only grow if she stayed by his side. Yet society would not let them be together as equals; he didn't know how to treat her as one, and she would accept no other arrangement. If their relationship was impossible, was it not better to end it now?

'I think I should go back north before Mr Thomas finds another actress to take my place. They're expecting me – in fact, I'm long past due. Mr Thomas wanted to put on *Measure for Measure* in Lancaster – I was to be Isabella.'

'No.' Jacob folded his arms, tone mulish.

'What do you mean "no"?'

'You are engaged in this case for Lord Elgin. You can't go back on your word.'

'That was all you. I gave no word.'

'It was implied.'

She threw up her hands. 'That's cank.'

'It is not cank. You were there.'

'Hardly. You wouldn't let me speak!'

'I said I was sorry!' Jacob turned away and kicked a lamppost. She had driven her gentleman doctor to the edge. He had not been so upset with her for weeks. Her heart began to soften.

No, she had to stand strong.

'Jacob, we must face facts. It's time for me to go back to my old life.'

'No, it's not.' He shoved his hands in his pockets. 'I don't want to let you go.'

'You can't hold me here.'

'But we have something extraordinary between us – a chance of happiness. Why would you sacrifice that?'

'Because I am a realist?'

'Or is it because you are afraid to reach for something better than you have now?'

'There's nothing wrong with being an actress.'

'I never said there was. Don't bend my words!' It was Jacob's turn to count to ten to reign in his temper. 'What I meant was that you have no one close, no family. I want to be that person to you, but you are too scared to let me try.'

Of course, she was scared. Letting people close meant they were able to hurt you the most.

'It's not that easy.'

'Naturally not. But difficult things are worth working for.' His blue eyes blazed with determination.

'Are you saying I'm a difficult thing?' Was it wrong to find him even more attractive when he was stubbornly furious like this?

His lips quirked. 'If the cap fits…'

She laughed, letting go of her anger – for now. They were both being ridiculous. 'Jacob—'

'Come back to the hotel with me.' He moved closer and put his hand under her chin. His warm fingers stroked her jaw. 'Let's talk where prophets of doom aren't eavesdropping.' He nodded to the preacher who was crouched at the railing, listening in on their argument.

'All right. We'll talk about this.' She accepted his arm and they turned towards Grillon's.

'Thank you.'

Gathering what was going on, the preacher leapt up and pointed a shaking finger at her. 'Repent, you scarlet woman! You Jezebel!'

Dora rolled her eyes at the harbinger of doom. Of course, he'd point at her and not Jacob. 'Oh, we're doing insults now, are we? And I thought we were getting along so well.'

'Harlot!'

Jacob tugged her away. 'Ignore him – he's a madman.'

'There's a lot of that about.'

'Then we, as the only two sane members of society, must stick together.' He gave her a rueful smile. 'And Dora, what exactly is cank?'

She chuckled. 'A slang word for foolishness. And I think, Jacob, you might be mine.'

Chapter Five

Grillon's Hotel

Dora was sleeping peacefully on the finest linens, much better than the straw of the barn where they had spent their first eventful night together a month ago. Jacob lay on his side and toyed with one of her corkscrew curls. So strong and resilient, like Dora herself, it sprang back even when crushed. With her sun-bronzed complexion and abundant figure, she represented warmth and life to him, so much more attractive than the marble-white ladies found in society ballrooms.

After their argument on the street, they had come back to his room 'to talk things over'. As ever with them, there came a point where their mutual desire had distracted them and instead they'd mended their quarrel in bed. Sometimes it was where they best communicated, so simple, away from the obstacles that the world outside put in their way.

He had no regrets, but there was still much to settle this morning. He was horribly aware that the time given the first stage of their relationship had ticked away – Dora had said as much.

They'd lived in a soap bubble created by events. Would he be able to keep her with him as normal life resumed? He was desperate to find the magic words that would persuade her to stay.

The sound of the clanging urns on a milk-delivery cart reminded him they must soon get up and deal with the other pressing issue: Elgin's commission. A letter had arrived late last night with the official appointment and down payment of expenses.

He let the curl go. So far Dora had rejected all the usual arrangements a woman made with her lover, insisting on independence. Her pride was admirable. She was an actress and could earn her own way. It was he who wanted to regularise the situation; in part because he worried about her and wanted to provide her with security, but also, he feared, because he wanted to make sure it was known that she was his. He wasn't proud of that side of his character. Would the lure to return to her life acting on the northern circuit prove stronger than her desire to stay with him? He had almost lost her yesterday. She had come within an inch of leaping onto the next coach to Lancashire.

But then Elgin had engaged them in a new investigation. The timing could allow Jacob to kill two birds with one stone, though that might be an unfortunate phrase considering the murdered man in Soho.

Dora turned over and opened her eyes. Deep brown, they blinked sleepily as her wits returned. She was a slow riser.

'Good morning, beautiful.'

She smiled and that was his true sunrise. 'Good morning.'

He danced his fingers down her bare shoulder. 'I've been thinking. We should head north today.'

'You've accepted that I'm going back to Mr Thomas' company?' She looked a little disappointed, which he found encouraging. Part of her wanted to stay with him – or so he hoped.

'Maybe eventually, if that's what you still want,' he said lightly, with no wish to reopen their argument. 'However, I thought we should see if Elgin's divorced wife and new husband are behind the threats. The Fergusons live near Edinburgh.'

'Scotland?' she groaned. 'But that's a week's journey at least!'

'Three or four days, if we travel by the mail coach.'

'We'll be churned up like butter even on the turnpike roads.' She ran a finger along his forearm. 'You think they're involved?'

'I don't know, but it is possible.' He brushed aside the sheet and kissed her breast. He could feel the faint throb of her heart and smell his favourite perfume of her skin. 'Elgin is right: it is urgent. One man has already died. We must go at once.'

Not that he was doing a good job of conveying the urgency.

Dora hesitated, seemingly undecided whether to pull him closer or push him away. Sadly, she chose the latter. She slid out of the sheets on the far side of the bed and padded to the washbowl behind the screen.

'I still don't think you need me for the investigation,' she said. 'I've stayed away from my real life for too long as it is.'

He followed her and stood behind her resting his hands lightly on her waist. He kissed her neck. Was there anything more attractive than a naked Dora in morning sunlight? He itched to get out his pencils and sketch her like this. There was a freedom and ease in this moment that warmed him all the way down to his toes.

She sighed. 'Jacob, please don't make it harder for me to leave.'

That was exactly what he wanted to do. If he could use their attraction to bind her to him, he would. 'Come back to bed.' He kissed her again.

'Stop that, you tempter. I can't go back to bed because then I'll have to get up again and do the same thing. Our little holiday from our lives is over.' And yet she softened against him, bringing her back into full contact with his bare chest. She would know he was very interested in taking this back to the sheets from the state of his shaft, but he had something even more important to settle first.

'Get behind me, Satan, you say?' He cupped her breasts. Their weight was delicious, so round and responsive. He nuzzled the hollow under her ear. 'Stay with me. Please. Just for a little longer.'

Dora shivered. 'Jacob, you're not being fair!'

'I'll fight with all the weapons in my armoury, even infernal ones.'

She growled and turned in his arms. 'You're a beast.'

'No, I'm very tame. You have tamed me. Look, I eat out of your palm.' He laid a kiss there.

'But the theatre—'

'—Will wait.' The answer was obvious, wasn't it? They both needed to go north. 'Come with me to Scotland. Help me investigate Elgin's conspiracy and see if you like this life with me.' Pray God that she did. 'If you do, we can send Mr Thomas a generous amount to hire a new actress – in recognition of the loss of your services. If you don't like it, then you'll be nearer your people and can part from me there.'

She frowned adorably at him. 'I have to earn my living.'

'You could make this your living.'

'I don't know… I want to be useful, not a kept woman.'

He gave a choked laugh. 'A kept woman? My dear Dora, if anything, you will be keeping me! I've seen you at work. You can go places I can't, ask questions that come better from a woman. My damnable brain loves solving these puzzles and I need you to help it do it.'

'But would anyone pay us for that?' Dora was a practical woman, the sort who read the contract through all the way twice before signing. He liked that about her.

Jacob nodded. 'Elgin sent a bank draft. He will cover our expenses and give us a consideration on top of that.'

'How much?' She looked wary.

'Two hundred pounds.'

Her eyes rounded in surprise. 'Two hundred pounds! For asking questions? I wouldn't earn that in five years playing every theatre in the land.'

She wrinkled her nose and Jacob dropped a kiss on the tip. 'I don't need his money. You can have it.'

She pushed away from him, disappointingly covering herself in a dressing gown. He preferred their negotiations when they were both naked. 'No, no, this has to be fair, split down the middle.'

She was considering it – he took heart from that.

He picked up his own dressing gown and shrugged it on. 'Very well.'

The seesaw swung again. 'I have a good position in the company and I do love acting. If I give that up, I might never be able to go back.'

He caught her hand in his, meshing their fingers. 'Do you really want a life tramping through mud and icy winds from theatre to theatre over the Pennines? You said it was backbreaking work, tough on the constitution. How long does that last for an actress before her health breaks down?'

'It's a hard life, I grant you. But I like my friends in the company.'

'I'm glad. They seem admirable people from what you've told me. But I more than like you, Dora.'

She put her hand to his lips. 'Hush. Let me think about this.' She stalked to the sideboard and poured herself a glass of water from the carafe. She then got a second tumbler for him and carried it over. 'Just as far as Scotland and the Elgin investigation?'

'That sounds sensible.' Inside he was rejoicing, but he kept his expression sober.

'We will look into this conspiracy together. It sounds important – lives at stake. We don't want anyone else to die.'

'My thoughts exactly.'

She looked up at him over the rim of her glass. 'You're laughing at me.'

'No, never that.' He gulped his water – a gift from her so he treasured even such little gestures – then put it aside. Taking her glass from her fingers, he set it down. 'Partners in investigations. I like that.'

She scowled at him. 'So do I – if you let me ask the questions when and where I want.'

Ouch. He wasn't forgiven yet for the carriage. He'd better distract her from her anger. 'I like investigating.'

'I do, too.'

He eased the dressing gown off her shoulders. 'I like getting to the bottom of every mystery.'

She caught on. 'Oh, do you now, Jacob Sandys?'

'I do, Dora Fitz-Pennington. You are my most intriguing mystery.' He guided her to the bed so the back of her thighs hit the mattress. They toppled together. They had an hour before the carriage to Scotland left the coaching inn. 'But I've remembered that there is an inch of you I fear I haven't yet explored.'

'I find that hard to believe,' she said, trembling delightfully.

'Let me show you.'

Chapter Six

The Great North Road

'I gave in too easily.' Dora sat next to Jacob in the stagecoach as it clattered out of London. She bumped against his shoulder at every pothole and rut so he put his arm around her to steady her.

'I disagree. You made me work for your surrender,' he teased.

Her cheeks reddened but she attempted to ignore her blush. 'I'm not talking about that, and you know it.'

He was delighted by her flustered looks. It was rare Dora was out of countenance; she was normally so confident, or able to act so convincingly that you wouldn't know she felt any doubt. A tentative hope sprang up inside that she might – just might – be persuaded to give him this chance. Look at the two of them, heading north on their next investigation, when yesterday they had been arguing on the street about parting. What a marvel she was. She looked very smart in a navy-blue redingote with black buttons and matching hat – the outfit a gift from him. Her faithful great coat, the garment that had accompanied her the length of the kingdom on their last adventure, was packed in her trunk. It suited a vagabond, or when she masqueraded as a man, but was not the usual garb of a lady who could afford to sit inside the mail coach. The redingote was a feminine version of the great coat and, he had successfully argued, it would cause less comment when they arrived at the Fergusons. He would have to double the tip to the modiste for getting it ready so quickly. He suspected someone else was going without a coat they had ordered.

'I should have held out longer.' Two little lines appeared above her nose which he wished he could kiss away.

'I'm all for that: it increases the subsequent pleasure.' He wasn't normally one to make such comments; only Dora could draw out the playful side of him.

The passengers opposite were fortunately too occupied in a discussion of the latest scandal caused by Lord Byron and Lady Caroline Lamb to listen in on their exchange. Like many women in society, the married Lady Caroline had become obsessed with the poet and was following him everywhere.

Dora poked him in reproof. 'I meant about not going back to my company yet. I can't argue with you when I'm—' She cut herself off with a glance at their companions.

'When you're under the crushing weight of my persuasive arguments?' he suggested.

'Something like that.' She folded her arms, a stubborn tilt to her chin.

He felt renewed stirrings of fear. She was like a wild bird that he could lure only so close and then she would fly off again. 'Dora, I don't want to drag you into something you don't want to do.'

'I know, Jacob. You are a true gentleman – in that respect.'

He grinned, remembering some of the ungentlemanly things he had done with her. 'But I do want you, and a life together, on whatever terms you will allow.' He would offer her marriage if he thought that wouldn't make her jump out of the coach and run for the hills. His family would hate it, of course – such a blot on the escutcheon marrying an illegitimate daughter of a Liverpool alderman – but he wouldn't care. He'd love it. He'd seen her tested and knew she was brave and true.

And did he mention attractive?

A man could do far worse.

He didn't dare let her know how his thoughts had run so far ahead of them.

Their coach passed orchards and market gardens, thatched cottages and village churches, a shepherd with his flock, a girl herding geese to a pond. The birds honked in alarm as the team of horses galloped by.

'I don't think I know what I want,' Dora admitted after a while. 'I'm used to relying on myself.'

Since her brother's murder, which had thrown them together for the investigation of the Hellfire Club, Dora had been coming to grips with a life without any family in her corner. Her father was worse than useless in that regard. Jacob had to remember she would need time to trust him to provide that home for her. And, truth be told, he had to prove to himself that he was worthy of that trust. His relapse into taking opium on the night of the Hellfire Caves fire haunted him.

'Let's not borrow trouble,' he said, keeping back all the words he really wanted to say. 'We have a mystery to solve. Our client suspects his former wife has a hand in this. We start there.'

Her expression lightened with something else to ponder. 'You think her a likely suspect?'

Good. Dora was thinking about their case, not about leaping out at Lancaster to meet up with her acting pals.

'The divorce was bitter, so I can see that Mrs Ferguson might want revenge. I don't discount the possibility.'

A butterfly flew in from the cornfield and landed on his knee. Dora cupped it gently in her hand and let it out of the window.

'A Red Admiral,' said the lady opposite, her attention caught by the movement. 'Do a good deed and it'll bring you luck.'

'I'm pleased to hear it,' said Dora with a charming smile. 'Going far?'

'Doncaster. And you?'

'All the way to Edinburgh.'

The lady chattered on about her family and extracted a few fictitious details from Dora about her and Jacob. Dora implied they were married, which would make them journeying together unexceptional. Jacob found he did not mind at all. Fortunately, the inquisitive lady fell asleep on the shoulder of her companion somewhere north of Alconbury.

Dora turned back to Jacob. 'Finally!' she whispered. 'I'm dying to hear about what happened to bring about the divorce?'

Jacob pulled her hand into his lap and kept his voice low.

'Elgin was right that he had a run of bad luck. It all began to sour on the way home from Constantinople ten years ago. He was caught in France when the Peace of Amiens collapsed. He was Napoleon's most high-profile prisoner for four years and was not released until 1806.'

'No doubt he was kept in a silk-lined prison cell. I've seen how the law treats the nobility.'

'Not in revolutionary France. During that time, the conditions changed from house arrest in Paris, to the most isolated cell in Lourdes, back to Paris, then prison again – all dependent on the political tides rather than anything Elgin did. Napoleon was like a cat with a bird he'd dragged alive into the house, prolonging the misery. I think that drove Elgin to strike out at the one nearest to him.'

'His wife?'

He nodded. 'I kept in touch with them both after meeting them in Athens. I thought their endeavour to rescue the marbles inspiring and corresponded about the finds. They share my passion for preserving the past.'

Dora made a wry face. 'You antiquarians find interest in the strangest things.'

Was she insulting him? 'How can you not be fascinated in saving the relics of ancient—?'

Dora cut him off. 'I'm teasing you, Jacob. You have to admit that you and your fellow collectors can be a little obsessed. You are my best customers, after all.'

Jacob did not like the reminder that Dora had supplemented her income with literary forgeries, sold to gullible collectors in London. Not that he had fallen for one of her fakes – at least, he hoped not. He would have to check his collection when he got home.

She nudged him. 'Tell me about the divorce.'

'Very well. I understand from people in their circle that Mary, Lady Elgin, made the mistake of writing him cheering letters, first from Paris where she worked to secure his release, then from London, when the French let her go home after their infant son's death. That left the earl stranded. Cut off from his friends and powerless, Elgin began to suspect her of being unfaithful even before she left France.'

'I imagine he had nothing but his thoughts for company. That must've eaten at him.'

Dora was always quick to understand human nature, probably from her life of playing so many different characters. 'Mary had always been more popular than him—young, pretty, with a vulnerable air that makes gallant men want to shield her. Knowing she was free and going about society fed his insecurities until he became insanely jealous.'

Jacob was enjoying telling her this story. It was a rare person in his world who didn't already know the details.

'He sounds like Othello. If so, who was the Iago?'

'I'm not sure there was an Iago, or he created one by his behaviour. Robert Ferguson doesn't fit the charge.'

Dora patted her bottom lip with a finger. 'Perhaps *The Winter's Tale* is a better comparison – the husband distrusting anyone his wife liked?'

'From what I've heard Ferguson was sincerely Elgin's friend and helped look after his interests while he was in prison. However, somewhere along the way, Ferguson fell in love with Mary and that is when they most likely began to betray Elgin.'

'Or Elgin thought she had.'

Who knew what really went on in any marriage? Jacob felt little doubt that adultery was involved. 'Whatever the truth of their connection, he chose to think the worst and that threw the lovers together as they fought his accusations.'

'Then he likely created the very situation he feared.'

'Possibly. I'm a little more cynical about human failings than you. Anyway, the marriage had broken down even before he came home, but then Elgin intercepted a letter to his wife from Ferguson – some ill-considered profession of love – and he used that as grounds to sue for divorce. Ferguson did not contest, thinking he could spare Mary a trial. He was slapped with a ten-thousand-pound damages claim – only half what Elgin had asked for, so a mixed victory.'

'Ten thousand pounds! That's an expensive way to gain a wife.' Her eyes were comically round at the sum – the annual income of one of the upper orders in society.

'Ferguson said he considered it a price worth paying.' He kissed her knuckles.

'Love makes us fools,' said Dora, giving him a speaking look.

'Indeed, but that wasn't the end of the scandal.'

'He couldn't leave them alone?'

'Oh, no. Elgin obtained the Act of Parliament needed to

dissolve his marriage and then went after Mary in the Scottish courts.'

'Why? To punish her?'

'He wanted control of her inheritance from her parents.'

'Ah, so it is about money.' Dora nodded. 'Now I understand.'

'Servants were brought in to testify and there were all sorts of scurrilous tales of amorous tussles on the sofa with raised skirts, but no witness could definitively prove Mary's adultery.'

'Really?' Dora snorted, showing how much store she put by that assertion. 'You can have your skirts up around your waist for some other purpose with a male visitor, can you? I imagine the newspapers had a field day.'

'Indeed. One tends to think that the couple should've been more discreet.'

'Does one?' Dora mocked him gently.

He put his arm around her. 'Yes, I do. The Scottish case ended up with everyone losing something. Elgin was refused control of his wife's inheritance because it had not come to her while they were married.'

'Then how could he claim it?'

'He claimed it on behalf of her heirs, their children. His argument was that she was not morally competent.'

'Oh, that's not fair.'

'She had proved unfaithful.'

'Only after her husband stopped believing in her fidelity.'

'She broke her vows. I take a dim view of that, as do most in society.'

'Men do it all the time. What about you and Lady Tolworth?'

'That was different.' He felt the hit. This wasn't the time nor place to argue morality and he feared he might be on shaky ground since the aged Lord Tolworth had technically still been alive, even if in his dotage, when Jacob had his affair with Lady Tolworth. 'The Scottish court decided Elgin could not be trusted with the money and her financial connection to him was severed – ironically, his exorbitant spending on the Greek marbles with her money was considered proof of his profligacy. But she lost her children. Like most divorced men, he has not let her see them since.'

'Wretch!' muttered Dora. 'If I'd known that when we met, I wouldn't have been so polite.'

'He believes he is protecting them from her immoral influence. She had proved morally frail.'

'Humph!'

'And Ferguson also lost. He had to give up his parliamentary seat – a penalty of being an essentially honourable man willing to pay for his crimes.'

'I can see why this bitterness might cause them to send threatening notes to the earl. I'd want to extract revenge too, if I were Mary.'

'But not go as far as to kill one of his employees – no revenge should go so far.'

'I agree with that.'

'I don't want to suspect the lady I met in Athens.' He remembered the laughing young wife, six months into her pregnancy, chestnut curls escaping from her bonnet and flirting with the breeze off the Aegean. She had loved the Parthenon and the excavations as much as her husband. 'But she could well have changed over the last ten years. And the use of that Greek play, the one about a family feud, does suggest it is personal.'

The coach hit another pothole and Dora bounced against him. He helped her sit back in place, not that her weight on him had been unwelcome.

'Thank you. So our mission is to find out if Mary and Robert Ferguson are plotting against the man that divorced her and is keeping her from seeing her children.' Dora frowned. 'If he dies, would she get custody of the children?'

'That's a very interesting question. Very possibly she would, as long as no one suspects her of these attacks.'

'But why kill Robert Brooking? Elgin's their enemy. I'm not convinced the threats and the murder are linked.'

'That's what we are trying to establish. We'll find out more when we reach Raith House. Not that they'd likely admit it straight out if they are guilty, but we need to start somewhere.'

Dora snuggled against his shoulder. 'How are we going to go about this?'

He rested his cheek on her head.

'I've an idea about that. There is more than one stage you can act on, Dora.'

Chapter Seven

Raith House, Kircaldy, Scotland

'Dr Sandys, how utterly delightful to see you again!' Mrs Ferguson, formerly Lady Elgin, rose as he was shown into her drawing room. 'I've sent for Robert. He's out with the steward but he won't want to miss your visit.'

The expression in the lady's whisky-coloured eyes was a mix of openness shaded with vulnerability, like a puppy seeking affection while fearing the next blow. In her early thirties, she retained a youthful complexion of the kind termed strawberries-and-cream by writers of romance, and had an admirably neat, straight nose. Not a stunning beauty, though she managed to be very comely and doubtless still turned heads thanks to her vivacity. Touchingly, she seemed genuinely pleased to have company, even though it was but a travelling doctor.

'I am very grateful you agreed to see me,' said Jacob, bowing over her hand.

'I couldn't be happier to receive a visit. We are a little insular here, so delighted by callers – especially an old friend who knew me before … before.'

He had sent a note ahead last night to give her warning of his visit and he saw that she had prepared by dressing in her society best. Her muslin day dress – which looked to be in the latest fashion, as far as he could tell these things – secured under the bust with a blue satin ribbon embroidered with daisies, her cap lace frothy like sea foam. No one could fault her for her appearance. There was no backsliding into country fashions here. She had tea things waiting for him on the table, a sign that she hoped he would linger rather than just sit the twenty minutes that was the minimum for a duty visit in society. It had to be hard to be such a notorious personage – a divorcee – yet here she was, holding her head high and hoping for the best. Many society hostesses would refuse to invite her to their gatherings and cut her dead if their paths crossed. Fortunately, men were given more latitude to choose their acquaintances.

'And how have you been, Dr Sandys? Are you married yet?' asked Mrs Ferguson. The lady's tone was teasing as she gestured for him to sit.

Was her cheerfulness rooted in defiance or the result of a genuinely sunny disposition, he wondered? And if it were a mask, what else was she hiding? Could she be sending those threats and arranging for young men in Elgin's circle to be killed? It seemed unlikely sitting here in her parlour.

Then again, he had recently made the mistake of assuming an old acquaintance was a decent fellow and he had turned out to be a monster.

'Not yet,' said Jacob. 'I can't find anyone who'll have me.'

Mrs Ferguson's expression dimmed a fraction. 'I imagine you are still considered quite a catch. What brings you to Kirkcaldy?'

'I am here on business and thought I would call on an old friend.'

'Oh? Business in this part of the world? How intriguing.' Revived, she rang a little bell and a maid brought in hot water for the teapot. 'You must tell me more. We live very quietly here. Milk?'

'Thank you.' Jacob accepted the cup.

'Are you thinking to set up as a physician in the area?'

'No indeed. I've left the medical profession for the moment and have become what you might call a confidential agent, acting on the behalf of private clients. I take cases where I believe I can help solve their problems.'

Mrs Ferguson passed him a plate of cakes, trying to puzzle out what that would entail. 'I remember well your expertise in antiquities, Dr Sandys. Do I take it you find items for collectors or evidence of provenance? I might know some local people who would employ such services.'

Jacob recalled how this lady's reputation, before the divorce made her infamous, was of someone who was always thinking of ways in which she could help the people she met. He wished he did not have to spoil his friendly reception by mentioning her former husband.

'How very kind of you.' Jacob selected a cake. 'My partner and I might indeed take on such tasks if we believe we can help.'

Savouring the iced shortbread and listening to local news, Jacob thought of Dora. If he was to persuade her that they could make a success of their joint enterprise as confidential agents, work such as Mrs Ferguson proposed might well prove a productive area. Dora might enjoy hunting down a lost Caravaggio or medieval psalter. The satisfaction of doing that might wean her off her unfortunate habit of forgery. The thought made him smile.

'I think I can hear Robert,' said Mrs Ferguson happily, breaking off her account of the Highland Games.

A voice in the hall announced the return of the master of the house. Jacob braced himself. He had known it would be the laird rather than the lady who would be the true test of his welcome. Mr Ferguson strode in, bringing with him the scent of the woodlands that surrounded the house, and a beagle with a ferocious tail. Both made a beeline for Mrs Ferguson. The dog sat at her feet after a brief petting, the husband stood protectively at her shoulder. His wife patted his hand where it rested on her arm, a sign that all was well.

'Robert, allow me to introduce to you an old friend from Athens.' She skimmed lightly over the introductions.

Robert Ferguson, a gentleman of middle stature with receding hair made up for by luxuriant sideburns, assessed Jacob with a hostile stare. Jacob felt as if he'd just climbed over a fence into what he had thought an empty field, only to find a Highland bull in possession.

'Sir,' the laird said curtly.

'Robert, Dr Sandys has been very kind to me,' Mrs Ferguson reminded him. 'His correspondence has always been very civil and lightened my darkest hours in Paris. What he doesn't know about antiquities isn't worth knowing. And look, he has called in on us while he was on business in the area. That is exceedingly obliging of him. We receive very few visitors here,' she said wistfully.

Jacob wished he hadn't come on Elgin's business. That would dim the lady's happiness once she learned of what she was suspected.

The husband was made of sterner stuff, ploughing through such social niceties.

'State your business, sir,' said Mr Ferguson. 'My wife might believe you are here out of politeness—'

'No!' protested his wife. 'Dr Sandys has already explained. He is here on business as a confidential agent. Do I have that right, Dr Sandys?'

Jacob glanced at Ferguson. Delaying an explanation would only make it more awkward. 'Mr Ferguson, Mrs Ferguson, please believe me when I say that, had I been touring in the region on a party of pleasure, I still would have called in.'

Ferguson snorted but didn't go as far as to call him a liar.

'I perhaps should have explained in my note.' He hadn't because he hadn't wanted to be turned away. Looking at Ferguson, that might well have been the result and still could be. 'I travelled up from London with the sole purpose of seeing you today.'

'You did?' Mrs Ferguson was learning caution. She withdrew a little, like one of the daisies on her sash closing its petals at night.

'I have been asked by a client to ask you some questions.'

Ferguson threw up an arm. 'That's it. I've heard enough. He's here, Mary, because of that bounder, who failed to get at your fortune and will never let it rest. There will be some scheme or other, some new allegation. Send the doctor on his way.'

Jacob had a sudden grim thought that maybe Ferguson was right. Had Elgin invented the whole thing? Might he not be spinning this story of murder and threats merely to make his former wife look bad? If she were disgraced, the money might go to her children who were under his control. Hell hath no fury like a husband scorned.

Jacob held up placating hands. 'Please, sir, hear me out.'

'Why should we? Get out!' Ferguson hauled him up by the elbow, other fist clenched.

'Robert!' exclaimed Mrs Ferguson.

Jacob twisted his arm free. 'The questions are of the utmost importance.'

'We owe that scoundrel no explanations – not after what he put us both through!' bellowed Ferguson. The dog barked.

'Then answer not for his sake but for your own benefit.'

'Ha!'

Ferguson's exclamation alarmed the beagle, who leapt up, looking for the threat, in the process knocking over Mrs Ferguson's cup with its tail.

'Oh, no!' said the lady.

'Emma, bed!' growled Ferguson, pointing to a cushion in the window. The beagle retreated.

Jacob hurried with his napkin to help mop up the spillage. The white muslin skirt was now splotched with beige. The interruption did, however, serve to divert Ferguson from thoughts of doing violence to Jacob.

'Forgive my outburst, Mary. You should put that in to soak immediately,' he said. 'Leave me to talk to Dr Sandys.'

'I … I will.' The lady stood up. 'Please stay, Dr Sandys. I won't be long. Robert, be gentle.' She hurried out, her expression giving away how relieved she was to have a moment to recover her composure.

Ferguson waited for his wife to close the door before rounding on Jacob. 'If you offer that woman one insult, or make her suffer for one more moment than she has already, then you'll regret it! If you are from that damnable earl, you are not welcome here.'

Left to Ferguson, this was likely to end up with Jacob being thrown out on his ear. He had to act quickly.

'You may not believe me, sir, but I am here as her friend,' he said. 'I will come and go without being noted and I believe that the earl will accept my word. If I'm turned away, I fear he will have to send less subtle questioners in my place.'

'What's this about?'

'Threats and … a death.'

'A death? Not one of the children?' Of course, the stepfather would leap to that conclusion. Ferguson was certainly acting as if he had no knowledge of the case.

'No, no, nothing like that. Someone who worked for him.'

'Who would he send in your place?'

'The Bow Street Runners are involved in the case.' Elgin wouldn't send them but the inference was helpful.

The laird scowled but backed down a little. 'You're saying that you are the best of the bad options?'

Jacob settled back in his chair. 'I knew such a lovely lady would not have married a stupid man.'

Ferguson kicked the fire irons. 'You'd better tell me what this is about.'

Chapter Eight

Dora sat primly on the edge of the wooden chair and tried to look respectable. She was Charmian – no, not Charmian, as she had a saucy turn of phrase and ended up dead by asp with Cleopatra. Maria? No, that was no good as she carried on riotously with Sir Toby. Margaret? Absolutely not. The woman got seduced out of a window and plunged her mistress into trouble.

S'wounds Shakespeare, your lady's maids are terrible role models for those seeking employment.

Dora would have to navigate this without a script.

Presiding over the austere office belonging to the housekeeper, Mrs Cameron clicked her knuckles. She was a twig of a woman, a creature of bone and skin on whom the black gown hung like it was pegged on a washing line.

'You are well acquainted with the tasks of a lady's maid, you claim?' she asked Dora sceptically.

The lady had grounds to be wary. It wasn't every day a woman walked into her domain claiming she was qualified to fill a highly specialised position, but that was exactly what Dora had done.

Dora nodded. 'Yes, ma'am.' Privately, she was having second

thoughts about the wisdom of Jacob's plan. The long journey north had given them time to plot their best approach to the Fergusons, and he had suggested she try to enter the household as a servant while he went in as a guest. There was something annoying about that. He got tea and cake in the parlour while she got a duster and mop.

To prevent them from being associated with one another, they had parted on arrival on the outskirts of Kirkcaldy. Dora had walked the last mile into the Scottish town that stretched north-south along a brisk sandy beach. Years on the road had taught her the best places in a new town to find out the local gossip. Talking to the customers at the inn on the seafront had given Dora everything she wanted to know about vacancies at Raith House, the local manor. They had been prepared for her to go in as the lowliest scullery maid, but she had heard that the last lady's maid had left to be married and that the position was being filled by two upstairs maids who were considered ill-suited for the task. The relative isolation of Raith House and notoriety of the divorced Mrs Ferguson had made recruiting the post difficult and thus Dora's application would be attractive. That was, if she could get over the problem of being an unknown quantity in an area where most people knew each other and their ancestors for several generations back.

'Can anyone vouch for you?' Mrs Cameron tapped her fingers on the desk.

Producing an envelope with a deftness worthy of a stage magician, Dora laid it down by the housekeeper's restless fingers.

'I have a letter of recommendation from my last employer, Dowager Lady Tolworth.' At least she had a glowing forged note purporting to be from Jacob's old flame. The lady had come to their aid when they'd investigated the Hellfire Club. Dora judged that Lady Tolworth would not mind her name being used for a good cause – in fact, she would probably think it a lark. As expected, Jacob had protested at taking Lady Tolworth's name in vain – he was determined to wean Dora off her forgery hobby – but Dora had ignored him. Judicious use of turning a blind eye to forgery would help their relationship no end, she had argued. In any case, she was the one with the relevant experience. She had applied for positions before so knew how this would go without a reference. She would be turned away as a troublemaker if she couldn't conjure up anyone to say a good word on her behalf. That was the lesson she had learned at twenty when she had walked out of her father's house on a snowy Christmas Day totally unprepared for the cruel world beyond.

Mrs Cameron laid her hands flat on the letter and bent over it to read the flourishing handwriting, using a pince-nez to magnify the words.

'It says here that you are skilled in the dressing of hair and can make all the necessary small repairs to a lady's garments.'

'Indeed, Mrs Cameron.' Preparing to act five different roles in a week had taught Dora to change her hairstyle and mend her costumes with alacrity.

'How do you get a stain out of silk?'

'I would try a solution of lemon juice and warm water, if lemons are available. If not, I would use white wine vinegar. Dab, don't rub.'

Mrs Cameron unbent a little, the quick answer reassuring her. 'What is in fashion this season for the arranging of a lady's hair at a ball?'

'An antique Roman style is *à la mode*.' This had ironically been inspired by the antiquities the Elgins and other collectors had brought to London from the Mediterranean. 'The front hair is to be curled at the temples and the remaining hair swept up or braided in a low bun. For the best occasions, a string of pearls might be added. I would have to see the lady's hair to know the details of how I would achieve the look.'

The housekeeper nodded as if that was fair.

'But as a married lady, she might wish to consider a Parisian mob cap or a Moorish turban of white satin.'

'No turbans,' snapped the housekeeper.

Ah. Mary Ferguson did not want to be reminded of her time with Elgin in Constantinople. Noted.

'Perhaps the Ann of Denmark hat would be an acceptable alternative?'

The housekeeper let that pass, possibly because that dashing style of hat had not yet reached Scotland and she did not want to show ignorance. 'How did you come to hear of the position?'

Now for her tale. She had plenty of experience delivering speeches of character backstory.

'I recently lost my brother, who was my only family.' That was true and she did not have to feign the catch in her voice. 'I had no one to anchor me to a particular place and I found living in London brought up too many painful memories. I wished for a change.'

'And you chose Kirkcaldy?' Mrs Cameron could be forgiven for sounding sceptical. A wanderer would be more likely to go to Edinburgh which lay not many miles away to the south. There was far more employment there for lady's maids.

'You could say Kirkcaldy chose me. I went as far as my funds would allow and heard about the position in town.'

'Are you often subject to such recklessness, setting off into the unknown?'

Yes. 'No, ma'am. I can only offer the excuse that grief makes us do unexpected things.'

That thought was accepted by the housekeeper.

'My condolences for your loss. Mrs Ferguson will want to see you herself before we make a final decision.' Mrs Cameron paused, assessing the migratory bird who had been blown in on today's wind. 'I will suggest a week's trial. Is that acceptable?'

'Thank you. I am most grateful for the opportunity.'

Mrs Cameron sent Dora away to tidy herself in preparation for meeting the lady of the house. One of the upstairs maids showed Dora to a little room in the attic, a slope-roofed chamber with a view of the distant sea. There was a salty tang to the breeze that came in through the open window. With the cry of the seagulls wheeling overhead, it was like being in a cabin onboard a ship.

'This one belongs to the lady's maids,' the girl said. 'You have it all to yourself.'

There was a bed with a faded patchwork quilt and a straight-backed chair under a window. A small washstand was furnished with a basin and jug, both chipped but finely decorated with roses – probably a hand-me-down from the mistress. Pegs ran along the wall from which to hang her clothes. Dora slipped off her redingote and placed it on the middle peg, like a flag declaring that she – the room's captain – was in occupation.

'Och, that's a verra fine coat,' said the maid.

'A gift from my last mistress, Lady Tolworth.' Dora poured the water into the basin. The maid was still lingering. 'What's your name?'

'Jeannie, Miss—?'

'Miss Pence.' Dora had adopted that name as being not too distant from her real one but far enough away not to recall her association with Jacob and the Hellfire Club case should news of that had reached this household.

'I wanted to be the lady's maid, but I fear I lack the skill.' Jeannie knotted her apron strings.

The girl must be one of the two servants who had been drafted to fill the empty position. No wonder she was jealous of the luxury of a room of her own. She must have been dreaming of stepping into the place. Dora met Jeannie's eyes in the little mirror hung on a nail over the basin. Jeannie was a redheaded lass with a sprinkle of freckles, no more than five feet tall in her stockinged feet. Dora needed allies in the household for her brief stay under the Fergusons' roof. Besides, she liked the girl.

'Skills can be learned, Jeannie. Would you like me to teach you?'

Jeannie practically hopped on the spot. 'If you please, Miss Pence.'

'I do please – if Mrs Ferguson approves of me.'

'She will.' Jeannie darted forward, grabbed a clothes brush from Dora's open trunk, and knelt to remove the mud from her hem. 'Thank you, miss.'

The helpful Jeannie later conducted Dora downstairs to wait for her interview with the mistress. Voices rumbled in the parlour, Jacob comprising the undertone, which was topped by what sounded like an irate Scotsman.

'They have a guest in there,' Jeannie confided. 'A bonny laird from London. He is to bide here the night, so my lady will dress fine for dinner.'

'Very good.' Dora sat on one of the chairs that stood against the wall in the hall, hoping Jeannie would leave so she could eavesdrop. 'Thank you for your assistance.'

Hearing the note of dismissal, Jeannie nodded sheepishly and disappeared through the door to the servants' quarters.

Dora concentrated on the few words she could make out. 'Elgin', 'bastard' and 'blasted marbles' were among the ones that reached her. Mrs Ferguson remained silent. Was she even in there?

'*Ma foi*, what have we here?'

Lost in her eavesdropping, Dora had not noticed the gentleman who had just emerged from the Fergusons' library, book tucked under his arm. She got to her feet and bobbed a curtsy. 'Sir.'

The first thing she noticed about the man was that he was dressed in the latest fashions. He wore trousers tapered to a close fit around his ankles. His blue coat had tight sleeves at his wrists but gathered for more fullness around the shoulders. The most notable feature, however, was the row of buttonholes running down both lapels, a French design which had no utility as it was meant to be worn open. He wore two waistcoats, one plain, one striped, and his shirt had a standing collar fastened with a neckerchief tied in a bow. He could have been modelling for a Parisian fashion magazine.

'Has my luck changed and you are visiting the Fergusons?' he asked. His dark eyes shone with amusement, aware of his flattery. No real guest would be left waiting in the hall, nor would she be dressed in a plain grey, round gown, hand-sewn by the wearer.

'I'm here for the position of lady's maid, sir.'

'Ah. Then you will be a humble person seeking employment, like me.' He gave her a wry smile. 'One of those halfway between the kitchen and the parlour, no?'

He was too well dressed to be anyone's servant. 'And you are, sir?'

'Michel Percy, librarian and archivist, at your service. I rejoice that the dinner table for the upper servants will be so improved by such beauty.'

He was a delightful flirt – how amusing. 'Do such flatteries usually impress the ladies of your acquaintance?'

'Only the plain ones.' His lips quirked into a wicked moue.

'Ah, so you give me a choice. Either I accept your compliment and class myself as plain, or object and make claims for my looks that smack of arrogance. You are making me sail between Scylla and Charybdis.'

He clapped his hand to his forehead. 'And she has a classical education? *Mon Dieu*, this improves by the moment!'

'Not a classical education but a good one in literature. And fortunately, I am an excellent sailor. I will be neither plain nor a beauty and skim past both dangers.'

'Which will leave me to praise your intelligence rather than your appearance.'

'You must do as you will, sir.'

They smiled at each other, the exchange of compliments and denials having gone off like a satisfying rally at lawn tennis. Dora was cheered to pass such banter with a clever man. Jacob had many strengths, but light badinage was not one of them as he had the commendable fault of sincerity.

At that moment the door to the parlour opened and Jacob emerged with his host. The bluff, balding host whom Dora took to be Robert Ferguson ignored her but introduced Jacob to Mr Percy.

'Dr Sandys, may I introduce Mr Percy? He is an expert on manuscripts and advised my wife's parents on displaying their acquisitions from the Aegean. He has brought me some new acquisitions for my library.'

'Indeed, Mr Ferguson has a fine collection of architectural drawings both here and in his other houses. I've been purchasing rare books for him to fill the gaps,' said Mr Percy, no longer playing up his French origins and adopting a sober tone. A chameleon, Dora surmised. Like her.

Jacob took his cue from his host and gave all his attention to the librarian, though Dora could tell he was aware of her, his fingers twitching in her direction.

'Monsieur Percy.' He bowed.

'Please, call me Mister Percy. My parents were emigres from the Terror and I have barely lived in France. I count myself a thorough Englishman by now. Or should I say Scotsman?'

Ferguson shook his head. 'A few days north of the border is not enough to turn you native, Percy.'

'That is a shame as there has always been an auld alliance

between France and Scotland, has there not? There goes my dream of tartan trews.'

'Is that a Parisian accent I detect?' asked Jacob.

Percy gave him a disarming grin. '*Mais oui*. You must blame my parents, *cher docteur*. I was raised to speak French as my first language.'

'My brother knew the Percys, very good people,' added Robert. 'He helped them escape from Flanders where they had fled in 1793.'

Percy bowed to Ferguson. 'My family is greatly indebted to *la famille Ferguson*.'

'Robert?' A lady's voice came from within the parlour. 'Is there an applicant waiting for me? If so, send them in.'

Mr Ferguson waved Dora to go past him. 'My wife will see you now. Sandys, let us go to the library. Mr Percy will no doubt know which books in my collection would most interest a connoisseur like yourself.'

'That would be my pleasure,' said the librarian.

As Dora made to go in, she caught Percy's eye and he winked at her.

'I always enjoy encountering hidden treasures,' he said loudly. 'It is so stimulating, *n'est-ce pas*?'

The incorrigible man was flirting with her in the hearing of Jacob and Ferguson. Perhaps being relegated to the servants' hall would have its compensations.

Chapter Nine

Jacob paced the guest room. He was grateful that he had been allowed to stay. It had been in doubt, but Ferguson had eventually turned his anger not on the messenger but the one who sent him. Rather than being booted out to the local inn, he had been given comfortable lodgings. The chamber was very fine, decorated with blue silk wallpaper and a four-poster with gold-fringed drapes. Add to the picture the cheerful fire in the grate, needed this far north even though it was summer, and he would acknowledge that the bedroom had a homely atmosphere, conducive to slipping between the sheets and sinking into feather pillows. No question that the room was very much superior to the inns they had stayed in on the long journey north. Such a shame that he was finding it so difficult to relax and enjoy it. And it had the very great drawback of not containing Dora.

The kindness from his hosts was the main cause of his unease. Were Dora and he doing the right thing? He had suggested the plan but not really anticipated all that it involved. He quelled his protests about using a forged reference, but he was now plagued with doubts like wasps on an overripe plum. It did not sit well with Jacob that he was party to a deceit. Dora was more flexible when it came to right and wrong.

Should he leave and take Dora with him? It was his fault that she was now employed as a servant but he hadn't meant them to lie outright to secure the post.

His door opened and swiftly closed.

'Dora!' His heart leapt as it always did when he saw her.

'Shh!' Dora stood in her nightgown, back to the door. 'I'm not supposed to be here.'

'Clearly.' He checked his pocket watch. It was one in the morning. 'No one saw you?'

She shrugged. 'Hopefully not. And there's no one in the rooms either side of yours.'

'Well then.' He put the watch on the bedside table and undid his waistcoat. 'Come in.'

Dora grinned. 'I haven't come for that.'

He rather supposed she hadn't. Sadly, being a man, he had initially leapt to that conclusion. However, it would be an enormous risk on their first night under this roof. Better to turn his thoughts to less tempting subjects. 'How is your room?'

'Nothing like yours.' She ran her fingers over a bed curtain then danced them over the silken counterpane. With her hair falling about her shoulders, she reminded him of a Botticelli goddess, or one of his nymphs from *Primavera*. She was magnificent. 'I see the Fergusons are doing nicely for themselves.'

'They have her money.'

'Yes, so they do.' She swung on the bedpost.

'You seem happy.' He wanted to touch her, but, damn it all, he knew where that would lead. Instead, he busied himself untying his cravat.

'I am. Mrs Ferguson appears to be a pleasant lady. She liked what I did with her hair.'

'She looked very fine at dinner. I guessed it was your work.'

He hung the cravat on the back of a chair, adding his waistcoat and jacket to the pile. He had rejected Ferguson's loan of a valet, but he would need one tomorrow if he didn't want to come down in a wrinkled shirt and limp neckerchief.

Dora picked up the jacket and hung it in the armoire. 'She is shy, so I didn't get much out of her today. It is not wise to push things so quickly when trying to elicit information out of your suspect.'

'You are an expert already?'

'Just used to managing people. I sense that when she trusts me, she will be more forthcoming.' She straightened the sleeves of the coats that a servant had already hung up for him.

'Ah.'

Dora frowned at him in the long mirror on the door of the wardrobe. 'What does that "ah" mean?'

'I've been wondering if we should, how can I put this, be more truthful with the Fergusons? That reference…'

'Oh, Jacob.' She closed the armoire, took his hand and led him to an armchair by the fire. Once he was seated, she settled on his knee. With a sensation of something unfurling inside him, he put his arms around her. It was moments with her like this that he lived for. She warmed him more completely than the fire. He hadn't realised how lonely he had been in his life before Dora.

'You're going to tell me I'm too scrupulous, aren't you?'

She burrowed her head under his chin. 'Does that make me unscrupulous?'

'Hmm.'

'I had a conversation like this with Mr Percy. He gave me the sort of compliment it is dangerous to accept.'

'Did he now?' Was the dandy making advances already to his lady?

'I diagnosed him as a practised flirt. We enjoyed our little bout of fencing with words.'

The man had the polished manners many women preferred, unlike Jacob's less easy ways. 'He has too many buttonholes.'

She laughed softly. 'Perhaps. What did you learn from your tour of the library?'

'That both Ferguson and Percy know their ancient manuscripts. There is a copy of *The Oresteia* in the library – a very fine one. Estienne's first complete edition from the sixteenth century, printed in Geneva, with Vettori's additions.'

'Please translate for us mere mortals.'

'Ferguson has a much-sought-after copy of the play in Greek. I would've been more suspicious if Aeschylus had been omitted from the shelves.'

'Then my employer and his French librarian are both familiar with the language of the original?'

'Yes. But that would be true of most men of my acquaintance so that fact tells us little.'

Dora snorted. 'I imagine that most men of your acquaintance forget everything they have learned as soon as they leave the schoolroom. Their brains appear to be full of hunting, stock prices and gossip.' She wrinkled her brow and pointed to places on his head. 'No, I do them a disservice. Perhaps there is a bump for dance steps and another for land management and the tiniest place possible for their wives.'

He caught her finger and kissed it. 'That might be true of the Ton, but you forget I am friends with antiquarians.'

'All right, I accept that it is a common trait among men of your pursuits. Do the Fergusons remain on your list of suspects?'

'I've seen nothing yet to exclude them, hard as it is to imagine the lady involved in anything so wicked.'

'And what about this Monsieur Percy?'

'He has only been here a few days, but he is worth a closer look.'

'Because he's French and has too many buttonholes?'

'Because he is so quick to ingratiate himself with you. Highly suspicious.' He squeezed her, telling her he was joking. Or perhaps he wasn't?

'You are being ridiculous, Dr Sandys.'

'I know. But we should suspect everyone. If the Fergusons are doing away with Elgin's people in London, they would need someone like Percy to carry out their orders for them.' His hand had wandered up to cup her breast, but he forced it down. 'How go your enquiries?'

She took his hand and replaced it on her breast. 'I've made a friend among the maids. I'm going to wheedle my way into the good opinion of whomever deals with the letters to London. If there is a record of what was sent recently, we can see if a message went to Elgin a few days before he received the threat.'

'They might have used an intermediary.'

'Then I'll look for evidence of that too. It is a shame the note wasn't in English. I could then try to match the handwriting to the notes. But as the alphabet is so different, I would need something in the same language. If you can find a sample of Greek from Ferguson or Percy, please steal it away for me.'

'I'll see what I can do.'

'How much did you tell the Fergusons?'

'I mentioned that Elgin had been threatened and that one of his men had died in suspicious circumstances. I made it sound as if we were trying to clear them of involvement rather than that Elgin thought it was them. They were much exercised about even the tiniest suspicion falling on them – at least, *he* was; Mrs Ferguson is past the point of being surprised at anything Elgin says about her.'

'Could Ferguson have been acting his outrage?'

'It felt genuine. He even suggested that Elgin invented the whole thing to damage them.'

'How curious. Do you believe him?'

'If it is true, then Elgin has employed us to do his dirty work for him. He'll want us to find them guilty.'

'That is ... a tricky situation.'

'Indeed. But we have also to consider that Ferguson might be throwing that out as a distraction. He does have much to resent so he could have drawn on those feelings to hide what revenges he had chosen to take.'

'You think he would be the one to send the note, maybe even kill Brooking, without his wife's involvement?'

'Mary Ferguson is not a bitter woman. She strikes me as someone who is relieved to be out of her old marriage like one who limps away from a carriage accident. Why turn back and prolong the painful associations?'

Dora nodded thoughtfully. 'Add to that, the message threatened her own children by implication.'

'You're right. It was the household that was threatened, and they live with him now.'

'Ferguson might resent them for spurning their mother, but she is unlikely to wish them ill even as a pose to upset Elgin.' She turned towards him, causing all sorts of pleasurable sensations in his groin. 'I wouldn't do it. What would happen if one of them did become ill or die?' She ran her fingertip over his brows. 'Would a mother not feel her ill wishes had some part to play in that fate?'

'That's not logical.' And Jacob was finding it very difficult to be logical.

'No, but I'm talking about feelings rather than reason.' She shifted and felt his interest stir beneath her bottom. 'Speaking of feelings…'

'We said we wouldn't.' He helped her shift her weight so that she now straddled his lap.

'I know. Aren't we terrible liars?' She gave him a wicked smile.

He chuckled knowingly and helped her nightdress escape to the hearth rug.

The Elgin Conspiracy

The grandfather clock in the room below struck three. Dora sighed and snuggled against his chest in the big bed that cocooned them. She was asleep but he knew he'd have to send her away before the household stirred. In the long, Scottish summer days, first light was not that distant.

'Dora?'

'Hmm?'

'It's three in the morning.'

'I know.'

'You're in my bed.'

'Well spotted. It's better than mine.'

'You know full well why I'm waking you, you imp.'

She pinched him for that and slid away, her hair dragging across his chest. He wanted to tell her that if they were married, she'd not have to skulk away in the night like this – though if she were playing a part like she was now then perhaps the situation might still arise. He said instead, 'We see this through for another few days, see what falls when we shake the tree?'

Dora wriggled into her nightgown. 'Yes' came muffled from the folds of cotton. Her head popped out. 'We're not harming them, Jacob. We are seeking to clear them. While we do that, I train her next lady's maid and arrange her hair nicely. We all gain.'

'And I track down samples of Greek handwriting and any details about the overly buttonholed Frenchman. I'd like to find out if either of them knew Brooking. Could he have upset them in some way?'

'We need to find out more about the man, who he was besides Elgin's employee.'

'We have to be back down south to do that, but I agree that's a priority. For the moment, though, you search the records of messages sent to London.'

She knelt on the bed and kissed him. 'I will.'

He cupped the back of her head. 'I wish—'

She bounced off, guessing, he suspected, what he was going to say. 'Save your wishes for a well. We have a job to do.'

Dora was right: this wasn't the time to revisit their conversation about their relationship. 'Goodnight, sweet lady.'

She smiled at his *Hamlet* reference. 'Goodnight, goodnight, goodnight.' The last came with a final hand wave as she shut the door behind her.

Chapter Ten

Dora had almost reached the servants' staircase when she saw a light coming up from the floor below. Damn, this could be awkward. She hovered in the shadows. With any luck it would be a servant coming up to bed and so would pass her on their way up to the attics.

Luck was not with her. Michel Percy left the stairwell on the guest floor. She stepped further back into the alcove by the hall table, but his lamp illuminated the hem of her white gown. He held it up higher, revealing her caught like a rabbit in a pen.

'Miss Pence? What are you doing up at this hour?'

To claim she was sleepwalking would be a poor excuse. She needed one that hopped well enough to make him accept it.

'Exploring, Mr Percy. I am incorrigibly curious. I had not expected to meet anyone.' No excuses, just boldness. 'Were you working late?'

'*Tout à fait*. I fell asleep in my chair in the library.' He gestured to a pressure mark on his cheek that did appear to bear out his story. 'My bedchamber is along here.' He stepped a little closer. His coat did indeed have too many buttonholes. She bit her lip to suppress a smile. 'Do you perhaps want to join me for a nightcap? You can tell me about your ... explorations.'

He hadn't bought the story she was selling – and he was right to be dubious. She had been doing exactly what he suspected with the other house guest.

She folded her arms across her chest. 'A kind offer but I have my reputation to consider. I will be happy to tell you in daylight in the library one day. I have plenty of stories that might amuse you.' She backed away into the stairwell, skirting around him.

'I'm sure you do.' He held up his lamp. 'Take this. I wouldn't want you to stumble.'

And have a guest's lamp in her bedroom that she would then have to explain? 'I can see well enough but thank you for the thought.'

'Then, *bonne nuit, mademoiselle*.' He gave her a gallant bow.

'*Bonne nuit, monsieur*.'

Would Percy tell the Fergusons of her night-time rambling, wondered Dora as she laid out the dress she had selected for her mistress. Newly appointed to her position and still on trial, news that she had been wandering at night, in déshabillé, would see her on the road by noon.

The white muslin gown she had spread on the chair looked like a fallen angel. She hung the French lawn slip to be worn under it on the back of the washstand screen. Mrs Ferguson was still splashing at the basin. Jeannie was spending a very long time cleaning the mantlepiece with her duster, watching Dora's every move with avid interest. Dora winked at her.

'Do you have any remarks on my wardrobe?' Mrs Ferguson asked from her position at the washstand. 'What are the fashionable wearing this season?'

'Your gown is lovely but you might want to consider a Queen of Scots ruff.'

'A ruff?' Mrs Ferguson laughed. 'Good lord.'

'One of starched lace, in homage to the Tudors.' Dora had seen it in *Ackerman's Repository* and thought it very handsome. 'You can blame it on Walter Scott's poetry. He has started a hare and all the ladies are running after it.'

Her employer chuckled at the image. 'Then I must get one. As a good Scotswoman, I must be seen to support my namesake.' The slip disappeared and Mrs Ferguson emerged from behind the screen half-dressed with her hair around her shoulders. Dora gathered up the filmy gown and the lady raised her arms. Together they carefully lowered the overdress so that the fragile material did not rip. 'When we reach town, you must send out for one. I'll give you the name of a modiste that I've heard does good work.'

'Town? Do you mean Edinburgh, my lady?'

Mrs Ferguson moved to the dressing table stool. 'No indeed, Pence. We are removing to London.'

'London!' She had only just recovered from the carriage trip north.

'Yes. Something has come up – some news which has made me concerned for my children. We are going to be near them should they need me.' Her voice caught but she busied herself selecting a pendant to wear with her gown, her hazel eyes a match for the amber brooch she considered.

Dora hid her surprise and began brushing her lady's hair – a hundred strokes – before she put it up. They should have anticipated this. Jacob couldn't bring news of threats to Elgin and not expect his children's mother to take alarm that enemies of her former husband might harm her brood. That's what an innocent woman would do – but so would one wishing to snatch back custody should Elgin meet with an unfortunate *accident*.

The possibilities were making her head ache.

'When will you be leaving, ma'am?' Dora asked.

'As soon as possible. Please pack only the essentials for the journey. I have a full wardrobe of clothes in our rooms at Grandmama's house in Grosvenor Square.' Mrs Ferguson held up a carnelian necklace. 'What do you think?'

'That will look very well indeed.'

'The first thing I want you to do on arrival is examine what I have there and make sure I appear only in the very latest designs.' It was unlikely she would be invited out as a divorcee, but if anyone did risk their reputations and call in, she did not want to show signs of rusticating in her exile from polite society. 'I will send out for this month's magazines and we will come up with some stunning gowns for me. As I am to spend part of my summer in London, I wish to make the best use of my time.' Her eyes twinkled. 'We will amaze the society of Raith when we return – with my ruff.'

'Very good, my lady.'

Enthusiasm growing, Mrs Ferguson added an opal ring to her ensemble. 'In fact, send a note ahead. I'll want one of the Walther sisters to wait on me as soon as is convenient.'

Dora had heard of the Walthers of Cavendish Square as being among the most sought-after modistes. 'I'll do so immediately I've finished arranging your hair. The satin Flora cap?'

'With the yellow ribbon.'

When the lady had gone down to breakfast, Dora picked up the discarded nightclothes. Jeannie was now polishing the silver-backed brushes as earnestly as any bootblack after a tip.

'How am I to send a note to London, Jeannie?' Dora asked. 'Can you tell me whom I need to see?'

'That would be Mrs Cameron, miss. She sends out all the family letters. Nae doubt she'll be sending one today to warn

Lady Manners that the master and mistress are on the road. Yours can go in the packet if you're gleg.'

'Gleg?'

'Och, sorry, miss. I mean "quick". I'm trying to learn proper English. I wish I could come to London.' Jeannie squeezed her duster.

'One day you may. And you speak very well. I like to learn new words – they enliven the language.' The stage thrived on fresh ways of putting words together. 'Did you know that Shakespeare invented at least a thousand words?'

'Well, then!'

'What did you learn today?'

Jeannie chattered away as they headed for the housekeeper's office, revealing that she had both paid attention and taken note. She would be a valuable source of information on the goings on in the household if Dora could wrangle more time with her.

'Will you help me pack the lady's trunk, Jeannie?'

'Oh, yes please!'

'Then come back this afternoon and I'll show you how to fold clothes so they don't get wrinkled.' She paused at the housekeeper's door. 'Who else will be going, do you know?'

'I would guess yerself, Mr Hambleton, Mr Ferguson's man, most likely Mr Percy, and one or two of the footmen.' With a skip in her step, Jeannie hurried away before the housekeeper caught her loitering.

'Come!' said the housekeeper in answer to Dora's knock.

She found Mrs Cameron entering figures into the accounts, her spidery handwriting nothing like the bold strokes on Elgin's note.

'Ah, Miss Pence. How are your duties?'

'Very agreeable, thank you. I have a letter to send to London and Jeannie informs me that you are the person to see about that.'

'What letter?'

'To my lady's modistes.'

'It will have to go in the afternoon bag. You missed this morning's.' Mrs Cameron took a slim volume off a shelf behind her and opened it at the current page. 'Address?'

Dora handed her the letter. Mrs Cameron sniffed.

'Is there a problem?'

'No – well, yes. You understand the delicate situation in which Mrs Ferguson finds herself when she leaves home?'

'I do.'

'I fear that she lays herself open to rebuffs.'

'Rebuffs? From tradesmen? But she's wealthy!'

'And they are mindful that association with her might not ingratiate them with their other clients. Please, do not tell her if they refuse her request. It will hurt her so.'

'If they refuse, I'll march into their dress shop and give them a piece of my mind.'

'I rather hope you do.' Mrs Cameron blotted her record, a slight smile warming her features.

'Whom else has she written to, if you don't mind me asking? I wouldn't like to offend her by suggesting approaching someone who has already insulted her.'

Mrs Cameron turned the book around so Dora could see the directions of all the letters sent out. 'I've had to *lose* some of the ruder answers, naturally. Fortunately, there are many accidents that can make a note go astray so she does not yet realise the extent to which her name has been blackened.' She sighed. 'Such a sweet lady.'

'She is not what I expected from reputation,' ventured Dora.

'I had to admit I was angry at first – not that it is my place to be angry, but I've known Mr Ferguson since he was a boy. I thought she had to be a scheming woman to drag him into such disgrace. But you only have to meet her to know that she is but a lost lamb and he the shepherd who saved her.'

That fitted with Dora's estimation. 'Saved her from what?' She pretended ignorance.

'From Lord Elgin. He is a wolf! He might have a fine title, but he is no gentleman in my books. Accusing her of such terrible, indecent things!'

Like having a romp on the sofa with a man she loved? That wasn't too terrible. And, let us be honest here, thought Dora. The lady would have probably been guilty even if not driven to it by Elgin's shabby treatment. Mrs Cameron had proved herself blind to her employers' faults so might not notice if they were up to anything more nefarious.

'Do you mind if I look?' Dora was quickly scanning the recent pages, lodging in her memory as many names as she could. 'Who wrote back with a refusal to supply the household?'

'Miss Collins of New Bond Street was very curt in her reply.'

'I believe she had to close her business due to debt. I saw the notice in the news sheet.'

'Mrs Fiske.'

'She has patrons among the royal ladies and they don't like mention of divorce.' Not least because the Prince of Wales was desirous of getting one from his despised wife, threatening a constitutional crisis.

'Mrs George. That one hurt the most as her establishment is on the corner of Grosvenor Square and had regularly supplied Lady Manners.'

'Then Mrs George will not get any more custom from us. I will make sure of it.'

Having learned all she could, Dora handed back the book and turned to go. Then a final thought struck her. 'How do you know that their replies are rude before you give them to her, Mrs Cameron?'

Mrs Cameron's eyes went to her candle. 'Someone has to spare her the hurt. I'm under the master's orders to see nothing upsetting reaches her.'

She had melted the wax seal and resealed it – and the lady had suspected nothing. Dora was not the only spy in the household.

'That's very kind of you to take that upon yourself. I don't suppose you've intercepted any threats against the lady, have you?'

Mrs Cameron pursed her lips. 'You wouldn't believe the abuse people who have nothing to do with her feel free to send her way. And worse, the immodest suggestions! Madmen, harpies, malcontents: they all creep out of the shadows when they sense someone has been wounded.'

'Were there any threats in foreign languages?'

Mrs Cameron gave her a sharp look. 'Why do you ask?'

'I was merely wondering what I should be looking out for when we are in London. I can read a little French so I should be able to detect any abuse in that language.'

Mollified, Mrs Cameron nodded. 'I'm sure Mr Ferguson would be most grateful. But no French. There was one odd note, a couple of lines in some gibberish, only yesterday. I showed Mr Percy and he said it was Greek.'

Dora's heart missed a beat. 'Did you keep it?'

'No, he threw it on the fire. He said it was vicious and best destroyed.'

'But he didn't say exactly what it said?'

'No. Nor did I ask. I wasn't interested in such filth. Neither should you be.'

Dora had learned more than she expected and pressing her interest any further would undo what good she had done here. 'Naturally. If it is in Greek, I'll certainly make sure it doesn't reach my lady.'

But she would make sure it reached Jacob.

Chapter Eleven

Jeannie knelt by the trunk and spread the tissue paper between the silk gowns. 'Like this?' she asked Dora.

'Yes, exactly like that. A lady's maid should bear in mind creasing is only one hazard.' Didn't she sound the professional? Where had this teacherly tone come from? 'Worse is water damage, as dyes can seep out and ruin a whole trunk of clothes if you are unfortunate. Never use coloured paper or newsprint.' As Dora had learned one wet winter when her pink Titania costume had gained a prominent blue rectangle thanks to a damp volume of plays.

'Will ye be travelling with milady?' Jeannie counted out the correct number of shifts.

Dora tidied the dressing table. 'I believe I'm to be in the second carriage with Mr Percy and Mr Hambleton. Dr Sandys is travelling with the Fergusons.'

Jeannie giggled. 'Then ye'll have two gallants to squire you!'

Dora smiled at her in the mirror. 'Is Mr Hambleton a gallant? I'm not sure I can survive so many days of flattery.'

'Och no, nae that one. He is quiet and kind. He'll let Percy rattle on but if ye are distressed he will put a stop to it.'

'Hmm.' That went with Dora's estimation of Ferguson's valet who had barely spoken at the senior servants' dinner table. 'How long has he been with the master?'

'Years and years,' said Jeannie. 'He has been the only man in that position since Mr Ferguson came of age and took on his own valet. They were friendly as laddies and went fishing and snaring together. I heard they even shared a tutor when they were wee, before the laird went to school.'

And thus Hambleton would be an invaluable source of information, could he be persuaded to talk. Did those lessons include Greek, she wondered. As a loyal retainer, would he go to London to carry out the Fergusons' vendetta against Elgin? But how did that fit with Mrs Ferguson also being threatened? 'And Mr Percy?'

Jeannie blushed. 'He is charming.'

'Too charming. I hope you haven't paid any heed to his flattery.'

Jeannie wrinkled her nose. 'Nae me, miss. I'm not the kind to attract his eye. He prefers women o' yer stature.' She straightened the lace on a petticoat. 'But Rachel from the dairy went courting with him a couple of times when he visited before. He is very attentive, she says.'

And doubtless a very good lover. 'I hope Rachel is old enough to know that a man like that is not serious about courting a dairymaid.'

'Donna fash about that. If ye meet Rachel, ye'll ken what I mean. She is courted by all the lads and has them dancing to her tune.'

'I think Mr Percy is playing quite another song. What do you know about him?'

'He is often in London working for gentlemen of learning, and at Mr Ferguson's other estates, all because he is an expert in the books the laird likes to squirrel away.'

Dora smiled at the description, recalling that she knew another man who liked to collect his hoard. She would have to accuse Jacob of being a fluffy-tailed rodent and see what he said. She sorted out a casket of trinkets to add to the packing, mostly ornamental hairpins. The valuable items would go in Mr Ferguson's strong box. 'I hear he owes the Ferguson family for his family's rescue from the Terror.'

'His parents do, certie. I dinnae think that the laird expects Mr Percy to be grateful. He is verra fond of him – helped him in his schooling, according to Mr Hambleton.'

So Mr Hambleton wasn't always silent – that was good to know. And Percy might feel so grateful he would do what Ferguson asked – that was another thread to tug.

'Do you know where he studied?'

'One of those southern places – Oxford or Cambridge.' Jeannie waved vaguely in a direction she believed England lay, but approximated more to the sea. 'He is fearfully knowledgeable about auld books and subjects that are far beyond my ken. As they say, there's nae so queer as other folk.' Jeannie stood up and rubbed her knees. 'How is that?'

'Perfect. I will close the lid. You were saying about Mr Percy?'

'Only that he's always writing to other experts. Mrs Cameron says the message bag is full of letters going to and fro to his friends in London and even abroad when he's here. She keeps a tally on the cost and says he is using double the amount Mr Ferguson did when the laird was a member of Parliament!' Jeannie lifted the lid and let it drop down over the trunk's contents. 'Great packets come and go full of books and pamphlets on which she has to pay the carriage. He never lets anyone else open them.'

'Really?'

'Och, aye. He was furious when Mrs Cameron cut the string on one to see what was inside. It caused bad feeling in the servants' hall – it was almost as if he accused her of stealing.'

'I imagine that did not go down well.'

'Nae, it didnae. Mrs Cameron is always happier when Mr Percy goes away. We should all have a pleasant few days once you leave.' Jeannie cheered herself up with that silver lining to being left behind.

'Indeed.' But before they left, Dora wondered if either Jacob or she could sneak a look at one of those mysterious packages. She had a strong Pandora streak in her character, wanting to lift the lid on any secret.

Her packing duties complete, Dora decided her next step was to engineer an opportunity to encounter Jacob to tell him about the Greek threat sent to Mrs Ferguson, or, failing that, sneak into the library herself to search for evidence concerning Percy's dealings with parties beyond the household.

A footman stood on duty in the hall, a tall fellow with a boxer's cauliflower ears, who looked down his broken nose at all callers.

'Have you seen Dr Sandys, Andrew?' she asked. That didn't sound appropriate. She needed to be less direct with her questions or their connection would be obvious. 'I wish to ask him about a powder for the headache.' She smiled feebly and pressed a wrist to her forehead.

'You are out of luck, Miss Pence. He has gone ahead with the master, setting off but a few minutes before.' Andrew rocked with self-importance on his heels.

'Gone away, or out for a ride?'

'They are riding to secure lodgings in the first inn on the road. Mr Ferguson left orders that the family carriages follow as soon as the mistress is ready, but he expected her to be off within the hour.'

'I will check with her now.'

Jacob hadn't even had time to say goodbye. Dora supposed that would have been too risky. They had sailed far over the line last night. Morning had come with a dose of common sense.

She went in search of her mistress and found her writing notes at her desk in the morning room, a pretty parlour decorated in primrose yellow and white. Mrs Ferguson looked up as Dora came in.

'Yes, yes, I'm almost ready,' she said, as if Dora had questioned why she was lingering. 'I'm sending apologies to the family and friends we had promised to visit. As soon as this is done, we can leave. There's no need to fret: there will still be many hours of light left for our journey.'

This far north and approaching summer, the travellers would not have to seek their lodgings until at least ten at night. Oh, the joys of the north!

'Your trunks are ready to be stowed, ma'am. I have packed a small valise for the inn. Would you like me to add a book to pass the time?'

'A book?' Mrs Ferguson sounded distracted.

'I like travel stories myself when I'm on a journey.'

Mrs Ferguson sat back and turned from her writing to look at Dora properly. 'You are a most unusual lady's maid, Pence.'

That was indubitably true and she should remember to be less memorable. 'I apologise if I overstepped, ma'am.'

The lady returned to her writing. 'Not at all. A book is an excellent idea. I usually forget and have to do without until I arrive at my destination. Pick something for me from our library.'

'Any preference?'

'Surprise me – as you are already doing.' Mrs Ferguson's smile, a slight tilt of the lips, was charming. Here was a lady whose sense of humour had survived the trials she had undergone. No wonder Mr Ferguson and Mrs Cameron were so quick to shield her.

Dora really hoped she wasn't guilty.

Bobbing a curtsy, Dora took her leave. She hurried through the house, informing the footman that their mistress would be ready momentarily and the trunks should be fetched. That set him leaping into action, calling other servants, and ordering the coach to be brought to the front steps. He enjoyed his moment to be in command, bellowing like a sergeant major. The confusion gave her the chance to slip into the library unobserved.

It was a beautiful room: walnut shelves lined the walls and six tall windows allowed plenty of light for reading. Dora considered herself an expert on libraries, having visited many as a child with her brother as they hunted out examples of handwriting of the great and the good. This one she judged to be a gem and wished she had more time to appreciate it, but the clock was ticking – literally in this case as there was a gilded pendulum clock on the mantlepiece, the figure of Winged Victory pointing to it being past four.

She hurried to the shelves to choose a book for her mistress. At the very least, she needed one in hand to explain her presence ferreting among the room's contents should she be interrupted. Her eyes alighted upon Henry Fielding's *A Voyage to Lisbon*. Fielding was a good enough pick for a journey, she resolved, and it was a slim volume she could slip into her pocket while she got on with her hunt.

The first place she went to search for evidence was Percy's desk. This was in the furthest part of the library, the section reserved for the treasures of the collection. She quickly ascertained that his desk was clear of anything of interest. It contained the usual paraphernalia of a bibliophile – ink, catalogue slips, glue and a basic kit for repairing worn volumes. Sitting in his chair, drumming her fingers on the leather top, she studied the arrangement. This area held the old books that no one would take out without express permission of the master, a decree enforced by the locked cases – and the key hadn't been in the desk drawers. That was unfortunate since she quickly saw that several packages addressed to Mr Percy were on the lower shelves, still wrapped in their brown paper. The only way to get at them would be to pick the lock – and if she were caught doing that, her excuse of searching for a book for Mrs Ferguson would collapse. Kneeling by the shelf, she wormed her fingers through the grill to tug at a loose corner of the paper. All that did was reveal the edge of a volume bound in brown Moroccan leather. The gold leaf lettering on the topmost part of the spine spelt out the title of *Twelve Plates of*— but the rest was hidden. Could she rip the paper?

Before she could make up her mind, she heard the library door open. Percy was already speaking to a servant as he entered.

'That writing case is to go. Forward any letters that come for me to Grosvenor Square and any parcels from Fore's Print-shop on York Street must also be sent on to our new address. They are extremely delicate and must be dispatched at once – unopened.'

'Yes, Mr Percy.'

'Make sure everyone understands my orders, including that busybody, Mrs Cameron.'

Dora got up silently from her crouched position, slipped the book she had selected out of her pocket and drifted to the nearest window as if in search of better light.

'Moonshiny? Is that a real word, do you think, Mr Percy?' Dora said aloud as if she had absolutely nothing to hide by being here.

Percy took a second to take in her presence somewhere he did not expect her to be. He was not happy to see her, unlike their earlier interactions. 'I beg your pardon, Miss Pence?'

'"A calm and moonshiny night" – that's how Fielding describes the approach to Lisbon.' She held up the book. 'I thought my lady might enjoy it on the journey but I'm wondering now I've seen how he tortures the English language.'

Seeming to recalculate his mood, Percy approached her to examine the passage she indicated. 'A neologism is not a sin if it conveys understanding.' Dora noted how his eyes went to his packages in the locked bookcase and she was pleased now she hadn't ripped the paper. Was he a secretive bibliophile not wanting fellow collectors to know his finds until he was ready to reveal them, or did he have more to hide? Twelve plates of what? 'I think he describes Lisbon very well.'

'You have been to Portugal?' She held out her hand for the book.

'I'm an archivist, Miss Pence. My voyages happen in places like this.'

Dora gave a sweeping look around the collection. 'I would like to see what adventures these shelves contain, if I am allowed.'

He gave her a smile that suggested he found something more amusing about her remark than she knew. 'And I would be delighted to show you – on our return.' He met her eyes, making the invitation plain. They were nice eyes, full of humour and sly wit. She was a little tempted to encourage his flirting by a smart reply, but Jacob...

He gestured to the door. 'The carriages are ready. We have no time to linger to see the fruits of Mr Ferguson's collecting and my labours to catalogue them, but I would be happy to instruct you as to what delights the library holds when we return and are both off duty.'

She murmured thanks and reminded herself he was a suspect, not a safe man to banter with. On the surface he seemed pleasant enough, but his offer to entertain her last night suggested he might have other delights in mind. He bore watching, both in connection with the conspiracy and for her own sake. She had complicated feelings for one man; she did not want to add another.

It wasn't until she took her seat in the carriage next to Mr Hambleton that she realised Percy hadn't denied ever being in Lisbon.

Chapter Twelve

Road to Edinburgh

Jacob cursed the fact that he hadn't been able to warn Dora that he was off with Ferguson after a late breakfast. He would have preferred to stay and continue the search of the house with her but his host had other ideas. Not a trusting man, this Ferguson. The man's overnight conclusion had been that he needed to separate Jacob from his wife as soon as possible. Why otherwise assign a task to himself that would more normally be given to a groom? It would be unexceptional for a servant to go ahead and reserve lodgings; the master and his guest doing it was a little odd, even with the excuse of wanting a good ride. Jacob was left in no doubt his attendance on this errand was expected.

There had followed a brisk canter south. The two men were now on the approach to Edinburgh, making good time, unencumbered by luggage or the slower pace of a carriage. The old castle in the centre of the city rose above the roofs like an island in a slate-grey sea. The sun set behind them, flushing the sky pink and mauve. The windows of the fortress gleamed gold.

Jacob was about to remark on the painterly view, but Ferguson spoke first after many miles of stubborn silence.

'How serious do you think these threats are to Lord Elgin and the children?' he asked. From the tap of his whip on his boot, he had clearly been fretting over this question for some time.

'It is hard to say, sir. So far, there's been a message and a death – it remains to be seen if there is a connection. Perhaps Brooking really was in the wrong place at the wrong time.' But that ring, thought Jacob. He'd have to trace that lead. His instinct told him it was important.

'Are you sure about that?'

Jacob studied Ferguson's face in profile, features in shadow because he had the light behind him. There was a shrewd expression in his eyes. 'What do you mean?'

'Do you not think it strange that it was Lord Elgin and Mary who were singled out for such exceptionally cruel treatment by Napoleon?'

'You think this might go back that far? Back to 1802?'

The whip tapped. 'Evidence suggests it began then, does it not – the misfortune?'

Jacob nodded. 'Yes.'

Ferguson's horse stirred, eager to get on to a stable and a bag of oats. His rider patted him. 'Steady, boy. This smells political to me.'

'I thought it might be a personal grudge – *The Oresteia* is all about families.'

'But Napoleon's hatred for us British is very personal. Everyone else has crumbled but we've stood strong. He sees us as the greatest enemy behind his misfortunes.'

'What misfortunes? The man has his family on practically every throne in Europe!'

'I meant being restricted to the continent and soundly beaten at sea. His animus against British prisoners is well known. Napoleon did everything he could to ruin Elgin when he caught his fish in the net of closed borders.'

'Would Bonaparte stoop so low? Keep up the attack once he'd let him go?'

'The Corsican has an unrivalled talent for details and hard work. An important British lord would not be below his notice.'

'Then do you think the note a French contrivance?'

'And the death. That sounds more like warfare than a private grudge.' Ferguson nudged his horse onward. 'Being imprisoned was ruinously expensive and now Elgin is unable to hold any position of state, being on parole. To speak bluntly he is broken professionally and financially. That process continues. I would say that the person behind this started the persecution long before Elgin returned to these shores.'

And long before the Elgin-Ferguson marital drama came into the picture.

Jacob patted his horse's neck, giving himself time to consider this view of the case. Ferguson would say that, would he not, if he wished to put Jacob off the scent? However, giving the man his due, Jacob let himself run with the theory for a moment.

'You think it most likely that the French are behind it and always have been?'

Ferguson checked his pocket watch. 'Mary should have left by now. Shall we ride on?'

Jacob urged his horse into a trot.

'I wouldn't put it past Elgin to fabricate the whole thing, Dr Sandys, but last night I couldn't help thinking that it is a very convoluted way of getting at Mary. Her friends know she hasn't a vindictive bone in her body so they wouldn't believe it of her. A plot to make her look guilty is as likely to blow up in Elgin's face as damage her.'

'I can agree with that – but I believe Lord Elgin is sincerely shaken by events. Would he engage an investigator if he were doing it himself?'

'Who knows how his mind works these days? I thought I knew him but...' Ferguson's fall into silence spoke volumes for their broken friendship.

Not broken – the relationship had been raised to the ground and the earth salted.

'You think I should be looking for an enemy agent?'

Ferguson smiled wryly. 'That is more plausible than my wife, I hope you agree?'

Jacob met his eyes. 'I never seriously considered your wife.'

'But me? Ha!' Ferguson gave a bark of laughter. 'You have guts, Sandys, I'll give you that. And yes, I could come up with a scheme like this, not that I even knew the murdered man. But there is one irrefutable reason why I wouldn't.'

'And that is?'

'Mary. She wouldn't like it.' With that, he urged his horse into a canter and headed down the road to the city.

Inside the second carriage, Dora studied her travel companions from behind the barricade of a lady's magazine. Percy's brown eyes were too often turned to her – though admittedly it was hard to avoid looking at the person opposite you in such close confines. It was the amused appraisal that gave her pause. What was it about her that he found so humorous? To be fair, she had mocked his buttonholes, but once she had got past the fashionable clothing and seen him in daylight, she noticed dark circles under his eyes. Investigating with Jacob had encouraged her to start diagnosing everyone from such outward appearances and she wondered if he had trouble sleeping. A guilty conscience perhaps?

By contrast, Mr Hambleton had a face which immediately

made you feel at ease with him – a combination of favourite uncle and kind counsellor. Like his master, he had a bald crown which he made no attempt to disguise with swept-back grey hair. The most striking feature though were his navy-blue eyes under black brows. The expression in them made him look thoughtful. He wouldn't rattle away any secrets in front of Percy. If she wanted to find out anything from him, she would have to be subtle.

'It is remarkable how many gowns a lady requires to be fashionable,' said Percy, gesturing to her reading matter.

'I imagine it is a conspiracy with the modistes, Mr Percy. I see that you are *au courant* with what is in favour for a gentleman.' Dora noticed the smile on Mr Hambleton's face. She guessed that the younger man bemused the traditional valet with his flamboyant choices. Time to lay out her bait to bring Hambleton to her side. 'Those of us with limited incomes are best advised to stick to some sturdy and serviceable pieces.'

Hambleton snapped it up. 'Very true, Miss Pence. Throwing out clothes as often as bouquets of flowers is a foolish waste,' he said. 'The laird swears by his tweed jacket, made for him fifteen years ago. He willnae go hunting in anything else.'

Percy raised a brow, conveying his disproval. 'I'm afraid Miss Pence is lying to you, Hambleton. She is a fraud.'

Dora strived to hide her swell of alarm. 'I am? How so?'

Percy gestured to her. 'You may not recognise it, but her coat is the first word in fashion this season.'

'My last employer, Lady Tolworth, was very generous.' Damn Jacob for his insistence that she needed a new coat.

'Really? It does not look as though it had a previous owner – and I do not believe that was the fashion last year, or the one before.'

The man was too perceptive. 'My lady was always a step ahead of fashion.'

'I'm sure the giver of the coat is a very generous person.' He tapped his lower lip thoughtfully. 'And as for not discarding clothes, no lady's maid I know is ever against the practice because they are the beneficiaries, flaunting them to impress upon the other servants how they are a cut above the common herd.'

Dora snorted at this misapprehension. 'As if that is all that is achieved! I'll have you know, Mr Percy, that there is a lucrative market for such clothes. Many ladies sell their gowns to fund their new purchases, and lady's maids are often their agents in the transaction.' She had bought such garments for her costumes on several occasions. There was a steady trade down the servants' staircase to the second-hand shops.

'How enterprising of them. We all have something to sell, do we not?' Percy's amusement again seemed to leave her out of the joke. Had he worked out that she was not who she seemed? If so, why had he not spoken up? Percy was becoming more and more dangerous to her mission; she must consider him a worthy adversary. And, damn, it was fun matching wits with him.

Mr Hambleton was taking everything at its face value, missing the undercurrents to their discussion. 'I dinnae hold with selling the laird's cloots. What if he comes upon some local farmer at the assembly wearing a jacket he once appeared in at the verra same meeting?'

'Oh yes,' said Percy gleefully. 'The foundations of society would shake when all can see that sauce for the goose is sauce for the gander. Have I got that English expression right?'

'Not exactly,' said Dora. 'You might be better saying "a man's a man for a' that".' Had Percy just shown his radical colours?

'I like Burns's poetry in the main, but I dinnae approve of all his sentiments,' said Mr Hambleton stoutly, crossing his arms. 'The laird is a good man, worthy of our respect.'

'Oh, I couldn't agree more,' said Percy, rowing back from any revolutionary statements with a slanted look at the valet. 'I respect his judgement. His eye for rare manuscripts is almost as fine as my own.' He accompanied that statement with such an outrageous wink that Dora had to chuckle.

If he was a rebel, he was an entertainingly arrogant one.

Jacob rode inside the carriage with the Fergusons for the next stage of the journey. Mrs Ferguson proved a lively conversationalist, so the hours to the border passed pleasantly, if he could ignore the lowering cloud that was her husband.

'Ah, we're at Berwick!' announced the lady. 'We are making good time. Summer is so much better for travelling, do you not find?'

He agreed that indeed summer was as she described.

'It would be better if we could stay in our own home to enjoy it,' grumbled Ferguson.

'Robert.' She placed her hand lightly on his knee. 'You know why I have to go to London.'

'I know that you are letting yourself in for a world of pain, Mary. You won't be able to see them.'

'But I'll be there in case.'

Ferguson sighed and let the matter drop.

That little skirmish won, Mary turned back to the world passing by. 'Don't the soldiers look fine in their red coats? The young ladies will be in raptures to have such men attending their local parties and balls.'

'We always were given a welcome beyond our worth,' said Jacob. 'I hope the young ladies realise that the uniform covers a multitude of sins.'

Ferguson grunted his agreement.

'Oh, yes, I forget that you were with the army for ... how many years?' asked Mrs Ferguson.

'Seven years. I retired after the retreat from Corunna.'

'Poor Sir John Moore – such a courageous leader,' sighed Mrs Ferguson.

'He was a good leader. Fortunately for the army, Wellington is better.'

'But you aren't returning to Portugal, Sandys? You've had enough of patching up soldiers? I suppose there's not much money in that.' Ferguson made it sound like Jacob was eschewing his duty for personal gain.

'My career came to an end with a sabre cut – one inflicted on me when I was retrieving casualties.' The worse blow had been when he was struck down by an infection after sewing himself up on board the evacuation ship. He'd flirted with the grim reaper for a week. His friends had been ready to wave him off to the afterlife, but he'd pulled through.

Ferguson sniffed as if he smelled the gangrene that fortunately hadn't set in. 'You look well enough now.'

'Thank you.' The scar was hidden under his layers of jacket, waistcoat and shirt. He was no more going to display that than he would bare his soul to the man opposite. What did Ferguson know about the toll taken on all who came under fire, the despair of not being able to save young lives as they were carried into the army hospital with horrendous injuries. You could only do such work for a time and retain your humanity. Doctors who stayed too long on the frontlines either drank to forget or developed such fortifications about their feelings that they were barely living.

Or they took opium.

Jacob turned to the countryside outside the windows. They were taking an easterly route along the coast because the Fergusons had friends in Durham and were planning to stay there the night after next. It made a change from the sights of the Great North Road that he and Dora had so recently passed. Whitewashed cottages with productive gardens clustered by the road as they approached the border. This route had often seen armies marching through, but the last half century had been peaceful between Scotland and England. No Jacobins under Bonnie Prince Charlie challenging for the crown, no Henry VIII pushing north to subdue the Scots, just carts and carriages ferrying goods and passengers.

'Looks like the harvest might be better this year,' mused the landowner Ferguson. 'It was a hungry winter.'

Even with the signs of tightened belts, Jacob contrasted this scene to the ravaged landscape of the Peninsular, where both the French and the allies used scorched earth tactics to leave the opposition short of supplies. The Spanish campaign had been particularly cruel with atrocities on all sides. How refreshing to be somewhere where the enemy was the weather.

As if his thoughts of the war had summoned the military, the carriage slowed as it drew alongside a supply convoy of wagons.

'The garrison looks like it is heading out on manoeuvres,' said Mrs Ferguson.

'They must be making the most of the fine weather to practice for an invasion,' replied her husband.

Mrs Ferguson looked shocked. 'Surely not this far north?'

'Napoleon will attack us where we least expect it.'

'That doesn't bear thinking about. Perhaps the troops are going to Nottingham. Isn't there some trouble down there?' suggested Mrs Ferguson. The newspapers had been full of stories about the troubles among the stocking weavers and the militia had been sent in.

'How do you know that, darling? I didn't think you read the newspapers.'

'Lord Byron,' she replied with a blush.

Ferguson chuckled. 'That man! He makes framebreaking and stocking weavers the theme of his maiden speech in the House of Lords in February, and all the ladies of the nation become experts on the subject.'

Jacob returned the husband's smile with a wry one of his own, not that the subject was very amusing. Framebreaking had been made a capital crime. In this, Byron was right: how could a man protest his job being taken from him with that threat hanging over him?

Heading to quell their own people or the French, the movements of the troops were all too familiar to Jacob, though he didn't approve of the intermingling of weaponry and foodstuffs. It was hard to tell which were barrels of butter and which gunpowder. A more careful quartermaster would make sure that the flammable supplies were quarantined away from the entourage of cooks and camp followers that trailed after any troop movements. One overturned lamp, one pipe knocked out in the wrong place, one misfired gun – it didn't bear thinking about.

'What a shambles,' he muttered. Wellington would have had these men flogged for negligence. A neglectful waggoner had even left his cart under the command of a child holding the horses on the far side of the bridge – the driver was walking off, likely headed for the nearest tavern. Jacob was tempted to have words with him if he had returned by the time the coach drew level. The girl could hardly be expected to control the team should they take fright.

'I've always admired this bridge,' said Mrs Ferguson, her thoughts on nature now rather than troop movements. 'It's such a lovely day. Might we pause to see the view of the Tweed?'

They had been overtaking the slow-moving convoy for a mile now.

'Let us admire it from the southern side, my dear.' Ferguson clearly didn't want to get stuck behind the convoy again where the road narrowed to cross the Tweed.

The lady's hands clenched in her lap. 'I had hoped to step out in the middle so I could see the river.'

Ferguson was about to refuse, but Jacob intervened. It could do no harm.

'An excellent idea, Mrs Ferguson,' he said. 'Then we can claim we walked from Scotland to England.'

She laughed, cheered by his support. 'Exactly, Dr Sandys. You must all keep our secret so we can amaze our friends when we reach Durham.'

Giving into their joint pleas, Ferguson rapped on the carriage roof, indicating that they should pause by one of the embrasures. 'Coachman, stop here.'

They pulled over and the other carriage carrying Dora, Percy and the valet overtook them. Jacob caught a glimpse of Dora's bemused face as they rattled past.

'Pleased, my dear?' Ferguson smiled indulgently at his wife.

'Thank you, Robert. We won't take long.' She gathered her skirts to step out.

Jacob reached for the door to help Mrs Ferguson to the ground.

That was when the world exploded.

Chapter Thirteen

Berwick-on-Tweed, the Border of Scotland and England

Jacob was first to regain his wits. Having been under fire before, he knew the ringing in his ears was the result of being too close to an explosion and only time would repair the injury. The carriage jolted wildly as the terrified horses jerked and reared. Then it settled – a sign that their coachman had regained control. Quickly ascertaining that no one in his carriage was injured, Jacob leapt out to find a scene of carnage. The wagon he had spotted on the far bank had been obliterated. Fragments of horse and, he feared, human, scattered the ground in bloody disarray.

That poor child, he thought bleakly, remembering the little figure who had stood closest to the wagon. He desperately scanned the casualties lying on the road or draped half out of vehicles. The smoke was still billowing, but Dora's carriage was almost in one piece, thank God. Screams and cries sounded to his dulled hearing like distant seagulls.

There would be scores of casualties as the wagons had been

closely packed at the exit of the bridge. Quick action would save lives and there was no waiting for the garrison to send their surgeons.

'You there!' he shouted to the stunned soldiers quivering in the shelter of the bridge parapet. 'Bring the injured to me on the English side.' He accompanied the order with gestures so even the most deafened should catch his intention that he was heading towards trouble.

The smoke was clearing in the brisk breeze and the air stank of sulphur – confirmation that it had been the gunpowder that had exploded. The horribly sweet smell of scorched flesh wafted to his nostrils. Mostly horse, he guessed. His eyes stung. Flashes of similar scenes on battlefields swamped him so that for a moment he floundered and was hard-pressed to identify which was the present and which was a situation long over.

Dora. That thought snapped him back in focus.

Rounding the second carriage, he saw to his horror that his impression that it was intact had been entirely false. Only the rear wall had survived. The interior was a mess of mangled wood and even more mangled horses.

He swore in the vivid language of the Peninsula veteran. He should begin work on the casualties if he was to save whom he could, but he had to look for Dora first.

'Help me!' He yanked a dazed infantry officer off the ground. Blinking, the man followed him to the carriage and they began throwing aside the smashed wood. They found Michel Percy first. He was either dead or unconscious. One arm was shattered by shrapnel, the fashionable jacket in bloody tatters. If he lived, someone might have to amputate the limb. They lifted Percy out and passed him to two men who had shown more sense than most by rigging up a piece of canvas as a stretcher. Next came Hambleton, gasping like a fish – a fragment of wood had embedded itself in his back. Collapsed lung, guessed Jacob. He helped the valet out to be carried away by the next stretcher crew. Once he was out, Jacob saw Dora huddled in the well between the seats. It looked like the men had thrown themselves on top of her – a gallantry that he would have to thank them for later, if they survived. There was no sign of blood and she was saying something to him, not that he could hear her. Her eyes were round with shock, her hair dangling around her shoulders, and she was furious. Good enough. He hauled her up and lifted her down to the waiting stretcher crew.

Now he had to do his duty.

He commandeered two barrels and planks to set up an operating table in a field next to the river. The men around him, some of them veterans from the campaigns, saw what he was about and hurried to help. Jacob caught the arm of one younger man and shouted, 'Fetch me my surgeon's kit from that carriage.' He pointed and dispatched another to get clean linen for bandages.

He walked quickly down the rows of injured lying on the grass, dismissing those that were too far gone to be saved and indicating to his stretcher crew to bring the rest in turn as he pointed to them. He did not look at faces, or rank, he saw merely the injuries. Smashed arm. Shrapnel wound to a neck. A broken leg. A deep gouge to a thigh. Damaged eye.

'Neck,' he said, indicating that man should be brought forward first. His patient had been lucky – the carotid had been missed by a hair. 'Bandage,' he snapped to the woman who had come to his side to help. It was only when she passed him a torn-up sheet that he realised it was Dora. 'If you please,' he added, touching her hand lightly as he moved on.

An hour later, after he had been joined by the surgeons from the garrison and they had cleared the backlog of casualties, Jacob paused to swig water from a canteen Dora had found for him. The buzzing in his ears had subsided and he could now hear, if a little muffled, what was being said. The deafening had, in fact, helped him concentrate for the initial few minutes of his triage.

'Are you well?' he asked her.

'Yes, doctor.' Her expression warned him not to show too much care for the lady's maid with whom he was supposed to have no acquaintance. The Fergusons weren't far away, Mrs Ferguson offering water to the injured, Mr Ferguson helping restore order on the bridge. 'I'm concerned for Mr Percy.'

'I'll go to him,' he assured her.

'Do we know how many we lost?' asked the senior surgeon – Dr Bailly, also veteran of the British expeditionary force under Sir John Moore, though their paths had not crossed then. Bailly had known Jacob by repute – being a son of a nobleman did make him famous in the service.

Jacob looked at the sorry row of bodies drawn up next to a hedge. 'Five – and I fear we will never locate the child I saw holding the horses, so that says at least six fatalities to me.'

'I will report that as a provisional figure. I predict that some of the injured won't survive despite our best efforts.' The doctor wiped his hands on a rag. 'I'll have them moved to the hospital. You have my thanks for your assistance.'

Percy was in a bad way. Jacob had not taken off his arm as he might have done if this were a battlefield. Many soldiers were killed by moving them with their injured limbs still intact. Better a clean stump than further blood loss. But this was not the frontline and Percy was near a decent hospital. If the librarian survived, Jacob would leave the calculation on amputation to Bailly.

Jacob went to kneel by the librarian. Percy's pallor had been bled to a ghostly white and he was trembling in shock.

'Here.' Jacob pulled a blanket over him. 'We will get you moved somewhere more comfortable.'

Percy's eyes fluttered open.

'Sandys ... have to tell you...' His words were broken by his laboured breathing, and he drifted off, losing consciousness again.

Jacob held a cup to his lips and let a little water dribble in. 'Tell me what, *mon frère*?'

Percy began rambling but this time in French. His voice was so soft, Jacob had to lean over to catch what he said. *Gênant ... livres ... pas un accident... à cause de moi.*

From the rustle of skirts, he could tell that Dora had come to kneel beside him.

'What is he saying?' she whispered.

'Trouble or embarrassment. Something about books. The last is clearer – "not an accident" and "because of me".'

Dora looked over to where the soldiers were poking about in the crater left by the explosion. 'He thinks this was aimed at him? Why?'

'He's delirious.' Jacob signalled to a stretcher team to carry Percy away. 'Look after him, please. He saved this lady's life.' He offered a hand to help her up. 'We'll talk later. I believe the Fergusons want to go on to the next stage of the journey and recover there.'

'They're going on with their trip?' Dora sounded incredulous, gesturing around at the devastation.

'To them this was a horrible accident. As neither are injured, and there is nothing they can do for the casualties beyond leaving funds to see they are made comfortable at the hospital, I think they will want to journey on.' He brushed her fingers in the folds of her skirts so no one would see the gesture. 'How is Hambleton?'

'He is bandaged and claims he is well enough to continue but Mr Ferguson has insisted that he stay in lodgings and recover.'

'Quite right. The man had a collapsed lung, for God's sake, though I love him dearly for helping to save you.'

Dora gulped, controlling her emotions with difficulty. 'It was Mr Percy. He reacted so quickly, shoving us all down onto the floor.'

Jacob regretted his uncharitable thoughts towards the man. 'Not such a waste of buttonholes then.'

As they watched the librarian being carried off, the Fergusons joined them.

'Dr Sandys, are you still needed here?' asked Ferguson.

Jacob rolled his shoulders, trying to shed the tension of the past hour. 'No, the hospital has surgeons enough.'

'It was fortunate that you were on hand to render first aid,' said Mrs Ferguson, leaning on her husband's arm.

'And fortunate that you, my dear, called for a stop when you did,' Ferguson replied, 'else we would have been where the other carriage was and taken the brunt of the explosion.'

Indeed, thought Jacob. He would have urgently to consider if they were the target in this 'not an accident' happening. Percy might have got it wrong – or meant something else in his rambling.

'Miss Pence, are you well enough to continue the journey?' asked Ferguson, turning politely to Dora. 'My wife would understand if you preferred to return to Raith House. You've only been in our employ a day or two and you almost get blown up!'

'I am fit to travel, sir,' Dora said quietly.

'Good woman.' Ferguson gave her a pleased nod. 'We will continue in the same carriage, then. I've sent the coachman from yours back to carry the news. He was blown clear, lucky devil. Cuts, bruises and a slight concussion but he says he is fit to travel. He will make sure Hambleton and Percy are looked after and transferred home as soon as it is safe to move them.'

'Poor Mr Percy,' said Mrs Ferguson, her eyes filling with tears.

'There now, my dear. He's alive. Let's say our prayers and concentrate on that.'

Alive for now, thought Jacob grimly.

'I'll give orders for our carriage to be made ready. I think we've done all we can here. Miss Pence, please gather your things – if they survived.' Mr Ferguson turned away to help his wife return to their vehicle.

'I will assist Miss Pence in retrieving her trunk,' said Jacob.

They fell behind the Fergusons.

'I'm not hopeful that much remains,' said Dora grimly.

'The back of the coach was protected in the blast,' said Jacob. 'It would take more than an explosion to do for that coat of yours. I believe it to be indestructible.' That raised a smile, as he intended.

Dora shot him a look that had more of her usual spirit as she got a little distance from her shock. 'Would it be very bad, do you think, if we had to quickly search the belongings of my travel companions?'

They picked their way over the wreckage of several carts.

'Indeed not, I think it justified as we need to work out where to send the luggage. And if Percy is correct that this attack was aimed at him, then perhaps his belongings might give us a clue?'

Dora tugged as her hem got caught on a spike. 'Who would go to this extreme to blow up a librarian? Are the Fergusons not a more likely target?'

Jacob knelt and released it. 'Why would they be targeted? Thus far they haven't been victims, only suspects in our investigation.'

'Ah, of course, I haven't had a chance to tell you.' Dora squeezed his arm. 'Mrs Cameron intercepted a threat in Greek sent to Mrs Ferguson. She hadn't understood what it meant, believing it to be insults of some censorious busybody to a divorcée, but she told Mr Percy and he destroyed it.'

Jacob fell silent for a few paces, slotting this new piece into the puzzle. 'The lady is also being threatened?'

'Yes.'

'Why would anyone…' Jacob clicked his fingers. 'The marbles – she was there, she was as involved as her husband in removing the marbles from the Parthenon.'

'So maybe this isn't about a grudge against Elgin but a grudge someone holds against them both?'

'Why did Ferguson not tell me?'

'He doesn't know. In that household they all tiptoe around protecting her – but it seems from the wrong thing.'

They watched as Ferguson handed his wife back into the carriage, arranging a blanket over her knees.

'I'm not a believer in blissful ignorance,' said Jacob.

'What should we do?' asked Dora. 'Tell them?'

'And how can we do that without revealing that you've been digging for information in the household?'

'But if we say nothing and this attack was aimed at her…?'

'Yes, we have quite a dilemma, don't we?'

'What shall we do, then?'

'I'll say Percy told me – he's not here to deny that. Then we make sure they take precautions. Before we leave, I think we need to take a closer look at the source of the explosion.'

'What will that tell us?

'If there is no waggoner among the casualties – or no one has returned to explain why they left such a dangerous cargo in the care of a child –' His blood boiled to consider the callousness of such a cruel move, '– then a deliberate attack seems all the more likely.'

'That's unspeakably wicked.' She shoved her fingers into her tumbled hair and screwed it back into a knot. 'I don't understand. Who is behind this? Was it aimed at the Fergusons?'

'We pulled over at the last moment. Our carriage should have gone first.'

'So that is possible. But if Mr Percy was the target, and the person who drove the wagon is still at large, what's to stop him finishing the job at the hospital?'

Jacob's heart missed a beat. She was right. Had he just sent his patient off to his death?

'I'll hasten to the hospital; you do what you can here. Tell the Fergusons I'll meet you at the next inn.' With that he set off quickly, hoping he wouldn't be too late.

Chapter Fourteen

Dora watched Jacob disappear in the crowds gathering on the Berwick side of the bridge. He had been so impressive, dealing with the casualties with a sangfroid that spoke of familiarity. She realised as he'd stitched and swabbed that they hadn't spoken much about his war experience – and that was an oversight she should correct. To truly understand him she needed to know where he had been before meeting her. The puzzle about his weakness towards opium – that probably had a solution connected to battlefields like this.

But not now. She had her own investigation to conduct and only a short amount of time in which to do so.

She found her trunk intact; rather like her, it had been at the bottom of the pile. Percy's had been splintered so she had but a few qualms transferring the book and papers that were blowing around to hers. She could claim she was protecting them in order to return them. Hambleton's had been destroyed – or perhaps someone had run off with it? Human nature would mean some saw another's misfortune as their opportunity. Sending the coachman to retrieve what else could be salvaged from within the servants' carriage, Dora walked back to the crater. Jacob had said he'd seen a child holding the horses. There were plenty of barefoot children milling about now, drawn by the grisly spectacle. Perhaps one of them would know what happened. Unfortunately, a soldier on guard blocked her way.

'Who died, do we know yet?' she asked.

He gave her a cold look. 'Step back, miss. This is none of your business.'

'I was sent by the doctors. One of them saw a child near the wagon and asked me to enquire.' And that wasn't even a lie.

The soldier took a closer look at her, saw the blood flecks on her arms and the smears on her skirts. 'Are you a nurse, miss?'

'I've been assisting Dr Sandys.'

The soldier swung round and bellowed to his fellow on the other side of the crater. 'Any sign of a child among the victims, corporal?'

The corporal poked at the wreckage with his bayonet. 'Nothing yet, sir.'

'You can tell the doctors that there's no patient here for them, miss.' He leaned on his rifle, deciding she would benefit from hearing his wisdom. 'When a magazine goes up like this, there's usually nothing left at the centre of the blast. Smithereens – that's where anyone close to the wagon is now.'

She had feared as much. 'Do we know whose cart it was? That way we might be able to tell the family.'

He shook his head. 'The quartermaster said he hadn't got it on today's roster. Most likely the usual mix-up at headquarters. You'd best move along now.'

She did, but only as far as a woman she had spotted who had her arms around a sobbing boy of about eight or nine. They were by the water's edge near one of the arches of the bridge.

'Can I help?' she asked, kneeling beside them. 'Is he hurt?'

The woman had the weather-beaten complexion of a camp

follower, used to tramping across country in all weathers, making cookfires and taking in laundry. Such women, sturdy souls in their middle years, were the accepted but unofficial service that kept the ordinary soldier on his feet.

'Not that I can see, Miss,' she said, her accent that of a Yorkshire woman. 'The bairn is beside his'sen, poor lad.'

'He's not yours?'

'Nay, he's one of the strays about the camp. Come, lad, there's nowt solved by ruering. You'll do thi'sen an injury. Where's your sister?'

That only produced a fresh storm of tears. Dora brushed the boy's hair out of his eyes. The boy was a skinny, undersized specimen.

'Do you know his name?'

'We all call him Kir. That's short for Aboukir, after the naval victory. Outlandish name but memorable.'

'And his sister?'

'Hattie, short for Hathor. Their father went on that expedition to the East and picked up her mother somewhere in Egypt and gave them those foreign names.'

Jacob had been part of that campaign. 'And the parents?'

'Dead. Him first, then her.'

Leaving the children loosely attached to the army camp. Now she had a sinking feeling about the fate of the missing daughter.

'And I'm guessing Hattie and Kir earn their keep by doing small errands?' Like holding horses for a wagon driver.

'That's right.'

Dora cupped the boy's chin in her palm. 'Kir, was your sister near the wagon when it exploded?'

He nodded, eyes brimming with tears. The woman drew in a sharp breath.

'Did you see the driver of the wagon?'

He nodded again.

'Can you describe him?'

Kir gulped.

'Here.' Dora passed him a canteen of water.

'Man,' he whispered. 'Wagoner's smock but shiny boots. He had a pocket watch.'

'Good boy.' She patted his shoulder. That didn't sound like any ordinary driver. That sounded much more like someone poorly disguised as one. Did he drive up, pick on some unfortunate child that wouldn't ask too many questions, and run away, fuse lit, knowing what he'd left behind? Such devilry shook what little faith she had in humanity.

The boy turned his eyes to her. They were deep brown and fringed with dark lashes. He had the look of a stray kitten rescued from a sack that had been on its way to the river. 'Where's my sister, lady?'

Why did this have to fall to her? Hiding the truth would do him no favours.

'Do you know what gunpowder is?'

He scowled. 'I'm not a baby.'

'No, you're not. Well, when gunpowder explodes, everything near to it is destroyed very quickly – so quickly that there's no time for pain or any thought at all. I think your sister might have been standing too close to the explosion.'

He blinked, his world shifting into a new and horrible sharp focus. 'She's gone?'

'Yes, I think she's gone.'

The boy crumpled and folded himself up into a ball of misery. Dora rested her hand on his back to let him know she was there. There seemed little else she could do.

'Can you look after him?' she asked the woman.

The camp follower reared back, probably regretting her kindness in comforting the boy. 'Not me, miss. I'm off on manoeuvres. Can't afford to feed another mouth.'

'Does he have relatives?'

'Never heard of none. You'll have to send to Egypt for the mother's side.'

So that was no good, then.

The woman got up and shook out the pins and needles in her legs. 'You could take him to the orphanage,' she volunteered, 'but they aren't fond of foreigners from outside the parish. His sister tried to get them in last winter, but they were turned away.'

Dora nodded. 'I'll think of something.'

The woman scurried off before she got landed with unwanted responsibility. The boy had shifted to fold himself in Dora's skirts, burrowing as close to her as he could. His street wisdom had told him that she was his best bet and he looked set to hold on to her ankle should she try to walk away. Not that she could. She'd lost her brother but had long been old enough to look after herself. Kir had lost a sister and the only one who had cared for him. He needed someone to step up into her place.

Dora imagined herself talking to Jacob.

'Jacob, I thought our life wasn't complicated enough so I've picked up a stray.' That was perfectly reasonable, wasn't it, in the middle of an investigation where people were trying to kill them?

She couldn't see any other solution for the moment. The boy was a witness, a lead that might yield further clues as to the identity of the murderer. He was also an innocent victim with no one to look after him. Presenting him like that to the Fergusons might earn him a place in the carriage.

She bent down and scooped up Kir. He didn't smell too clean, but he weighed next to nothing.

'Kir, you're coming with me. I'll make sure you're safe.'

Chapter Fifteen

Berwick Hospital

Coat tails flying, Jacob sprinted through Berwick to the military hospital, pausing only to ask the way from the startled people he collared. He hadn't saved a man just to send him to his death, had he?

He was directed to a double-fronted building tucked behind a wall on the narrow street of Ravensdowne. Built of salmon-pink stone, it had the look of a gentleman's house, rather than the barrack-like buildings he was used to in most army camps.

Jacob was about to head inside but an orderly on duty stepped in front of him. A big man, the doorkeeper had a rust-red walrus moustache that made him look perennially melancholy, his manner lumbering like that sea-animal on land.

'Now then, not so fast. Your business, sir?' he asked with a world-weary sigh.

'Dr Sandys. I was at the bridge. One of my patients was brought here,' Jacob said between panting breaths. With the benefit of experience, he could tell that the place was efficiently run. The casualties had already been cleared from the wagons and taken into the wards. He could hear the cries of the wounded, but they were muffled by closed doors. Staff hurried across the hallway and upstairs but with purpose and no panic. Order had soon been restored after the influx of victims. Unfortunately, that also meant he was prevented from getting to where he needed to be this moment.

The orderly consulted a list with agonising slowness. 'Name of patient?'

'Michel Percy.'

Finger finding the name halfway down his list, he finally stood back to let Jacob pass. 'Popular man, sir. First floor. Second door. He's in a room for officers as we were told he's a gentleman.'

'Why do you say he's popular?'

'Well, sir, that would be because you aren't the first to ask for him.' But Walrus Moustache had still insisted on checking his list! He clearly liked messing with doctors, the petty revenge of a subordinate.

'Damnation!' Jacob hurried past him to the stairs, then climbed two at a time. He would strangle the orderly if his officiousness meant Jacob was not in time to stop disaster. He passed the first door – it was open, and a nurse was dressing a man's wounds. Not his patient. The second was closed. He tried the handle, but it was locked, or maybe barricaded? No one locked wards in a hospital unless the patient was raving, and Percy had been in his right mind when last seen. Jacob's foreboding grew. Through the observation window in the door, he could make out Percy lying on his back, injured arm swathed in bandages. His head had flopped to one side, the line of his throat and cheek exposed. Had he been drugged against the pain – or was he dead? Had someone already done the deed?

Then a man came into view – though all Jacob could see was his back. Broad-shouldered, dressed in a dark brown coat and breeches, he picked up a pillow from the second bed in the room and stole towards the patient, holding it in front of him. His intent was clear: he was going to smother his victim – a cause of death that left no trace. People would think Percy had died of his wounds. The assassin stooped—

'Open up!' Jacob hammered on the door, hoping to startle the man from his purpose and alert Percy to the danger. Next he tried ramming the door, then kicked, breaking the chair that had been wedged under the handle. As he tumbled into the room, the man was already lunging at the patient.

But then Percy moved. The Frenchman twisted out of the way of the pillow and swiped up with his uninjured arm, a scalpel in his grip that had been hidden in the sheets. He slashed the blade across the man's throat, releasing a spray that drenched the white sheets crimson. The assailant staggered back, pressing the pillow to his neck, but it was too late for him. Percy had cut the artery and death would follow in a few heartbeats. Percy collapsed back on his bloodstained bed with a gasp, pain of the sudden movement and the exertion of what he'd been forced to do, depriving him of his momentary strength. The man clattered into a trolley, then collapsed to the floor. Jacob was left the only one standing in a scene of bloodshed.

'I need help in here!' Jacob bellowed into the corridor. He rushed to the attacker's side, but the man was already dead. The face was unfamiliar – flattened features of a pugilist, scar on his eyebrow, and unshaven. Shabby and none too clean. If he had to guess, this was a man down on his luck and not above being hired for an assassin's duty. Such men usually had little idea what they had been employed to do, or why, nothing past the name of his victim. That type of desperate man was easily catalogued, but not so his intended victim. The librarian was an enigma. Confirming the lack of pulse under his fingertips, Jacob looked up at Percy. 'Very effective defence.'

Percy grunted, looking down at his own arm. '*Putain*, that hurt like hell. Am I bleeding or is it his?'

Jacob got up to check. 'I wonder where you learned to do that?'

Percy winced, dropping the scalpel from his cramping fingers. 'The best school – the school of life.'

'Very drole. It's mostly his blood, but you'll need a fresh dressing.' Jacob turned and patted down the man's pockets, transferring any papers or identifying items into his own for later examination. Percy watched but made no protest at what was effectively robbing a corpse. 'Your answer begs the question: what kind of life led to such unexpected skills?'

Jacob got up from the body as doctors and orderlies hurried into the room. It took some minutes to explain that, no, he, Jacob had had nothing to do with the man's death and that he had witnessed the attempt to murder the patient. His story was assisted by the arrival of Dr Bailly who was able to vouch for him. This produced much fussing around Percy and a fresh examination of his arm to see if he had further injured himself. When the patient was declared stable, the body was carried off for the coroner's examination. Three men lifted Percy into the clean bed. An orderly helped him into a fresh nightshirt while two others hauled the blood-soaked mattress out into the corridor and swabbed the floor.

Finally, only Jacob and Percy were left in the room. Dr Bailly had gone to prepare a sleeping draught and double the guard. The walrus orderly would no doubt catch it for not screening Percy's visitors better despite his officious ways.

Jacob sat in the surviving chair, only now his heart rate was returning to normal. A strange silence fell between him and Percy, each absorbed in their own thoughts. Jacob was reminded of the silence in a ceasefire. Places were never so tangibly quiet as after the thunder of action had stopped. He could hear the birds in the trees outside and footsteps on the cobbles of Ravensdowne. They had met first in a hallway that smelt of flowers and beeswax polish; now they were face to face in a room that smelt of blood and damp flagstones.

'Do you know who is trying to kill you?' asked Jacob.

Percy gave a very French shrug which caused him more pain. He hissed, '*Merde.*'

'Steady, man. Lie still. I'm surprised you were able to defend yourself with that arm. When they carried you away from the explosion, I thought you were only hanging on by a thread.'

'I still am,' said Percy. '*Un fil de coton.*' He sighed, his pallor looking worse than it had a few moments ago as the excitement drained from his limbs. 'But I knew they might come after me. So I prepared.'

'You stole one of the doctor's scalpels?'

'I would put it as borrowed, until the danger had passed.'

The will to survive was a strange thing. Jacob had seen men walk on broken legs when it was a matter of survival. He rubbed his jaw, considering the man before him. That move was not something a beginner could have pulled off, not while lying prone with a serious injury. The man had training.

'Who are you really, Percy? You're no ordinary librarian.'

'Who wants to be ordinary?' Percy's eyes went to the birds in the trees outside but there would be no escape from this questioning.

'You've been in the military.' Jacob made it a statement.

'Haven't we all?'

'But for which side, I wonder?'

Percy smiled and closed his eyes. 'Sides change. When I was born, France was trying to kill my kind merely because we were noble. These days, since Napoleon made himself emperor, everyone in Paris is aspiring to be a duke or a prince. They will welcome you back if you swear allegiance to the new order.'

'Is that what you did?'

'I merely say it is a possibility, not necessarily a path I have trodden.'

A man with access to the libraries of rich gentlemen would be well-placed to be a foreign agent. If Jacob oversaw the French secret police, he would place agents in just such a position.

'I don't expect you to tell me the truth, Percy, but I do expect you to tell me enough to keep yourself alive. I'll ask again: who is trying to kill you?'

Percy kept his eyes closed. 'I'm feeling very tired. How is Miss Pence, if that's her name?'

Damn slippery creature, this man, like a fish that escapes to the river when you remove the hook. He was using Jacob's gratitude against him. 'She is well. Thank you for protecting her.'

'I rather thought she was under your protection.' A little of his customary mischief came back into his expression as he smiled to himself.

'You know what I mean. That was a brave thing you did.'

'Instinct merely.'

'Then it was a good instinct.' Jacob wondered how he could get the man to talk. Was the threat to Percy connected to those against Elgin? Or had they stumbled upon a separate plot? He wasn't much of a believer in coincidences – they did happen but two different groups scheming to kill or threaten the same circle of people strained his credulity. No, there was likely a link. He just had to dig for it. 'Let me present some theories to you, Percy. When you thought you were dying, you mentioned books – and that you felt shame or embarrassment.'

Percy turned his face away. 'Forget I said anything. I was raving. That is nothing to do with this.'

'Nothing to do with the attempt on your life?'

'I think not.'

'Then why, with what might have been your last words, did you mention them?'

Percy turned his weary gaze back to him. 'Oh, Dr Sandys, don't tell me that you have your life in order? If you had died today, would there be parts of your life you'd prefer did not come to light?'

Jacob smiled wryly. 'That's why I've given instruction in my will for my brothers to burn my correspondence and diaries without reading them.'

'Very wise. Put what I said about the books to one side. They are irrelevant. There are things moving in this country that neither you nor I can control. We have enemies on all sides.'

'Are you talking about France?'

'Not everything is about the war. Some of us are engaged in a battle that started long before Napoleon, long before even the house of Hanover that sits on your throne.'

'You are speaking in riddles.'

'That is the only way I can speak in my trade.'

'Then you are a spy?'

Percy waved that away as if it were an inadequate term. 'Say, for the sake of argument, I was indeed somewhat attached to a foreign power and tasked to gather what little bits of information I can – I'm not admitting to anything of the sort, merely presenting it as a—'

'Possibility. Yes, I understand.'

'Mostly that work would be reporting the true state of public opinion in an enemy country on what might bring said country to make peace.'

Jacob sat back, letting Percy tell this in his own roundabout fashion.

'What if, in the course of those patriotic duties, I discovered that there were others, not representing either country but, shall we say, a group of people with special interests.'

'Go on.'

'This group is active both here and in other capitals in Europe.'

'A secret society?'

Percy inclined his head. 'You've had experience of these before I believe. Was it not you who tangled with the Hellfire Club?'

Percy was well informed if he had heard about that investigation. 'They have been tamed for now and the leadership decapitated.'

'How French of you. I heard as much – and also that it was thanks in part to your lovely companion. You see, you and I, and the lady, are all doing essentially the same task – trying to uncover dangerous secrets.'

Percy knew about Dora, which he would have done, of course, if he was rigorous about collecting gossip in the highest circles. That explained a lot. 'What group are you talking about? Not the Illuminati?' He thought he and Dora had silenced them for a while, too.

'Thankfully not, those *salauds* are hard to track down. They have too much money and are too well connected.'

'Freemasons, then?'

Percy shook his head slightly, weariness overcoming him. 'No, no. I'm so tired.'

'Then who?'

'There are others with designs on the marbles.' His eyelids fluttered. The man was barely conscious.

Dr Bailly entered with Percy's medicine. 'That's enough talking for now. Mr Percy, we will have to take a view on your arm tomorrow. I've put a guard on your door. You need not fear there will be any repeat of the outrageous attack on you. Do you know why that man went for you as he did?'

'Perhaps because I am French?' said Percy, reaching for the laudanum with relief. 'I think I will take this now I've spoken to Dr Sandys. I find it hard to think while plagued with the sensation of daggers sticking into my arm.' He drained the cup. 'If I survive, Sandys, I'll endeavour to join you in London and tell you what I know.' He flicked his eyes to Dr Bailly, indicating he would not say any more in front of the other man.

Frustrated, Jacob wished he could squeeze more answers out of him, but the man was seriously wounded. An interrogation had to wait. 'You know more than you're telling me.'

'Another hazard of my profession but it's all I can tell you today. Asking questions is what brought this on me so be careful. My arm...' He touched it with his good hand.

Dr Bailly interposed. 'Dr Sandys, Mr Percy needs rest.'

Jacob nodded. 'Have courage, man. You might yet keep the arm – and, if not, many better men have survived the operation.'

'And many worse.' Percy's smile was bitter.

'We'll talk when you come through it.' Jacob left one of his calling cards on the bedside table and followed Dr Bailly out into the corridor.

'What an extraordinary day,' said the local man. 'Is the gentleman right? Was that some misguided patriot taking advantage of the explosion to attack an enemy national?'

'I couldn't say. But I would be obliged if you would guard him well. The danger might not be over.'

'We'll do our best, but you know the risks better than most, I'd say.' Bailly's mind had gone to the medical challenges.

Jacob agreed that operations were hazardous, but he feared Percy's secrets were going to bring them all into even worse peril than going under the surgeon's knife.

Chapter Sixteen

Alnwick, Northumberland

Jacob caught up with the Fergusons at Alnwick, a market town huddled by the walls of a magnificent castle. The ruling family in these parts were the Dukes of Northumberland, whose ancestor, Harry Hotspur, was made famous by Shakespeare. Their descendants still occupied the castle, a reminder to Jacob, a proud northerner, that not all parts of the country marched to the beat of Westminster.

The Ferguson party was already taking supper in a private room. On entering, stamping the mud from his boots, Jacob was taken aback to find their numbers had increased by one: a little boy with big eyes and freshly scrubbed skin. The ragamuffin was seated on a stool by the fire wolfing down a serving of stew like he'd not seen food for weeks. Where on earth had the urchin come from?

'I see I've been supplanted,' he remarked wryly as he joined them at the table. 'No doubt the child is somewhat cleaner than me so the ladies will prefer his company in the carriage.' Jacob now carried on his coattails what felt like half the road as he had made haste to join them.

'Miss Pence took pity on the boy,' said Mr Ferguson. 'She thinks he might be the only surviving witness of the blast.'

Ah, so that explained it.

'And the child was left with no parents or relatives,' said Mrs Ferguson. 'I said we could do something for him. I couldn't turn my back knowing he had nowhere to go.'

'Hmm,' said her husband, but in a way that suggested he hadn't put up much opposition to the act of charity.

'We brought him here. I must say he looks much more presentable in clean clothes and after a scrub with lye soap in the inn's scullery. Perhaps he will do as a kitchen boy?'

Mr Ferguson merely smiled, not committing himself.

'Did you ask the boy for a description, Miss Pence?' asked Jacob.

Dora rolled her eyes at him over her tankard, but not so that the Fergusons could see. 'I have, sir,' her tone less pert than her expression. 'He says that the man who abandoned the wagon to his sister's charge had shiny boots and a pocket watch. Is that not right, Kir?'

The child nodded vigorously. He swallowed his mouthful. 'A gentleman. He shouldn't have been driving a wagon, sir.'

Not the dead man at the hospital, then. That one had had battered boots and no watch. The contents of his pockets had yielded a handful of coppers, a latch key, and a bundle of leaflets for a forthcoming prize fight in Glasgow. Kir's information suggested there was at least still one man at large. Jacob had to hope Dr Bailly's precautions at the hospital kept Percy alive, but perhaps they should look to their own security, too?

'I fear that the boy's information confirms what I found at the hospital. The explosion was no accident. We are being hunted.'

The Fergusons were understandably alarmed, particularly when they heard that their archivist had been assaulted at the hospital and that Mrs Ferguson had also received a threat in Greek a few days ago, one that had been kept from her. The only major detail Jacob held back was that Dora was working with him.

'Damn Elgin, dragging us into his trouble,' was Ferguson's verdict. 'Why can't he just leave us in peace?'

They dined swiftly and retired, meaning to make an early start. The inn's servants were ordered to stand guard. With an admirable instinct for self-preservation, Kir stuck to Dora's side like a self-appointed bodyguard. He slept on the floor by her bed and showed no signs of making way when they got back in the carriage the following morning, blocking any attempts Jacob might make at a private conversation. He had many questions for her.

Like what she thought they could do with the boy once they arrived in London. If the Fergusons didn't find a place for him, it would be left to Jacob and Dora to take responsibility for a child who could be no more than eight or nine.

Jacob imagined her thoughts hadn't travelled that far yet. Her impulsiveness was part of her charm, though it drove him to his wits' end on occasion.

He had plenty of time to consider their situation as they headed south. He rode as guard to the carriage, keeping a few yards behind where he could keep a watchful eye on anyone attempting to overtake their vehicle. He spotted no one suspicious approaching them from that direction. Did that mean the missing man was still after Percy and had stayed in Berwick to pursue that target? Maybe he had gone into hiding when he discovered his attempt had failed and he was preparing for the next assault? Jacob would very much prefer to be riding back to the trouble that awaited in London knowing they had cleared away the problems behind them, but that had not been possible with the wagon driver disappearing so effectively.

To put pursuit off the scent they avoided coaching inns as much as possible. When they reached the Fergusons' friends in Durham, their accommodations were more spacious than at the inn the night before and they had the security of a loyal household staff. The housekeeper insisted that Kir was put with the stable boys, which meant Dora had a room to herself as befitted a lady's maid. She had whispered the location to Jacob when they passed in the corridor.

Once the family retired, Jacob made his way to Dora's door and slipped inside. He found her sitting up in bed studying some papers by candlelight, a shawl over her nightgown.

'Finally!' he whispered.

She put her finger to her lip, nodding to either side of her. The servants' floor was fully occupied and the walls none of the thickest. Sliding from the bed, she padded on bare feet to him. He put his arms around her and hugged her tightly, then put his lips to her ear.

'Thank God you're safe.'

'Thank God you are, too,' she whispered.

'I've never been so scared – never been so relieved.'

'Not even on the battlefield?'

'I didn't have someone there I cared for as I care for you.' He brushed his hand over her cheek.

'Not even yourself?'

'Like most soldiers, I was philosophical about my own chance of surviving. You don't hear the bullet or cannonball that kills you so there's no need to worry over much.'

'But we survived.'

'Yes, we did.'

They stood enjoying the fact that both were alive. He also

began to enjoy the warmth of her body beneath the cotton – rather too much when they could not act on that awareness. He gently pulled away and sat down on the edge of the bed.

'We need to catch up on what we know.' He told her about the hospital – an account he had made in brief to the Fergusons. Now he told her the full story.

'Percy thinks he was the target? But who would aim at him?'

'I don't know yet, but it may link to the ring we haven't yet identified. Elgin and I both thought it a society emblem. It would tie the two separate strands together.'

Dora smoothed her gown over her knees. 'How has Elgin, Brooking, Percy and Mrs Ferguson upset a secret society? Is it something to do with the marbles?'

'I don't know. Ferguson suggested to me that it might be political.'

'How can marbles be political?'

'When they become a grievance between nations. Elgin's coup bringing the marbles to London was a blow for the French, who had been hoping to add them to their spoils of war. The emperor is cherry-picking the artefacts he desires and getting his generals to drag them back to Paris. He makes Elgin look like a rank amateur in that respect. The Louvre is stuffed to the gunnels with iconic pieces and there will be many nations who will want their artworks returned should he ever be defeated – Venetians, Egyptians, Spaniards, the list goes on.'

'He takes their artworks and in exchange sends his brothers and sisters to be their monarchs.'

'That's about right. Collecting is one of Napoleon's obsessions.'

'I can see why he might hate the Elgins for beating him to the marbles. But what then has Percy to do with it? If Mrs Ferguson was the target of the explosion, why go after him at the hospital?'

Jacob leaned back on the pillows, his arm around her. She tucked up her legs and pulled a cover over them both.

'It could be that the explosion was aimed at us. We, after all, are investigating for Elgin.' And didn't that make him feel guilty, putting them all in danger. He'd taken no precautions to disguise that he was leaving town. If someone in Elgin's household was feeding information to the enemy, it would be child's play to discover that Elgin had engaged his and Dora's services, thanks to the letter of appointment and the conversation in the carriage after the Newgate hanging.

'You think someone followed us?'

'And decided to get rid of half of his targets in one fell swoop – Elgin's investigators and the Fergusons? Possibly.'

'That means we brought the trouble with us.'

'It would. We should've been at the exit from the bridge when the fuse reached the gunpowder, but Mrs Ferguson asked to stop on a whim.'

'And we slowed down, too, to pass you. Both carriages were slightly delayed. We had a lucky escape.'

'However, there's another possibility. From his hints, I think we can assume that Percy is working for Napoleon. He implied that he was the target because he had asked too many questions.'

'But why murder Hattie and other bystanders?'

'Because it's war.' The wagon had been a messy attack, predictably imprecise in its victims. It reminded Jacob of an assassination attempt on Napoleon in 1800, which had similar aspects – a wagon of gunpowder, an innocent left holding the horses, the deaths of bystanders but not of the targets. 'Maybe it isn't an either-or case, but let's kill two birds with one stone? Try for all of us. Make it look an accident and no one would come after them for it.'

Dora was silent for a moment, turning that idea over. 'And what does Percy know that is so dangerous?'

'I wanted to ask him more questions, but he was in no

condition for a longer interrogation. I fear we will only get the answers from him if he survives and joins us in London.'

'Maybe we can find out quicker than that.' Dora slid from his arms and hefted out of her trunk a parcel of books and papers. She dumped them on his lap. 'I haven't had a chance to go through them yet as Kir watched my every move last night. It was most unnerving.'

'He probably thought you were going to abandon him as everyone else has.' Jacob lifted one eyebrow, amused when he recognised the handwriting. 'You didn't?'

'Oh, I did.'

'I am amazed you had time.'

'The trunk had been damaged in the blast and they were sitting on top. I was doing him a service.'

'That you were.' Jacob leafed through the letters. Most were in French and appeared to be innocuous orders for books. That could well be a code. He would need a closer look at them.

'If you find proof he is working for the enemy, what are you going to do?' Dora asked.

That was a very good question. 'I know people in government. I think that the Home Office often takes the view that it is better to identify the agents Napoleon has among us and watch them. Percy's access is limited and, if he is to be believed, he is merely reporting on the public mood.'

'You think he was being truthful?'

Jacob paused, considering. 'For the moment I do. I reserve the right to change my mind.'

Dora reached for the book. 'This looks like the one bound in Morocco leather that I spotted in the library at Raith House. My curiosity was pricked because it was in a locked cabinet, wrapped in brown paper. It's the same or part of the same set.' She flicked it open. 'Oh. Well now.'

The title read *Twelve Plates of Amorous Scenes by Thomas*

Rowlandson. The publisher was in York Street – one of the addresses Percy had frequently written to, according to Mrs Cameron's book. 'I see Mr Percy has a taste for naughty drawings.' The scenes included mostly naked men and women, all with optimistically-sized breasts and cocks, in beds, in carriages, or behind screens while husbands dozed.

Jacob had seen many Rowlandson cartoons before, but none so carnal. 'I would call this beyond naughty. Hardly a book you would keep in your library for anyone to pick up.'

'He did have them under lock and key. I had assumed that was for more nefarious reasons.'

'Perhaps he had those, too. Yet it does make sense of something he said. He was worried about his books coming to light. He might have meant these.'

'Is it so shocking? I doubt there are many gentlemen in the land who do not own the odd print or two that they would not share with their maiden sisters or daughters.'

'A few in a collection might be overlooked as a peccadillo, but what if you were the one supplying the images? There are censorship laws against public indecency.' And the image of the woman hiding nothing as she displayed herself splay-legged to an audience in the one called *The Congregation* sailed well beyond the usual cheek of the caricaturist, if he could be forgiven his pun. There was no political message he could detect, just salacious imaginings.

'These are horrible but it's all very silly,' said Dora, not appearing in the least scandalised. 'Men have been at this since ancient times, drawing, sculpting, writing about sex.'

Jacob had to agree. The ruins of Pompeii were full of similar images, though when he'd seen reproductions, he'd considered them somehow softened by the passage of ages. In the Rowlandson pictures, it was possible to identify some of the subjects being lampooned. These were dangerously current. 'But think about it this way. Indecent materials are a ripe field for a spy to harvest. If Percy knows which society gentlemen are customers for such books, he has a hold over them. He could blackmail them into telling him what they know, or perhaps more subtly, be accepted as a confidante as he is in possession of a secret and appears to keep it.'

'I like that explanation. Do you think Mr Ferguson…?'

He squeezed her shoulder. 'That Mr Ferguson knows? I doubt it. There's too much of the dour Scot about him. Remember what lengths Percy went to to hide it from the household, locking the books away?'

'The servants said he flew into a rage when Mrs Cameron tried to open a parcel.'

Jacob smiled grimly, imagining Percy's terror that the stern housekeeper might have been confronted with such bacchanalian images. 'No doubt. Perhaps this is a little side business that Percy conducts and never thought would be exposed, not until his secret life was literally blown up.'

Dora closed the book. 'I don't like them. Too cruel.'

'I'm afraid that if I spent too long looking at them they'd rot my brain – so I'd better take myself off to my own room before my innocent mind is polluted.'

'Ha!' She smothered a laugh and handed the book to him. 'You'd better keep these. Imagine what would happen if I was found with them.'

He kissed her in farewell. 'I'll make sure no one finds them.'

'Wouldn't that be embarrassing?'

'And very hard to explain.'

She teasingly rubbed against his crotch. 'Hard?'

'Stop that,' he growled.

'All right.' She removed her hand to safer territory. 'But only until we are back in our room. Then I think we must revisit this conversation and make some good images to drive out these nasty ones.'

Jacob kissed her soundly again and left her with a whispered 'good night'.

As he crept back to his own room, he decided that Dora's teasing was going to be the death of him. And he found he didn't mind a bit.

Chapter Seventeen

Grosvenor Square, London

It was a relief to reach London with no further attempts on their lives. Dora felt an unexpected sense of homecoming as the carriage arrived in the capital after five days on the road. By far the largest city in the nation, it was an exciting stage to enter after lingering in the wings of rural towns. Maybe she was more of a city girl than she thought. Where were Jacob and she now in their enquiry, she wondered? Act three, scene one? That sounded about right – the answers they were getting were leading to more questions. The Fergusons were no longer suspects but targets. They had a possible political plot, an elusive librarian, and a mysterious group with designs on the marbles to investigate. The villains were hidden, and the challenge was to unmask them before anyone else died.

Jacob's warning that they had not left danger behind had produced a feeling that something might leap out of the dark at any moment. Alert for trouble, Dora watched the traffic-choked streets. It would be hard to spot an attack with these crowds. That man with the cherry-red coat and the leer? He was loitering with intent. Or what about that woman with the blue shawl and overly large basket? She had a shifty look. Dora shook her head at herself and her imaginings. They were both probably ordinary criminals looking for targets, not members of some sophisticated conspiracy about collectors of Greek statues.

The carriage bumped and jolted on. London was a city of contrasts: fine squares that paid homage to classical architecture and squalid slums that did not; the parks, shops and markets bustling with some people in fancy clothes, others in rags. The season was playing to its crescendo, so the rich families were in their mansions and social engagements at their height. That in turn meant servants were running errands, shopkeepers rushing to fulfil orders, and debt collectors lurking to settle bills before the nobility fled to the country. Fortunately, no one seemed to be interested in a dusty carriage arriving from Scotland.

It was only when they turned into Grosvenor Square that Dora remembered she had originally been planning to return to her theatre company when she travelled north. The explosion at the bridge and the fear of pursuit had driven that from her mind to the point that she hadn't even asked herself whether she still wanted to go back on the boards. Jacob hadn't raised her intention again, which he wouldn't because he had made no secret of his desire to keep her with him.

She swore under her breath with words that would've shocked her employer had she heard them. It was late to be having the debate but was she happy to be here rather than on a stage in a northern town? Surely she could not leave while the case was still in so dangerous an unresolved state? Leaving would not stop her being a target now she was involved so she could imperil her friends. Dora shuddered to imagine another explosion in a packed provincial theatre. It was not safe to depart until this was resolved.

But even so, hadn't the decision always been about Jacob? Did she want to leave him? She remembered the special connection she had felt to him in the aftermath of the Berwick incident. It had felt even closer than lovemaking, working together in the carnage and danger. She had needed him desperately, and he her – and that thought unsettled her. She wasn't used to needing anyone.

'You're very quiet, Miss Pence,' said Mrs Ferguson. 'Are you overwhelmed? I thought you were familiar with London?'

'I am, ma'am. I just hadn't expected to be back here so soon.'

'Thoughts of your brother?'

Dora's heart squeezed. Trust the sensitive Mrs Ferguson to remember that element of truth in her explanation for going to Scotland.

'Yes, ma'am.'

Mrs Ferguson nodded. She tweaked her kid gloves in place. 'I find keeping busy stops me dwelling on the things I am powerless to change.'

Like losing one's children to a vengeful husband. 'Wise advice. Thank you, ma'am.'

As they reached Marylebone, Jacob parted from them to return to his lodgings. Nero found renewed energy as the horse sensed his home stables to be nearby. Jacob's eyes held hers as they separated, but they could risk no clearer sign of affection as they made their farewells. What was she going to do about him?

Reaching the house of Mrs Ferguson's grandmother, Lady Robert, the Scottish party disembarked like survivors of a shipwreck making it to shore. The elderly lady of the house met them in the grand foyer. Life-sized statues of demigods and full-length family portraits by Gainsborough and Reynolds stood as spectators to the reunion. A froth of white curls framed the lady's face, her cap was crimped with tucks, and she sported a frilly ruff, showing Lady Robert's lady's maid was aware of what was fashionable this season.

'Mary, Mary, what is all this I've been hearing?' the lady cried. 'Your message was most alarming.'

'We are well – you can see that we are.' Mary Ferguson bent to kiss her grandmother. 'At least this time the scandal is nothing to do with me.'

'Oh, my dear: what happened? Tell me at once.'

'A wagon of gunpowder exploded on the bridge at Berwick. We were lucky to escape with our lives.'

'Oh, I can't bear to think what might-have-been!'

Mr Ferguson bowed over Lady Robert's wrinkled hand. 'It could have been a lot worse. However, we kept our presence at the scene out of the reports, ma'am. We have no wish to attract renewed public attention.' He looked around him, taking in the butler who was hovering. 'And that goes for our presence here, Rogers. We would prefer to keep it quiet. I left word at Raith that we were going on a summer excursion, and we are not inviting callers while we stay in London.'

Dora prayed that would also keep them safer.

'Then why are you here?' The old lady could be forgiven her confusion. 'I had hoped it was because you wished to call on me?'

'That is always a pleasure.' Mrs Ferguson took her arm gently and prodded her to move to a less public area in the house. 'Let's have tea, Grandmama, and I'll tell you what brought us here.'

As the Fergusons disappeared into the parlour to explain the danger to the lady, Dora and Kir were left facing the household servants. Kir slipped his hand in hers.

The butler scowled. Mr Rogers was clearly the stern sort who stood as Cerberus to the home of the wealthy. 'And you are?'

Dora had to bite back her many witty retorts to that impolite enquiry. 'Miss Pence, Mrs Ferguson's lady's maid.' As the man probably knew. He was just stamping his authority on a new servant.

He lifted his chin and looked down his nose. 'And he is?'

'I'm Miss Pence's boy,' Kir said quickly. He was not so ignorant that he missed the raised eyebrows this remark was met with. 'I'm her servant,' he clarified.

That was news to Dora. She put a hand on the lad's shoulder. 'This young man is called Aboukir after the victory in Egypt. Kir for short. He is not my servant, but I did recommend him to the Fergusons.'

'Is he to be taken on as a member of staff?' asked Mr Rogers.

'His status is undecided. Kir is the orphaned son of one of our brave army officers who lost his life serving our country.' That might have been a promotion, and she had no idea how Kir's father had died, but there was no one around to gainsay her. Kir had been vague on the details of his parents, being too young to remember much when they died. 'Mr and Mrs Ferguson have taken him under their wing as an act of charity and in recognition of that sacrifice.' She'd be having the maids all weeping if she kept this up.

'You can call me Kir,' said Kir, as if granting the butler a great honour.

'What are we supposed to do with him?' asked the butler with a sniff.

Difficult audience, this one. 'How do you mean?' asked Dora, cocking her head to one side.

'Where do we put him?'

She had no idea. This wasn't her house, after all. 'I imagine he would be happiest if he were close to my room.'

'I can sleep on the floor,' said Kir.

Mr Rogers was on the move, heading to the servants' quarters. 'No need for that, Master Kir. Miss Pence, if you would follow me?'

Mounting the servants' stairs, Dora pondered how much longer she should continue this subterfuge. It had seemed a good idea in Scotland but there was a chance that she would be recognised in London, particularly if she went anywhere with Jacob. And how much more could they find out from the Ferguson household? They'd already uncovered one spy and discovered that Mary Ferguson had received threats. Surely that was enough to report to Lord Elgin that Mary could be taken off his list of suspects? This investigating lark was less fun if it meant being under the thumb of martinets like Mr Rogers. Was it time to bow out of the lady's-maid game?

But how to disengage from her employment? And would she be leaving Mary less well protected if she did remain?

And what about Kir?

If Dora had been on her own, she would have thumped her own forehead. She had the talent of getting herself into situations for what felt like very good reasons and only later discovering the escape ladder was missing.

'I'll put you in this room, next to Miss Mitkou, Lady Robert's maid.' The butler gestured to a small chamber at the end of the corridor. 'She is known as Mitty to the household. I will request she shows you what you need to know to fulfil your duties.'

The name snared Dora's attention. Maybe she should not be in such a hurry to leave? 'Is Miss Mitkou from Greece by any chance, Mr Rogers?'

'Miss *Mitty*. And yes, I believe so. She came back from Athens with Mrs Ferguson – who wasn't Mrs Ferguson then, of course – and was given to Lady Robert.'

'How interesting. A well-travelled woman.' The maid might know more about people the Elgins had met in Athens who might bear a long-term grudge against them. 'And my mistress's dressing room?'

'On the floor below. I'll send someone to take you there in ten minutes. You, young man, follow me.' The butler tapped Kir on the shoulder. 'You can sleep in the dormitory with the junior footmen until your status is decided.'

Dora only had a moment to herself to wash and change as she would be expected downstairs to care for her lady's clothes. She splashed her face in the basin of water to drive away dust and weariness. Here was another task for her to do in the investigation. Servants were the unseen presence in every household, able to go everywhere and overhear so much without their employers giving them a second thought. Dimitra Mitkou was worth a closer look.

Dora's chance to meet the lady's maid came sooner than expected. She was waiting for Dora by Mrs Ferguson's trunks in the suite of rooms assigned to the couple. A small woman of no more than five feet, Miss Mitkou still projected an air of command as befitted one of the senior female servants. Her straight black hair was curled up and hidden under a cap, leaving her strong dark brows to frame her brown eyes. Her nose was on the larger side, but it gave her face character and made her handsome rather than forgettably pretty.

The Greek woman shook Dora's hand in a strong grip.

'Welcome. I was told you are newly employed by Mrs Ferguson so have not been to this house before. May I help you unpack?' Her accent was barely perceptible. She had acclimatised to her situation, and, with her anglicised name, Dora would've been hard-pressed to guess she was originally from Greece had she not already known.

'I'm delighted to meet you. I'm Dora Pence.'

'Dimitra Mitkou, though Mr Rogers insists on calling me Mitty. It caught on.' She pulled a wry smile. 'He is not an admirer of foreigners.'

Dora chuckled as the tone invited her to do so. 'Miss Mitkou.'

Dimitra bent over the first trunk and unstrapped the buckle. 'I don't mind Mitty. It is strange what you can get used to.'

'Yes, like bad weather and English food?'

The woman's eyes sparkled. 'Well, maybe not everything.'

The two women chatted about fashion and modistes while they hung up the clothes for an airing. Dora looked for an opportunity to steer the conversation towards Dimitra and the origins of her employment, but perhaps it would be best to wait to ask after Dimitra had first shown interest in hers?

She didn't have to wait long.

'You don't sound Scottish to me, not like Mr and Mrs Fergusons' other servants,' said Dimitra, unfolding the tissue paper hiding the next layer in the trunk.

'That's because I'm not. I grew up near Liverpool.' Dora brushed off a light splatter of mud from the hem of a skirt with a silver-backed brush. 'I'm not sure where my accent has settled but I have worked in London for fashionable ladies.' And that had the benefit of being partly true. Performing for audiences across England, her regional dialect had been trained out of her. 'And you?'

'I was born in Athens. I entered service with Mrs Ferguson as a girl when she was in Constantinople, on the embassy with Lord Elgin to the Sublime Porte.'

'How marvellous – Greece! And Constantinople! You must've seen so much of the world.' Dora gave Dimitra a quick survey, trying to gauge her age. 'You had to have been very young at the time. That's more than twelve years ago, is it not?'

'About that.' Dimitra shook out a petticoat. 'I was fourteen. Finding employment with a European lady was a very lucky chance for me.'

'And she passed you on to her grandmother?' Dora wondered if there was any lingering bitterness about that.

'Oh, yes. She saw I was happier in London and thought I

would not feel at home in Raith where she told me there were no other Greeks for miles. I'd have to go to Edinburgh or further if I wanted to taste *raki* or *souvlaki*.' Dimitra brushed down a gown as she hung it, taking care that suggested affection for the owner. 'She's a very thoughtful lady.'

'That she is. What is raki?'

'Alcohol – a spirit. Souvlaki is grilled meat on a skewer – though that doesn't do it justice.'

Dora didn't press Dimitra for more information, though she could tell the woman was homesick. Seeming overly interested in her too early would work counter to persuading Dimitra to confide further. Dora changed the subject and, after finishing unpacking Mrs Ferguson's clothes, she went down to the servants' hall to see about her own dinner. All that talk of Greek food had whetted her appetite.

She was delighted – and surprised – to find Jacob there. He was casually dressed, probably to put the staff at ease as he invaded their territory. Dora liked how comfortable he looked in his old jacket and breeches that she remembered from their first journey together from Kendal to West Wycombe. His painting clothes, he'd once explained, suitable for traipsing over the Lake District with easel and oils. He was now sitting on a stool by the kitchen fire, looking very much at home. He had one foot on the opposite knee, cradling a sketchpad on this impromptu rest. Kir stood at his shoulder and was looking down on the picture and commenting on what he had drawn. Dora didn't want to interrupt them so merely lightly touched Kir's arm in greeting and then took a seat at a nearby table to select her meal from the dishes that had been left out. From the looks of the food, the staff were benefiting from the leftovers from the Fergusons' dinner.

'How about this?' Jacob lightly sketched a nose on the face he was drawing.

Kir squinted. 'I think so.'

'Eyes like this, or further apart, like this?'

Dora helped herself to tepid lamb cutlets and thought of spiced meat on skewers. Jacob was carefully taking Kir through the process of shaping each feature, trying to get a portrait of their mystery wagon driver.

Kir sucked on his bottom lip. 'I think a little lower, like the brows were more like this.' He scowled to show what he meant. 'Like Mr Rogers.'

'The butler,' Dora supplied when Jacob looked blank.

'Oh. Yes, that fellow. Now?'

Kir nodded enthusiastically. 'Yes, sir, like that.'

This went on for another ten minutes and at the end Kir pronounced himself content with the sketch. Dora was also content, but in her case from having consumed a hearty meal.

Jacob turned his artwork round to face Dora. It wasn't anyone she recognised: square-faced, nose on the thin side for the breadth of cheeks, light brown hair, deep-set eyes.

'I've not seen him, Dr Sandys,' she said.

'Neither have I. I'll take this to the Fergusons and to … my employer and see if they have more luck. Now who's next?' Jacob looked around the kitchen with the staff busy preparing the next round of meals. The cook, a red-cheeked woman with a suitably dumpling-like figure, was beaming at them indulgently. She was clearly enjoying the afternoon's entertainment. 'Miss Pence, I must draw you. And then Mrs Widgeon, I must capture your likeness.'

The cook, Mrs Widgeon, went into gales of laughter and shook her head at him. 'You don't want my old face, sir. Besides, I never have two moments to sit down. Draw the pretty ones, like Miss Pence here.'

Clever Jacob, finding an excuse to prolong their conversation.

'Miss Pence?'

'Very well,' said Dora, 'but I only have a few minutes before I must return upstairs.'

'How are you settling in?' Jacob turned to a fresh page. Kir didn't budge from his post but seemed content to watch the next sketch take shape.

Dora swivelled in her seat to face him. She reminded herself they must only show the familiarity of two travelling companions of very different stations. 'Very well, sir. Lady George's woman, Dimitra Mitkou, has made me very welcome.'

He met her gaze. 'She has? How interesting.' He held up the pencil as if measuring Dora's features.

'Miss Mitkou was with Mrs Ferguson in Constantinople.' She hoped her expression was saying all that she could not in front of the servants. The scullery maid at the sink was shooting interested looks in their direction while she washed the pans. They might pretend not to listen, but they surely were. Servants thrived on gossip and would leap on any gesture that betrayed their intimacy. 'She has served Mrs Ferguson's grandmother since their return to London. I thought perhaps you might have met her in Athens when your paths crossed with the lady?'

'I don't remember meeting any of the female servants, but I'll mention it to Miss Mitkou should I come across her in the house. Perhaps she will like her picture drawn?'

That was a good idea, a chance for Jacob to question her. 'I'll be sure to ask her – if you don't make my own countenance look like a gorgon. I won't recommend you to anyone if you do that.'

Jacob gave her one of his little lopsided smiles that she adored. She tried to keep her features straight. 'The gorgons were supposed to be great beauties.'

'Until cursed,' she countered.

His eyes smiled at her. He always enjoyed it when she showed she hadn't wasted her youth spent in libraries. 'True. Ovid says Athena took exception to one with golden locks.'

'That's not what the goddess disliked.'

'Ah yes. Some unseemly goings on with Poseidon in her

temple.' Jacob looked around and realised their audience might think this venturing onto too familiar ground for a servant and a gentleman. 'Miss Pence, you are well read for your station.' Dora wanted to scowl at that condescension but knew he was acting. 'The Greek culture is so vivid. I imagine Miss Mitkou would enjoy reminiscing about home when she has been away for so long. I fell in love with Greece and its treasures in my brief sojourn there. She'll find me a most enthusiastic conversationalist.'

He turned his sketch around. Dora had to admit it was excellent for a brief drawing, though she did look rather more glamorous than she thought herself to be in her lady's-maid uniform of sober dress.

'Oh, larks, sir!' clucked the cook. 'You'll have all the girls lining up for their portrait before you've finished. You'll turn their heads for certain. I'm not sure we should let you loose in the household.'

Dora risked a grin at Jacob. 'He is a flatterer, is he not, Mrs Widgeon?'

The cook patted Dora's cheek in passing, showing she was from the motherly school of cooks and no gorgon herself. 'Some of us give him better material to work with than others.' She handed Kir a raisin scone, which the boy took with a whisper of thanks and the look of a worshipper receiving a favour from his goddess.

Jacob turned to the cook. 'Exactly, Dame of the Kitchen. Who shall I do next? I can sketch you while you work.'

Dora got up from her seat and held out her hand. 'My portrait?'

Jacob had already turned to a fresh page. 'I'll keep that one. I wasn't quite happy with it and will work on it further. Now, Mrs Widgeon, tell me about yourself.'

Dora left Jacob charming the most important personage on the staff and returned upstairs with a smile.

Chapter Eighteen

Lord Elgin's House

Lord Elgin paced his study while Jacob delivered his report standing. He felt like an aide-de-camp describing enemy movements to a general. Sunlight poured in from Hyde Park where leaves were in their freshest green but somehow it failed to warm Elgin and his surroundings. The room had the gloomy atmosphere of a man of high station with too many debts and too little money.

'Miss Fitz-Pennington remains in Mrs Ferguson's service?' the peer asked when Jacob completed his account.

'For the moment. She is pursuing the possibility that there may be knowledge of other enemies of you and your former wife among the long-serving servants, and some of them came back with you from Constantinople.' He put his sketch of Dimitra on the table.

Elgin glanced at it. 'I remember her. My wife's maid. My *former* wife's maid,' he corrected. He moved to the window and stood looking out on the garden with its exhibition shed. A steady trickle of well-to-do visitors passed through to admire the marbles for a small consideration handed to the guide on duty. Elgin had been reduced to turning his house into a tourist attraction. That must gall the proud man. 'I would ask my own servants, too, but none have been with me for long. You concluded that the Fergusons are targets, not suspects?'

'I can say with considerable certainty that Mary and Robert Ferguson have nothing to do with the threat you've received. The explosion that nearly killed us all weighs against that. However, Miss Fitz-Pennington also discovered that Mrs Ferguson was sent a threat shortly before that, though it did not reach her. The housekeeper intercepted it, not knowing that it was part of a larger pattern.'

Elgin frowned, like he'd tasted something sour. 'Then why has the blasted woman come to London and not stayed in Scotland?'

'She fears for her children.'

'Children she abandoned by her disgraceful conduct.'

Jacob was not going to get into the middle of a divorce – that was like stepping between a warship and the dock when the sea was swelling. 'She has a mother's feelings, sir.'

'Ha!' Elgin was dismissive but Jacob thought he detected sincere hurt in his expression. A difficult man to know, Elgin was suffering from the deep betrayal of his first marriage.

Jacob was relieved that Elgin did not pursue the topic, instead he took a seat at the desk and gestured for Jacob to sit opposite him. The peer folded his hands together, ready to puzzle through the information Jacob had delivered.

'What about this attack in Berwick? Gunpowder? That sounds like Napoleon's plots to me. Were they targeting the troops?'

Ironic that like Ferguson he thought that politics were involved. 'You think agents mounted an attack on the army and we merely had the misfortune to be passing? Have the French done anything like this before?'

Elgin shook his head slowly, reworking his assumptions. 'No, you're right, that doesn't seem likely. Berwick is an obscure place to begin such a campaign. A naval dockyard or a London barracks would make more sense.'

'I believe our presence was the cause, not a coincidence. Someone had to know we were travelling that route and knew roughly when we would be there. That means they either had a source in the household or they were watching us. We didn't think to hide our plans when we stopped in Edinburgh – no one saw the need. We thought the danger was in London.'

'But why target the Fergusons or this Percy fellow? I'd be the better target, surely?'

Be careful what you wish for, thought Jacob. 'They also might've been trying for Miss Fitz-Pennington and I.'

'Ah, yes, as an extension of me, like Brooking.'

'However, we should also consider the presence of the Frenchman. Normally I would dismiss Percy's suggestion that it was aimed at him but the follow-up attack at the hospital gives weight to his opinion.'

'Any word on the man who tried to kill him?'

'I received a letter from Dr Bailly, the chief surgeon at Berwick Hospital. The dead man was identified as a local troublemaker, Kit Parker, a washed-up regimental boxer, dismissed from the army for repeated drunkenness and behaviour unbecoming. He apparently knew the man on the door and talked his way in.'

Elgin grimaced. 'He must've been a bad piece of work to warrant dismissal. The dregs of society are usually swept up into the ranks.'

'It would seem the local commander does have some basic standards.'

Elgin leaned back in his chair and looked up at the ceiling, fingers steepled. 'Let us work with this Percy's theory. A secretive group targeted him because he was asking questions in the wrong places. His motive for doing so is obscure but possibly because he is an enemy spy. He was in possession of obscene material that he might have been using to blackmail a highly placed person – another motive for doing away with him.'

'For all his charm, he has a formidable number of enemies.'

'In some way it goes back to the group he mentioned. Could that connect to Brooking's murder and the threats against Mary and myself? Did Percy catch their attention because he was getting close to unmasking their plot? He has been ferreting out the secrets of British high society and this was one he stumbled over. He was the one who read the threat and destroyed it. Was he there because he suspected someone was going to threaten Mary?'

Jacob couldn't answer these questions – not yet.

He drew out another sketch. 'Do you recognise this man?'

'Is that the devil who blew up that poor girl and the other victims?' Elgin pulled the picture closer.

'Yes, sir. The boy who survived says it is a good likeness.'

Elgin gave a disappointed frown. 'I don't recognise him.'

'We don't yet know if he's another paid assassin, or the one behind the plot. In my mind, it is more likely he is – or was working for – the same person as the hospital attacker, but he had a greater sense of self-preservation. He made sure he was far from the scene when the wagon exploded and didn't care tuppence what the outcome was. The person who planned the attack didn't have long to put the elements in place as our departure was a quick decision. He scrambled the plan using local resources to hit us at a strategic spot and might've guessed casualties would be brought to the hospital. He had a man in place to follow up in case Percy survived – as he did.'

Elgin held the picture up to the light. 'If I may keep this overnight? I'll show it to my staff and have a copy made by my man – he's skilled at drawing. You know him – Harold Fisher.'

The hair on the back of Jacob's neck prickled. He hadn't

paused to consider whether his old friend might be also at risk – or involved. 'Ah, yes, his sketches of the Parthenon were wonderful. I'm sure he'll be able to produce a good copy. I'd be pleased to renew my acquaintance.'

'I'll have him bring this back to you, then.'

'Thank you.' Fisher was a source that Jacob could press for information. 'I've not seen him since the breakfast you arranged.'

'Which breakfast?'

'The one with the boxers a few years back.' It had been an odd way to introduce the British public to the Elgin marbles when first put on display in the earl's garden. Elgin had arranged for prize fighters to pose bare-chested alongside the statues. The propaganda point had been that British brawn rivalled that of the Greek heroes. The audience was to understand that the marbles had found their natural home in London, the new centre of European culture and art – not Paris.

'Ah, that.' Elgin gave another of his little smiles. It seemed the way to his heart was through his collection. 'The French hated that. I take my revenges where I can within the limit of my parole.' Elgin stood up, signalling their interview was over. 'Good work, Sandys. Please convey my thanks to Miss Fitz-Pennington.'

'Sir, I believe we should also investigate Richard Brooking. There is much that is murky around the circumstances of his death.'

The earl nodded. 'You can't do better than talking to Fisher about him. They were friends, I believe.'

That was helpful, but Jacob also wanted to talk to the people who found the body.

'Do you have the address where he died?'

'Indeed.' Elgin wrote it down for him. 'There will be no trace left by now.'

There were always traces, even if only in the recollection of those nearby. 'What do you want me to do about Michel Percy?'

'The man's injured and out of action. Leave him free for now. I'll have a word with the Alien Office, let them know your suspicions. I'll be very surprised if he isn't already on their watch list.'

'On the basis of "keep your friends close, and your enemies closer"?'

'Yes – though that isn't without its dangers. Take care of yourself and that partner of yours. We've already seen that these people are serious about their threats.'

'I will try my best. Any last orders?'

'The question I'd like you to investigate most urgently is where they will strike next? I don't want any of this touching my family.'

'Very good, sir.'

Jacob had his hand on the door handle when Elgin added, looking down in the diffident way he had, 'You know, Sandys, you should take a look at Byron. If you are hunting for a man who would be attracted to the flummery of a secret society and might want to kill me, it would be a hothead like him.'

Jacob left Elgin's house and walked back to his rooms. Take a look at Byron? All of society was doing exactly that. The young poet had achieved a fame far beyond the merits of his title, which was only distinguished as a line of scoundrels. Jacob had, of course, read *Childe Harold* because everyone was talking about it. Reluctantly, he had borrowed a copy and corrected his ignorance. He'd found it faintly annoying. He recognised that Byron had a gift for verse and some stirring passages, but it did not appeal to him. The young man travelled round Europe striking poses on rocky outcrops with the sun setting behind him, declaiming self-righteously about freedom. Meanwhile his contemporaries, Jacob and his army friends, were risking their lives and spilling blood to settle the same matter on the battlefields. Byron undeniably had glamour, though that was something Jacob found suspect. Society periodically lost its head over a handsome young man, and today it was Byron's turn. How long would it last? One day, his charm would vanish, and he'd be mauled by the vengeful mob, Jacob could predict that now as a certainty. That trajectory was all too like a Greek story.

An idea flamed in Jacob's brain casting a new light on the case. That had been the fate with which the Furies threatened Orestes, was it not? Byron was exactly the kind of person who would use *The Oresteia* to make threats against his enemy, histrionically perceiving himself as the wronged son, and Elgin the usurper.

Could this poet have the organisation to be behind a plot to assault Elgin and his associates? It was public knowledge that he had attacked Elgin in his verse. How did it go? 'The last, the worst, dull spoiler' with a barren mind and hard heart. Sitting on his picturesque rock – naturally, it was a rock – Byron appealed to Pallas Athena to defend her temple, as Orestes appeals to Athens' goddess to defend him against the Furies.

But was this battle worth killing for? Wasn't it far-fetched to think a poet would do something so extreme? Yet Byron was also a gentleman. Jacob reminded himself that gentlemen had taken aim at each other for less. Only three years ago, government ministers, Canning and Castlereagh, had fought a duel over a political slight. In this case, two cultural visions were in conflict. Byron argued that the marbles should have stayed in Greece; Elgin felt entitled to take them for Britain and to stop them falling into the hands of the French. In a perfect world, the marbles should have found a home in a restored Parthenon in a flourishing Greece, but the Acropolis was an army camp ruled over by the Ottomans who cared little for the relics. Byron was naïve if he thought the marbles would have survived if Elgin had not taken them. But Byron's poetic attacks had hurt the earl. Little wonder

Elgin was eager to find his critic guilty. The poet had undermined the earl's grand aim to preserve culture and made it out to be little more than grave-robbing. If Byron's version of events prevailed, he would destroy Elgin's last chance at leaving a great legacy.

But would a poet turn man-of-action, taking the step to sabotage and murder?

Jacob paused at a street crossing as carriages passed. There was no choice but to go in search of Lord Byron to find out.

Chapter Nineteen

Melbourne House

An inquiry at his club quickly produced the most likely whereabouts of the poet. From the knowing gleam in the porter's eye, Jacob suspected he wasn't the first to ask the question. Byron was at present an intimate of the Whiggish Melbourne circle – by intimate, Jacob understood 'lover' of Lady Caroline Lamb, the married daughter of the house, whose complacent husband, the Honourable William Lamb, dealt with his wife's infatuation by ignoring it. The aristocracy played games with their marriages that would make most people of the middling sort blush.

The odds were good that Byron would be there now. During the week there were daily dance parties at Melbourne House that started at noon. The excuse was that those gathered – some forty or so friends – were there to practise the quadrille. It had grown to be the most coveted daytime invitation and expanded to serve a luncheon and continued to late in the afternoon.

Armed with this information, Jacob went to Melbourne House

which lay opposite the Banqueting Hall, scene of Charles I's execution. He hoped that his father's name would gain him admittance. Lord Sandys had voted with the Whigs while he was still active in the Lords. The Melbournes were likely to welcome all his sons with the aim to recruit the next generation to vote with them. He was proved right: 'Sandys' was the 'Open Sesame' required. He gave his name to the footman on duty and was granted access through the pillared portico that fronted the wide, cobbled street of Whitehall.

Away from the bustle of the king-killing thoroughfare, he could hear strains of music playing. He was shown into the ballroom where couples were arranged into groups of four to learn the intricate moves of the dance. This was no evening ball, so the ladies were dressed in light gowns suitable for exercise, with no heavy jewellery or complicated hairstyles. Likewise, the gentlemen were in morning coats and snug pantaloons. They had left off the silk, knee breeches and stockings that they would adopt for the evening social events. They came together in twos, retreated, wove, passed to the opposite partner. Having just been considering the marital behaviour of high society, it was easy to imagine the dance was an illustration of their wayward habits.

Jacob had not come intending to dance – if he'd wished to join in that would have necessitated a return to his rooms to choose more appropriate footwear than his mud-splattered Hessian boots. His hope was that he could watch the goings on and look for an opportunity to make Byron's acquaintance, though with so many wanting a moment with the celebrated writer he wasn't optimistic that this would be possible. He could learn much by observing.

He spotted his female quarry easily. Lady Caroline Lamb loved dancing and she was in the middle of the floor, teasing her partner over some misstep. Her hair curled around her gamine face; hazel eyes, big and limpid like a child's, though the lady herself was twenty-seven. Her slight frame was boyish in its lack of curves. Society was buzzing about her delight in going about as a page, and he could see how she could easily pass as one where her face was not already known.

'Again, again!' she called when the set came to an end. 'Sir Michael hasn't learned the steps. We must take him back to school.'

The poor young man who was the object of her teasing blushed and bowed over her hand. Obediently the musicians started over.

Jacob moved along the edge of the room, weaving his way between the other onlookers. Some were waiting their chance to join the practice while others had come to gawk. There was no sign of Lord Byron. He wouldn't be among the dancers. He had a slight infirmity and avoided dancing in public. He famously hated to be caught in any awkwardness that took away from his appeal to his admirers.

Maybe that was why he preferred striking poses on rocks?

Jacob allowed himself the mean-spirited thought. Taking potshots at those riding high in society favour was catching.

'Dr Sandys?'

Jacob had been so caught up in watching the dancers that he was surprised to find himself addressed by Alexander Smith, formerly a lieutenant colonel in the 1st Battalion 2nd Foot Guard. Smith was a tall, golden-haired Adonis of a man, just the kind of dancing partner many debutantes dreamed of having on their dance card. When Jacob had met him before, he'd been resplendent in a scarlet uniform. Now he was dressed in sober dark blue.

'Smith, how are you?' They shook hands warmly. 'I haven't seen you since that day at the House of Commons.' Having arranged for Dora to meet her brother's lover in the aftermath of the Hellfire scandal, they had all been present when the prime minister was assassinated. That had cut short their introduction as Smith had hurried over to help with crowd control in the lobby while Jacob ushered Dora out to safety. Not an auspicious first meeting.

'A grim business.' Smith leaned against the wall next to Jacob, taking them out of the circulating spectators. Jacob had the sensation of the world swirling around them while they were the only ones to be still. 'Hasn't the world had enough of killing? How is Miss Fitz-Pennington?'

'She is well, though she's still grieving.'

A muscle twitched in Smith's jaw and he looked down.

'As I'm sure you do,' Jacob added softly. Smith and Anthony Pennington's desire to conduct their illegal relationship out of the public eye had led to their involvement in the Hellfire Club and, in turn, that had led to Smith's fatal decision to entrust state secrets to the group as price of entry. These papers – military orders – almost fell into enemy hands but were saved when Jacob and Dora exposed the plot. Smith had lost his commission as punishment, but he had escaped worse penalties because the government did not want the security breach to be known. Smith had been quietly shuffled into civilian life under a cloud. Jacob had thought the man a fool for betraying his secrets to such unsafe hands, but then again, he himself had been a fool going into the caves high on opium, so he did not consider himself the superior in wisdom. Love could be a kind of madness – as bad as an addiction to laudanum.

'Please send her my best wishes,' said Smith.

Jacob nodded. 'She would like to see you again. She has no one else with whom she can share her memories of Anthony.'

'And I would like to see her.' Smith's face brightened at the prospect. 'Is she in London?'

'Ah.' Jacob scanned the room. Still no Byron. 'We are working on a new case together and she is currently living under an assumed name as part of our enquiries.'

'How intriguing. And is your presence here today due to the same investigation?'

The man was quick. Jacob folded his arms and relaxed beside him. To all the world they would look like two acquaintances catching up on the news. 'It may be. I'm not sure.'

Smith nodded sagely. 'No doubt you have to turn over many stones to find what you are looking for.'

'Exactly.' Jacob glanced at the young officer. 'What are you doing these days?'

'Since my disgrace?' Smith said in a low voice, his tone self-mocking. 'Well, my father won't speak to me, which I have to say I deserve; and my mother refuses to understand that her son has lost his commission and thinks it all some terrible mistake. She threatens to go to Wellington himself about it, which nobody deserves, not even old Beaky – she can be terrifying when she is on the warpath.' Jacob gave a sour smile, thinking of the steely general facing an irate mother – that would be one for the caricaturists to capture. 'What else? Oh yes. The whispers and rumours have been such that my sisters don't want me anywhere near them in case I pollute their chances this season. I am barred from Almack's.'

Almack's was the famous marriage mart and assembly room. Smith might not have enjoyed the weak punch and insipid conversation but one way out of his predicament would've been to marry some innocent heiress and pretend to be the devoted husband. That would've quietened tongues as people liked to think young men 'grew out' of attraction to their own sex, dismissing it as a schoolboy humour. 'Lucky you. Almack's is a bore. Yet you are allowed to come here?'

'The Melbournes welcome fashionable young men willing to partner the wallflowers. Dangerous ones only add to the lure, as a certain poet proves. I get a free luncheon out of it and, so far, my sisters have not banned me from attending. I'll keep coming until my shoes wear out and I can no longer pass myself off as presentable.'

It sounded like his father had cut off his support and, without a commission, Alexander Smith was in a financial quandary: having to live like a member of society without having a penny coming in.

He wouldn't be the first, nor the last.

At that moment, Jacob was drawn from his thoughts by the arrival of a dark curly-haired man with striking blue eyes, dressed in an impeccable morning suit. The noise fell away then swelled in excitement. What Jacob had not expected was how pale Byron was. If he were to present himself as a patient, Jacob would recommend a hearty meal and a dose of sunshine. Byron stalked into the room, any lameness masked by his resolute demeanour, and the occupants orientated themselves so he was at their centre.

'There is he,' murmured Smith. 'Childe Harold himself. I'm swooning already.'

'Do you believe in the version of himself as a traveller that he created?'

Smith gave him a sardonic look. 'You haven't heard the stories?'

'One hardly knows what to believe when it comes to Byron.'

'I can tell you one thing that he failed to mention in his poem: he is well known to men of my persuasion; indeed famous at Harrow for it. He has had many boys in his service who were there for their attractions, just as were the maids at Newstead. He is indiscriminate in where he bestows his favours.' Byron was scowling at the assembly, cutting dead many of the young ladies angling for his attention. His eyes were on his current lover and her inept partner. 'Lady Caroline,' Smith nodded to the dancer, 'combines the looks he prefers with a socially acceptable amour. Adultery is preferable to sodomy.'

'So I understand.'

'You're not shocked, sir? Not going to summon the law officers to take us into custody?'

Jacob took a moment to work out what Smith was really asking. He was probing as to whether he was accepted by Sandys. There was real vulnerability in the man's expression as he awaited the verdict.

'Smith, you are an idiot not because of whom you loved, but because of what you did.'

'I see,' the man said tightly. He looked like he wanted to throw a punch.

'However, I too am an idiot for what I did during that investigation.'

Smith's belligerence went down a notch. 'What did you do?'

Jacob waved that away. 'I'd have to know you a hell of a lot better before I bare my soul to you.'

Smith grinned, showing the charm that had hooked Anthony Pennington. 'Feel free to bare anything else you'd like.'

'Very funny. I am also a doctor and have seen everything life offers. I don't stand in judgement on people. I'll leave that to God, if there is one.'

'And if there isn't, what does it matter anyway?'

Jacob shrugged. It was hard to believe in a merciful God when standing in the guts of boys disembowelled by cannon balls, but he hadn't quite shaken the sense that there was something more to life, something spiritual. He felt it when he painted, he felt it when reading Wordsworth's poetry, or Coleridge's, he felt it when he laughed with Dora. He just didn't feel it standing listening to the annoying strains of a quadrille, contemplating the ridiculousness of the London season. He didn't feel it when reading *Childe Harold*. He would be the last person someone like Byron would befriend.

Then an idea came to him.

'Smith, would you be interested in helping Miss Fitz-Pennington and me with this investigation?'

Smith stood up from where he had been lounging, a warhorse hearing the drums. 'Help? But of course. I owe you both so much.'

'You can share in the fee – this wouldn't be repaying a favour.'

'Sandys—'

'Before you agree, you should hear what this is all about.'

'But what do I bring that you need? I'm a disgraced ex-officer with shady connections.'

Jacob slapped him on the back. 'That, dear sir, is exactly what you bring.'

Smith's eyes gleamed with intelligence and humour. 'I see. How ironic – my fall is my greatest asset.'

'Like Milton's Satan, you are far more interesting now. You can start this moment. Make the acquaintance of Byron. I can't muster a reason to beg an introduction, whereas he will find you ... shall we say ... intriguing.'

'And what do you want me to do once I've done that?'

'Meet me later at Lady Tolworth's and I'll explain. This isn't for so public a place. I will try to arrange for Dora to join us.'

'Lady Tolworth's?' Smith frowned, probably fearing being turned away from the termagant's door.

'Don't worry, she'll make us all welcome. The lady fears to be bored and she has found Dora and me very amusing of late. She will think you delicious even if disgraceful.'

In answer, Smith gave Jacob a smart salute and went off to tempt Byron's attention away from his current lover.

Lady Caroline wouldn't stand a chance, mused Jacob. If Byron really did prefer his own sex, then few could defend against Alexander Smith with his disreputable allure. And if there was one thing Jacob had learned about the poet, he was unable to resist scandal.

Chapter Twenty

Soho

Leaving Smith to charm Byron, Jacob followed up the address that Elgin had given him in Soho. This area of London was changing fast. Respectable families still lived around the garden square but in the side streets people slipped into penury, occupying houses divided into tenements. The area was becoming shabby, but not yet quite as dire as the nearby Rookeries a street or two north, where the beggars, orphans and thieves took shelter in crumbling warehouses. That made it the perfect halfway point between the streetwalkers and their gentleman clients.

Finding the entrance to the townhouse on Rose Street, Jacob noted the flaking blue paint of the door and a cracked window stuffed with rags. He knocked. After a shout from deep within the house that they were coming, he waited, keeping alert for both ordinary thieves and the assailant Kir had described. Humanity streamed by, pushing carts, carrying burdens, rushing on their unknowable tasks and oblivious to him. Except one. Was that man at the end of the alley familiar? He wore a hat pulled low over his brow and his collar up, despite it being a warm summer's day. Half in mind to confront him, Jacob was about to turn away, but the door opened.

'What you want?' asked an elderly woman, puffing on a clay pipe. She smelled sour and he suspected water did not often touch her skin. She wore the stained rags of a gown that had been fashionable thirty years ago. Her gaze skittered behind him. 'Where's your wench?'

'I'm not here for that.' He tipped his hat to her.

Rather than being charmed, she narrowed her eyes and scratched at a flea bite. 'Are you a shoulder-clapper?'

He quickly parsed what she might mean. 'No, I'm not here to arrest anyone for debt.'

'Then what are you 'ere for?'

He offered her two shillings. 'Information – and a look at the room where the man died.'

She didn't take the coins. 'Which man?'

Had there been so many? 'The young man. Richard Brooking.'

Giving him a thorough examination, she then looked down at the coins. 'It'll cost more than two shillings.'

He'd thought as much. He produced a crown. 'What about now?'

'What's going on, Joanna?' wailed a voice from an inner room.

The servant rolled her eyes. 'Now I'll have to ask my mistress. You should keep your voice down.'

'You aren't the landlady?'

She scoffed at that. 'Nah, my mistress owns the house, but she's confined to 'er bed these days. I'll go ask 'er.' The door snapped shut.

Jacob could hear voices in the ground-floor room. He moved nearer the window, eavesdropping.

'It's another gentleman, Miss Beamish, askin' questions about the man that got 'imself killed.'

'Make him pay,' came the querulous reply.

'I always do, ma'am.'

'Only respectable people, mind, in my house. You know my instructions.'

'Yes, ma'am, they're all very respectable, every single one.' There was the sound of a pillow being plumped.

'My father was a gentleman.'

'So 'e was.'

'Taught music.'

'That he did.'

The servant returned a minute later. 'She says it's all right. You can come up.'

Jacob had surmised that the loyal maid was protecting, or was it exploiting, her mistress by not letting her know that the rooms she rented were to all-comers.

'What ails your mistress?'

'Age,' said the woman simply.

She showed him up to the miserable room in which Brooking had died. It had a bed in one corner, sheets pulled straight though they looked none too clean. A deal table sat in the window, two chairs either side, a plain candlestick in the centre. The remnant of former glory clung on in the panelling that ended halfway up the wall. Above the panels a few pictures were nailed, portraits of forgotten ancestors and a surprisingly fine landscape of Stonehenge at sunrise. That last looked out of place, too modern. The occupants hadn't been purchasing artwork in the recent decades from the appearance of everything else.

'Did Brooking come here often?' Jacob asked, taking a closer look at the painting.

She shrugged. 'About once a week.'

'Since when?'

She scratched her head, dislodging her mob cap. 'It's so hard to remember with so many coming and going.'

He held up another coin. 'Does this help?'

'Since last September.'

'Alone or with company?' He placed the coin on the table but kept his finger on it.

'Never brought a woman with him.' She crossed her arms over her skinny chest.

'Men?'

'Not like that. But 'e sometimes met another man 'ere. They never used the bed before you ask. They'd sit here and play cards, talk – strange goings on but who am I to say?'

'Did you ever hear what they said?'

'Nah, they talked funny.'

'Funny how?'

'In a foreign language.'

'Do you know which one?'

'Who the 'ell do you think I am? Dr Johnson?'

That was a 'no' then.

'Did he meet a man on the night he died?'

'Must've done, seeing how he was killed.'

'You didn't open the door?'

'No, they'd knock, and 'e used to let them in 'imself. Told me not to bother stirring from my kitchen.' Her face wrinkled. 'Nice gent,'e was, as they go.'

'You told the Runners this?'

Now her face took on a hard look. 'You're not working for them?'

'No.'

'Course I told those buggers, but you know what they said? They said as I didn't see nothing then they'd make up their own minds. They knew better. A man don't hire a room for any other reason, not in their world.'

Jacob nodded at the picture. 'What about that?'

Her expression went sly. 'What about it?' She picked nervously at her fraying apron.

'Was it Richard Brooking's?'

'Do you recognise it – are you looking for it?' Her mind was clearly scrambling to come up with an excuse. 'I was just taking care of it. Couldn't give it to the Runners now, could I?'

'So you put it up on the wall and hoped no one would notice. Where did you find it?'

She nodded to the side of the room by the bed.

'Did he have it with him when he arrived?'

She shook her head.

'Then the killer brought it with him.' Jacob took the watercolour down, the phrase 'Beware of Greeks bearing gifts' coming to his mind. He looked at the title: *Before the Great Fall of 1797*. It showed the henge as it had appeared before one of the trilithon – a three-stone arch – had collapsed. Why would Brooking be given this picture just before he died?

'You won't tell the Runners?' A desperate note entered her voice. 'Please, sir. You know what they're like. They'll say I stole it, greedy bastards. Miss Beamish wouldn't survive if I weren't 'ere to look after 'er.'

She was probably right about that. Perhaps the woman wasn't as mercenary as she'd first appeared. Maybe she was just doing her best to see them both through their old age with no other support than a house to rent.

'Thank you for looking after it.' He tipped his hat again. 'I will see it is returned to the rightful owner.'

When he'd worked out who that was.

Chapter Twenty-One

Bruton Street

In the long twilight of late spring, Dora knocked on the area door of Lady Tolworth's house and was let in by a servant. Only a few lamps had been lit and the windows shone with the reflection of a sky tinged with purple and green like an old bruise. Crepuscular – that was the word for this kind of light, but it didn't sound a very good omen.

'This way, miss,' said the maid, a pert girl barely out of her teens, clearly happy to be part of the intrigue. 'My lady and the gentlemen are expecting you.'

A note had arrived from Jacob asking Dora to meet them at ten. As Mrs Ferguson was unable to take part in the social events of the London season and had no private invitations for that night, it had been easy enough to request the evening off from her duties. Mrs Ferguson had even sounded pleased that bereaved Dora had friends, though Dora had been vague about the details of those she was visiting. She had claimed to have once worked for Lady Tolworth so a visit to the staff there would fit with that story, should anyone press for an explanation.

Shedding her servant persona as she mounted the stairs, Dora entered the drawing room as Miss Fitz-Pennington, Jacob's partner in this investigation. The relief of sloughing off the lady's maid made Dora realise that she must at all costs avoid a life that led to being a domestic servant. It would kill her like a case of slow arsenic poisoning.

Maybe she should go back to the stage where she could be a queen or a courtesan all in the same evening?

'Miss Fitz-Pennington,' declared Lady Tolworth with a dramatic manner that would have stood her in good stead in the theatre, 'I am delighted to see you.' The comely blonde widow in her middle years bustled over and bussed Dora on the cheeks signalling that she considered them firm intimates. Their friendship was something that existed outside of society constraints, forged when they were caught up in the Hellfire investigation. 'You know my guests, of course.' She arched an amused brow at Jacob. As an ex-lover, Lady Tolworth claimed teasing rights now that Dora and Jacob were together. The lady had the strength of character to know her time with Jacob was past even if she would've liked to reignite the flame. From the little rumble of jealousy in Dora's chest at the thought of relinquishing Jacob to Lady Tolworth, she decided she was not yet ready to return to her old life.

'Dr Sandys ... Jacob,' said Dora with a smile that let him know they would speak later. 'And Lieutenant Colonel Smith – I'm so pleased we have another chance to meet.'

Alexander Smith bowed. 'Lieutenant Colonel no longer. I'm plain Mr Smith.'

'There's nothing plain about you, young man, as you well know,' said Lady Tolworth, taking her seat on the sofa. 'Besides, it is quite the thing to carry on claiming your rank even when kicked out.'

'I believe, my lady, my rank is considered to have been stripped away. If they could have taken the scissors to my stripes in front of the regiment, they would've done.'

She waved at the company to take their seats. 'Ah, yes, but they aren't saying so in public so you needn't make a point of humbling yourself – it will only prompt questions no one wants asked.'

Smith smiled wryly at that presentation of his case. 'Then I will not hurry to correct them in future.'

'Just so. Brandy?' Lady Tolworth rang a bell and her formidably organised butler entered with four glasses already poured. He left rapidly and closed the door to stand guard at the entrance. Dora got the impression that Lady Tolworth's household enjoyed this variance to an unimpeachable life of a society widow as much as their mistress. Perhaps they would all have been much happier if the lady turned pirate captain and took them all as her rascal crew?

Lady Tolworth swirled her spirit, admiring the amber liquid. Her relaxed pose showed they no longer need stand on company manners. 'So, Jacob, Dora, what mischief are we up to today?'

'There's a new investigation, Ginnie. Elgin's marbles are stirring up deadly trouble,' said Jacob.

'How?' The lady tasted the brandy. 'Wonderful things in their way, but I don't see why the government should pay for them. Let collectors pay for their own collecting.'

'You think Elgin wants the government to buy them?' asked Jacob.

'That's what my friends are saying. You know he's washed up since he divorced himself from that silly girl, Mary Nisbet – Mrs Ferguson now? She was lucky Robert Ferguson stood by her.

Lifting her skirts to him when her poor husband was in captivity – she must have the heart of a harlot.'

'That's not fair,' said Dora, stung on Mrs Ferguson's behalf. 'Lord Elgin was as madly jealous as Leontes and it would have been unfair to condemn her to live as a statue until he saw sense.'

'You see it as *A Winter's Tale*, do you?' Lady Tolworth's eyes laughed at Dora from over the rim of her glass. She enjoyed provoking her audience, her tone betraying that she was not invested in taking sides in the Elgin divorce. 'I always saw it more as Clytemnestra making love to Aegisthus while her man was away. Elgin was lucky he wasn't murdered in his bath when he returned from France.'

Jacob and Dora exchanged a quick look.

'What made you think of that comparison?' asked Jacob.

Lady Tolworth crossed her feet at her ankles. 'Oh, I'm not being clever, Jacob. That's not my line. It was what was said generally at the time. Don't you remember?'

'I was away with the army, only back for short periods of leave,' said Jacob.

'And I'd never heard of the Elgins, for what it is worth,' muttered Dora.

'I remember,' Smith spoke up unexpectedly. 'There was a salacious print to that effect that made the rounds of the clubs. The lady with her heels in the air "entertaining" her husband's best friend, a latter-day Clytemnestra.'

'See!' said Lady Tolworth. 'That must've lodged in my memory. I am glad you invited him, Jacob. It makes a change to meet a clever fellow about town, even if he was a knave and traitor over that Hellfire business.'

Smith swallowed and looked abashed, as well he might. Everyone in the room knew how close the country had come to disaster thanks to him. But they weren't a judgemental lot, thought Dora, or if they were – like Lady Tolworth – it was only because she judged everyone and found them wanting.

'Shall we move on?' Seizing the awkward pause in the conversation, Jacob swiftly laid out what had happened so far in their investigation for the benefit of Smith and Lady Tolworth. He added in the most recent twist that had taken him to Melbourne House, which produced the inspiration to include Smith, and ended in Rose Street with the watercolour.

Dora studied the painting. 'You have been busy.' She envied him the freedom that allowed him to gad about town.

'We agreed we needed to know more about the first victim,' said Jacob defensively.

'So we did.' She passed the picture back.

'Stonehenge is not so far from Salisbury where his family is from.'

'An odd murderer,' said Dora dryly. 'Here's a memento of home, and by the way, here's a dagger in your throat.'

'I agree that it is perplexing. How did you get on with Byron?' Jacob asked Smith.

Smith checked his pocket watch. 'Very well. I'm invited to join him and his friends this evening. They keep late hours, so I'll still be welcome if I leave in about half an hour.'

Lady Tolworth opened her mouth to make a remark but thought better of it. That was so unexpected from the forthright dame that they all turned to look at her.

'My lady?' asked Dora.

The Dowager Viscountess let out a hiss of breath. 'I shouldn't.'

'Shouldn't what?' prodded Jacob, amused.

'Even I have my limits.'

'Now we really are all interested,' said Dora. 'You can't stop. We'll die of curiosity.'

The lady gave way, as she clearly had wanted to do after her brief show of restraint. 'The young man might not know but Lord

Byron and his friends are rumoured to be of the Grecian persuasion – and I'm not talking about marbles. It is wise to take care after the Vere Street affair the other year.'

From Smith's glower, it appeared the name meant something to him.

'What happened at Vere Street?' asked Dora.

'A group of male friends had the habit of gathering in the back parlour of the White Swan on Vere Street, off Bond Street,' said Smith in a tight voice.

'It was a molly-house,' said Lady Tolworth stridently, so that even the butler outside the door would hear. 'An infamous place.'

'It was a private room, and no one was forced into doing anything they did not want to do,' snapped back Smith in a much lower tone.

Lady Tolworth gave him an assessing look, drawing a conclusion that Jacob and Dora already knew.

'They were betrayed. The Bow Street Runners broke in and arrested twenty-seven of us. The usual bribes were exchanged, and the majority were released without charge, but even so, six unfortunates were pilloried at the Haymarket. Two were sentenced to death and hanged, despite not even being present at the time of the raid.' Smith turned to Dora. 'Now do you see why we needed the Hellfire Club?'

That could've been her brother Anthony – that could have been Lieutenant Colonel Smith: hanged for whom they loved and how they chose to express it.

'I don't hold with all this fiddling about with the same sex, but neither is it right to kill someone over it,' said Lady Tolworth. 'Less we poke our noses into other people's bedrooms, the better.'

'I'm sorry, Lieutenant Colonel Smith—' began Dora.

He turned his devastatingly blue eyes on her – eyes the colour of forget-me-nots fringed with long fair lashes. He still managed to be entirely masculine despite these elements of outrageous beauty. If one of Elgin's marble gods had come to life, he would look like Smith. No wonder Anthony had fallen for him hook, line and sinker. 'Please, call me Alex, Dora. With Anthony gone, and my family not on speaking terms, you would be the only one that does.'

'I can do that. I'm sorry, Alex. You were there? At Vere Street?'

'No, but friends of mine were. Those that sat in the stocks on Haymarket fared little better than the condemned. The crowd was ugly – men *and* women – throwing filth, rotten fish, even dead cats. Most of those punished are scarred for life and can't show their face in London again. How in the name of civilisation can a society let this happen?'

'It's our Furies – the underbelly of civil society, if you will,' said Jacob. 'It is the same question I had when I saw what I'd thought of as good men pillaging and raping their way through the towns and cities that they conquered. If a superior officer was not on the spot to make sure they behaved, the soldiers acted worse than beasts – it was a kind of terrible release from the tension of war, and the innocent suffered.'

Alex took a moment to govern his temper. 'Yes, you're right, of course. I should not be surprised that humanity is nasty and brutish – the philosophers warn us that this is so. But returning to Lady Tolworth's warning, Lord Byron and friends are taking care. Our meeting is in a private house, not a public one, and there should be no reason for anyone to disturb us at what is merely a card party. What is it you wish me to do with this new friendship you're encouraging?'

'We want to find out what Lord Byron would do to harm Elgin. How far would he go?' said Jacob.

'I know he is all for the Greeks and for leaving their antiquities in place, but you think he has been arranging assassination attempts in Berwick?' Alex could be forgiven for sounding sceptical.

'Maybe not, but if someone is, it stands to reason they may move in the same circles as Byron – Whiggish or radical, pro-Greek, anti-Elgin and all he stands for. We are also looking for any evidence that someone belongs to a group who wears this ring.' He showed Alex the bronze ring that had been found on Brooking. 'If you can, find out if anyone knew Richard Brooking.'

'I'll do my best.'

'Take it slowly,' advised Dora. 'Don't rush out all your questions on first meeting. Let him tell you by making comments about yourself that invite him to reciprocate.'

'It will do you no harm that many in his circle know that you are under a cloud,' added Jacob.

'Lord, no! That boy loves a rebel: just look at his poetry! And he admires Bonaparte.' Lady Tolworth said the latter as if it were a clinching argument.

'Haven't we all to some extent?' said Jacob.

'He is our enemy!'

'But he is also a formidable general and gained his position through brilliance not birth.'

Dora saw that Jacob and Ginnie were about to begin another of their arguments – one a staunch Tory, the other with radical leanings. 'I for one hope that Wellington proves his match,' she said brightly, attempting to move the conversation along.

'Napoleon is on the border with Russia; Wellington is in Spain: I doubt their paths will cross,' said Alex as he got up. 'I'd better go to keep my appointment. How shall I pass on anything I learn?'

'I have rooms in Albemarle Street,' said Jacob, passing him a visiting card. 'Though we should look for something more convenient.'

'You are always welcome here,' said Lady Tolworth.

Jacob gave her a bow. 'Thank you, but I was thinking of somewhere more discreet.'

'You can take my steward's office in Bruton's Mews if you

like,' she said. 'He's a useless fellow and happy enough in the library in the main house. There's even a room above that you can sleep in if living in a hotel has begun to dim.'

Dora watched the thoughts pass over Jacob's face. It would damage his reputation for independence if he was considered a hanger-on of his ex-lover, living in her servants' quarters, but it would also be very convenient, tucked behind the lady's house on Bruton Street. It would suit Dora, too, as she could slip away from Grosvenor Square very easily and be there in five minutes.

Coming to a decision, Jacob turned to Alex:

'What about you, Alex: would you like to man our office and live above? It would solve some immediate issues for us all. You can receive new customers for our services and take reports from us both.'

'It sounds a Godsend, but who is "us"?' asked Alex.

'Sandys and Fitz-Pennington, private enquiry agents,' said Jacob with a grin at Dora.

'Have we just set up a company?' she asked, bemused. 'I thought that was yet to be settled.'

'I believe we have, temporarily, and we even have our first employee. If that is agreeable to you and to our hostess?'

Lady Tolworth raised her glass. 'It sounds most amusing. With the prospect of so much intrigue, I will delay my return to the north until at least the end of the Season. Who knows: I might even be able to help?'

Chapter Twenty-Two

Bruton Mews

Jacob insisted on walking Dora home, even though it was only a street away in one of the safest areas of the capital. He had mentioned he had glimpsed someone who might've been watching him, so she agreed that it was better not to walk in the dark alone. Neither of them should, but she doubted he'd like that idea as it would curtail his freedom.

'And I think we should look at our new office, don't you?' he said with a gleam in his eye that told her this was a thin excuse to delay their parting.

'I'll have Yarton show you the rooms,' said Lady Tolworth, swishing the emerald satin of her gown aside. She bade them farewell and handed them over to her major-domo. The unflappable butler escorted them downstairs and across the cobbled yard at the back of the house. The mews served all the houses on this side of Bruton Street. It was a semi-private courtyard used for stables and coachhouses, though parts were used for accommodation and there was even an inn, *The Three*

Chairman, at the far end by the entrance, popular with the domestic staff of the surrounding area. Yarton led them to a house next-door-but-one to the inn and used his key to unlock the entrance. This would be perfect: not too far into the mews to deter customers but secreted sufficiently to offer some privacy.

'My lady has given me orders to clear out the steward's belongings and set it up however you wish. Please let me know tomorrow what you desire and I will see it done.' He gave them a bow and left.

Dora sighed. 'I want a Yarton. It is almost as good as having a genie in a lamp.'

'I always thought employing a good butler was one of the points of being rich,' said Jacob, standing back to let her go first.

'And yet you don't?'

'I'm not settled enough for a butler. I haven't even got myself a valet. My family think I'm eccentric. I prefer the word "private".' Jacob moved around the room, inspecting the shelves and running his finger over the desk. 'Ginnie doesn't lie about the steward not using this for work. He's let the dust settle.'

Dora clasped her hands to her chest and revolved in a circle. 'Are we really doing this?'

He looked up from the bookshelf and gave her one of his shy smiles that made her want to kiss him. 'If you want. You know I'd do this and much more for you if you'd accept it.'

Give a lover an inch and they take a mile. Her instinctive defence of her boundaries flared but she made sure she did not sound too harsh when she turned him down. 'Somehow it feels right that it comes from Lady Tolworth and not you.'

'Ginnie is playing matchmaker – a worrisome thought.'

'Heaven forbid. You know I'm still not convinced we can be together.'

'I know.' His tone was solemn. 'You know what I think. I won't push you any further.'

And wasn't that exactly why she ... she hesitated on the word ... felt ... so very much for him? Dora sat on a padded bench under the window. A change of subject was in order. 'This is where our clients can wait.'

Jacob took the chair at the desk. 'And this is where we – the terribly important enquiry agents – will sit scribbling vital information until we have sufficiently cowed our petitioners with our greatness.'

She laughed at that. 'I imagine most of our customers will be like Lord Elgin – ones who summon us to come to them and will treat us as a higher form of servant. Or summon you, at least.'

'But they will be the ones who pay best, allowing us to help those who don't turn their nose up at waiting on a bench.'

'True.' Dora smoothed her skirts, taking in the room and the promise of all it might be. 'Will it pay, I wonder?'

Jacob rose from the desk and came to crouch before her. He rested his hands on her knees. 'Dora, look at me.'

She smiled and tapped his nose. 'I am. You are really quite something, Dr Sandys.'

He nipped her finger. 'I am selfishly glad you are happy to extend this experiment between us.'

'Experiment?'

'A relationship that is not a rich man and kept woman, but two people who are deeply in *like* with each other willing to work together.' He said like in such a way that she heard something else.

She cupped his jaw, feeling the bristle scratch her palm. He pressed her hand more firmly against his skin then took it and brushed a kiss in the middle. This was the problem with Jacob – and why she lost her head around him. Every time he touched her like this, so loving and gentle, she felt like her skin was prickling with silver shivers of delight. She'd not had enough kindness from men in her life, and he was intent on correcting that oversight. She adored his dark hair, the way it swept back from his brow, his earnest blue-grey eyes. He was one of the strongest men she knew, not because he went around like a bully demanding his way, but because he stood firm on his principles and knew his faults well enough not to claim he was perfect. They often disagreed and he didn't pretend to think like her just to please or woo her. It took strength of character to do that. And now he was kissing her palm. Her breasts grew heavy, rubbing against her too-tight stays, and her body warmed with desire. To make love with him was an appetite that was only growing the longer they spent together. The intensity of what she was feeling was terrifying and wonderful.

'They've left us alone,' said Jacob, smiling roguishly at her. Neither of them was a plaster saint, thank God.

She stuffed her fears away and reached behind to close the shutters. 'How fortunate.'

He undid her coat and pushed it off her shoulders. 'Aren't you too warm in that? It's a mild night.'

'Aren't you too hot in all those layers?' she responded, undoing his waistcoat buttons.

'Boiling.'

With a flutter of laughter, they undressed each other, pausing to kiss and worship each part revealed – the notch in his shoulder by his collar bone, the sensitive underside of her breast, the middle of his chest with its scar, her navel – oh lord, her navel! She hadn't realised that it had a direct connection to her most sensitive areas. Once they were both naked, he cupped her bottom and lifted her so that her legs clasped around his waist. He strode to the desk.

'Really?' she teased gently, setting her hand against the muscles of his chest. He was toned by riding and exercise, a deep tan line at the neck which told her he was fond of dropping the gentleman and going about without a cravat like a vagabond. She had a vision of him striding on the fells in the Lakes, sketchbook in hand, gloriously free from social restrictions. She would love to see him like that one day. Perhaps they could make love under the sky?

'We need to christen our partnership appropriately, don't you think?' He pressed her gently to lie back. 'Fitz-Pennington and Sandys.'

'Or Sandys and Fitz-Pennington.' She stretched on the cool wooden surface and a ledger clattered to the floor. 'Oops. Are you sure this is a good idea?'

'It's the best one I've had all day.' He leaned down to take her breast in his mouth.

Very soon she was vocally agreeing with him.

A good while later, once they were restored to fully-dressed respectability, they let themselves out of the office. The inn was closed, but there was a lamp over the entrance lighting their way to the exit from the mews. Dora rested her head on Jacob's shoulder, a final farewell before they reached a more public thoroughfare. He caressed her hand. Reluctantly she put her bonnet back on; even if the other servants did gossip about her late return, she did not want to give them any tangible reasons to criticise her.

As they approached Lady George's house, Kir burst out of the area steps.

'Where have you been?' he said, his eyes wild with panic.

That was not a question Dora wanted to answer. 'Hush now.' She gathered him into a hug. 'I'm back now. You needn't wait up. I'm not going to abandon you.'

Kir shoved her away, too angry, too scared to listen. 'You should've been here!'

Jacob stepped in and took the boy by the shoulder. 'Listen, Kir,

Miss Pence can't always be around for you, but she will come back. You have to learn patience.'

Kir looked up at Jacob mutinously, tears glistening. 'You don't understand. I know you two are prigging. I don't care.' So much for the innocence of youth. 'But I saw him!'

There could only be one 'him' that would send Kir into such a lather.

'Where?' asked Dora.

'He was watching the house from over there.' He pointed across the square. 'I saw him from upstairs but when I got out, he was gone. I think he followed you. I ran the way you went but I couldn't find you.'

The thought of the boy on his own with the enemy so close made her feel sick. Kir had been watching Dora leave – of course he had. His anxiety that he would be abandoned meant he would always be keeping an eye on her.

'Are you sure it was him?' It would've been getting dark.

Kir looked lost for a second, then nodded fervently as his resolve grew. 'Yes, it was him. He was standing under a lamppost. He didn't think anyone was watching him.'

'If he followed you, Dora, he would've seen you go into the lady's house,' said Jacob.

'By the servants' entrance,' she reminded him. 'That should not immediately raise suspicions as she is my former employer after all.' She gave him a look to remind him not to drop that story in front of the boy. 'I have friends in the household.'

'It is more worrying that it is you that was being followed.'

'More worrying than him following you earlier?' This was very bad news. He might even have watched her question and then take Kir under her wing at the Berwick.

'Perhaps it's the boy they want?' she said in a low voice. 'They know he's a witness.'

'That's possible.' Jacob turned to search the street for a sign that they were still being watched. Dora couldn't spot anyone unless they were hiding in the bushes of the garden square. Their delay to christen the office had possibly put the watcher off the scent, and they had emerged from a different exit than the one she went in.

Jacob pressed her hand in parting. 'You'd better get off the street – and stay indoors, Kir. We don't want this man snatching you.' And doing much worse, was the thought behind that warning.

Kir gave a little growl. 'I want him to come for me.' He pulled a paring knife out of his pocket and thrust it at the belly of an invisible enemy. 'I want to stick him for what he did to my sister.'

Dora gently removed the knife from his hand. 'This belongs to the cook. We will talk about how to catch this man, but it won't be by putting you at risk, my lad. And there will be no sticking knives in anyone.'

Kir didn't protest the removal, possibly because he had more than one weapon on him. An angry, fearful boy would not stop at one little knife, she thought. But that was a subject to be tackled when they were indoors.

Jacob ushered them inside. 'I'll send a message tomorrow with any news. Both of you, look after each other. I'm relying on you, Kir.'

That was a better tactic to gain the boy's compliance than her attempt to curb him. Kir immediately set a firm hold of Dora's hand. 'Yes, sir. I'll make sure she's safe.'

To be guarded by a mite of eight years – what a strange twist her life had taken.

Chapter Twenty-Three

Bruton Mews

When Jacob returned to the mews the next morning, he found that Yarton had already swung into action. The place had been emptied, surfaces polished, and there was little trace, only memories of the visit the night before.

Memory was enough, though, Jacob thought, unable to stop smiling. He knew that he was the luckiest man in London to have Dora as his partner – temporarily. He could not grow complacent; she was like a migratory bird that sang in the garden all summer – look out of the window one day and she would be gone. He had to make sure she never saw their relationship as a cage.

A creak of a floorboard upstairs alerted him to the presence of someone else in the building. His heart picked up its pace. Had their watcher got here already? Was he lying in wait?

'Is anyone there?' he called upstairs. He grabbed a poker from the fireplace.

A groan was his answer, followed by:

'Coming!' Alex Smith stumbled down the stairs, a damp cloth pressed to his temples.

'Heavy night?' asked Jacob wryly, putting the fire iron back on the hook. He did not need his medical studies to diagnose a hangover.

'You could say that. I must be out of practice.' Alex slumped in the visitor's chair that Yarton had added to the office furniture. His golden hair was in disarray and his face sickly pale.

'I imagine Lady Tolworth's butler will have a cure for what ails you.'

'He does. It tastes like cat piss.'

'And how would you know what that tastes like?' Jacob sat opposite him and opened the desk drawer, giving Alex a chance to fight his way out of his foggy brain. A clean ledger and pens occupied the space, plus a closed bottle of ink. He set these out and got ready to take his first notes. He inscribed the date and then wondered what kind of cipher they should use. Only a fool would make plain records of a case where they had reason to suspect spies were involved. In honour of the Greeks, he decided to use that alphabet to stand for their client and the other people involved, going in the order that he had been introduced to them rather than any connection to their name. That should at least obscure the identities to a casual reader as only he and Dora would be in possession of that detail. Under this system, alpha meant Fisher, beta Lord Elgin, gamma Mrs Ferguson, and so on. Following that method through to the two attackers in Berwick, Jacob was amused to find Lord Byron by chance reached iota. The lord would not like to be associated with so minuscule a sign.

'How did you find your new friend?' he asked when he decided Alex had had enough time.

Alex pressed his brows then dropped his hands. 'He is remarkable – truly, Sandys, you must meet him. I prefer the private Byron to the public one. He is informed, witty, and, as you might expect, eloquent. He is also completely immoral.'

To the extent that taking lives would be nothing but a game to him, wondered Jacob. 'I am not surprised to find he has an attractive air to him or his rise to fame would be hard to explain, but what made you decide on the latter?'

Alex wrinkled his brow. 'Maybe immoral is too harsh. Perhaps he is amoral? I think he has his own code of conduct, rather like the Stoics. He is without religion and so not bound by the usual rules.'

'How do you know this so quickly?'

'He doesn't hide it. Take last night. He mentioned over cards that his mother died last year – he rushed back from his travels, he said, but wasn't in time to be with her as she breathed her last. When one of his friends made the usual expressions of sympathy, resting in peace and such, Byron snapped that he would have nothing to do with immortality. He said we are miserable enough in this life, without the absurdity of speculating upon another. He then laid down his winning hand as if to cap the point.' Alex smiled softly. 'I have to say I found that refreshing.'

'That must be the secret of his success. He is like a shot of brandy to our palate after poetic tea-drinking for decades.' Jacob added to his notes. 'Don't you dare fall for him, Alex. First rule of investigating is to keep ourselves out of emotional entanglements.'

Alex gave him a sour look. 'Like you and Dora keep out of such things?'

'That's different.' Jacob could feel his cheeks heat. Why had he thought it a good idea to christen their place of work?

'Don't worry.' Alex massaged his aching forehead. 'I'm not in danger of falling for Byron. I can see the path of broken hearts that he has rolled over in his golden chariot. He is not a man who cares deeply for another – or not for long.'

'Anything else to add to the record?'

'Two things. I have an invitation to return.'

'Excellent.'

'In fact, I think I might be able to get you in to meet him, too. We are due to gather at Angelo and Jackson's. It would not be remarked on if I brought an ex-military colleague with me for the exercise.'

Jacob groaned. 'I hate fencing.'

'I'll go easy on you.'

'I didn't say I wasn't any good at it. What about the second thing?'

Alex settled back, for the first time looking as if his headache might be lifting, some of the lines of tension smoothing away. 'Byron has two fierce Greeks in his service, ones he brought back with him from his travels. They are among his most trusted servants. If Byron is employing people to strike at Elgin and his circle to avenge the marbles, I'll stake my non-existent fortune on them being part of it.'

Byron's circle were such hardened drinkers that the meeting at Angelo and Jackson's was due to take place that same morning, everyone expected to have shaken off the revels of the night before. After dunking his head in a basin of cold water and towelling dry, Alex declared himself restored sufficiently to accompany Jacob to the rendezvous. It was a short walk to Bond Street where the fencing studio was located – a perfect spot to attract the young men of the Ton who wanted to brush up on their skills as both swordsmen and boxers. Jacob had time to remember that Jackson was one of the boxers at the exhibition breakfast that Elgin was so proud to have hosted. That showed how closely knit was their society. Even someone who you would not suspect of being involved in a plot about Ancient Greek marbles had already been scooped up into the mix and weighed in the scales – Jackson on Elgin's side.

Thinking of scales... One scrawny gentleman was being judged, a process that involved sitting on a swing seat and having weights put on the other side of the balance beam to accurately adjudicate this. He was being mocked by his friends for how few of the weights were needed. Jacob and Alex joined the men changing at the side of the room given over to fencing mats and a boxing ring. Serious hobbyists would bring their own equipment, but Jacob was relieved to find that boxing gloves and fencing gear were available to hire. Sporting prints lined the walls to inspire those that flocked here to imitate the greats, including prints of Jackson himself in his prime when he was national champion. These could be purchased by members at a club discount. The room smelt of sweat and sawdust, with not a hint of effeminacy. This was no place for a woman or a dandy, it declared with its bare boards and unpainted benches. Men came here to be men, sweat, punch, and not worry about petticoat government at home.

Suspicious of the keen sportsmen who had always been the worst bullies at school, Jacob did not feel at ease here; Alex, by contrast, glowed. That was literal as he happened to be standing in a shaft of sunlight, but also his expression showed how much he loved this kind of exercise.

'I'm getting the impression that you might make mincemeat of me with the epee,' murmured Jacob, strapping on his padding.

Alex merely smiled.

All right, then. Jacob would need to dredge up the long-neglected training he'd had with his brothers. Their tutor had claimed he could've been a great fencer if his heart had been in it. Perhaps he should've listened?

As if summoned by the memory, who should arrive at his side but his brother William, towel around his neck, perspiring from a bout with one of the club trainers. Cheerful and golden-haired in stark contrast to Jacob's saturnine looks, William was the family optimist, the sunny child. He had blithely accepted his role as spare to the heir, Arthur, and was the one whom everyone secretly loved most of the three sons of Viscount Sandys.

'Jacob! Do my eyes deceive me? What on earth has brought you in here?'

Trust his brother to destroy at the top of his voice any chance that Jacob's presence would go unremarked. He could see some of the men who were here primarily to catch up on society gossip peering at him with new interest. The brothers were not often seen together in company.

'I came with my friend here. Alexander Smith. Smith, this is my older brother, William.'

Smith gave William a deep bow. 'Sir.'

William, usually the kindest of souls, surprised Jacob by snubbing Alex's overture. Instead, he caught Jacob's arm.

'A word, brother.'

With an apologetic look at Alex, Jacob let William pull him aside.

'Look, Jacob, I know you are your own man—'

'Thank you for remembering that—'

'But I feel obliged as your older brother to warn you about him. He's not quite the ticket.'

'Meaning?' Jacob was interested in how much William had heard.

'He has been cashiered.'

'I'm aware.'

William blinked. 'I see. But there's worse.'

'Is there?'

'He's a … one of them.'

'Is he, indeed?'

'I know you aren't of that persuasion – you're not of that persuasion, are you?' William now looked deeply worried.

'I'm not.'

'Well, then. Good. Not that I wouldn't support you whatever you decide to do, as I did when you went idiotically into the army as a doctor – a doctor! Father would've purchased you a decent commission in a senior rank.'

That old family argument again! But William was right: he had stood by Jacob's right to be wrong.

'Thank you for backing me.'

'But Smith – it is merely that men are executed for doing things like that.'

'I am aware.'

'*And* their associates suffer.'

So that was what he was most anxious about: that Jacob would be tarred with the same brush. Vere Street had made everyone afraid.

'How old am I?'

William smiled, knowing exactly what Jacob meant. 'You're still two years younger than me.'

'I know what I'm doing. Smith is a good man. He has made mistakes, but he regrets them, and I believe in second chances. Don't you?'

His brother's smile turned self-mocking. 'Indeed, or Charlotte would have booted me out of the house long ago.'

William's wife was a forthright character who had quite fooled him by playing the shy doe during their courtship. Jacob rather admired her, certainly preferring the real Charlotte to the insipid miss she had pretended to be during their engagement. William needed a lady in his life to give him backbone against their older brother's demands. Arthur was a splendid fellow in many ways, but he could take them both for granted, expecting his brothers to dance attendance on him as their father had made them do. 'Give Smith a chance, that's all I ask.'

'And watch your back, that's all *I* ask.' William clapped him on the aforesaid area and went over to his peg where he had left his clothes to get changed.

Jacob made his way back to Alex, more conscious now of the looks they were attracting. Let the watchers be damned by their own evil thoughts, he decided, daring the scandalmongers to do their worst.

'Everything settled?' asked Alex softly.

'Yes.' Jacob resumed changing into his fencing gear.

'It's good to see a brother caring for his sibling.'

'Even if it comes at your expense?'

'Even so. Ready?'

They walked out onto one of the mats that had become vacant. A fencing master approached them and asked if they wanted instruction.

'We are here for a warm-up bout, Senor Luigi,' said Alex. 'We've not fought before so we want to take each other's measure.'

'Very good, sir,' said Luigi. 'Call me if you want my observations.'

Jacob was relieved not to have an expert audience for his first fencing bout in years. But he was aware that William had stayed to watch, which was almost as bad.

'Remember what you said about going easy?' muttered Jacob.

Alex grinned and launched into a balestra move forward and a compound attack, purposely a little showy. Jacob had to duck sideways to avoid being hit.

'Come on, Jacob! Don't let the family down!' called William.

Jacob parried but kept on the defence. From the vicious joy Alex was taking in making his moves, he had a lot of pent-up rage, and he had decided Jacob would be a good vent for it. Jacob had underestimated the man, thinking handsome looks meant handsome manners. There was a killer in Alex just as there was in any soldier worth his salt. Fortunately, as Jacob's muscles warmed, so did his memory of some of the moves that he'd once had drilled into him. He came up with a compound riposte that gave him some respite, and he recovered to the 'on guard' position.

'Coming back to you, is it?' asked Alex smugly, swishing his blade in the air.

'Slowly.' He moved even as he spoke, knowing that would take Alex by surprise. He got in a redoublement and landed a hit on the middle line. He glanced over to his brother and received a nod. The family honour was salvaged, even if he was going to lose this 'friendly' bout by a great many points.

Ten minutes later they stepped back and saluted each other.

'Good match,' said Alex.

'I thought it was a warm-up bout,' said Jacob wryly.

'I never fight unless I mean to win.'

'Hear, hear!' said a man from the sidelines.

Lord Byron had arrived.

Chapter Twenty-Four

Grosvenor Square

Dora sat with Dimitra in the housekeeper's room, both using the excellent light coming through the sash windows to mend their ladies' garments. They had the place to themselves as Lady George was giving Mrs Simmonds her orders for the day. Sewing was the time-honoured occasion for the women in a household to talk and Dora made sure they kept up the tradition. They had exhausted the topics of the best seamstresses, the most reasonable hat shops, and the fairest of the second-hand clothes dealers. Inside she was screaming at being confined. If she could swap places with Jacob and stride around the capital investigating this case, she would do it in an instant. With an internal sigh, Dora introduced the topic of the pastimes in the capital open to servants, from boating on the river to visiting the animals in the Tower of London, so thought it safe to move on to the question she had been aiming for.

'Speaking of sights, have you ever seen Lord Elgin's marbles?' she asked, threading her needle.

Dimitra huffed and smoothed the stocking she was darning over the wooden mushroom. 'I saw them in their rightful place long ago when I was a girl.'

Dora pretended ignorance. 'But aren't they in London now? I heard something about being able to see them if you can pay the entrance fee.'

Dimitra bristled. 'Why should I, a citizen of Athens, pay to see what is mine?'

Interesting. She had hit a sore spot. 'Oh, I don't know, because you're curious?' Dora grinned at her, showing she meant no disrespect by her words. 'I've been told they used to be high up on a building—'

'The Parthenon, Athena's temple.'

'That's the place. But now you can look at them close-up. It would be like being allowed to wear the Crown Jewels that we can only see from afar in a glass cabinet, or glimpse when the Prince Regent goes past in his carriage.'

Dimitra looked thoughtful. Good: she wasn't disagreeing.

'I was thinking of going to have a look, if Mrs Ferguson can spare me for an hour or two. They can't be far.'

'They're in Lord Elgin's garden,' Dimitra supplied, showing she was well aware of the fate of the statues and friezes from the Parthenon.

'I would value the company of someone who knows what they are looking at. Otherwise, they're all Greek to me.'

Dimitra smiled despite herself at the apposite use of the phrase.

'I will go with you,' she conceded. 'I should check that he is looking after them properly.'

'This afternoon?' pressed Dora. 'How about once the ladies are at their afternoon tea party?' Lady George had invited some intimate friends who had been supporters of Mrs Ferguson during her divorce. That should give the two lady's maids a few hours off their duties.

Dimitra havered. 'I have an errand to run –' Dora's hopes fell '– but it could take me in that direction, I suppose.'

'Then we have a plan.'

'We do indeed.'

Dora glanced up and saw that Dimitra's smile was a little worrying. The woman was plotting something, but whether that was a private intrigue, or connected with their mystery, only time would tell.

The two women slipped out after the arrival of the guests for the afternoon party. Mr Rogers was occupied ferrying the ladies to the parlour so was not on hand to make disapproving comments on servants 'gadding about' in the daytime. Kir was not so easily shaken. He fell into step with Dora as soon as they climbed the area steps to the street. Dora shooed him back but he shook his head. He was determined to be a limpet.

'Is he yours?' Dimitra asked, taking a closer look at the waif. 'I will not tell if you say he is.'

That would be the logical conclusion to the boy's evident loyalty to her. Dora put a hand lightly on his shoulder.

'He's not mine, but I have promised to look after him.'

Kir looked up at her. 'And I promised him I'd look after you.'

Less said about the 'him' in question the better. 'And so you did.' She ruffled his hair, which he hated and so would be too preoccupied smoothing it to say anything else about Jacob. 'You heard of the accident at the bridge in Berwick?'

'I did indeed.' Dimitra quickly moved off, leading the way along the pavement. Did the topic unnerve her?

'Kir's sister died in that explosion.'

Dimitra faltered. 'Oh, I'm sorry.' She looked down at the boy with new pity. 'Then he must come with us on this treat.'

'Thank you.' Dora held out her hand for Kir's. 'All right, then, pest. We are going to see some famous statues. You must be on your best behaviour.'

Kir didn't look too excited about the idea of statues, but he nodded solemnly. 'I will be good.'

The party of three resumed their walk. Dimitra was careful to make way for any of their betters who were strolling in the sunshine. This involved lots of stepping aside, even into the street, so as not to disturb the ladies and gentlemen who owned this world. Dora had to remind herself to do so, such deference not coming naturally to her.

'You mentioned you were there with the Elgins in Athens,' Dora said. 'Did anyone object strongly to what they were doing – enough to bear a grudge against them?'

'A grudge? We all did,' snapped Dimitra. 'How would you like someone to go into your house and carry off your furniture because he told you you couldn't be trusted with it?'

'Oh.' Dora hadn't paused to consider the Greek perspective on Elgin's collection. Jacob had been so adamant that the earl had been doing world culture a favour by rescuing them. 'I would hate that – and I'd fight to stop them.'

Dimitra grimaced. 'That's easy for you to say. We would've done, but our house is now under a new landlord and the earl said he had their permission.'

'Still, I imagine there were those who will not let the matter rest there?'

'Absolutely. We'll get them back one day.'

From the fierce expression on the Greek woman's face, Dora rather thought she might. But would she turn to violence to do so? That was what she and Jacob needed to consider. They were looking for a secret group and political intrigue, but might it not be as simple as outraged patriots?

As they approached Lord Elgin's house, Dimitra's expression turned to one of doubt.

'Will they let us in, do you think? I've heard that the lower classes aren't usually allowed into the earl's grounds.'

Dora wasn't going to be put off by such petty concerns. She had heard so much about the marbles that she had to see them. 'Leave that to me. Just play along. But be prepared for Kir's elevation in rank.'

The entrance to the garden lay at the side of the house and it was manned during visiting hours by a porter at the gate.

'Kir, you are my pupil, understood?' Dora whispered.

Kir had lived the raggle-taggle life of a camp follower long enough to know when to fall into a con without protest. 'Yes, Miss Pence.'

Dora approached the porter with an assured manner and felt in her purse for coins to pay the entry fee. 'My good man, one entry ticket for my charge, Lord Howard, for the marbles. Is that half price for a minor?'

The porter peered at Kir who had adopted the stance of an officer on parade. Fortunately, the clothes that had been found for him were of the best quality, cast-offs from Lady George's family, so it was not possible to dismiss that he was a lord by what he wore. If he had looked scruffy, Dora would not be trying this tactic. 'Humph. And who are you two?'

'She's my governess,' piped up Kir. The boy was blessedly quick on the uptake. The Scottish burr made it hard to place his social position. 'And that's –' his invention faltered when it came to Dimitra '– my valet?'

'He means nursery nurse,' said Dora with a confidential smile at the porter. 'He is so eager to grow up that his papa, the viscount, humours him in that way.'

The porter gave a throaty chuckle, forgetting suspicion. 'I reckon I can let him in for two shillings, then – such a sharp lad.' He opened the gate. 'In you go, ladies, and you, young sir.' He made a little salute that Kir, bless him, returned, further earning the porter's approbation.

The party of three progressed swiftly down the garden path with Dora reflecting that she and Kir made a good team.

Dimitra was still reeling from not having to pay for her entry. 'You cheated!'

Dora fixed her with a quizzical look. 'Please, do go back and fork over your hard-earned money to see marbles that you believe you Greeks own. Be my guest.'

Dimitra gave a snort. 'I can see you need watching, Dora Pence, and you, Lord Kir.'

The boy sniggered at that.

'And on the way out, if the porter asks, remember to tell him how much you enjoyed the marbles. You can say I'm going to make you write a poem about them,' said Dora.

Kir's face fell. 'Really?'

Dora rolled her eyes. 'No, Kir, not really. But I'm your governess, remember?'

'Good. 'Cause if you want a poem, you'd have to teach me to read and write first.'

Dimitra elbowed Dora in a friendly fashion. 'You *are* neglecting your duties in the schoolroom, Miss Pence.'

'Yes, yes, laugh at me, both of you. But you've done it now, Kir. I really will start on your lessons when we get back.'

Kir gave her a thoughtful look, beyond his years. 'I think I'd like that.'

They fell into a respectful silence as they entered the exhibition shed. It was hot in the summer sunshine, light falling in rectangles through the open doors and windows. Statues were lit at random – a god here, a centaur there. It felt like figures from Greek myths had been put under the Medusa's spell and could come awake at any moment.

'Why aren't they wearing any clothes?' Kir asked, not keeping his voice down. Happily, there weren't many other visitors this afternoon. It felt like a church in the middle of the week, holy but empty.

Dimitra was standing transfixed, tears in her eyes. The woman was in no state to answer.

'I think, Kir,' said Dora, 'that the sculptors of old thought the human body a worthy subject. These are mainly images of gods and goddesses so they are perfect specimens. Heroes.' She took him over to a male lying on his back. 'See all those muscles? It is like a lesson in anatomy.'

Kir looked puzzled. 'Anat—?'

'Study of what goes on inside the body,' she clarified. 'And Greece is a hot country. At that time, I don't think they wore clothes like ours, but loose tunics.'

'We wore chitons,' said Dimitra, coming over to join them. 'Knee length for the men, longer for the women. See, lots of them are wearing them sashed around the waist, or higher up, under the bust. Very simple clothing. However, you are right that many are naked.' She took Kir over to a frieze of two fighters. 'We weren't as bashful then about being unclothed, not in the right arena. Gymnasts competed unclothed. People bathed together unclothed. A healthy body was celebrated.'

'There was a lot less darning for the lady's maids,' said Dora with a smile.

'Why are they all in bits?' asked the boy, frowning at the stump where a hand once would have been.

'They are very old. Over two thousand years,' said Dimitra. 'A lot can happen in that time.'

'Perhaps it is more remarkable that there is anything left, rather than that a few things are missing?' suggested Dora.

Kir wandered over to a metope of a man and a centaur fighting. The human had his fist at the centaur's temple and his opponent had his hand around the man's neck. 'I like this one.'

Dimitra stood beside him. 'I can see why you like it. It tells a story, doesn't it? These are the tales of my people, how our heroes fought with the centaurs – that's the half-man half-horse creature. Everything here tells a story. Many of these are meant to be seen together as they show a procession in honour of Athena, the goddess of wisdom. They were supposed to be on her temple for all time so that the goddess was always being honoured with the gifts of the people of Athens. But now they are here. In a shed in London.' Her anger was palpable.

Kir turned to look up at her, his expression puzzled. 'Do you believe in this goddess Athena? Aren't you a Christian?'

Dimitra bit her lip, his question making her smile. 'My child, every Greek believes in their gods and goddesses just as we believe in old friends we haven't seen for a long while. I am, however, a Christian. In fact, I'm Greek Orthodox.'

'Ortho…' The word was new to the boy so he looked up at Dora. 'Grown-ups are confusing.'

'Only because we've had more time to get ourselves into muddles than you. The Greek Orthodox church is the one in Dimitra's homeland, like the Church of England is the one here. And then there are a few other little points of difference, but you needn't worry about that.' Dora gave Dimitra a look that suggested they didn't get into hashing out the doctrinal disputes of a millennium of Christianity thanks to the artful questioning of a boy wanting to understand the world. 'Do you like the marbles, Kir, now you know they are so old?'

He looked around the exhibition. 'I like the animals. And the ones that are almost all there. I don't like the ones that are in bits. They look injured—' He broke off and buried his face in Dora's skirts. 'Can we go home now?'

Of course, they look like those killed in the explosion, body parts scattered on the road at Berwick, and he had just made the connection. The boy had seen too much recently. She should've thought of that before bringing him here. To dispel that memory, she had to make him think of them as stones, not people.

'The amazing thing is that they are still finding parts of the marbles. Maybe one day someone will be able to put most of them back together, like a big jigsaw puzzle. Where do you think this horse head should go?'

Distracted by this new game, Kir lifted his head. 'With the other one.' He took her over to another fragment.

Dimitra stayed behind. When Dora looked back, the Greek woman was standing in front of the broken god with a ferocious look on her face.

They spent half an hour touring the exhibition. As they came out, Dimitra roused herself from the place her thoughts had taken her and smiled brightly at Kir.

'Was that not something, young man? We are privileged to see such masterworks.'

Kir nodded, though his good behaviour for the last fifteen minutes had been secured not by art appreciation but by the promise of an iced bun on the way home.

'Do you mind if we take a little detour? I want to call on my cousin,' said Dimitra as they left the porter behind with an extra tip, handed over with great solemnity by Kir.

'Not at all,' said Dora, who was enjoying this excursion. It beat sewing. 'Where are we going?'

'St James Street. It won't take long.'

This was but a stone's throw from Jacob's rooms. The area was popular with single gentlemen, being near their clubs and societies. Who did Dimitra know there?

The Greek woman left them waiting on the pavement as she went in by the servant's entrance to Number 8. Bun consumed, Kir wandered over to make friends with a horse in the traces of a handsom cab. He looked very small compared to the sturdy mare.

'Do you mind?' Dora asked the jarvey. Cab drivers could be a jealous lot.

'No skin off my nose,' said the man with a magisterial shrug. He was a thin man in a big coat, like a crab whose shell was too large for him. 'It's his fingers he's risking.'

'Does your horse bite?' Dora wondered if she should intervene.

'Nah, she's a sweetheart. Is he your nipper?'

That question again. Was there some resemblance between them that Dora didn't see?

'I'm just looking after him for the afternoon. My friend went in there.' She nodded to Number 8. 'We're waiting for her to come out.'

The jarvey gave her an impudent grin. 'Good-looking, is she?'

'Pardon?'

'Lots of good-looking girls go in there. They stay for a bit and sometimes take a cab home with their newfound riches.' His reason for hovering outside became clear. 'Or sometimes they talk their way in just to have a look at where he sleeps. You wouldn't believe what some girls get up to.'

'Where who sleeps?'

The jarvey grinned wider, showing the gap in his teeth. 'That Lord Byron. Bees to a honeypot.'

Dora recovered her surprise in time to inform him that she and Dimitra were both servants on errands, not admirers of the poets.

The jarvey shook his head. 'That doesn't stop you women.

Take poor Taffy. She hangs round here sometime. Oh, yes, the charwoman told me all about Taffy.'

'Taffy? Who is that?'

'That's what he calls her. No doubt she had some decent Christian name before he got his hands on the wench. She was his favourite at his place out in the country but then the fur flew when his nibs discovered she and his other favourite maid were both sleeping with his page, who, would you believe it, was also the lord's favourite. Quite a threesome.' The jarvey gave a rumble of laughter, clearly enjoying telling this tale. 'His nibs found out and banished the girls, though he kept the boy, mind. Shows you where his loyalties lie, eh?' He winked at Dora. 'Poor Taffy, she who thought she was his one true love, now hangs around here trying to get back in his favour. I told her to go find another gentleman. But she won't listen. She's stalking him like a huntress does a stag, like that Artemis woman.'

Even London cabbies knew a few stories about Greek goddesses it seemed. Probably from the Drury Lane pantomime.

A man whistled further up the street.

'Right, that's my signal.' The jarvey flicked his whip to get his mare in motion. 'Do your friend a favour: tell her not to be daft like Taffy.'

'I will.'

Dimitra emerged from the house a few minutes later. There was no disorder in her attire, nothing to suggest she had been 'doing a Taffy turn' as Dora now called it in her mind.

'Everything all right?' Dora asked, not able to probe more directly.

'Everything is fine,' Dimitra replied. 'We'd better hurry. The tea party will not last much longer.'

Collecting Kir from the pavement hopscotch he was playing with some other children, they headed home, Dora with even more questions unanswered.

The Elgin Conspiracy

Was Lord Byron at the heart of this conspiracy?

Chapter Twenty-Five

Hummums, Covent Garden

Jacob had not begun the day planning to end up in a bagnio in Covent Garden, but being part of Byron's circle made such interesting destinations inevitable. After a thorough session sparring and fencing, the young men voted to retire to Hummums in the Covent Garden Piazza to bathe and recover. Unlike the many Covent Garden bagnios that were little better than brothels, this one did offer a Turkish bath and massage and was owned by a respectable man and wife. The husband dealt with the gentlemen and his wife took the ladies to a separate area for their treatments – all very decent as long as you ignored the line of prostitutes under the portico on the way in.

Lying on his belly, Jacob could see no sign of any of the staff inside offering other kinds of services, especially as his masseur was a huge man, with bulging arm muscles, a bald head and thick black moustache that framed his lips into a perpetual frown. The love he was offering Jacob was the tough kind that made his body ache.

Thanks to some subtle manoeuvring by Alex, Byron was stretched out on the table next to Jacob, face-down on his arms, head to one side looking straight at him when his blue eyes weren't hidden by his heavy lids. The steam rose between them from the water running in a channel to the hottest of the plunge baths, Moroccan tiles in azure, yellow and cream were arranged on the walls in the shape of geometric flowers. The air smelt of rosemary and mint soap. It was easy to imagine you had been whisked away from London and landed in Constantinople or Alexandria.

Jacob hissed as his torturer worked on a particularly stubborn knot in his shoulders.

'It's best when they go hard,' said Byron. 'You'll feel a new man once he's finished with you.'

'I always tell myself that.'

'Not your first time, then?'

'When I was in Egypt, I learned to enjoy them.'

'Navy?'

'Army. We were there to see the French hand Egypt back to the Ottomans after the treat of Amiens.'

'Not much fighting, then?'

'Not unless you count against disease. I'm a doctor.'

'And yet you have a very impressive scar. Don't tell me this was a childhood accident with a penknife.' Byron's masseur worked his way down his customer's arm, even manipulating the very tips of his fingers. Byron purred. 'That's very good. I like a little pain with my pleasure.'

Jacob considered that too much information. 'The penknife was a French sabre, and the location was Corunna some years later.'

'Ah, the glorious defeat. Napoleon wins victories by the bushel and yet we celebrate a successful retreat in small boats.'

'You admire him?' Jacob kept his tone carefree. Byron would

not be alone in society praising the Corsican; many a Whig dinner table had made a toast to him, when he defeated foes other than the British. The emperor was yet to win a resounding victory over British land forces, so it felt safe to give him his due as a remarkable man. The greatest man of the new century perhaps?

'How can you not admire him?' Byron gave a groan. 'Yes, that's the spot. Press there.' The masseur leaned in and did so. 'But in truth – harder, Salim – I detest all existing governments. The only truth I see is that riches are power, and poverty is slavery all over the earth, and one sort of establishment is no better, nor worse, for a people than another. That's enough.' Byron swung his legs to sit up, draping a towel over the leg that so worried him.

'Then you are indifferent to the outcome of the war?'

'My blessing is indifference. Others get themselves in a lather like this soap.' He flicked off a bubble from a soap dish standing on the table of oils and perfumes. 'While I smile at their antics.'

Jacob gave his masseur the nod that he too had had enough. He sat up and towelled off the excess oil. 'I always thought you a man of action, my lord.' That was stretching the truth. He had always assumed that the poet of *Childe Harold* was happiest as a wry observer of humanity. To get involved was messy and it was easier to snipe from a distance.

'Oh, I could be, if only there was something I felt worthy of my sacrifice. I'm going to the plunge pool. Are you coming?'

Jacob slid from the table in answer.

'Do you see anything worth fighting for, Sandys? Did being in the army convince you of the righteousness of our cause against the French?' Byron dropped his towel and walked into the tepid water of the cool plunge bath.

'Far from it. It convinced me that war was an idiotic way of settling matters, but we are yet to come up with a better one.' Jacob sank up to his waist. 'I saw it as a *necessary evil*.' He said the last phrase in Greek – Αναγκαίο Κακο.

Seated at the side, Byron slapped the water at him. 'Necessary evil!' Byron translated it without trouble. 'People say that as if it means something. If you really think it necessary then surely it is not evil?'

Wiping the spray from his eyes, Jacob had to concede him a point. 'Then perhaps I mean that the behaviour that accompanies the necessity is all too often wicked, the by-product of aggression.' Jacob joined him on the ledge at the side of the pool. 'It does not have to be that way. In fact, Napoleon's most admirable quality is his insistence that his armies should not batten on the land like locusts. He breaks them up into units fitting the resources and they pay for what they take.'

Byron smiled to hear his hero praised. 'He is the kind of leader I would like to be.' He laid his head back and closed his eyes.

'If you weren't indifferent.'

'If I could rouse myself to care.'

The groans of men undergoing the massage treatment and the lap of the water filled the silence between them. Jacob heard the echo of the cries of the battlefield after the fighting ceased. It was never far away. He felt a pang of longing for opium to help him forget.

'Surely you must care for something? What about Greece?' Jacob asked.

'If I could see a way to help, maybe I could care about that,' agreed Byron.

'You have already taken up your greatest weapon against Lord Elgin.'

Byron gave a hoot of derision. 'That's me – I run at people with pen and ink. How brave.'

'You are very effective, probably doing more damage than a thousand armies could. If you take the long view.'

'If you take the long view. But in the short, I'm a rebellious soul yet to find my cause. I don't find myself very admirable.'

Byron sank under the water, bringing the conversation to an end.

Alex and Jacob strolled back to the office in the mews.

'What did you make of him?' Alex asked. There was a note in his voice that suggested he rather hoped Jacob would endorse his positive opinion of the poet, like a friend who is hoping his new acquaintances would get on.

How to explain his reaction to the poetic thunderstorm that was Byron? 'If I were a Greek doctor at the time of Plato, I would say he had too much of the saturnine humour in him.'

'You think he's melancholic?'

'I think he at root doesn't like himself very much – that's why he grumbles and flashes out at society.'

Alex hummed at that. 'He wouldn't be alone.'

'He has found a public stage on which to brood in a way that sells books and makes him a rich man.'

Alex chuckled. 'I think *you* are the true cynic, Sandys, not Byron.'

Reaching the office, Jacob went to the desk and made notes in his case book about the conversation. Byron was about surfaces, a glittering semi-precious stone in the diadem of English writers, not quite a true diamond. He would be no gem because he deliberately kept things superficial and flippant. Even though they had both been stripped to the skin, sharing a private moment, that conversation had been no true heart to heart. Jacob didn't fault him for that. Byron would be too aware that anyone he spoke to could run off to the press and sell his story since gossip about Byron was selling newspapers in their thousands. His words were chosen as an artful confession to impress a new person he found mildly interesting, calculated to give the effect of frankness.

So where did it leave their case? Sifting through the verbiage to what grains of truth he had allowed to get through, Byron hoped he would act if he had a cause that justified it, but he feared that he would fail the test of his manhood. It would be hard to see that aspiration being expressed by using assassins and gunpowder at a remove, keeping himself above the fray. Maybe he could feel strongly enough about the wrongs done to Greece to throw in his lot with them, and he might've done so had he stayed in the Aegean for longer, but now it also seemed Byron could equally become impassioned for the frame breakers in Nottingham that he defended in the House of Lords. But his efforts had only gone as far as giving a speech. That left Byron still looking for a cause and he was whiling away the time flirting and getting himself into scandalous liaisons. In the quiet of his own bedchamber, he likely hated this version of himself and itched to break free. Jacob for once felt a little fellow feeling for the man. He knew what those dark hours were like.

Alex returned having changed into his blue jacket and loose trousers. He sat in the client chair and waited for Jacob to blot the page.

'The verdict on Byron?'

'Sending coded threats to Elgin? Unlikely. He prefers to make his gestures in public. But he could, however, be stirring up the campaign against Elgin's circle with his words.'

'He is creating an atmosphere where it is permissible to hate. That does sound like he bears some responsibility, then.'

'That's one for the philosophers. I'm not looking directly at him, but I'm interested if you have any suspicions about others in his circle.'

'You mean Hobhouse and Tom Moore and the rest?'

'Or their hangers-on. It could be some misguided admirer thinking to please his idol.'

'He does inspire fanatical devotion.' Alex rubbed his newly

shaved chin. 'I'll keep on the watch for anyone answering that description.'

'And when you are comfortable, ask about Brooking, see if anyone knew him.'

'What if I wear the ring? If it's a secret club, then maybe it would shake out another member.'

Would that put him in danger? Possibly, but Alex was no clergyman's son like Brooking, sheltered from the ways of the world. He passed him the ring and Alex slipped it on his right hand middle finger.

'Try not to lose it – or your head.'

Alex nodded and stretched out his long legs. 'What are you going to call this place?'

'I don't think my family would thank me for using our name.'

'And Ezra Pennington would love his daughter to put his name over the door.'

They both chuckled at the idea of annoying the alderman.

'We must ask Dora. Then we can take out an advertisement in the news sheets and spread the word. I'd prefer it if our only client wasn't Lord Elgin.' Jacob opened the newspaper he had collected and scanned for any similar companies offering discreet services. His eyes fell on a report of a murder of a printer in York Street, Covent Garden, near where they had just been. Why did that address seem familiar?

He remembered the parcel that he had taken over from Dora that was still in his rooms – the book of Rowlandson prints. It had come from York Street, had it not? How many printers were there on that street and was this dead man the same as the one with whom Percy had been in correspondence?

He stood up. Another thread they hadn't yet tugged.

'Are we going somewhere?' asked Alex, grabbing his hat.

'To see a dead publisher of erotic artworks.'

Alex tapped his hat onto the crown of his head. 'My, my, working for you is far more entertaining than I expected.'

Chapter Twenty-Six

Grosvenor Square

Mrs Ferguson had gone down for dinner in a cream silk gown that Dora had spent the last hour ironing – it was skilled work not to scorch the fabric but not the kind that brought her much satisfaction. She was just on the point of rewarding herself with dinner when Kir arrived with a message for her. They met on a turn of the stairs as Dora went down to the servants' hall. She held the note up to the window.

Can you come out for a few hours? There is something you need to see at York Street. J

'He's waiting outside with the other gent,' Kir whispered.

That was awkward. Her curiosity was running wild but what if she wasn't back in time to help Mrs Ferguson disrobe? Entering the servants' hall, Dora checked the clock on the mantlepiece. The soup had only just gone up. If she was quick, she should be able to make it.

Mrs Simmonds, the housekeeper, looked up from her post at head of the senior staff table as Dora passed her, Kir in tow. In her fifties, she had a coronet of grey hair under her cap, a remarkably unlined face and the competent manner of a naval captain running a tight ship.

'Going somewhere, Miss Pence? Second outing in the same day.' The note of disapproval was clear. 'Wasn't your excursion with Miss Mitty enough?'

Dimitra helped herself to the Irish stew that sat in a tureen between her and the housekeeper but kept her counsel. Mrs Widgeon bustled in with some bread rolls that smelt heavenly.

Dora needed an excuse – and quickly. Her eyes alighted on a chipped Staffordshire dog next to the clock. 'I have a little secret to confess.'

Kir's eyes rounded in alarm and he tugged at her skirt in warning.

'My old employer, Lady Tolworth, has the most adorable spaniel – he was my particular pet when I worked there. The usual walker is ill so I promised I would take him out this evening. I hope that is all right with you?' Dora beamed at the gathered servants. As a nation of dog lovers, few people could resist the excuse of a spaniel.

'I do wish Lady George would get a dog,' sighed Mrs Widgeon. 'I love a good hound in a house.'

'Then I'd be stuck cleaning up after it,' muttered a footman.

Ignoring the byplay, Dora continued. 'I thought Kir would enjoy the fresh air. It would stop him dwelling on things.' She was going to be struck by lightning for using his grief again in this way, but from the boy's swift grin, he seemed to enjoy the games she was playing. Lord forgive her for the duplicity she was teaching him.

Mrs Simmonds considered the matter and came down on the side of dogs and fresh air. 'That sounds very commendable.'

'I will put a plate aside for each of you,' added Mrs Widgeon.

'Make sure you are back before nine. I can't see the family staying up late today.' Mrs Simmonds nodded her permission.

With muttered thanks, Dora hurried Kir out of the servants' hall, selecting a cap for him and a hooded cloak for her from the selection of garments on the pegs by the outside door.

Their escorts, Jacob and Alex, did not greet them as they saw them emerge from the house. They fell into step with them on the opposite pavement, pretending it was pure coincidence that had them walking in the same direction. Covering her head with her hood, Dora took a swift survey of the street.

'Any sign of the man you saw, Kir?' she asked the boy in a low voice. She pressed his shoulder. 'Don't make it obvious but have a look around.'

The boy did as asked, taking a good long look at everyone within sight, then turned his gaze up to her. 'No, miss. Do you think he's gone for good?'

They wouldn't be so lucky. It was more likely that one man couldn't keep watch at all hours on his own. Either he wasn't expecting them to go out tonight and had given up for the day, or someone else was watching in his place.

'It is safer to assume we are being followed and hope to lose them in a busier street.' They picked up their pace and plunged into the crowds on Bond Street, weaving between the shoppers, and the clerks attempting to bring customers inside their establishments. After they'd crossed the road a few times, she felt confident that none of the people in sight had been on Grosvenor Square when they left Lady George's. She caught up with Jacob and Alex, who had been discreetly leading the way.

'I didn't think you'd bring the boy,' said Jacob, tipping his hat to her.

'I had to have some excuse to leave during dinner. We are walking a dog in the park.'

'That's the first time I've heard a visit to the scene of a murder called so.'

Her heart squeezed with alarm. 'Someone is dead?' She checked Kir wasn't in earshot, but Alex had him in hand, discussing the window displays on the Bond Street shops.

'A Mr Stokes, who worked for Mr Fores, printer and bookbinder.'

The connection clicked in her mind. 'Does he by any chance provide interesting etchings to the upper classes?'

'Ones bound in Moroccan leather? Indeed. Unless there is more than one print shop on that street, I believe we've found Percy's supplier.'

Dora revolved the possibilities in her mind. 'What connection can this have to the attack in Berwick?'

'Let's puzzle it out.' He placed her hand on his forearm, finding a comfortable pace to match hers. 'What changed after that? Percy didn't die as was intended but I've been putting it about that Percy is a suspected French agent. Elgin was asking questions in the Alien Office.'

'That means the whispers will be circulating. Such a titbit would travel faster than a cannonball. If Stokes was part of the spy network, perhaps even part of a scheme blackmailing influential gentlemen, then someone might have gone to the source to destroy evidence of their questionable little habit.'

'Or simply to end the blackmail. As Percy is out of the picture with his injuries, it would have been a good time to cut off one head of the hydra and deal with Percy if he survives and when he is weakened. Or…'

'Or what?' They paused to let three carriages pass before crossing the road. Jacob tipped the sweeper who cleared the horse dung out of their path.

'Or the shop is more than a seller of risqué material. Let's return to the subject once we've checked that it is the right printer's assistant who has died.'

As the killing had happened the day before, the body had already been removed for the coroner and the print shop was shuttered.

'It is the same address as recorded in the book by the housekeeper at Raith,' said Dora, who had excellent recall. The premises was no backstreet operation but a respectable brick building with Doric columns. The prints in the window were scurrilous but nothing as extreme as the graphic images in the books they had intercepted. Naturally not. That would get the print seller marched to nearby Bow Street Magistrates Court and charged with distribution of obscene works.

They walked on so as not to draw attention to their interest.

'Smith, see what you can find out in the tavern,' said Jacob, indicating that Alex tackle the regulars in The Fleece that stood on the corner of Brydges Street. It had fancy plate glass windows and flaring oil lamps over the entrance marking it out as a gin palace.

Alex grinned. 'If I must. It has a reputation.'

'For what?' asked Jacob.

'Violence.'

'Ah.'

'Maybe I should go?' volunteered Dora.

'No!' both men said in unison.

'I'm less likely to get in a fight.'

'I'm not so sure about that,' muttered Jacob.

Alex gave her a salute. 'This is my share of the work, Dora. I'm the disreputable ex-army officer. Getting into a bar brawl will only help my reputation. I'll meet you back at the office in an hour. Come on, Kir.'

'You're taking the boy with you?' asked Jacob.

'I need someone to watch my back who no one will try to fight or flirt with for the evening.' With a wink at Dora, Alex drew the lad away. 'Look lively, lad.'

Dora didn't like seeing Kir vanish into an alehouse. She told herself that Kir had the wit to behave as fitted the company – he had shown as much already. Alex was right in that boys were ten a penny. No one would pay him a second's attention. Would he be safer with Alex than with her and Jacob?

Then why did she think she'd just done wrong?

Chapter Twenty-Seven

She pulled her mind back to the problem of searching the premises.

'This case is frustrating. There are too many parts that don't seem connected,' she said. 'Maybe the death here is a coincidence?'

Jacob strolled with the ease of a gentleman about town. 'I think of it more like an octopus – there's a mind in the middle with tentacles spreading off in different directions.'

They paused to admire the display in the cheesemonger's next door to the printer's.

'I found out today that Dimitra has a cousin who works for Byron,' she said, pretending interest in a wheel of Cheddar cheese.

Jacob squeezed her arm. 'That's very interesting. The community of Greek servants in London must be very small. I'd wager they all know each other.'

'And they are furious that Elgin stole their marbles.'

'He didn't steal them.'

'Of course he did.'

'He rescued them.'

'From what?'

'Time – and poor guardianship.'

'*Temporis Vtrivsqve Vindex*? Wasn't that something about championing the past? Elgin said he wasn't a member of that secret society, but he's doing the same work, isn't he? Did he lie to us about not knowing the group?'

'I don't think so.'

Dora shrugged. 'I don't trust him. He should send those marbles back to Greece and maybe all this would go away.'

Jacob stiffened. 'I didn't think you would be so simple-minded, Dora. If not Elgin, it would be Napoleon. Until the Greeks rise up and gain independence, they won't be a fit nation to look after the marbles.'

'But they belong to them.'

'Do they? I rather believe that they belong to all of us. Ancient Greek culture belongs to the world, not one small nation who has changed so much over the last two thousand years that the very idea of who and what is Greek would not be recognisable to a Plato or an Aeschylus.'

'You're just saying that because you're a collector yourself and like to have these things where you can see them.'

'And what's wrong with that? Here they can be studied and sheltered.'

Angry that she didn't have a good retort, she changed the subject. 'Let's agree to disagree. We've got a job to do.'

Jacob tried the most obvious route: he knocked on the front door. There was no reply – but the window in the house opposite opened like a shot.

'Ain't nobody in,' said the old biddy who stuck her head out. 'Not since Mr Stokes got himself dead.' It was likely that Stokes had been the live-in member of staff. The owner, if he was doing well for himself, would have a house in one of the nicer areas.

'Do you know when it will be open? I'm waiting for a book I ordered,' said Jacob pleasantly.

'Oh, are you?' The woman gave him a leer. 'You'll just have to wait for your thrills, won't ya?'

Jacob gave her a politer bow than she warranted, and the woman shut the window with a snap. Dora and Jacob began walking slowly away.

'How are we going to get in?' asked Dora. She didn't have her lock picks with her, and, in any case, they were suited for small locks, such as writing desks and cabinets, not a house door. Plus, the lady opposite would notice if they tried anything of that nature on the entrance.

'We go round the back.' Offering her his arm, Jacob took her to the alley down the side of the premises.

'You know what people will think seeing you take me down here,' said Dora. She could already imagine the old woman sneering at them out of her window.

'I hope they do. It will stop them wondering why we are taking so long.' Jacob found a good place where he could give her a helping hand over the wall. Dora gathered her skirts between her legs and tucked the material into her waistband to make a pair of loose breeches. 'You should've told me – I would've worn my Viola costume.'

Jacob boosted her up. 'And deprive myself of this sight?'

'Eyes down, Jacob Sandys.' Dora made sure she gave him a little kick in the face as she wriggled over the wall and swung down on the other side. As the material caught on a nail, her skirts were practically around her ears as she landed but there was no audience on this side. She smoothed them down and waited for Jacob to drop into the yard. She would have her own mending to do tonight.

'What now?' Dora was already searching among the pots and crates by the backdoor. In her experience, most householders thought that they were the only ones to come up with novel places to hide the spare key.

'I could break a window?' offered Jacob, lifting a brick next to the ash bucket.

'Let me just check…' Dora took a twig with a suspiciously ashy end that leaned against the wall and poked it into the bucket. It came up with a key on a ring. 'Ta-dah!'

'Excellent.' Jacob wiped it off on his handkerchief.

'Do you think this means they have nothing to hide?'

'I think it means they aren't expecting anyone to be breaking in, which is quite different.'

He opened the door and they waited for their eyes to adjust to the gloom. In the long twilight they wouldn't need a lamp, which was just as well as the lady opposite would spot them in a trice. They entered the kitchen. The stone floor was slightly damp as if it had been mopped recently.

'Where did he die, do you know?' asked Dora.

'He was found right here – dead at dinner. The news report said he dined early, probably so that he could open the shop for the evening trade.'

'I imagine that is his busiest hour, considering what he was selling. Drinking, whoring and theatre-going, then take home a little something to pass the time in your chamber. Look, the table has two glasses, two plates, two sets of cutlery.'

'He knew his attacker, then?'

'Or thought he did. They didn't get as far as eating.' Dora checked the larder. Day-old bread, ham and cheese were set out on the marble-topped cool shelf. 'I think the maid or whoever does the chores for this household had prepared this for him.'

'Then it sounds like he sent her away so he could be on his own when his visitor came. That's like Brooking. He also knew the one who killed him – invited him right up to the chamber where he died.'

Dora shut the door. 'That was a stabbing. How did the man here die?'

'The Bow Street Runners said he was struck over the head by a hammer. Their theory was that he likely surprised a burglar. There has been a number of violent attacks round here recently—'

'Yes, like Brooking.'

'Sadly, many others, too. And there are people looking to pick up petty cash to buy their next shot of gin or twist of opium.'

'Hmm. I doubt the magistrate is going to believe that story if his men reported the meal set out in the kitchen.'

'You have more faith in the observational powers of the Runners than I do. They wouldn't look into Richard Brooking's death even with a witness who told them he didn't arrive with a woman – *and* Brooking works for an earl.'

'Two men dead not so very far from each other. I wonder if Stokes had a bronze ring?'

'Let's see what the print shop will tell us. Keep low. I don't want anyone peering in and spotting us poking around.'

They crept in, using the counter for cover. From her position crouched on the floor, Dora could make out the organisational principle behind the shop. To her left was a section for fine art prints, copies of great works of art, etchings of famous sights like the pyramids, and other architectural wonders. If she looked further, she would probably find the Parthenon and the marbles among them. Likenesses of the leading members of society dominated one wall on the right – a print of Byron was placed at the front of these. The wall behind the counter was for the most popular sellers, mainly cartoons about politics and the foibles of the famous – these two sections merged when it came to the Prince Regent and his brothers. Nothing in view was out of the ordinary level of the rude, bold drawings that were accepted in cartoons.

A drawer next to her nose begged for her attention. She raised a brow at Jacob.

'Under the counter?' he murmured.

'It's a classic for a reason,' she said. It was also locked. Reaching into her hair she pulled out a pin and shaped herself a lockpick, then straightened a second. 'Wish me luck.' On her knees, she eased the hooked pin into the hole and used the straight one to keep the tension as she twiddled the mechanism. Then with a snick, she turned her wrist and the lock opened.

'I don't think you needed luck.'

'It's an easy one, fortunately, and kept well-oiled.' She pulled the drawer out.

'You must teach me to do that. It's a useful skill.'

'Look what we have here – or don't look as these will make your eyes burn.' Inside were the salacious prints they had seen in Percy's parcel, plus some others that hadn't been bound in that collection.

'I'll take the risk.' Jacob took one out and examined it closely.

'See something you like?' She didn't like watching him studying this material – it felt as far from the sex they enjoyed together as east was from west. No tenderness – no respect.

He turned it over, searching for markings on the back. 'I'm looking for anything that suggests its provenance. There is a market across Europe for such things. If the owner Mr Fores, or perhaps Mr Stokes alone, was part of that exchange, this shop would make an excellent postal service to the French, the route by which Percy received and sent his reports.'

'Why do you think that?' Dora found many of the images stomach churning, violent even, like a punch in the midriff. The good humour of the cartoonist morphed into the cynical taste of the rake where women only had to be available, not necessarily willing.

'Technically, we aren't trading with France, apart from some exempt goods such as corn.' Jacob took one of the images that had been in Percy' book and put it in his coat pocket.

'Well, they had to do that. We'd be starving after the poor harvest if that wasn't an exception.' Dora relocked the drawer.

'But I see no lack of French brandy or Belgian lace in society drawing rooms, do you? Even Paris fashion journals are found only a week or two after first publication on the tables of well-to-do ladies. Smuggling is a lucrative trade.'

'Oh, I see how it would work. You could send erotic prints and, if opened, everyone would be too taken aback by the content to ask if they aren't a disguise for something else.'

'We must take a closer look at the book you took from Percy's trunk and compare it to one of these prints. There may be messages in it that we missed on first look.'

It was at this moment that they both heard the jingle of keys at the front door.

'Damnation,' muttered Jacob, risking a look over the counter. 'Retreat.'

But there was little chance they could cross the floor to the kitchen unobserved if someone stood in the shop. The bell over the door jingled.

'Mr Fores! Mr Fores!' the old lady opposite shrieked from her window.

The man at the door paused. 'Yes, Mrs Chesham?'

'There was a suspicious couple asking when you were next open.'

'When was this?' There was a long-suffering weariness to his tone.

'About quarter of an hour ago,' said the lady in her trumpet voice.

Dora grinned. The woman was so eager to share her news that she had drawn the shopkeeper back onto the street again. Seizing their chance, she followed Jacob into the backroom.

'Do you think they did it – killed your Mr Stokes?' shouted the lady.

'I hardly think a housebreaker would come back and knock at the front.'

'I suppose not,' agreed the dame.

'Might they have been customers?'

'Well now you say it, the man did ask when you'd be open as he wanted to collect an order.'

Mr Fores sighed. 'Thank you for your vigilance, Mrs Chesham. Let me know if they come back. You can tell them normal opening hours resume next week.'

At this point of the conversation, Dora and Jacob reached the backyard and silently closed the door on the speakers.

Jacob bent to her ear to whisper as she replaced the key. 'We can't risk climbing over. Let's hide in the shadows and see what he does.'

'And if he looks out here?'

'That would be a problem.' He held her hand.

They waited but the owner did not come out. Dora could feel her heart thumping. Jacob could surely hear it, too. Mr Fores checked that the backdoor was locked, collected some things from the kitchen – possibly the perishable food – and then let himself out of the front.

They waited another five minutes. It was nearly dark. Dora had the sinking feeling that she had prolonged her outing too long.

'I'm so late. I've got to get back.'

Jacob nodded and helped her over the wall. There was no more teasing. They emerged from the alley and turned to walk on so as not to go past the vigilant neighbour.

'Will you get in trouble?'

Dora grimaced. 'Know anyone with a spaniel I can borrow?'

Chapter Twenty-Eight

Bruton Mews

Dora paced the office, anxious that Kir was not back yet. This was a disaster. It was already gone eleven. Her employer would have her guts for garters – pretty, lace-edged ones as this was Mrs Ferguson – but garters nonetheless.

'You go. I'll bring him home later,' suggested Jacob. He was studying the cartoon he'd stolen from the print shop. His calm was incredibly annoying.

'And how would I explain that?'

'Say you bumped into me and I took him somewhere. The Fergusons are aware I know him already and have taken an interest in the lad.'

'He's eight, Jacob. A responsible woman doesn't let a boy go off for a night on the town.' She thumped her forehead. 'That's what I've done, haven't I? I'm so stupid. Alex used to go to Hellfire Club parties. I don't even know him, really – neither do you.'

'Your brother loved him.'

'Oh, yes, and Anthony was such a great judge of character. An associate of my brother is hardly going to flinch at getting a boy drunk down The Fleece gin palace!'

'You're not being fair to Alex. I've seen no such recklessness.'

'*Yet*. No such recklessness *yet*. Not until tonight.' She felt sick. It was her brother all over again, careless with the lives of others. 'Kir is my responsibility.'

'And mine.'

Her fragile control snapped. 'I haven't noticed you stepping up. I'm the one shepherding him around Grosvenor Square, worried some madman will scoop him up off the street. I'm the one darning and ironing and pretending to be all meek and mild while you get to go play in bagnios with dissolute lords!'

Jacob looked up, shocked. 'Dora, where has this all come from?'

She didn't know, but the last few days had seen a steady winding up of tension and Jacob was getting the full blast of her resentment.

'It's why we don't work, Jacob. Am I always going to be doing the wretched tasks while you lord it about in fine company, thinking great thoughts and arranging us all to your satisfaction?'

'No!'

'Where's your proof?'

Their eyes met, his desperate, hers angry.

Hurried footsteps outside signalled the end of her vigil. At last!

'Dora—'

'Later.' She didn't even let Kir enter but hurried out of the door. 'Alex, I'm furious with you. We've got to go.' She grabbed the boy's hand and ran towards Grosvenor Square, leaving Alex open-mouthed in her wake. 'You don't smell of gin, do you?'

'Me? No!' The boy sounded affronted. 'I had a few sips of ale, no more.'

That had better be true or she'd wring Alex's neck.

'Say nothing about what we've done tonight, do you understand?'

'But they'll ask. What's the name of the dog?' Kir asked as they reached the steps to the basement.

'What?' She checked for the mystery watcher but couldn't see anyone suspicious.

'The spaniel.'

He was right: they needed to agree a story. Damn it all. 'Desdemona.' That was a stupid name but the only one she could come up with on the fly.

'I'm hungry.' He was making the cry of children everywhere who had missed supper as she pushed him ahead of her into the passageway. Putting his cap and her cloak back on the pegs, she marched him to the kitchen.

'Let's see if there's any left for us,' she said with forced brightness, acting as if they weren't hours late. 'Mrs Widgeon said she'd put it aside.'

Dimitra appeared behind her. 'You're wanted upstairs, Miss Pence.'

'Oh, thank you.' Where had Dimitra come from? Had she heard Kir ask about the dog's name?

The camaraderie they'd struck up earlier was entirely missing in the Greek woman's demeanour. 'Mrs Ferguson had a headache. She asked for you an hour ago.'

Blast! Of course she had. 'Oh, I'm so sorry I'm terribly late. Did someone else go to her?' Her performance was a little frayed, she was that rattled.

'I took her a powder and helped her undress. She wants a word.'

Of course she did. Her lady's maid had gone out without permission. 'I'll go up directly. Kir, eat your supper.' Pretending for the rest of the staff that all was well, Dora bounded up the servants' staircase two at a time.

Pausing to catch her breath, she knocked on Mrs Ferguson's door.

'Come!' said a feeble voice.

Meek and mild, Dora reminded herself.

She entered and shut the door quietly behind her. 'I do apologise, Mrs Ferguson.' The room was dimly lit, only a lamp set to a low flame on the dressing table. Bed-cover pulled under her arms, Mrs Ferguson had propped herself up on her pillows.

'Pence, I think you are taking advantage of me. Do you dislike your duties?' There were shadows under her eyes, and she was very pale. The anxiety for her children was getting to her and a disappearing maid adding to it.

'No, ma'am.'

'Since we arrived back in London, you've been out and about as if your duties as my maid were but a secondary consideration. You appear to think your valuable time is better spent sight-seeing and amusing the boy.'

That was accurate, Dora had to give her that. 'I apologise.'

'Where were you tonight?'

'I took Kir out for a stroll.'

'Until a quarter after eleven? Mitty said something about a dog.'

'A spaniel. Desdemona.'

'Not an auspicious name.' Mrs Ferguson cocked her head to one side and considered her. 'Pence, is there something you aren't telling me?'

Oh, so many things.

'Mitty mentioned that she'd seen Dr Sandys outside when you left.'

Was Dimitra spying on her? 'Yes, I saw him, too. He was passing by with a friend.' *Nothing to see here. Let's change the subject.*

'Oh, Pence. Do I have to warn you about the fate of servants who set their cap at their social superiors? Do not believe the dreams encouraged by novels. There is rarely a happy ending; the maid does not get to wed the master.'

At least Mrs Ferguson only suspected her of an illicit affair, not the fact that she was investigating the household on behalf of her ex-husband. Small mercies. 'Yes, ma'am.'

'You have only been in my employ for a week – an eventful week, to be sure. I was very impressed by your work for the first few days, but I am changing my opinion rapidly. Consider this your first and final warning.'

The lady had some backbone. Dora liked her all the better for it.

'If you go missing again on any day apart from your Wednesday half day and your Sunday off, I will dismiss you without a reference.'

'Understood.' She couldn't promise it wouldn't happen. Her real purpose for being here meant that another conflict between duties and investigating was all too likely.

'You may go.'

Dora bobbed a curtsey. As she closed the door behind her, she heard a male voice rumbling in the room. Mr Ferguson must have just come in from his adjoining chamber. Dora pressed her ear against the door.

'You dismissed her?' he asked.

'No, Robert, I gave her a warning. I was very stern.'

There was the sound of a kiss. 'I doubt that. She's a bad'un if she's already skimping on her duties within a few days of being appointed.'

'But she was so good in the aftermath of the explosion. She didn't mind getting her hands dirty, helped nurse the injured, while I just hovered stupidly offering water.'

'A gesture that was greatly appreciated by the men. You mustn't let her take advantage of your good nature.'

'I suppose not, dear. But she didn't abandon us even when Dr Sandys explained there was a chance we were the target of the explosion.'

'I disagree. She's clearly flighty – running up to Scotland on a whim, running about London on another.'

Mrs Ferguson sighed. 'Maybe you're right. I'll start making enquiries about a replacement when we get home. Pence might prefer to be left here. There are more chances for employment.'

'There you go again, considering her wishes over your own. If I had—'

The rattle of a tray warned Dora that her eavesdropping was over. She moved quickly away from the door and hurried past the butler bringing up a nightcap for the master. He stared down his nose at her.

'Good evening, Mr Rogers,' Dora said politely.

'Some people are simply not suited to domestic service,' he said with a sniff.

He was right about that.

Knowing her time in the household was ticking to the end, Dora felt there was little left to lose. After that row with Jacob, she could be on a coach back north to her place in the acting troupe tomorrow. She might as well see what setting the cat among the pigeons would achieve. If Dimitra was part of those in Byron's circle plotting against the Elgins, how would she react if Dora challenged her in front of others?

She didn't have to pretend as the whole evening had lit the fuse on her temper. Straightening her shoulders, she sailed into the kitchen in high dudgeon.

'Oh, there she is!' she declared. 'Miss Tattletale.' She pointed an accusing finger at Dimitra who was sitting with Mrs Simmonds and Mrs Widgeon by the fire, enjoying a tot of sherry. The other staff in the dining room fell silent in shock. Kir looked up from his bowl and blinked. He had never seen her like this. 'I go out for a stroll, and she makes it into a sordid dalliance, dropping me in trouble with the mistress!'

Dimitra swallowed. 'I merely said I saw Dr Sandys and another man on the street when you left. They looked like they were waiting for you.'

'So, it's *two* men now, is it?' Dora stood centre stage, arms akimbo. The woman had as good as implied she was meeting them for an assignation – which she had been – but not as to take them two at a time with a boy in tow! 'Oh, really? You *merely* said. Why say anything at all? Why spy on my comings and goings?'

'We weren't with the doctor. We were with Desdemona,' said Kir, rather protesting too much. 'A spaniel.'

'I'm not the one making secret assignations!' Dora tilted her chin, daring Dimitra to take the bait.

'Now look here, Miss Pence—' began Dimitra.

'No, you look here. You've got me in trouble with my mistress. Other servants who support their fellows would have stepped in and covered for my brief absence.'

'We couldn't help that. Desdemona ran away,' Kir told the nearest footman. The boy had a good imagination. 'We had to rescue her from footpads who wanted to cook her and eat her.' Strike that: his imagination was running riot.

'They wouldn't –' Dora raised her voice over the dog-eating comments '– throw their fellow servant in front of the carriage by making insinuations.'

'She was with me the whole time,' said Kir in his role as her own little Greek chorus. 'She never went off on her own with Dr Sandys.'

'Kir, please.' Dora patted his head in a gesture of 'pipe down'.

'Why?' sneered Dimitra, her own anger now rising to match Dora's outrage. 'Are you afraid he might tell the truth? You encourage him to lie – I've seen it.'

'Oh, you want to do this now, do you? I talked our way into that exhibition so we all could enjoy it, and you went along with it. And what happened next? You left us standing on the pavement when you went into Lord Byron's house *on your own* and stayed there for at least fifteen minutes. What exhibition were you involved in in there, Miss Mitkou? I hear his lordship is famous for his attractions.'

'Lord Byron was from home!' Dimitra snapped, then she flushed, realising she had just admitted to her visit.

'Oh, I'm sure his household is exactly the kind of place a decent servant should be visiting.'

'I have friends there, all right? My cousin is one of his servants.'

Could she wind her up to make more confessions? 'Is that a kissing cousin?'

Mrs Simmonds stood up. 'Miss Pence, Miss Mitty, that's enough. I'm shocked at the pair of you. It seems neither of you can be trusted to go about the neighbourhood without risking the reputation of this family. Miss Pence, you do not fall under my authority, but I will be having words with Mrs Ferguson. I will not stand for such scenes in my domain. Miss Mitty, I suggest you go upstairs and consider where your loyalties lie.'

Dimitra shot Dora a fulminating look and flounced out. Dora strode over to the table and pulled a plate in front of her. She lifted the lid on the stew.

'You didn't leave me much, did you?' she told Kir.

He again blinked at her, not able to reconcile this calm Dora with the angry one who had just created a storm in the servants' hall.

Dora scooped up the remains of the meal. Oh, well. It was better than many a dinner she had scraped together. Gradually the servants turned their attention from her, intent on gossiping about the argument and probably tearing Dimitra's reputation to shreds. Dora as a newcomer was far less interesting.

'By the way, those footpads?' she said in a low voice to Kir.

Kir winced. He probably realised that he'd gone too far with that piece of invention.

'They don't eat dogs.'

'They might – if they're starving.' The boy had evidently seen desperate times.

'It looks like I'm confined to the house for a few days. Run messages for me – but only if no one is watching the house,' she said in a low voice.

'Yes, Miss Pence. Whatever you need.'

'Good lad.' Every confidential agency needed a messenger boy, didn't it? It seemed as if she had just recruited theirs.

Chapter Twenty-Nine

Bruton Mews

Sitting at his desk in the office, Jacob tossed a cricket ball he'd found in a cupboard, a relic from some old game of footmen versus stableboys that had been played in the mews behind the great houses. Each throw, each catch, helped him settle his thoughts.

Jacob understood all too well that, with her position under threat, Dora was unable to take off to see him as she had on previous days. However, they needed a consultation and he needed to repair the holes they'd torn in their relationship yesterday with their argument. First they'd fallen out over the ownership of the marbles and then she'd pretty much accused him of taking her for granted and sending her to do all the menial jobs.

The ball thunked into his palm. He was guilty of having assumed that as a member of the lower orders she would be happy to masquerade as such. He hadn't even considered volunteering himself for a similar role. What did that say about him?

Alex came down smartly attired and looking far less hungover than he had after a night with Byron. 'Penny for them?'

Jacob threw Alex the ball, which he managed to catch. And yes, his reflexes were also in tiptop form. Good to know their employee was fit for action. 'I'm considering how we can get Dora here. We need to talk about our next steps and compare notes on what we've learned.'

Alex took a seat in the window, basking in the sunlight streaming through. 'I half expected her to be here ready to kick my arse some more. She wasn't dismissed for being late then?'

'Not yet, though it does show that we need to put a better communication strategy in place when one of us is working under cover of another identity.' Jacob made a note in his ledger.

Alex stretched his arms up and rolled his head, working out the stiffness of the night before. 'The point is that she can't come to us, and we can't go to her.'

'Exactly. Lady's maids do not go about with gentlemen.'

'But they do deal with ladies.' Alex nodded to the main house.

Jacob smiled, following his thought. 'They do indeed.'

'You should recruit her.'

There came a little tap at the door and Kir slid inside. 'Miss sent me,' he said, holding out a message.

Jacob unfolded the paper then laughed. 'Perhaps we do not think so differently after all.'

Dowager Lady Tolworth scowled at Jacob across the breakfast table. 'You want me to invite a divorcee to my house?'

'We do.' Jacob helped himself to a warm muffin and slathered on the butter while Yarton hovered, ready to assist in anything that was lacking.

Alex speared a sausage from the warmer and put it on Kir's plate. 'You have invited us to breakfast, so I'd say you were halfway to scandal already.'

'You, young man, have good looks to recommend you. People will simply think I'm engaging in a flirtation.' Ginnie tapped her teacup and Yarton refilled it. 'The boy ... no one notices a boy.'

'The morals of the town are beyond my comprehension,' admitted Jacob. 'A woman, now respectfully married to a Scottish laird after a stormy time in the divorce courts, is still beyond the Pale; whereas the idea that you might be engaging in an affair with a disgraced officer is barely blinked at.'

Ginnie's pearl earrings jiggled a warning at him that she found his observation annoying. 'I'm a widow. I'm allowed my follies.'

'You are indeed,' Alex murmured placatingly. He gave her his most outrageous rakish smile, aware that he was safe from her advances. In fact, mused Jacob, they could both be of use to each other, one in scotching rumours about his preference for his own sex, the other in burnishing her reputation as a desirable widow. Alex would make an incomparable escort.

'Why care what anyone thinks? You are allowed to host a divorcee to a quiet tête-à-tête,' Jacob pressed. 'It wouldn't be as if you were forcing her upon others. Just the two of you. She's good company and very kind.'

Ginnie wavered.

'You said you wanted to help and this is what we need. Isn't it better than respectable boredom?'

The latter argument clinched it.

'Lord, yes, you're right.' Ginnie turned to her butler. 'Yarton, send a message to Mrs Ferguson. Tea, this afternoon.'

Kir looked up from his plate, egg smeared on his cheek. 'You need to get a dog and call her Desdemona.'

The adults all blinked at him.

'It's true,' he said defensively. 'Ask Miss Pence.'

Jacob was dispatched to find a spaniel – again, not what he had thought he would be doing with his day in pursuance of their investigation. At least his new profession was far from predictable. Fortunately, he knew where he could get one at short notice – Mount Street, where his brother's family were living for the Season. William's wife was a dog lover and had a spaniel – the only problem was that he was male. Close enough, Jacob decided, as he picked up the long-eared, tan-and-cream dog who decided this was his cue to lick Jacob's chin.

'I didn't know you liked dogs,' said Charlotte, a diminutive redhead with a sprinkling of freckles and big grey eyes. The newest addition to the nursery was already showing that she took after her mother with her fluff of ginger locks. Jacob had admired the baby, as was expected of an uncle, and declared her in good health, as was expected of a doctor, and was now rewarded with temporary custody of a spaniel.

'I do.' Jacob hesitated as to whether he should tell his sister-in-law the truth as he sat in her fine parlour stroking the designated pup on his lap while her other hounds playfought on the rug. The house had an air of restrained chaos, which he had to admit was fun and far from the stultifying atmosphere in many a society marriage. He could imagine his brother striding in, kissing the wife, then the baby, followed by rolling around on the rug with his other children and the pups as he let them best him in wrestling. William was lucky in his wife. Unfortunately, though, Charlotte was also an astute woman and would smell a lie. Jacob would be safer telling her what he was up to than inventing some moonshine she would instantly dismiss. 'Patch is for a case I'm investigating.'

Charlotte eyed him with curiosity as she presided over the tea tray. 'Jacob, I didn't think you'd added lawyer to your other qualifications, or are you talking about a medical case?'

'I mean, I'm helping a friend –' Elgin could loosely be termed a friend, couldn't he? '– who is being threatened. He brought the case – the mystery – to me to diagnose unofficially.'

'I can't for the life of me see how Patch would come into it.'

'It's a long story.'

Charlotte passed him a cup of coffee, knowing he preferred a stronger brew to tea at this time of day. 'Does William know about it? He worries about you.'

'No.'

She pursed her lips. 'Shame he's out in the City.'

'Do you need his permission?'

She laughed. That was a 'no' then. 'I was thinking he could warn you to take care. He is worried that you are reckless.'

Compared to Dora, Jacob thought himself a model of restraint. 'I can look after myself.'

'And you promise me you'll take care of Patch?'

'You have my word that he will be returned later today without a hair on his head out of place.' He ruffled the dog's ears affectionately. Patch rolled onto his back and showed his tummy in adoration. Sadly, that also declared his gender unambiguously. Never mind: the important thing was they had a spaniel.

Patch, undercover as Desdemona, had a pink bow around his neck. He scratched at it but put up with the indignity in exchange for several biscuits. Lady Tolworth eyed him suspiciously.

'He won't ruin my upholstery?'

'That's cats, Ginnie,' said Jacob. 'Dogs are far less destructive.' Usually.

A ring on the doorbell announced their guests. Alex exited, but Jacob remained. They had decided it would be no bad thing if Mrs Ferguson felt grateful to Jacob for the introduction. It might smooth over any other suspicions she might have about Jacob's familiarity with her lady's maid and explain the sudden invitation.

Yarton showed Mrs Ferguson into the room. She was dressed in a white muslin dress embroidered with forget-me-nots, and sported what Jacob understood was a fashionable ruff. She curtsied deeply.

'Lady Tolworth, it is an honour.'

Jacob could tell from Ginnie's expression she very much wanted to agree. She was showing great condescension to invite her. Fortunately, she resisted making the barbed comment.

'Mrs Ferguson, you are very welcome. Dr Sandys told me in confidence that you had come to town and might welcome a quiet invitation or two?'

'That's very kind of him.'

'I thought you might appreciate the diversion,' he murmured. 'It has been a trying week.'

'Dr Sandys mentioned something about an accident in Berwick. He said my Pence did a sterling job assisting as a nurse. Fancy her ending up with you! I was very sorry she left my employ. I hope she is giving satisfaction?'

A faint flicker of doubt passed over Mrs Ferguson's face before she mustered a polite agreement. 'I understand she is fond of your sweet spaniel and still visits to see her?' The lady leaned down to pet the animal, who naturally did one of his all-too-revealing back wriggles. 'Oh, it's a he.'

Jacob scrabbled to think up an excuse, but Lady Tolworth was there before him. 'Oh yes. I suppose I should call him Desmond but I have called all my spaniels Desdemona ever since I was a girl, like I call all my footmen James – so much less taxing on the brain and none of them mind.'

The rich were known to be eccentric, so Mrs Ferguson merely smiled faintly. 'How economical.'

'Quite. I don't even have to change the name on his collar – or her collar – whichever it is. Foolish waste of money to get new things for each pet, wouldn't you agree? I'm not sentimental about my pets.'

'I … er … suppose that's so.'

'I must be going,' said Jacob, rising. 'I'll leave you two ladies to talk. I'll only be in the way.'

'Thank you for your advice, Dr Sandys. I'll send for a tonic immediately.' Lady Tolworth invited Mrs Ferguson to take the chair next to hers. 'Would you be so kind as to take Desdemona to see Pence on your way out, doctor? It's time for his walk.'

'My pleasure.' Jacob bowed and called for the dog. He, of course, did not recognise his new name and was quite happy rolling on the hearthrug. Jacob had to scoop him up and bundle him from the room.

Yarton had made his office available to them for their consultation as it was thought too risky for Dora to leave the house, even by so short a distance as going over to the mews. Kir was sent off with the spaniel to exercise him with the ball in the yard.

Jacob wondered if he could give Dora a quick hug. Her expression was not encouraging so he settled for a kiss on her cheek. 'All well?'

'It's … fragile.'

Alex waved to her. 'Dora. Good to see you.'

'Alex.' Her tone was far less friendly than before and Alex

noticed. Was she still upset about being made late the night before?

'Do we need to clear the air?' he asked tentatively. 'I'm not sure what I did wrong—'

'No. What do we have to report?' Dora asked briskly. 'Shall I go first?' She described her insecure position in the Ferguson household and her instigation of a row with Dimitra. 'The more I think about her, the more I see that she could be involved. She loves the marbles and hates that they are in London. She is clearly in communication with Byron's staff and, as a trusted servant in Lady George's house, she would know where the Fergusons were and could easily send them a threat in her native tongue. She reads, so *The Oresteia* would be well within her grasp. She was also with the Elgins in Athens at the start of this and would have known where they were in France and now in London and Scotland.'

'We agree she had the opportunity and ability but what about her character? Do you see her sending the messages?' asked Jacob.

'Oh, yes. On their own, the messages aren't so bad, are they? They could merely be a righteous outlet for the anger of a population who see their precious artefacts being taken out of their country. Perhaps they are to be understood in the sense that wrongs rebound on the evildoer? We author our own punishments with our actions. That's not so much a death threat as "you'll get your comeuppance".'

'Richard Brooking?'

'I hate to say it, but it is possible the Runners were right. Wrong place at the wrong time. It was Elgin who added two and two and made sixty-three.'

'But what about the attack in Berwick?' asked Alex.

'We only have Percy's inference that it is connected to the Greek cause,' said Jacob, seeing where she was going with this. 'It could be something quite different and connected to the fact that he is spying for Napoleon. That would link to Stokes' untimely end.'

Alex frowned. 'The British government was trying to stop Percy so blew up the bridge?'

'Hardly. The right course of action would be to arrest him, not kill innocent bystanders with so cruel a tactic,' said Dora shortly, indicating she thought the suggestion foolish. 'It will be some deeper game than that.'

Alex glanced at Jacob, clearly wondering why Dora was showing so little patience with his questions. 'Dora, have I done something to offend you?'

Dora looked down at her hands. 'We don't have time for this.'

'Make time. Please,' said Alex.

'It wouldn't be constructive as you can't help it. Tell us what you learned at The Fleece.'

Alex sighed, though from his expression it appeared he had decided to let it go for now. Jacob hoped Dora wasn't going to insist they get rid of Alex. He was proving invaluable.

'Mr Fores is regarded with a high degree of respect as a successful printer,' said Alex. 'No one in that taproom knows him well, so I understand he isn't the sort drawn to a dubious tavern. Stokes was different, often seen propping up the bar, not slow in standing his friends a round. They seem to regard him as one of them and were anxious to lay hands on the person who did for him.'

'They weren't looking for that person among their number?' asked Jacob.

'No. The violence at The Fleece is the sort driven by gin and drunken brawls, not blackmail plots and politics. If the killer was there, he was hiding his presence well.'

'What did they think of Stokes' goings on outside the tavern? Or did you not get to that?'

'He was well known in the area for his willingness to supply fruity material.'

'Fruity?' Dora raised a brow. 'That's a rather mild word.'

'Did anyone see anything on the night he was killed?' asked Jacob quickly.

'Not that lot. And I think they would have told me as I followed in Stokes' tradition and bought them all a drink.' Alex smiled at Jacob, finding him a more sympathetic audience. 'I trust that can be regarded as a company expense?'

'Naturally. I'll set up a cashbox and account.'

'It must only be spent on legitimate purchases,' said Dora severely. 'Nothing for yourself, no personal debts or habits.'

Alex gave her a hurt look. 'You don't need to explain that to me. As a gentleman, I know what is mine to pay, and what is not.'

She gave a little snort at the word 'gentleman'.

Jacob laid his hand on her knee through the layers of skirt and petticoat. 'Dora, we need to trust each other.'

She seemed to gather herself and then shot them both a brittle smile. 'Yes, of course. I apologise if you took any words amiss. I did not mean to be rude.'

Jacob studied her. Something was up with his Dora. She was normally far more relaxed with them. She would be making jokes, encouraging Alex, but since last night, she had gone very cold towards them both. What could he do to mend things? He knew she didn't think he was pulling his weight with the boy.

'Dora, would you like us to keep Kir here? He'd be happy enough sleeping in the office and we'd look after him.'

'I'm perfectly able to look after him, thank you, Jacob. There's a whole household at the Fergusons to help me and I'm not convinced either of you are good for him.'

'Is that an insult?' asked Alex. 'If you were a man, I'd call that a challenge.'

She shrugged. 'Call it what you like. What do you have to report?'

Jacob wanted to snap back but that would only pour oil on the fire. Alex and Dora would be crying 'pistols at dawn' if this carried on. One of them had to be the adult in this room.

He took a breath in and let it go slowly. 'Let's lay out our findings.'

Dora opened her mouth.

'Politely,' he added.

By the time they'd finished comparing stories, they were left with two theories. One was that the notes were the work of Greek supporters – Byron and his circle – who wished to scare Lord Elgin but were unlikely to go further than that. In that explanation, the Brooking, Berwick and Stokes killings were not linked to the marbles and had been aimed at Percy and his associates because of something someone knew about them – blackmail, or some skulduggery of the spying kind. Brooking had just been a victim of a crime.

The second theory connected the gunpowder sabotage and murders to the notes and suggested a more worrisome conspiracy, perhaps with people of power and influence at the top.

'We must discover whose ring this is,' said Jacob. 'I would wager they are well-connected.'

Alex twisted the ring that he wore. 'I'll flaunt it more plainly, see if anyone at Byron's notices it.'

'You've given Alex the ring? Is that wise?' asked Dora.

'I'm not going to pawn it if that's what you mean,' said Alex acerbically.

Dora scowled. 'I didn't, but now you mention it…'

'Enough, you two.' Jacob gave a weary sigh. 'Maybe there is no conspiracy, no connection between the parts. Rings, pictures of Stonehenge, threats in Greek – a bundle of coincidences.'

They sat for a moment contemplating that depressing description of the case, then Dora spoke.

'I've just thought of something. If there's no connection, then why is the person Kir recognised from Berwick watching us? We have nothing to do with Percy's spying or blackmail.'

She made an excellent point. 'My guess would be that he suspects you have the book from Percy's trunk,' suggested Jacob. 'He could have been watching from the shadows as we cleared up after the explosion. Perhaps there is something in that which makes it imperative that he gets it back?'

Dora nodded slowly, accepting the idea. 'Then we must look at that again. I wonder if our mystery man was Stokes's killer – and Brooking's? Unless London is suddenly flooded with assassins it would make sense that someone who killed once might be willing to do so again.'

'It's a shame no one at The Fleece saw him,' said Alex.

'That drunken crew didn't, but I'll wager we know someone who did.' Dora's eyes lit up with excitement. 'Jacob, do you have the sketch back from Lord Elgin yet?'

'He's sending it back today.'

'Then I think Alex should make the acquaintance of the lady who lives opposite. He is best for the task as she'll remember us and, besides, every woman loves a man in uniform.'

Alex grimaced. 'I'm not supposed to be wearing that any longer.'

'Fiddlesticks,' said Dora. 'If I can pretend to be a lady's maid, you can pretend to be an officer. At least you've played the role for years. Oh, and Jacob, why not include the sketch you made of Dimitra – and add in some others so the neighbour doesn't pick them out to please Alex?'

'I've heard of this.' Alex sounded more enthusiastic with his task now. 'Don't they do something similar at Bow Street?'

'Correct,' said Jacob. 'The Blind Beak, John Fielding,

introduced the procedure to the Runners, though he used line-ups of ordinary people. Ironic it took a blindman to see that the sighted could be prejudiced.'

Yarton knocked at the door and then put his head around. 'You're wanted, Miss.'

'That's my signal to go,' said Dora. 'What are you going to be doing, Jacob, while Alex tackles the neighbourhood watcher?'

'I'm going to meet with Harold Fisher, the friend who first introduced me to the Elgins. He might know about the ring and he worked with Brooking.' He escorted her to the door and risked another kiss, on the cheek, not the mouth. 'We have to talk.'

Dora frowned. 'I know. But I don't think you'll like what I have to say.'

Chapter Thirty

Piccadilly

Jacob had received a note from Fisher inviting him to luncheon at a chophouse on Piccadilly. As he walked to his rendezvous, he had a sneaking suspicion that Dora had been right with her complaints. He was getting the pleasanter end of their investigation.

But didn't she see that it was necessary? Could that not be part of the fun?

Fisher was sitting in a booth, perusing the newspapers. Straw-haired and freckled from his fieldwork, he wore his suit like a sack, boyish despite reaching his mid-thirties. Jacob suspected he would always have that air to him, even in his dotage. His mind was always in 600 BC, not the fashions of 1812 AD.

'Fisher.' He held out a hand.

'Sandys.' Fisher gave it a firm shake. 'Long time since we last met.'

'Indeed. How are you?' Jacob slid onto the bench opposite.

'As well as can be expected stuck in this rainy old country.'

'What can I get you, sirs?' interrupted the waitress. London chophouses didn't like their clients to occupy their booths for too long. They both gave their luncheon order to the brisk maid.

Fisher pushed over the folder containing the portraits. 'I see you've gained a skill since Athens.'

'A hobby.'

'But it comes in useful no doubt in your work.'

'In surprising ways. Tell me how you've been.'

Fisher adjusted his cuff to hide a frayed edge. 'I miss Greece. Those were good days, working in the sunshine, my pay making me a rich man, whereas here it barely buys me a decent luncheon. Damn Elgin for divorcing his wife.' He said it with a self-mocking smile. 'That's selfish, I know. He couldn't stay with her after what she did.'

'But with her money gone with her, the excavations had to cease?'

'Yes. We all came back to London or took employment with other collectors. I was lucky he kept me on.'

'And here you are still, working on the marbles?'

Fisher nodded. 'Their beauty makes up for other inconveniences. I sometimes think of myself as the most recent champion devoted to their care.'

An interesting choice of word – one of the translations of 'vindex' on the ring, though 'avenger' was also possible.

'What does Elgin want to do with them?'

'Their current lodging is only a temporary solution. He'd like the nation to buy them.'

Lady Tolworth had been correct as usual. 'A nation who is pouring all its money into the war effort?'

'He sees it as part of that – the British cause versus the French. He wants us to have something to rival the collection at the Louvre.' Fisher leaned closer and dropped his voice. 'There's also the fact that he's close to bankruptcy. Selling them might just save him.'

Which made the earl doubly vulnerable to the campaign of threats and intimidation. 'But you are managing despite your employer being short of funds?'

'He's not on the breadline yet. And working for Elgin is a good reference. I'm piecing together an income from other collectors, keeping an eye on auctions, suggesting purchases, you know the sort of small services someone like me can offer.'

It was difficult being the second son of a gentleman who only has a small living to support his family. Fisher was doing well to make a profession of what was his passion.

'There seem to be plenty of collectors for you to approach in London.'

'I don't think there's been a time to rival this, what with gentlemen making it into a national competition. It is us versus the French and they are ahead by many points.' Fisher tapped the paper. 'Did you read the latest? The horses of St Mark are now on top of the Arc de Triomphe. Napoleon has no shame. He should send those back to the Venetians.'

'Why not to Constantinople? That's where they came from when the Venetians looted them.'

Fisher poured him a mug of ale from the jug. 'So you are content with the French ransacking of Europe?'

'Content? No. Philosophical? Yes. Anyway, did you not help Elgin bring the marbles to London?'

Fisher flushed. 'That's different. If we hadn't, they'd be in the Louvre. The French still want them desperately and are doing their damnedest to ruin the earl.'

'Then you know?'

'About the threat? Naturally. I open the earl's letters.'

'And do you agree with him that Brooking's death is connected?'

Fisher tugged at his collar. 'I do, and that's a damned scary thought. I believed studying antiquities would be safe, but I've found since that there are more mad people in the collecting world than in the asylums. I'm certainly not going out to meet people on my own – present company excepted – until this business is settled.'

'Very wise. Tell me about Brooking.'

The maid delivered their chops. These were perfectly cooked, the meat a little rare, plated curled on top of creamy mashed potatoes and slavered in gravy. Fisher took a bite.

'Good, eh?'

Jacob agreed and tucked in.

Fisher speared a morsel of meat and waved it at Jacob. 'Brooking lived and breathed those marbles. When one of the ships carrying the marbles went down on the way home, he wept.'

'The *Mentor* shipwreck?'

'Exactly. When we arranged for pearl fishers to salvage the cargo, he cried tears of joy.'

'So you wouldn't describe him as being moderate in his attachment to Elgin's marbles?'

'I really think he'd die for them – and perhaps he did. Though he had been mentioning of late that he didn't like the idea that they go to the nation. Then someone cut his throat.' Fisher looked down at his plate and pushed aside the rest of his meal. 'I've lost my appetite.'

'The night he died, he was wearing a bronze ring.'

Fisher nodded. 'The earl showed me. I didn't recognise it.'

'It's so distinctive, there must be someone who does. He was also given a picture of Stonehenge.'

'How peculiar.' Fisher sounded genuinely baffled.

'One of my sources suggested I investigate a secret group with designs on the marbles.' Percy would be amused to find himself described as a source. 'I think the ring might belong to them.

You've been working with collectors. Who do you think would know?'

'You need an expert with a longer memory than mine.' Fisher wiped his mouth on his handkerchief and put down the coins to pay for the meal. 'Happily, I know the very man – and you do, too, by reputation.'

Jacob pushed the coins back to Fisher, paid and added a tip for the maid. 'Is it far?'

With a nod of thanks, Fisher pocketed his money. 'No, and on the way there's something I'd like to show you to prove my point.'

Jacob followed Fisher out onto the street. 'What point?'

'That the world has gone mad for collecting. It's become a dangerous business with a lot of money at stake, not to mention national pride.'

They went a few doors down and stopped outside a building on Piccadilly. Shire horses were drawing away the last cartload of scaffolding revealing the project in all its glory, so they weren't alone in pausing to admire the frontage. There were many puzzled looks.

'What is it?' asked Jacob.

'Bullock's Egyptian Hall, built for Mr Bullock to house his collection. I got him the inside track on a sarcophagus from Luxor.'

'To think someone has the money to spend like a Pharoah.'

'What do you think of it?'

The two friends studied the façade – an Egyptian temple elbowing aside the terrace houses either side. Three angular apertures stood over the pillared entrance, the central one flanked by two full-length statues of an Egyptian god and goddess supporting the building on their heads, caryatid style. Above them was a horned ox head on the back of sphinxes. At the top a pediment curved out like geometric palm leaves waving over the heads of the bemused Londoners. Hieroglyphs decorated the stonework. As no one could read them, Jacob wondered what this ribbon of signs was saying. It could be curses and insults for all the architect knew.

'I think it's a folly.'

'They knocked down the White Hart for this,' mused Fisher. 'I rather liked that tavern.'

'I blame the Prince Regent. His Brighton Pavilion is another whimsy in this vein.'

'You do? I think the blame lies with Napoleon. He was the one to start the Egyptian craze. I'm dying of curiosity to see what it's like inside. I'm told that Bullock's built a huge hall with pillars and a dome. Do you want to go in?' Fisher was clearly persuadable.

Jacob drew him away. 'Not today. I'd prefer to get answers on the ring.'

Professor John Soane, architect to the Bank of England and Royal Academician, was at home to callers. Jacob and Fisher were shown into his office at 13 Lincoln Inn Fields, next door to his extensively remodelled home and famous collection. On the north of the square, Soane's office had a fine view over the garden in the centre. Young lawyers and their clerks were playing a game of cricket, making the most of the sunshine. As the wheels of justice ground very slowly, Jacob suspected they had time for many innings.

Professor Soane stood up to greet him. A kindly looking man of middle years with softly curling auburn hair and warm brown eyes, Soane made Jacob immediately feel at his ease.

'Dr Sandys, Mr Fisher, what a treat. I do hope you've come to sell me something?' said Soane.

'Professor Soane, thank you for seeing us. I have nothing to sell you today, I'm afraid, but I will keep an eye out for anything that I think you would like to buy at auction,' said Fisher.

'Dr Sandys, I'm so delighted to make your acquaintance.' Soane gestured him to a chair. 'I hear you have started on a little collection of your own and keep it in the Lake District? You've beaten me to a couple of manuscripts recently.'

'A modest one. Nothing to yours.' Looking around the room at the priceless volumes and drawers that doubtless contained many unique manuscripts and drawings, Jacob made a mental note not to bring Dora here. This was a forger's dream, and she could create havoc amongst antiquarians copying the samples. 'What a fine place you have.'

'You think so?' Soane glanced around. 'I'm tearing it down next month and rebuilding it so you may bid it farewell today.'

'Rebuilding it?'

'Houses are so awkward for displaying antiquities. The only solution is to start again like Bullock has done on Piccadilly. Have you seen his Egyptian creation yet?' He rubbed his hands together.

'On our way here. It is—'

'Impressive, is it not?'

'It is certainly that.'

'Ordinary people cannot understand the power of touching something so old, so historic, it is like transporting ourselves back to be with our ancestors.' Soane looked around his study and his eyes alighted on an illuminated manuscript. He lifted it up like a delicate baby and placed it in Jacob's hands. 'And thank goodness we are given such things to comfort us.'

'Dante?'

'Exactly. Fifteenth century. Each page has a little picture into which the reader can vanish when the world outside gets too trying.'

Jacob murmured his agreement as he turned the pages. It was

magnificent, the blues and golds like jewels. He wondered if that was what Soane was attempting to do with his houses – hollow them out and fill them with his own little illuminations of ancient civilisations. You could disappear into his collection for days, months even, and ignore the war and any personal troubles. If he was fanatical about his artefacts, it was the pure devotion, close on religious, not the fixation to possess an object to fight a cultural war. Jacob felt closer to Soane than to Elgin in that respect.

Soane sat down. 'Right, Dr Sandys, Fisher, to business. Please do satisfy my curiosity and tell me what has brought you to my door?'

Jacob carefully placed the Dante on the desk. 'I wish I could say it was for that book – my thanks for sharing that with me.'

Soane nodded. 'I often wonder if I would have been happier as a monk in a monastic library, spending my days illuminating capital letters.' He chuckled. 'But then I wouldn't have had Eliza in my life, and it would've been much poorer for it.'

Jacob smiled an acknowledgement. 'And in answer to your question, I'm here about Lord Elgin's marbles.'

Soane perked up. 'What? Has he finally decided to sell them? Maybe I can buy another house on the square…?'

Before Soane's ideas ran away with him, Jacob held up a hand. 'Not to my knowledge – not to a private collector.' Taking a strong liking to Soane, he decided to risk trusting him. He was hardly a Bow Street Runner who would go to the press with stories. Soane was a gentleman. 'It is about some threats he and those close to him have received, very nasty ones.'

Soane sank back in his chair. 'Poor man. Bad enough being imprisoned by the French, so hardly fair to come home to this.'

'He has been unfortunate.' Jacob described the content of the messages. 'I was wondering who you think among your fellow collectors might feel moved to attack him in this way?'

Soane drummed his fingers on the leather-topped desk. 'Using

The Oresteia? It all sounds very cloak-and-dagger. At least Byron takes his run at him in public.'

'You don't agree with Byron?'

'Naturally not.' Soane gestured to his own collection. 'I don't like ill-educated people sniping at us collectors. Without us, the classical past would be lost to future generations, used for building materials as happened to half of the Colosseum, or knocked about to make a church or mosque, as happened to many a Greek temple. If people like us didn't care, there would be nothing left by the end of the century.'

Dora should be listening to this, then she wouldn't get swept away by Dimitra's impossible dreams for the marbles.

'But if you were to guess?' pressed Jacob.

'I really don't know.' Soane leaned back in his chair and studied the ceiling, tapping his fingertips together. 'Though us collectors can be a rum lot to each other. I'd look out for a jealous type.'

'I'm afraid to say that we have reason to fear that the attacks have gone further than words. One of Elgin's archivists was killed.'

'You mean Brooking? A great loss – his Greek was exceptional, and his Latin. I heard about that. Robbed and done away with by a prostitute, wasn't he?'

'That doesn't fit the facts. It is possible he was dabbling in something quite different. Have you heard of a secret group among the antiquarians? We think they each wear a bronze ring with the inscription *Temporis Vtrivsqve Vindex*.'

Soane started to shake his head, then paused. 'Wait a moment. I think ... yes, let me check.' He got up and plucked a book from the shelf. *Palaeographia Britannica, Discourses on British Antiquities*. 'There's only one group that comes to mind.'

'What would that be?'

'The Society of Roman Knights. It was very fashionable last

century and an offshoot from the Antiquarian Society to which I belong myself. I thought that had mostly died out when William Stukeley passed away, but it sounds like some devotees continue to carry the torch. How interesting.'

'Stukeley?'

'He wrote this book and I believe that was his motto.' He placed it on the desk in front of Jacob and Fisher.

'What brought the knights together?'

Soane opened the book to an illustration of Stonehenge. Jacob's heart gave a leap. 'Stukeley and his fellows were set on the idea that Britain should become more Roman. They wanted us to value its Roman and Druidic past. Rule Britannia, and all that.'

'I thought our grandfathers were all for Greek neo-classicism,' said Fisher. 'How on earth did he come to this opinion?'

'He swam against the tide. While others of that generation made the Grand Tour, Stukeley stayed at home and marvelled at Stonehenge and Avebury, Hadrian's Wall and Glastonbury. He wanted a Roman Britain for a modern age. We were to model ourselves on Ancient Britons and Romans, tough and virile.'

'That sounds amusing,' said Fisher. 'I can imagine enjoying a society like that, tramping around the countryside looking for Roman ruins.'

Soane smiled at the younger man. 'Oh, I'm sure it was, particularly with scholarly young ladies involved. Stukeley was very progressive when it came to the fairer sex.'

'That aspiration sounds harmless,' said Jacob. He feared they had run into a dead end, but at least the picture now made more sense. If Brooking was meeting – or thought he was meeting – another knight, then a picture of one of their sacred places was an appropriate gift.

'Ah. Don't be fooled by the air of scholarly learning,' warned Soane. 'The knights were serious, too. And some of those who followed on after Stukeley's death might well have kept their appetite for the Roman past. A Roman Britain would not be a country for milksops but gladiators. Elgin would be their foe.'

Jacob suddenly saw where this was going. 'You mean that Elgin's desire to place Greek marbles, from a culture whose empire never reached here, at the heart of British culture, would be seen as dangerously diverting us from our true Roman heritage?'

'Exactly. And warning him off in the blood-soaked language of a Greek playwright would appeal to this group.'

But would the Roman Knights take their vows to acts of violence? That would suggest the group, or one of them at least, had descended into fanaticism. Jacob needed more than ever to discover who they were and where they could be found.

'Do you know where they meet these days?'

Soane frowned. 'I can make some enquiries but I'm not sure I should. If they still exist and are mixed up in murder and whatnot, none of us should go near them. They should be committed to an asylum.'

Jacob gave him a wry smile. 'Unfortunately, being mixed up in murder is exactly why I need the introduction.'

Chapter Thirty-One

Grosvenor Square

Dora took out her frustration on a black velvet cloak she was brushing clean of mud. Her attitude to Alex had been poor that afternoon, emotional rather than fair. She wasn't a simpleton. She knew exactly what was going on. Every time she saw him, she saw her brother; it was like someone put a pair of Anthony spectacles over her eyes. Watching Alex swagger off to The Fleece the night before and then wander back carelessly late had pitchforked her memory to the numerous times in her own childhood when her brother had done something similar. She also felt guilty for persuading herself that it was fine to let Kir go with him.

But didn't she have a point? Alex had been neck deep in the Hellfire Club and yet Jacob had not thought twice to recruit him. Nor had he asked her opinion.

True, she might well have come to the same conclusion that he would be helpful, but Jacob should have asked.

Men! Even the most enlightened still thought they were God's gift to womankind, able to make decisions on her behalf. If Jacob dared say it was for her own good, she would skewer him.

'What did that poor cloak ever do to you?' a familiar voice asked.

'Mr Percy!' Dora swung round in shock and found the man she thought they had left at death's door standing in the entrance to Mrs Ferguson's dressing room. He had his arm in a sling so clearly no amputation had taken place, but he was very pale and bruised. His face on the left side was swollen, a magnificent black eye swelling the lid shut.

Percy put a finger to his lips. 'Shh. I'm not supposed to be here.'

'You're supposed to be dead!'

'Reports of my demise are happily exaggerated. It would take more than a little gunpowder to do for me.'

Dora had to smile. For all they knew and suspected about him, she couldn't rid herself of an instinct to like him. 'But Dr Sandys said—?'

'Ah yes, the good doctor. May I sit down? Reports of death might be exaggerated but I do feel like I've gone ten rounds with Gentleman Jackson. The arm is killing me – hopefully not literally as, so far, I have escaped infection.'

'Of course – sit down.' She helped him over to the stool in front of her mistress's dressing table. From his reflection she could see he had lost part of his hair at the back and had stitches in that place. 'You poor thing.'

'Yes, my allure has been severely dented.'

She smiled. 'I'm sure you'll get over it. Do the Fergusons know you are here?'

'*Bien sur*. I'm not up to breaking into a gentle lady's house in Mayfair at present. There was much rejoicing, killing of a fatted calf et cetera and they sent me off to rest from my journey.'

'How on earth did you survive a trip to London?' The man had to be seriously motivated to drag himself off his sick bed.

'My dear Miss Pence, did none of you consider coming by sea? It is far more comfortable for a recuperating patient than a rattletrap of a carriage.'

'You came by sea? How?'

His eyes danced. 'Shall I torment your curiosity or satisfy it? Will I be cruel or kind? Delayed pleasure can be so exquisite.'

She rolled her eyes at him. 'I thought that a brush with death might put a stop to your flirting.'

'The day I stop trying to charm a beautiful woman is the day I am dead indeed.' He caught her hand and laid a kiss on the back of it. 'I have missed you, Dora.'

'No, you haven't – and it's Miss Pence.'

'Is it, really?' His eyes were laughing at her.

'Mr Percy,' she said sternly.

'Yes, yes, I will behave. I have no energy to torment you in ways we would both enjoy. The story is simple, dear lady: one of my friends has a pleasure boat – a yacht. This is prime boating season. He sent it for me. The wind was fair, the weather perfect, and we had a trip *formidable* to London. Behold, I sit before you a veritable sailor.'

'But you were so ill!'

'It's done me far more good than lying in a bed in a pestilential hospital surrounded by grumbling soldiers. Since being wafted on the waves from the Tweed to the Thames, I doubt I'll travel by mail coach again if I can avoid it.'

Dora returned to brushing the velvet, more to give herself time to gather her thoughts. What was he really doing here? Any sensible person caught up in that explosion would allow time for their bruises and stitches to heal at the very least and lay low. 'What did Dr Bailly say when you took off?'

'He said I'd die on the voyage, but see, I proved him wrong.' He gave a little bow.

'But why did you risk it?'

'Because,' he said, his smile turning hard, 'I discovered that some little bird flew off with my book. What have you done with it, Miss Fitz-Pennington?'

She barely flinched at her true name. Jacob had said Percy had worked out her identity.

His expression changed as he noted his sternness did not daunt her. 'I won't be cross with you. Just tell me you have it secure. It wouldn't do if it fell into the wrong hands.'

'And which would be the wrong hands, Mr Percy?'

He rounded his eyes, a vision of stage innocence. He could have been used as an illustration in the manual for actors. 'Why the French, of course. Whom else could I mean?'

As ever, Dora was confused by the man's ability never to give an honest answer. If Percy was a French agent, shouldn't he have taken the opportunity to flee once on board that yacht, seeing that he had half-confessed to Jacob? And if he wasn't, what was he? He'd let Jacob go away with the impression that he was working for Napoleon. Had he been speaking the truth when he thought he might die, or was he telling the truth now? He was lying, but about what?

'I don't understand you,' said Dora. She put down the brush and hung the cloak in the wardrobe.

He didn't move his gaze from her. 'My dear, you don't need to understand me. You simply have to reunite me with my belongings. Once I have it, I will leave you in peace.'

'I don't have the book.'

'And if you don't,' he continued as if she hadn't spoken, *malheureusement*, then I'll have to tell Mrs Ferguson what you are really doing under her roof. I wager she had no idea, poor lamb, that Lord Elgin sent you.'

The Elgin Conspiracy

A gasp came from the doorway. Dimitra stood there with a stack of ironed linen. Perfect – just perfect. Today was turning out to be a complete disaster. Percy looked comically discomposed to discover he'd made his threat before a witness, but he had no idea how dangerous a one he had chosen.

'Dimitra, I can explain—' Dora said quickly. Though what excuse she was going to make was beyond her at that moment.

'You're a spy for that man – that despoiler!' hissed the Greek woman. She dropped the linen and turned tail.

'*Merde*!' said Percy.

'For once I agree with you.'

They could hear her shouting for Mr Ferguson. Too late to do anything to stop her now.

Dora knelt and picked up the linen. 'The thing about threats, Mr Percy, is you really shouldn't make them so carelessly. They should be hoarded like diamonds, not scattered like acorns.'

He grimaced. 'You are right, *cherie*. I appear to have planted a rather ugly oak tree in my haste to regain my property.'

Mr Rogers appeared at the door. 'Miss Pence, you are wanted in the library.'

Mr Percy got up. 'That was quick.'

'I fear they were already primed against me.' Dora grimaced.

'So it will be both barrels?'

'Indubitably.'

'Not you,' said the butler.

'Ah, but the library is my domain, my good man,' Percy said affably. 'I need Miss Pence's arm to manage the stairs.'

Percy had evidently decided not to lose sight of her. Dora couldn't decide if his presence would help or hinder. She had been skating on thin ice with her absences. It was likely, thanks to him, they had both just fallen through that surface and were destined for a very cold reception.

Mr Ferguson was standing in front of the fireplace, the heat of his fury greater than any fire that might blaze there in the winter. Dimitra stood to one side, arms folded in victory.

'Is it true?' Mr Ferguson snapped as soon as she entered. 'Are you working for Elgin?'

How to play this, wondered Dora? Straight bat or try to hook it over to Dimitra to catch in the face? 'I'm here for your wife's protection, sir. Dr Sandys and I agreed that was prudent.'

'What nonsense is this?'

'I am working with Dr Sandys. The reason I went out to meet him was to report progress on the case.' That was partly true.

'Why did no one tell me?' thundered Mr Ferguson.

'We wished to keep it secret.'

'So you could spy on my wife?'

'*So* we could find out what enemies you both might have in the household. It would have to be from someone who knew Greek and knew the earl and Mrs Ferguson well. Perhaps someone who has been here since the marbles were taken from Athens ten years ago. Do you know anyone like that, Miss Mitkou?'

Dimitra shook her head and wagged her finger. 'Oh no, don't you go pushing this off on me. I'm not the one working for my lady's enemy.'

'I rather thought the enemy was the person who sent the threats,' said Dora. 'You hate those who raided your homeland, don't you? Why not get a little revenge on them? It would be so easy to scare them with a few well-chosen lines from a play all about revenge. Are you and your people willing to go further?'

'What n-nonsense is this?' Dimitra spluttered indignantly.

Mr Ferguson looked like he was going to intervene and wrestle the direction of this interview back under his control, but Dora shot him a look that made him back down. This was her true task here and she was going to do it while she still had the chance.

'Are you willing to kill for your cause, Dimitra?'

'Of course I'm willing to die for Greece, if it would do any good!' she retorted. 'People are dying for the cause every day!'

'I didn't ask if you were willing to die but if you were willing to kill. Kir's sister and the other victims on the bridge – were they the first casualties when you tried to punish the woman who had funded the removal of the marbles from Athens?'

Dimitra threw up her hands in exasperation. 'This is madness! You are the one who is in the wrong. You're probably digging for more scandal to hurt Mrs Ferguson. Sir, you can't trust a word she says. She's working for the earl.'

Percy had taken a seat and was watching the confrontation like a judge at a horse show seeing the fillies put through their paces. 'Miss Pence is telling the truth about the threat being in Greek, sir. I read it myself. It was a cry of the Furies, a quotation about feeling miles of pain. That's a very fine speech, if I remember.'

Mr Ferguson ran his hands through his hair, his aim to kick Dora out thwarted by these new revelations. Dora knew that it would still end with her leaving, though. She couldn't stay with her identity revealed.

'My wife is still in danger?' he said at last, circling back to the most important thing.

Dora glanced at Percy, wondering if he would claim the explosion was aimed at him, but he was sitting smiling benevolently. Would it help if she exposed him as a possible spy? Would she even be believed as that was the accusation she faced? No. Information should not be shared without thinking through the full ramifications of what the revelation would do.

'It is a strong possibility, as Dr Sandys told us in Alnwick. I do not deny that I'm working here under false pretences, but our aim is to save lives. You need to take this threat seriously, sir. We aren't sure, but we think that at least two people in London have been murdered and it might relate to this.'

'Two? Sandys only mentioned one.'

'There's been another.' She wondered if Percy knew yet about Stokes. Could he have already been in London a few days ago? Jacob and she needed to have a long talk with the librarian. 'If at all possible, I suggest you persuade your wife to take that tour of the Highlands that you told your neighbours you were on and leave London. It is too dangerous here without us knowing from which direction the next attack might come.' She shot a significant look at Dimitra who glared back at her.

Mr Ferguson gave her a sharp nod. 'You may have the right of it, Miss Pence.'

Dora gave an internal sigh of relief. At least she could get someone out of harm's way.

'However, I won't forget how you abused my wife's trust. You are dismissed. Do not expect pay or a reference. Seeing how you were always working for someone else, I'm sure you don't expect it.'

But it would've been nice, thought Dora, regretting the many hours she had put into looking after Mrs Ferguson's clothes. 'Very well. I'll leave immediately. You might mention to your wife that Jeannie would do very well if given a chance to be her lady's maid.'

'And the boy?' Ferguson asked as she made to leave. 'Is he involved in this?'

'Kir is eight. What do you think?' Dora left with her head held high.

Chapter Thirty-Two

Bruton Mews

Jacob looked up from his notes when he heard the door open. Dora walked into the office with Kir – not unexpected – *and* Michel Percy – miraculous – in tow.

'What is he doing here?' Jacob asked, shocked to see the man on his feet so soon. Percy looked ghostly white, apart from the colourful bruises, but very much alive.

Percy took a chair. 'I told you I'd join you in London, doctor. *Et voilà.*'

'I'm sorry. I can't shake him. He's sticking to my skirts like a burr.' Dora put down her valise, which Kir promptly sat on holding a bundle on his lap.

'Your employment has ended?' Jacob offered her his chair, but she shook her head and remained standing.

'Thanks to that *imbecile*. He only went and blurted out that I was working for Lord Elgin.'

Jacob gave her a hug in commiseration. 'Bad luck, but you

might have done all you could there. It will be better with you being able to govern your own time.'

She hugged him back. 'I thought so. I put the Fergusons on their guard too against Dimitra, not that I think she's really involved in this. Her indignation was genuine.' With a little sigh, she rested against him for a moment. His hope that they could mend their argument revived. 'I also thought Kir was safer with us, as that man is in London.'

'What man?' asked Percy brightly, not even pretending to give their murmured conversation any privacy.

Jacob considered the Frenchman. What was going on in that complicated brain of his? While they would keep most of what they had discovered from him, Percy did need to know about the possible threat to his life. 'We believe the other man involved in the attack in Berwick, the wagon-driver, has made it to London and is taking an interest in our proceedings.'

'How curious,' said Percy.

'When did you arrive in London? You didn't say,' said Dora, sitting on the edge of the desk and folding her arms.

'Ooo, is this the interrogation?' His eyes glinted with mischief.

'Would you like it to be? I'm sure I can find some thumbscrews for you.'

'You may think she's joking,' added Jacob, 'but she's not.'

'I adore a vicious woman, so much more deadly than the male.' Percy held out his hand, 'Screw away, my dear.'

Dora huffed in disgust. 'Why does almost everything he says sound rude?'

'Because you saw my book. Did you like it? Come, come, no need to be shy.'

Dora got up to put more distance between them. 'Kir, why don't you run over to Lady Tolworth's kitchen and see if they can give you some supper?'

Kir frowned up at her and whispered, 'I don't like that man.'

'You, my dear boy, are an excellent judge of character. You can smell the stink of lies on him.' She wiggled his nose affectionately. 'Now run along. Perhaps you can bring back something for me?'

'I can do that.' Kir loved an errand even more than he did food. Jacob considered it a sad sign that Kir was continually trying to earn his keep, fearful of being abandoned. Hopefully he would learn to trust them.

Once the door banged shut behind the boy, Dora swung around to face Percy.

'Time to tell us what is really going on, particularly if you want that book back.'

Percy gave her an enigmatic smile. 'I thought the pictures told their own story. I have more if you're interested. Anything you don't understand, I can educate you on the finer points.'

That was enough of that. Jacob took a position between them before Dora dropped a ledger on their guest. She was known for taking direct action against liars.

'Percy, cut the claptrap. It doesn't impress either of us. When did you arrive?'

'So impatient! This afternoon, *mon brave*. We came in on the tide. No doubt the customs officials would confirm that.'

'And where is your ship moored?'

'The distrust wounds me.' He put his hand to his chest. 'We tied up near Garlickhythe.'

'Name of the vessel?'

He hesitated, then smiled. 'The *Lucia*.'

Jacob made a note. He would send a footman to check. He was inclined to believe Percy. There were too many details to his story that could easily be proved wrong, and the man had to have had time to get well enough to haul himself out of his sickbed and transfer to a boat. It was highly unlikely it could have been done any faster, certainly not two days ago when the York Street murder took place.

'Did you tell him about the second?'

Dora shook her head. Good.

'Do you know that Stokes is dead?' He sprang the question on Percy and watched for the reaction. The man's cheerful façade flickered, then smoothed out to become puzzlement.

'Who is Stokes?'

'You know full well as you write to him regularly,' said Dora. 'I saw Mrs Cameron's mail book.'

Percy smiled sourly. 'Not just a pretty face, then.'

'We've worked out that Stokes supplied you with the prints, but what did you do with them, and did he know?' asked Jacob. 'Was he aware that you had entangled him in something more serious than titillating the jaded palates of society men?'

'And women,' added Percy. 'You'd be surprised at some of the society ladies.'

Jacob held his gaze. 'No, I really wouldn't.'

'Mr Percy, please stop acting as if we are old maids to be easily shocked. Nothing you've circulated in your little side trade surprises us,' said Dora coldly. 'Sickens us, yes, but not surprise.'

'Sicken? How so?' asked Percy, sounding sincerely interested.

'Are they all drawn from the imagination? No, I can see from your expression that they were not. Some poor girls and boys were paid to pose for them so that rich patrons can get their pleasures. It is a kind of artistic prostitution, but worse than the street trade because the images never pass away. The models know pictures of them are circulating for all eternity. How do you think that makes them feel?'

'Glad to have a full belly with their pay? Isn't that a fair exchange?'

'You think we only worry about the next meal? Believe me, the poor have hearts and souls as tender as anyone.'

Jacob rested his hand on Dora's shoulder in sympathy. 'For the purposes of this conversation we should agree to disagree with our guest about the morality of making such images.'

'Don't you find her so unsophisticated?' said Percy, appealing to Jacob.

'I find her lionhearted in the cause of the lower orders, but that is neither here nor there today. You've successfully diverted us from our questions but now we must get back to business. Who do you think killed Stokes?'

'*Bof! Je ne sais pas.*'

'Becoming more French to avoid a straight answer won't work,' said Dora. From her fierce expression, Jacob surmised she was imagining sticking sharp objects into the objectionable man.

'Then give me back my book and I will show you.'

Dora checked her hair and then flicked at her skirts. 'Jacob, can you see the bits of shell? Surely he must think I'm newly hatched to fall for such a simple ploy.'

Percy leaned back in his chair and winced. 'I'm tired, Dora. Sincerely tired. Take pity on me. Look, you are not meeting me at my best.' He had been managing remarkably well for a man who had been so badly injured. Jacob believed him when he claimed to be lacking in energy. Anyone would be in his shoes. 'I need that book and I don't know who killed Stokes.'

'Why do you need the book?' asked Dora, letting pass the use of her first name, doubtless another of Percy's diversionary tactics. Jacob didn't like the familiarity.

'Because I will be in deep trouble if I don't restore it to its owner. I am merely a custodian.'

Jacob thought that this might be partly the truth. 'Who is the owner?'

'Ah, now there my word as a gentleman conflicts with my desire to be straight with you.'

Dora huffed. 'You are never straight with anyone, *Mr* Percy.'

'Maybe not often but I am today. I have a proposition – a

decent proposition,' he added with a wink at Dora. 'I help you discover who killed Stokes. The boy was harmless. He merely wished to make a little money on the side dealing in material his master did not approve. He did not deserve death.'

Possibly, but he also could have liked the money brought in by blackmail, thought Jacob. 'And how do you think to help us?'

'Only a few people knew that Stokes was involved in this trade. If it was that connection that killed him, I should be able to give you their names if I'm left to ask around. If I do that and give you your killer, will you then give me my book in trade?'

Leaving Percy to investigate this part of the mystery did seem a reasonable course. They could watch him and see what he did. He was likely to reveal more about his motives than continuing with this questioning. Added to that, the time that would elapse would give them an opportunity to see if there was anything else in the book.

'Dora?' murmured Jacob.

She nodded. 'That seems fair.'

'We agree, Percy. Bring us the name and we will bring the book.'

Percy stood up. 'Then I will go and rest and begin my enquiries tomorrow. I hope to have news for you in two days.'

'Very good.'

They both watched the Frenchman leave. He paused outside, wavered on his feet, then set out in the direction of Grosvenor Square. Another act or real fragility? Jacob thought it most likely that it was a combination of the two: a deliberate moment to make them discount him as a threat.

'Verdict?' asked Jacob.

'We have just embraced a snake – an injured, charming one, but he will still turn and bite us if he can,' said Dora.

'My thoughts exactly. When Alex gets back, we will set him to watch Percy. The Frenchman won't recognise him.'

'He'll need help. One man can't watch alone.'

Jacob took out a strong box from the desk drawer and drew out some coins. 'It looks like we need to find ourselves some more employees. Any ideas where we can find them?'

Dora smiled and took the purse. 'Funnily enough, I know just the place.'

Chapter Thirty-Three

Having arranged with Yarton for a truckle bed to be set up for Kir in the office, Dora took charge of their expedition. Changing into her disreputable great coat, she was ready to enjoy the next part of their investigation, all traces of the lady's maid cast off.

'Are you not going to tell me where we are bound?' asked Jacob, his expression telling her that he was amused by her insistence that she wanted to surprise him.

'I am not. And I am very much enjoying my freedom. I don't have to answer to you, to Mrs Ferguson, or to anyone for how I spend my evening.' Being independent was costly but it was a price worth paying, she had to remember that.

'Dora, I'm sorry that you felt it unfair that you were the one to enter service.'

So they were going to talk about it, were they? Dora sighed. 'I was upset. Of course, it had to be me, but sometimes I'm just so angry with the way things are.'

'I understand that but I'm not sure what I can do to make

things fair. I certainly don't want you to run back to the theatre just because we encountered difficulties at the first hurdle.'

'I'm not leaving – not yet, at least.'

'Please don't leave without talking about this properly with me.'

'I won't. There's more than us to discuss. We must think of what's best for Kir, too. The theatre would look after him.'

'So can we.'

They turned down Piccadilly, heading in the same direction as they had the night before.

'Are you taking me back to York Street?' asked Jacob.

'Oh, no. I'd soon as not revisit that place again.' Thoughts of The Fleece left a sour taste in her mouth.

'I wish we could get a message to Alex. I'm intrigued to find out how my sketches went down with the Lady Argus.'

'I'm sure she is having a rare old time with a handsome young man flattering her espionage skills.' Dora could feel his eyes on her for that snippy remark and her damn cheeks would flush in shame, wouldn't they, for her ungenerous tone?

'Dora, that's another thing we need to discuss. Why have you turned so cold towards Alex?'

Naturally, Jacob would have noticed, but did she owe him an explanation? 'You didn't ask me if I agreed to taking him on.'

'Is that all?' He seemed irritated but swallowed it. 'Then I apologise. Do you disagree with the decision? Do you want me to cease employing him?'

She shook her head. Alex was useful, she agreed with that. Just look at how he got Jacob to see Byron and was even now going places they couldn't. 'No, Jacob, he can stay.'

'All right. Then, if you accept that he is in our employ, we have a duty to treat him well.'

'Meaning I'm not doing so?'

'Meaning ... forgive me for saying this, but I think your problem isn't really with him but with your grief.'

'My grief?' That was a low blow. 'You mean my emotions are running away with me. Next you'll be saying I'm hysterical!' She tried to pull away.

He held firm. 'Nothing of the kind. Both you and Alex are grieving, and you must know that mourners go through seasons, that is why we allow at least a year to mark the passing of a loved one.'

Dora looked down at her dress, reminded that she had stopped wearing a black armband for her brother, not wanting to answer questions about him while pretending to be someone else. A wave of guilt washed over her. Was she failing to honour Anthony? Was that part of her problem?

'The loss is very raw, barely a month old. After your shock and disbelief that he was taken from you, it is natural that you should feel angry with him for getting mixed up in a dangerous game that killed him.'

Jacob was using his reasonable, calm, doctor's voice on her which lit her short fuse. 'Hardly a game!'

'I said that badly. There was nothing playful about it. A dangerous *gamble* with his life. However, I think you are lashing out at Alex because he shared the blame with your brother for the entanglement with the Hellfire Club. Anthony is gone so whom else are you going to take to task?'

Damn Jacob for knowing her so well so soon. She had already had similar thoughts, hadn't she? 'You think I'm not being fair?'

'I think you aren't giving Alex the chance to prove himself that you would give anyone else.'

Dora groaned. 'Jacob, we mustn't be naïve. Anthony always, *always* let me down.'

He drew her to his side and gave her a comforting squeeze. 'But Alex isn't Anthony.'

・・・

The rest of the walk gave Dora time to consider his words. Jacob had a point and maybe she would try to get past her fear that Alex would repeat her brother's pattern – but she needed Alex to prove himself or she would always see him as yet another Anthony.

Pushing those thoughts aside for now, she stopped Jacob in front of the Shakespeare's Head tavern, a venerable place serving theatre folk which was located conveniently between the two great stages of Covent Garden and Drury Lane.

'Behold, the home of out-of-work actors.'

With the quickness she loved about him, Jacob caught her meaning. 'People adept at disguises?'

'Just so. And probably desperate for money as Drury Lane is still being rebuilt. There is half the work around with only Covent Garden playing this season.'

Jacob leaned down and kissed her soundly. It was an excellent kiss and did a lot to heal the wounds they'd inflicted on each other. 'You are brilliant.' The compliment was possibly even better.

'I know. And you, my friend, in this circumstance are the moneybags.' Without further preamble, she pulled him into the public bar.

The noise of the early evening crowd was deafening. Little flocks of dancers sipped sherry punch and massaged their calves, preparing for the night's balletic interlude at Covent Garden. Carpenters washed away the sawdust with tankards of beer, grumbling about management. A couple of old timers regaled anyone who came within earshot of how they once were famed for their Malvolio or Dr Faustus and begged a drink in exchange for some anecdotes about Garrick or Kemble.

'Promising, very promising.' Dora looked around for likely

recruits and spotted what she wanted in one booth. 'Fetch me a drink, would you?'

Jacob headed for the bar. 'Any preference?'

'Wine if they have anything decent. Punch if not. Bring a tray over to the booth at the back.' A lot of sins could be hidden with spices and orange peel.

Dora headed for the booth and sat down at the end of the padded bench, not waiting for an invitation. 'Ladies and gentlemen, this is your lucky night.'

The mixed company, two men and a woman, looked startled at the interloper.

'Don't mind if you do,' muttered the woman in rebuke to Dora's ill manners. She was about fifty with a beauty spot on the corner of her cheek. Someone was clinging to the fashions of yesteryear.

'Do you mind if I offer you a drink?'

The heavy-set man, who could have played Falstaff with no padding, chuckled. 'You may offer us that, to be sure.' He had a hint of Ireland in his voice.

'The drinks are already on their way.'

'It's not every day a young lady marches in and offers us a tipple. What's your game?' asked the third of their company, a tiny man whose feet did not reach the floor while sitting in this booth.

'My name is Dora Fitz-Pennington.'

The woman scowled. 'Doesn't mean anything to me. Never heard of you.'

'I didn't expect you to, unless, that is, you've recently been on the northern circuit?'

Their eyes brightened at that.

'Are you recruiting?' asked the Falstaff. 'I can do any character part you like – Sir Toby, Tony Lumpkin, the Friar.'

'My Cleopatra was well received in Lincoln,' said the lady. 'Mr

Garrick himself encouraged me to go on the stage.' That must have been decades ago as the great actor-manager died in 1779 but Dora was too diplomatic to mention that.

'Tom Thumb is my most famous role,' said the small man. 'I'm ready for anything, though.'

Dora smiled at him. 'I do hope so.'

Jacob arrived with a tray of drinks and passed them out. 'Ladies, gentlemen, apologies for the interruption to your evening. You've met Dora. I'm Jacob Sandys.' Dora was impressed that Jacob had adapted his manner for the company. Maybe some of her ways were rubbing off on him?

'Never heard of him, either,' whispered the lady, looking more suspicious. Good, thought Dora, they didn't want to employ gullible fools.

'I should hope not,' said Jacob, smiling charmingly at the lady. 'Though I believe I've seen you before. Were you all not in the last pantomime before the fire?' The afterpiece – or pantomime – was usually a comedy to lighten the main fare; character actors such as these would likely find a spot.

All three beamed at him. As Jacob had told Dora that he had avoided the old Drury Lane as he did not like the size of the auditorium, it had to be a lucky guess.

'Word is that it will open again this autumn,' said the lady. 'We are hoping to be taken back on for the Christmas season.'

'And I'm sure you will be. What my companion and I are proposing is something to help keep the wolf from the door in the interim.'

'Let's say we're interested,' said the small man. 'What's the job?'

Jacob gestured to Dora and himself. 'We are investigators.'

Falstaff frowned, an expression that did not suit his round face. 'Of what?'

'Of mysteries,' said Jacob with a smile. 'I know it sounds unusual, but it is what we do.'

'That's a profession?'

'It is when there's a rich man paying you to answer his questions,' said Dora bluntly.

'What? You're like the Bow Street Runners, but private?' asked the woman.

'I suppose there is a resemblance, though we don't work for a magistrate. We work for ourselves.'

The smaller man downed his ale. 'All right, what do you want us to do? I'm not doing anything dangerous or illegal, let's get that straight. Been in a prison once and never again.'

Jacob nodded as if he appreciated the man's forthrightness. 'First, might we have your names?'

The woman shrugged. 'Names won't cost you nothing. I'm Susan Napper.'

'Hugo Ingles,' said Falstaff.

'Goliath Renfrew – my parents had a twisted sense of humour also being in the miniature line. You can call me Ren,' said the third.

Susan cracked her knuckles. 'Let's get down to the brass tacks, duckie. What do you want us to do and how much are you paying?'

Susan, Hugo and Ren were happy to swap the drinks they had been eking out for the past hour for a brisk walk across town to the office in Bruton Mews. The three men walking ahead of the two women were quite a sight as they cut so different a silhouette.

'Is one of them yours?' asked Dora.

'No, love. I lost my man five years ago. Jerry Napper, best

scenery painter at Drury Lane. He said it was the paints that did for him. Lungs packed up.'

'I'm sorry.'

'Those two? They're good men, though. I always say there are no friends like those you make backstage.'

Dora smiled in agreement. She was missing her friends from the northern circuit. They weren't great letter writers, but she had heard from Ruby Plum, mainly with questions as to when she would return.

'And what about you?' asked Susan. 'I can't make you out. Are you with the gentleman?'

Nor could Dora. Their relationship was a tangle. 'Yes, we work together.'

'You know that isn't what I meant.'

'Our private life is private.'

Susan nodded as if something had been confirmed. 'Good for you, duckie. He's a catch. Ask for jewels. Many a retired actress has lived on the gems her admirers have sent her over the years.'

Dora felt irritated at the assumption, but it was muted. Perhaps she was getting used to something she couldn't change? 'Not this one.'

'No? Hmm, we'll see. Maybe you're too young to worry about things like that, but it won't be long before you are on the shelf and there's a younger lady hanging off his arm.'

Susan was only saying what most people thought, Dora told herself. The blaze of anger at the idea of Jacob moving on to another woman was hardly fair to him – she'd made him no promises of constancy – nor him her. Yet she believed him when he said she wasn't just another one in a line of lovers. Didn't she?

'Live for today, don't worry about tomorrow,' advised Susan, catching her consternation.

'For today has enough worries of its own?'

'Something like that.'

When they arrived back in the mews, Alex was seated with his feet up on the desk. Kir was asleep in a corner. He stirred when they came in but Dora patted his shoulder that all was well so he turned over and went back to his dreams.

Jacob found seats for the new recruits and made the introductions.

'We need to keep a watch on this man.' Taking up his drawing book, Jacob sketched Percy for them, summoning up in a few lines the likeness of the Frenchman. 'He's distinctive as he was recently in an accident and has a scar here –' he sketched a back view '– and an arm in a sling. He is staying at this address in Grosvenor Square. We don't expect him to leave tonight but we should keep watch just in case. Alex, I want you to organise a rotating watch in pairs so that you all get enough rest. Follow him if he leaves the house, but I want one of you to bring us a message that he reaches his destination. Let us know if you lose him.'

'We won't lose him,' said Susan. 'A man like that doesn't disappear into a crowd.'

'Let's find out. But I would warn against complacency. Michel Percy is clever and skilled. If he thinks he is being watched, he will make an effort to lose you.'

'Make sure he doesn't suspect you,' said Dora.

Susan and Ren agreed to take the first part of the night so set off to begin their vigil. Hugo went home to catch a few hours of sleep.

'So, Alex, how did your meeting with the neighbour go?' asked Jacob as soon as they were alone.

Dora realised that she was feeling very tired and Camden was a long way away. She looked with longing at the truckle bed occupied by Kir. Would there be room if he budged up a little?

'Mrs Chesham? I think you gave me my most dangerous mission yet.' Alex gave Jacob a rueful smile, avoiding Dora's eye. 'She is a hoarder. Her room is filled with news sheets and bottles, rags and Lord knows what. I dread to think what plague she might be brewing up there.'

'It sounds like she let you in?'

'Oh yes. I said I was helping the Bow Street Runners with their enquiries – which we are in a way. They aren't enquiring in the right places, so we are. The uniform, as Dora rightly guessed, did the rest.'

'And the sketches?' asked Dora, stifling a yawn.

'She enjoyed looking through those. Gave me comments on all the faces, telling me which ones were doubtless villains and which had the look of a victim. When she reached our mystery man, she said she thought she'd seen him – and yes, it could have been the man who went in to see Stokes on the evening he died.'

'That's something. How sure was she?'

'She said he had a hat on, pulled low over his eyes, but Stokes met him at the door and made him welcome. He put up the closed sign when he invited him in.'

'Did she see the visitor come out?' asked Jacob.

'Yes, only a short while later. She assumed he was a customer because he only spent five minutes in the shop, but she is now convinced he's a villain. The jaw should have warned her, apparently.'

'A villainous jaw. If only detecting criminals was that easy. Thank you, that helps fill in the details. Let's assume this is the same man. He came to London when we did. He checked where Kir and Dora were but took no action against them. Stokes was not so lucky. He arranged to meet him and killed him.'

'How do we know it was arranged?' asked Alex.

'There were two plates of food in the pantry,' said Dora.

'Of course. I should've thought of that. Sorry.'

'What's the betting that Percy knows exactly who this man is?' said Jacob.

'Almost certain. If he doesn't know who he is by name, he will know who sent him,' said Dora. 'And I don't believe it is Byron or any of his servants, do you? I can't see the link.'

'For what it is worth,' said Alex, 'the lady didn't recognise Dimitra Mitkou. Her only pronouncement was that she looked like a victim and asked was she dead?'

'That's a chilling question.'

'Well, I was showing her pictures of potential murderers so it would be a logical leap to think some of the images were of those they have killed.'

'Do you think she'll tell the Bow Street Runners what she told you?'

Alex shrugged. 'She will if they come back but they'd already questioned her before I reached her. She gave them a description of a villainous-looking man in a hat. You can imagine what they made of that.'

'It supported their idea that it was part of the violence in those parts carried out by ne'er-do-wells. Unless Mr Fores pays them to dig deeper, I doubt they'll go back to her,' said Jacob.

'But a woman like that, keeping an eye on the street all day, might well be one of their regular informants,' said Dora. 'What if she mentions Alex? He could get in trouble.'

'I would say I'll have a word with the magistrate but last time I went near him he consigned me to Bedlam and a man died,' said Jacob laconically.

'I didn't give my true name,' said Alex. 'It is unlikely to blow back on me unless we are very unlucky.'

Dora gave him a searching look. 'How lucky have you been feeling recently, Alex?'

He pulled a face. 'Good point.'

'Let's report it to Elgin,' said Jacob. 'He can send word to the magistrate that we are asking questions. An earl is a useful trump card to hold in our hand. Perhaps he can arrange for us to meet one of the Runners? It would be good to have them on our side and not trying to arrest us for making inquiries on their patch.'

'I'm happy to do that,' said Alex.

Jacob shook his head. 'Oh no, with Dora's agreement,' he gave her a rueful look, 'I think this is woman's work.'

Jacob might be trainable, thought Dora. Now he was asking permission in advance rather than for forgiveness after the fact. 'How so?'

'The Runners will feel competitive with Alex and me; but with Dora they will feel…'

'Feel what?' she asked suspiciously.

'The need to impress.'

Chapter Thirty-Four

Grillon's Hotel

Professor Soane was as good as his word – and had gone one better. Jacob received an invitation, written in Latin – naturally – on a parchment scroll, inviting him to meet with the Society of Roman Knights that night at Tower Hill.

'The pre-eminent collector in London has got us a break in the case,' said Jacob, showing Dora the note. 'But the knights aren't hiding that deep in society if they come up for the first bait laid out for them.'

Sunlight streamed into his room in Grillon's Hotel where Dora had spent the night with him. She was sitting up in his bed, watching him dress, her shoulders bare and gilded by the sun.

'I wonder what that says about them?' She yawned and threw back the covers. 'And here was I enjoying a lazy lie-in after my short spell in service.'

'I'm afraid you aren't included in the invitation.'

'You can't meet them on your own.'

'Why would they want to harm me?'

'Because they know you are investigating them and they want to shut you up?'

He grimaced. 'That is a possibility.'

'Take Alex with you.'

'You've changed your tune about him.'

'I don't doubt he'd back you in a fight.'

Jacob came over and kissed her. 'It won't be a fight.'

She looped her fingers in his shirt front. 'You take care tonight, Jacob. There can be very bad apples in a barrel of otherwise sound ones.'

Jacob smiled at her as he returned to tie his cravat in front of the mirror. 'I know – and I will.'

She bunched her hair up and let it fall again. 'Argh, it all sounds so foolish – killing over statues. What do I care about Rome? I certainly don't feel I inherited anything from Ancient Romans here in England.'

'And yet you've walked the Roman roads they left us and crossed the wall that separated the empire from the Picts.'

She gave a rude snort. 'I think I'm the wrong audience for their arguments. I struggle to accept that I've inherited anything from my parents so I really would prefer not to be told I also have to take on an identity forged over a thousand years ago by ancient ancestors – a civilisation that withered into the heaths and or vanished under new buildings when the legions left.'

'How very poetically expressed.'

She grinned. 'I do have my moments.'

Satisfied with the knot on his cravat, he shrugged on his jacket.

'I like you in blue,' Dora said. 'Very dashing.'

'Why thank you, kind lady. What are you going to be doing while I check in on our team and prepare to take my oath to the ghost of the legions?'

'If the earl gets me that meeting with the Runners, I'll do that.' She slid out of bed and went to the basin behind a screen for a wash. Jacob loved these domestic moments with her – it felt so, and here was a forbidden word, *married*. 'And I'll see about finding myself a place to stay closer to our office.'

'Is that so? But you are always welcome here.'

She stepped out from the screen and pulled on a clean shift. 'I know, Jacob, but the hotel will only look the other way until one of the guests complains. In their eyes I'm a lady of ill repute – and that's rather tiresome. Besides, I can afford a room closer to town than Camden, can I not? Somewhere with room enough for Kir.'

Don't press or she will fly away. 'Indeed. Take a cab please – or borrow one of Lady Tolworth's footmen.'

She wrinkled her nose. 'Really? It's so expensive to hire a hansom cab for every little journey.'

'It's a legitimate expense. Take what you need from the strong box in the office. Have my key.' He pulled it from his waistcoat pocket and pressed it into her palm. 'I've an account book set up so just note down what you take. I'll do the same.'

She stood up on tiptoes and kissed him. 'Thank you. Any advice where I should lodge?'

Here, with me. 'In your place, I'd ask Yarton.'

'Jacob, you genius! Of course! I swear that man knows everything. Can we recruit him?'

He kissed her back. 'I think we already have.'

Chapter Thirty-Five

Bow Street Office

'Miss Fitz-Pennington, I understand from the Earl of Elgin that you are undertaking an enquiry for him, have I got that right?' The head of the Bow Street Runners guided her to an upright chair in their spartan office next to the magistrate's court. With his slick hair and oiled moustache, this Runner was what Dora would call a cockney gallant – the kind to turn up at the stage door with flowers and invitations to dine, a polite way of inviting an actress to bed. She knew how to handle his type.

Two of his colleagues stood behind him, expressions sceptical. They had more in common with the bruisers who caused trouble in the Pit, beaten and weary but not past rousing themselves to a punch-up if one offered. They were best avoided.

One feigned a cough. 'Enquiry, my arse,' he said behind his hand, not even attempting to keep his voice down.

'Gentlemen.' Dora favoured them with what she hoped was her most beguiling smile. 'There are some questions a lady can ask that fine men such as yourselves are not able to, some matters which require a gentle touch.'

'That's very true,' said the gallant, Josiah Watkins.

'Myself and my associates are interested in the death that took place in York Street last week because it may connect with a little bit of business we are doing for the earl.' Look at her: she hadn't even had to lie yet! 'We started asking questions of the inhabitants and then realised that you might feel we are trespassing on your own investigation. Hence, we asked Lord Elgin to intercede for us.' Dora wished she was getting paid by the syllable because she had just trotted out some impressive words. They would think she had swallowed Dr Johnson's Dictionary.

'You meant that business at Fores's printshop? Break-in weren't it?' remarked one of the sceptics.

'We are not so sure. My associate spoke with the lady who lives across the road and was told she had seen a man go in with the victim and come out five minutes later alone.'

'Oh, yes, batty Mrs Chesham's mysterious man in a hat. Could've been a customer. Could've been anyone,' muttered the bruiser. 'What do you want us to do? Arrest everyone who wears a hat of that description?'

'Naturally not, sir.' Dora wasn't going to waste their sketch of the likely suspect on these men, particularly as they had not bothered to question the neighbour more closely, bypassing their best eyewitness. They would plaster the likeness up on every street corner and drive him away. The best she could hope for was a truce of sorts so that she, Jacob and Alex weren't arrested for interfering with the case.

'What business does the earl have with Mr Fores?' asked Watkins, demonstrating he had earned his position thanks to quicker wits.

'I'm afraid I can't say. It's a private matter.'

Watkins rubbed his chin and looked at her with a pensive

expression. 'You might want to ask the earl to send you to a more decent company. Fores is well known for his … shall we say, questionable material?'

Oh, lord, they were going to be left with the impression that the earl was buying the obscene prints. It was a logical deduction after all. He wouldn't thank her for letting that whisper do the rounds.

'Questionable? I hadn't heard the reproductions of his Greek marbles called that. Beautiful depictions of classical ideals, yes. The prints are selling well, second only to the pyramids.'

Watkins gave her a steady look, showing he was clever enough not to take her act at face value. 'Well, then, I suppose artistic prints can't do anyone any harm. However, while it is acceptable for you to make a few ladylike enquiries in the neighbourhood, it will not excuse anything that gets in the way of one of our cases. And if you have any evidence leading to the identification of Stokes's killer then you must hand it over directly.'

Now her ground was getting a little shaky and staying would only jeopardise it further. Dora got up and smoothed her skirts. 'Indeed, you will be the first to know, Mr Watkins, if we are so fortunate as to solve that particular mystery.'

'If you get a name, don't approach them, miss. They've killed once and I dare say they won't blink to do so again.'

'I do agree with you. Absolutely. No approaching of murderers. That makes complete sense. Thank you for your time.'

The gallant Watkins hurried to open the door for her. Outside waited a line of woebegone people petitioning for help from the Runners – some on the hunt for stolen goods, others looking for missing children, a few wanting their loved ones released from custody. She had felt bad walking straight past them earlier all because she had a letter from an earl.

Mr Watkins blocked her exit for a second. 'Miss Fitz-Pennington, you didn't say who your associates were, but if you would pass the message on to the ladies, tell them what we discussed? Mention we will be watching you – for your own safety, naturally.'

'Oh, indeed, I will tell them.'

Watkins bowed over her hand and she made her escape.

Dora smiled to herself as she walked down Bow Street. It looked like the only safe way for Jacob and Alex to carry out investigations in the area around Bow Street would be to don petticoats – how refreshing to have the tables turned.

Dora went back to Camden to change her clothes and pack a bag in case she couldn't get back for a few days. Returning to Bruton Street, she had a brief discussion with Yarton, who assured her that he would have the solution to her housing issue by the end of the day. He was hopeful something in the mews could be found for her too. Lady Tolworth's household was aware of the danger so, while Dora and Jacob were busy elsewhere, the butler had taken Kir under his wing. The boy was following him around the house, mimicking his gestures, which raised many smiles from the staff. Kir couldn't hope for a better role model if he aspired to be a butler.

Dora crossed the cobbles from the house to the office to find a note from Jacob. The team had reported that Percy had gone out at ten and headed straight for Lord Elgin's exhibition. Last word was that he was still in there. Jacob had gone to see what he was up to and warn Elgin.

Sitting at the desk, Dora made a note in their ledger, using the same scheme as Jacob had instigated. He had given her a list of the Greek letters and suspects which she had memorised and destroyed. *Epsilon gone to Beta's.*

She tapped her fingers on the page. Percy was supposed to be investigating who killed Stokes. Why take the time out for tourism? Of course, as an antiquarian and librarian, he could be expected to be among the admirers of the marbles but why was it his first stop on return from Scotland? He must've had chances to see them before. With his limited strength, why wasn't he putting every ounce into getting his book back?

Unless he knew the name of the suspect already and was merely pretending to let a decent amount of time pass.

But why the marbles?

Dora looked to the door, willing Jacob to return. He might not have time to come back before his meeting that evening. The knights had summoned him to the Tower of London; Tower Hill, to be more precise. As it was the traditional place for beheadings it did not seem a very peaceable choice. She hoped he would take her advice and go with Alex.

Still, she wished he would come by. She wanted to discuss Percy's odd behaviour with him. She wanted to see him.

She had it bad, didn't she?

Shaking her head at herself, she turned back to the case. For the first time in days, she had a moment to think. She decided her time was best spent studying the book of Rowlandson prints. Jacob had transferred it from his hotel room to Lady Tolworth's library on the grounds that Percy wouldn't be above sending in burglars to get it back. The office and a hotel were vulnerable. No one would dare invade Lady Tolworth's home.

Leaving a note of her own to say where she was, Dora crossed the mews and entered Lady Tolworth's kitchen by the backdoor. The servants were used to her presence by now and merely nodded as she passed. Kir was turning the spit of capons and looked happy, so she left him there, telling him to go back to the office when he had tired of the task. The cook, a delightful Frenchman by the name of Jacques, handed her a meat pie in a napkin as she passed.

'For the beautiful lady who works too hard,' he said with a flourish.

Dora blew him a kiss. 'For the handsome chef who knows how to flatter.'

His chuckle accompanied her up the servants' staircase. These Frenchmen: too charming for their own good.

The library was empty, Lady Tolworth not often darkening its doors. Dora went directly to the large globe in the window. It was hinged with a little compartment inside, meant for brandy and glasses. The cubby hole made a good hiding place for a book so that casual visitors did not come across it. Splitting the world along the equator, she lifted the book out and took it to a table.

'All right,' she muttered. 'Look past the obvious.' It was easier to do so with no one watching; the pictures became just lines and colours. She regarded it with her forger's mindset, first checking the lettering. Rowlandson's prints were often covered with speech bubbles and subtitles, using a recognisable hand. Was there anything added that could amount to a secret code? She couldn't see any additions, no ink that stood out from the printing plate marks. She next checked for additions to the pictures, comparing it to the print they'd taken from the print shop. Nothing had been corrected or added to the images.

That left the book itself. The first thing she had noticed was the fine Moroccan binding. Collectors typically bought prints loose and bound them to match their libraries. If any part of the book was going to be interfered with, that would be the easiest to adapt. She pushed a letter opener down the spine, feeling for anything hidden in that narrow channel.

Nothing.

Next she examined the marbled fore and after pages, feeling for bumps or slits where messages might be concealed. Again nothing. Short of disassembling the book, she could go no further in that direction.

She flicked through the pages again, her frustration mounting. She wouldn't let this cynical, woman-hating cartoonist defeat her! So, what did she know?

It was a puzzle. Percy wanted it back – this particular book. He could find the prints again if he was so minded, so it was something about the volume in front of her that mattered. What had he been able to influence through his communication with Stokes? Not the cartoonist, as some of these prints had been done years ago. There had been no meddling with the prints themselves that she could detect, but perhaps that was too obvious. If you are trying to conceal something, you want it to be well hidden, preferably understandable only to the recipient.

What about the order in which the prints were bound?

Dora noted down the titles, taking care to preserve which letters were capitalised. She was left with a long list that didn't immediately reveal a message in either French or English.

Dash it all! Why wasn't this easier?

Because you are dealing with international espionage, not a children's game, her mind responded sourly.

Steady steps announced the arrival of Jacob. He placed his hands on her shoulders and bent down to kiss her cheek.

'Anything?'

'Perhaps but no eureka moment.' She pulled out the chair next to her. 'You came.'

'I've just got time before I have to go to the Tower.'

'And doesn't that sound ominous? You're taking Alex, aren't you?'

He nodded. 'He's just getting changed. He's spent the afternoon disguised as a grocer. I've asked him to wait nearby – and asked Fisher to come with me.'

'That's good. I didn't want to think of you going in alone. But will they admit Mr Fisher?'

'As a proven archaeologist, I think they'll let him in.'

Dora leaned back in her chair. 'I think you're enjoying this?'

He took a seat. 'Your friends from the theatre are very entertaining. They brought me reports in the coffee house where I waited and stayed long enough to regale me with stories.'

'Actors tend to like the sound of our own voices.' She brushed a smudge of soot from his jaw. 'And don't pass up someone buying them a drink.'

'And I like listening. What about the Runners?'

'I and my team of lady investigators should take care and let them know when we solve the case.'

Jacob laughed and pulled her list towards him. 'What's this?'

'The titles and captions in the book. I wondered if the order was significant, but I can't see how.'

'That would be because most ciphers of this nature rely on a key – and we don't have the key. For example, a could stand for z if it is a simple reversal of the alphabet, but this isn't the case here as they are using proper words which would give a too frequent use of less used consonants.'

'It could also be just one letter on each page, or only the capitalised ones.'

'Agreed. However, I like your thinking. It would be an excellent way of passing information. No one could detect a pattern as they could a message hidden in the binding.'

Dora rubbed her hands over her face, trying to cudgel her brains into order. 'Can we restate the facts and see if we can detect our own pattern?'

'Yes, let's do it.'

'Lord Elgin and Mrs Ferguson receive threats in Ancient Greek within a week of the earl's man, Richard Brooking's, death. We now know Brooking regularly met with someone in Rose Street, talked to them in a foreign language, and on the last occasion was given a picture.' Dora shook her head. 'The watercolour doesn't make sense.'

'What do you mean?'

'If you were going to murder someone, even if you brought the picture as a diversion, wouldn't you take it away with you again?'

Jacob nodded slowly. 'You're right. No one disturbed the killer, so he had time to take it back. Either he wanted it found with the body and the maid spoiled that plan by hanging it on the wall, or—'

'Or the murderer didn't know it didn't belong there. Could there have been two visitors that night?'

Jacob rubbed his chin. 'I wonder if the old lady in the front room noticed. I'd wager the Runners didn't even think to ask her. Let's add that to our column of things we must follow up.'

'I'll do that while you are meeting the knights.'

Jacob nodded reluctantly. 'Take—'

'A footman. I know, Jacob.' She shook her head at him.

'Going back to our involvement…' He waved his hand in a gesture to continue.

'Right, the earl first suspects his embittered former wife, but our enquiries and the attack at Berwick removes the Fergusons from our suspects and transfers them to the victim column.'

Jacob took up the narrative. 'But we meet Michel Percy in their household who reveals in a weak moment after what might have been an attempt on his life, that he is an informant, possibly a blackmailer, for the French. His greatest concern after the explosion is this book. An attacker comes to silence him but fails thanks to Percy's skills at self-defence. The attempt, though, suggests Percy is right that he was the target, or one of the targets, of the explosion.'

'True, we shouldn't forget that the wagon might have been a "two birds with one stone" strategy. It was messy enough and we were also a possible target.'

'Percy's words – which never mean what he says – set us on the trail of other groups with a grudge against Elgin. Elgin suggests Byron, and that leads us to the pro-Greek party in London. They do have motive, but do they have the will to take their campaign in this direction? The poet is waging his campaign with a pen in public, not private threats.'

Dora rubbed her arms. 'As for the Greek servants like Dimitra, I sense that they are angry, but I didn't detect any murderous intentions. Messages, yes, maybe; wagons exploding, men dying, no.'

'And, of course, the ever-reliable Mrs Chesham said Dimitra had the face of a victim.'

'Oh, yes,' said Dora sardonically, 'let's accuse people on the basis of how villainous they look. However, I think we need to consider the politics. The Greek party want support for their struggle. Surely blowing up British dignitaries sets their cause back rather than advances it? Even if they somehow got hold of the marbles through such tactics, they have no country to take them to.'

'All excellent points. I think Elgin sent us in that direction because he has a loathing for Byron. Let's not get distracted by that when we have a much more likely suspect – this unidentified man who set up the wagon attack and followed us to London. He probably killed Brooking, and was seen, we think, with Stokes, who is linked by this book –' Jacob tapped the Rowlandson '– to Percy.'

'Do you think we were on the wrong scent with them jointly blackmailing influential men? Perhaps Stokes was doing Percy's bidding only so far as it came to binding?'

'That's another good thought and would simplify their relationship. Fewer secrets.'

'Stokes might not even have known what he was doing.'

'Or chose not to know. He could claim Percy was nothing but an eccentric client.'

'But hold on a moment!' Dora felt a swell of excitement. 'There has to be another party in the exchange, doesn't there, for it to make sense? Percy was *receiving* as well as sending books. Someone else was ordering the prints to be bound like this and sending them to Percy, else why dispatch them all the way to Scotland? Percy was getting his instructions when he received this book, not just sending them. I wonder what he was told to do?'

'We must also remember that the man who came to the shop and killed Stokes was known to the printer. That would be the other party to the communication or someone who discovered how messages were being sent beneath the noses of the authorities.'

'Then who is he? What if the mystery man out to kill Percy is one of our spies eliminating the enemy within?'

'Or a Russian agent, or one of our allies? They would be less careful of British lives.'

Dora bent her head to the table, resting it on her arms. 'Oh, dear. I seem to have only increased our list of suspects.'

'No, this has been worthwhile. We keep narrowing our hunt – and we are right to think Percy is the key. All we need to do is find a way of making him talk.'

Dora sat up and groaned. 'Is that all?'

'There is one thing that we haven't tried.'

'More than one, surely?'

He smiled. 'True. But we haven't yet ascertained how far back Percy's connections go to this. He is cagey about his past.'

'I think he's been to Lisbon at the very least.'

'Oh?'

'It was something that he was quick to deflect when I was discussing a book with him in Scotland.'

'He also hinted that he had been in military service of some kind. He knew how to defend himself from an attacker while at a disadvantage, lying on his back with his injury hampering him. Maybe he has had to fight for his life before, but his story is of a sheltered upbringing with émigré parents, resulting in a bookish life of scholarship. I don't buy what he is selling.'

'Hardly bookish. Remember the buttonholes?'

'How could I forget? You're right, that shows a vanity of someone with a more worldly outlook. And that swipe cutting his attacker's throat? That's the kind of experience our men get when they're serving as Wellington's exploring officers, going behind enemy lines with the partisans – brutish and up close.'

'So we can't believe anything he tells us? Next you will tell me water is wet.'

'That might be the only thing we can be sure of.'

'Then how can we get to the bottom of his story?'

Jacob went to the window. Dora joined him. A light rain was falling, the pavements shining. He put his arm around her and she rested her head on his shoulder. It was a peaceful moment, the calm between the storms.

Jacob dropped a kiss on her crown. 'Why don't you work on that when you get back from Rose Street, see if you can come up with some incentives to make him talk. You can tell me your ideas when I get back from my knightly excursion.'

'Make sure you come back, won't you?'

'If I know you're waiting, nothing will keep me away.'

Chapter Thirty-Six

Soho

Dora knocked on the door of Miss Beamish's house and waited for the pipe-smoking maid to shuffle out of her kitchen. Dora's escort, a capable footman, stood behind her, carrying the basket prepared from Lady Tolworth's well-stocked larder.

The servant opened the door and blew out a plume of smoke.

'Two shillings for— Oh.' She looked at Dora, then at the footman, and scowled. 'What you want?'

'I'm here to see your mistress,' said Dora politely.

The maid blinked. 'My mistress?'

'Yes. Miss Beamish.'

'But nobody calls on her.' Her frown deepened. 'If you're some distant cousin 'opin' to get your mitts on 'er house then you can sling yer hook! She don't want nothing to do with you lot – leavin' 'er high and dry in 'er time of need!'

'I'm not a cousin.'

'Oh, really? Then what are you?'

That was a complicated answer. 'I've brought her some treats – cherry pies, chicken pies, some fresh rolls…'

The elderly maid's eyes glistened and she wet her lips. 'You brought food?'

'Yes.'

'Show me.'

The footman stepped forward and opened the lid. As the woman stretched out to seize on a roll, he snapped it shut.

'Is the price of admission acceptable?' Dora asked.

'All right, you can come in. I'll just tell my mistress she 'as callers.'

Dora was allowed as far as the passageway while the maid ventured into the front room. There was a sour smell in the house, much of it clinging to the servant, but Dora had been in worse places.

'Neil, please take the basket to the kitchen.' She didn't want the looming presence of a footman to put Miss Beamish off answering her questions.

'Very good, miss. Then I'll wait for you here.'

'You could sit in the kitchen by the fire.'

'And be dismissed for failing to fulfil my orders? I'll wait for you here, within call. Mr Yarton was most precise with his instructions.'

The maid came out of the room and saw her food parcel heading further into the house.

'I sent him to the kitchen,' Dora explained.

The maid looked between her mistress and the basket – appetite won.

'I don't reckon you mean 'er harm. But watch it, all right?' She shook a finger under Dora's nose and set off in pursuit of the footman.

The late afternoon sunshine barely penetrated the front room. A lace curtain, much yellowed with age, stopped people peeking in but gave the occupant of the bed a view of those who walked by. As for the bedbound lady, she was no bigger than a baby bird in her cotton nest, as scrawny and lacking in fine feathers as one newly hatched. Arthritis twisted her fingers into claws as she scrabbled at the sheets. Her eyes, though, were bright.

'Who are you?' she asked. 'I've not met you, have I?'

'No, Miss Beamish.' Dora dipped a curtsey. 'I'm Dora Fitz-Pennington.'

'What are you doing here, Miss Fitz-Pennington?'

'Sticking my nose into business that you probably don't think I should.'

A creaky chuckle came from the lady. 'What kind of business?'

'I investigate crimes with my partner, Dr Sandys. He called yesterday.'

'I remember. He had a nice voice.' She sat forward, strings on her nightcap dangling. 'You are investigating with him? I didn't think women did that kind of work.'

'I don't feel obliged to ask anyone's permission.'

The lady slumped back on her pillows. 'Oh, I wish I'd been like you when I were your age.' Her finger plucked the linen, in a ghostly piano-playing motion. 'My father taught music.'

Dora took a seat on a stool by the bed. 'He did?'

'I wanted to sing, I was good at it, but he said it wasn't ladylike. No one would want to marry a woman who performed in public.'

Except Jacob. Dora's heart warmed at the thought. 'That's a shame.'

'Isn't it? I should've done like you, stuck my nose where I wanted it to go, not where people told me I should.'

'Their loss.'

'No, dear, it was mine.'

This was such a familiar and sad story. The country was full of maiden ladies who lived in expectation of a match and were regarded as worthless when they failed to attract a husband. It made Dora's blood boil at the unfairness.

'I'm sorry.'

Miss Beamish gave a deep sigh. 'Ask me your questions, Miss Fitz-Pennington.'

'It's about the night of Richard Brooking's murder.'

'Answers don't come free. I can't afford it.' A glint of steel in her gaze explained how Miss Beamish had survived a life of disappointments.

'I brought with me a basket of exceptionally fine food worth at least three guineas. You can keep that even if you decide not to tell me anything.'

'That's very decent of you – so I'll repay the favour. What's your question?'

'You hear and see more than people suspect.'

Miss Beamish gave a snort. 'Naturally. Nothing else left to do.' She waved to the ceiling. 'I know what goes on here, but Joanna would prefer to believe that I don't, so we both pretend.'

'I imagine some of your temporary guests are not quiet about their business?'

'They are not – though your Mr Brooking was. He only wanted to talk with his friend when he came.'

'Did you hear what language they spoke?'

'French in the main, sometimes Latin – gentlemen like to show off their learning, don't they? But I had lessons as a girl and know enough to recognise it.'

Interesting. 'On the night he died, did you see him arrive?'

'Yes. He came as usual just as it was getting dark.'

'When did his visitor arrive?'

'Immediately after him. He called up from outside my window to be let in.'

'Was he carrying anything?'

Miss Beamish smiled. 'Oh, you clever thing. Yes. He said he had something for Mr Brooking – a thank you gift. "The one you admired so much".'

'This was said in English?'

'Yes, you can't go shouting French on the streets – there's a war on, don't you know?'

Dora smiled. 'I do know.'

'But I can tell you the visitor had a French accent.'

'Can you tell me anything more about him.'

'He had a ridiculous number of buttonholes on his jacket.'

Percy had killed Brooking? That came as a rude shock. Dora had liked him too much to think him capable of cold-blooded murder. But she didn't really know him, did she?

Her skin felt clammy. 'How long did he stay?'

'About half an hour. Not as long as usual. When they parted in the hall, he said he had a boat to catch.'

That damn yacht! Dora and Jacob had been put off considering Percy a suspect as they thought he wouldn't have had time to make the long journey from London to Raith. However, the man had been travelling around the country at twice the speed thanks to his private boat. What was the betting that the supposed friend who had it available for him was Napoleon Bonaparte himself, furnishing his agents with means to carry out their work? Percy had probably rushed north to beat Dora and Jacob to the Fergusons' household to find out what they were doing.

Wait a moment... *When they parted in the hall...*

'Brooking was alive when that gentleman left?'

'Yes. Very much so. He said he would go back up to fetch his gift and he didn't come down again. I heard a few bumps but thought nothing of it – it could've been the couple in the other room – and the next thing we know is that Joanna finds him dead.'

'That same night?'

'About an hour later. She thought it strange he hadn't left so went to check – we were going to charge him extra.'

Joanna chose this interesting moment to come in carrying a platter filled with choice cuts from the gift basket. Miss Beamish looked back at Dora.

'You did bring the best, I see.'

'Have you finished with the mistress yet?' asked Joanna in a tone that suggested she thought Dora had got her money's worth.

'One moment. Miss Beamish, did Mr Brooking let anyone else in after the gentleman left?'

'No. Never heard a peep from him again.'

'Joanna, the couple in the other room, when did they leave?'

The maid glanced at her mistress. 'I wouldn't like to say.'

'Joanna!' warned Miss Beamish. 'This is murder.'

'Had they gone before you found Mr Brooking?'

The maid nodded.

'When did they arrive? After Mr Brooking greeted his guest?'

Joanna nodded again. 'They engaged a room. I recognised the woman. She's a usual customer.'

'The man?'

'Never seen him before or since.'

Dora wished she had the sketches with her. 'Can you describe him?'

'Medium height, wide-brimmed hat, brown coat. He didn't look at me. The gentlemen usually don't.'

That wasn't conclusive but it left open the possibility that Percy or Brooking had been followed here and the man had hired a prostitute to give him an excuse for entering the house.

'His companion's name?'

'Cathy Dean? You can find her most nights in Covent Garden. Tall, dark-haired, usually wears a pink cloak.'

Dora stood up. She had a lady of the night to locate. 'Thank you. Did either of you tell the Runners about the second man – or Cathy Dean?'

They looked at each other and shook their heads.

'You didn't?'

Joanna shrugged. 'They didn't ask.'

Chapter Thirty-Seven

Roman Wall, Tower Hill

Opposite him in the hansom cab, Fisher straightened his cuffs nervously. He was wearing his most fashionable jacket, but it was sadly rumpled and one of the buttons was missing. Here was a man in need of a well-paying archaeological commission if ever there was one.

'Are you sure they'll receive me?'

Jacob had told Dora that the knights would, but now the moment drew near he was less sanguine.

'If I go in alone, they might be quicker to silence me.'

Fisher gulped.

Alex checked his pistols. Tonight he had swapped his uniform for a dark coat and trousers. He would be almost invisible as he stood sentry in the shadows beyond the meeting place.

'Buck up, man. Sandys can't have you folding on him before the hand is even played.'

The cab turned past the pale walls of the Tower of London. Moonlight illuminated the stretch of Thames called The Pool where scores of ships were moored, waiting for passengers, cargo, or the tide, their masts a leafless forest. Wolves howled in the Tower Menagerie, interrupted by the grumbling of the lions. The windows of the barracks housing the Tower garrison glowed as troops settled in for the night. Lonely figures, those who had drawn the short straw of night watch, patrolled the ramparts.

The cab drew up on the northern edge of the Tower.

''Ere you are, sir. The London walls,' said the jarvey.

Jacob handed over the fare. 'Will you wait?' He added a generous tip.

The jarvey tipped his hat. 'For money like that I will. I'll be over there.' Other carriages were waiting on the side of the road indicating the Roman Knights had come in advance of them.

Alex slid out on the side hidden from the grassy mound of Tower Hill. 'Watch your backs,' he said.

'Because Romans like stabbing them?' quipped Fisher in a high-pitched voice.

Jacob slapped his friend on the shoulder consolingly. 'This may be nothing – just a meeting of the kind of men who will give you employment.'

Fisher took a deep breath and let it out. 'Yes, I'm making connections, developing my career. This is all very normal.'

And perhaps it was, for those obsessed with the past. Jacob had to admire their choice of venue. There were few traces left above ground of the Roman occupation of London, but one sizeable piece that had survived was the stretch of wall found a stone's throw from William the Conqueror's White Tower. It was at least two storeys tall, marked as Roman by the horizontal band of red tiles at every fifth or sixth course of stone. The most famous invaders of Britain, both the Romans and the Normans had left their stamp on the nation on this strategic place, the old entrance to the city from the east.

Would Napoleon be the next, wondered Jacob. Englishmen

had become used to their island fortress, but the Frenchman did have a realistic chance of being the next conqueror to come across the Channel once he defeated the armies of Europe. Would London be destroyed again by war? It didn't bear thinking about.

As Jacob crossed the grass with Fisher, the noise of the city dropped away. He could almost persuade himself that they were travelling back in time to meet their ancestors. Men clustered at the base of the wall, a line of flaming torches marking out their meeting ground. All wore white robes with deep hoods. No doubt, if he checked their fingers he'd also find bronze rings.

One man stepped forward, their designated leader.

'Dr Sandys, we understand that you are interested in joining our legion.' He spoke in the clipped tones of the upper class but with a hint of northern vowels like Jacob's own. 'Who is this you have brought with you?'

Fisher must have 'bucked up' as Alex had urged him because he gave a decent bow and said:

'Harold Fisher, MA Oxon. I'm a member of the Society of Antiquarians and another friend of Professor Soane.'

Eyes glinted in the depths of the hood. 'I believe I have read your monograph on the Colosseum.'

Fisher looked delighted, forgetting his trepidation. 'I'm so glad someone has.'

'I am Caractacus.' He dipped his head. 'If you choose to join us, then you, like us, will select a name from Roman or Celtic Britain to honour our forebears.'

Jacob wondered if the leader's choice of name was an indication of character. Caractacus had resisted Roman invaders for decades before being betrayed and captured. Legend said that once, in Rome, he gave an eloquent speech that persuaded Claudius to spare his life. Thereafter he lived as an honoured prisoner and a convert to the superiority of Rome. Was that kind of proud accommodation of Briton to Rome what these men stood for?

'Our joining ceremony is very simple,' said Caractacus. 'You swear allegiance. You then receive a ring and a new name. From thence forward, you adhere to the behaviour expected of a Roman Knight.'

'And might I enquire what behaviour that is?' asked Jacob.

'As our founder stated, we fight to keep Britain free of foreign taint, rescuing the relics of our ancestors from that most envious power, time.'

'You go as far as fighting?'

'We are knights first, scholars second. Yes, we fight. If necessary.'

'Too long has ignorance and neglect of Roman greatness spread a dark and almost indissoluble cloud over our island,' added a man on his right.

'And our duty,' added a third, 'nay, our glory, if we are blessed with the means, is to adorn the noble monuments of the Romans in Britain and give them a Roman eternity.'

'These knights are the second and third in our order,' said Caractacus. 'Togodumus and Praesutagus.'

Jacob bowed to them. 'And you do not limit yourself to Roman remains but value the Celtic, too, I understand?'

'Oh, indeed, there is little that is more sublime than standing in Stonehenge at midsummer to witness the wisdom of the ancients in their placing,' said Togodumnus with a slight smile. 'Many have stood there and found a new purpose in life.'

The picture left with Brooking was then a very fitting gift between society members.

'This sounds capital,' said Fisher. 'I don't suppose any of you gentlemen – knights – have a Roman villa on your land that needs excavating?'

'Then you wish to join us?' asked Caractacus.

'If you will have me.'

'And you, Dr Sandys?'

'It is an intriguing proposition, but I do have more questions.'

'As do we for you.' Caractacus gestured to them to take the bench seats placed at the foot of the wall. 'We suspect you have come here for quite another reason than a wish to join our ranks. We hear reports from some of our members that you are close to the Earl of Elgin.'

So that explained their haste in inviting him. They wanted to find out what he knew. 'And is that a problem?'

'Not if you disagree with his abominable plan to place the Parthenon marbles at the heart of our national museum. That would skew our identity just as we are coming to understand it. We are Celts, Britons, Romans, Anglo-Saxons, not Greeks.'

And there was their motive.

'You fear he will succeed in persuading the government to buy them?'

'He has influence. And even that idiot Lord Byron is not helping by kicking up a fuss among the radicals. The government is leaning towards supporting Elgin, the noble victim of Bonaparte, rather than the emperor's celebrated defender.'

'And you are working to change the government's mind against the earl?'

'We are.' Caractacus gestured to a boy dressed in a toga to approach with a tray of wine. It was a warm summer's evening so it did not seem strange to be drinking wine with possible enemies beneath the stars, as the Romans must have done when the English rain let up. 'A libation to the gods to confound Elgin's plans.' And then he surprised Jacob by casting back his hood. A man conscious of guilt surely would have hidden his identity for longer? Jacob recognised him as Colonel Patrick Campbell, a landowner in Cumbria who had part of a Roman fort on his estate. They had met several times in Keswick and Kendal.

Sandys stood up and saluted. 'Colonel.'

'Dr Sandys, I'm Caractacus in these circles.' He took a seat placed in front of the wall, the stance of a centurion defending it against those who would attack it. 'I know you are a good man from your service to our country, so I was eager to straighten things out with you when Soane made his inquiries. You are investigating us, am I right?'

Hard to deny when put like that. 'I do have questions, yes.'

'Our cause is a noble one. What do you suspect us of doing?'

Killing people, blowing up innocent bystanders, sending threats…

'Have you taken actions against Elgin?'

'Specifically?' Caractacus tapped his knee.

Jacob was acutely aware of the cluster of robed men standing around them listening to their conversation. He'd brought Fisher as his witness, thinking that would deter them spiriting him away, but now he wondered if he hadn't dropped his friend in danger. Alex had better be ready to rescue them if this went badly.

'Have you ever threatened the earl, sir?'

Caractacus gave a bark of a laugh. 'He took fright at an anonymous note, did he? Our campaign is having more effect than expected.'

'It's not just the threats.'

The man's gaze sharpened. 'What do you mean?'

'Did you know that Richard Brooking is dead?'

'He was known as Cador to us. Yes, very regrettable. I wouldn't have thought him the kind to live so dangerously, picking up prostitutes.'

'He didn't. It was no robbery gone wrong. He was murdered. Maybe by one of you.'

The leader's expression changed to one of recognition. There was a scuffle at the back of the circle as one man seemed to be trying to leave without permission. Caractacus stood up and gave an imperious beckon.

'Brother Quintus, would you care to explain?'

Chapter Thirty-Eight

The knights jostled Quintus to the front. The man's hood was still pulled over his face.

'We tasked you to work with Cador to undermine Elgin's plans for the marbles. What happened?' thundered Caractacus.

With a huff, accepting he could not escape, Quintus shook back his hood and gave the company a wry look. The dancing shadows and a black eye gave his face a distorted appearance, more gargoyle than knight.

'Surprised?' Michel Percy asked Jacob.

That damned man! He had slipped the watch they'd placed on him. 'You were conspiring with Brooking—'

'Cador,' corrected Percy.

'To send threats to Elgin – and to Mary Ferguson?'

'What? You threatened a woman?' Caractacus sounded furious.

Percy shrugged. 'That was only to mislead the good doctor when I knew he was on the way. I wrote that one myself, allowed the housekeeper to intercept it and destroyed it. I hoped word would reach our intrepid investigators and send them running in the wrong direction.' He smiled weakly. 'I thought it rather clever myself.'

'But you also sent me looking for this society,' said Jacob, remembering the words spoken in the hospital.

'Did I? I only said you should look for others who have designs on the marbles. So many people do. It wasn't meant to be helpful.'

Jacob had a strong desire to strangle the man.

Caractacus scowled at his brother knight. 'We discovered that Quintus enjoyed blackmailing his customers – taking his payment in secrets and favours. We thought to put him to good use turning his talents on Elgin.'

'The man is paranoid about his family, so I suggested to Brooking that we should make him worry to the extent he gave up on the marbles to keep them safe,' said Percy. 'We searched *The Oresteia* for suitable quotations. Brooking then slipped that threat into the correspondence but died before it was delivered.'

'That's not the behaviour of a gentleman,' protested Fisher. He had been the one to open the letter, Jacob recalled.

'We aren't gentlemen, we are Roman knights,' said Caractacus.

'I rescind my desire to join you,' Fisher muttered.

Good man, thought Jacob.

'But we draw the line at involving the ladies in our fight.' Caractacus pointed at Quintus. 'That was badly done.'

'Not as bad as murder,' said Jacob. 'Percy—'

'Quintus.' Percy sounded too pleased with himself.

Yes, strangling was the only option.

'Michel Percy, Brother Quintus, whoever the hell you are, did you kill Richard Brooking?' Jacob thought he knew the answer but he wanted to get it straight from Percy's lips.

Percy took a step closer so that the light fell full on his face. 'No, I did not, Sandys.'

Fisher reared back in surprise.

'Good lord, Archambeau, what on earth has brought you to London?'

Percy's smile became rigid. 'You are mistaken, sir. I am Michel Percy. Or Quintus.'

Fisher shook his head. 'No, you're not. Or if you are, you are also Michel Archambeau. Don't you remember: we were at the Voivode's reception in Athens to celebrate the Treaty of Amiens? I never forget the name of someone whose work on antiquities I would want to read. I thought your understanding of the Acropolis second to none.'

Percy struggled to hide his irritation. 'I'm sorry, sir, but I've never been in Athens.'

Fisher wasn't giving it up. He peered at him. 'Do you have a twin? I swear you're the same chap. You were most put out when Elgin nabbed the marbles before you could get to them. You said your master at the Louvre would be furious.'

The tide turned against him and Percy now found himself in the middle of a ring of hostile Englishmen.

'I fear, sir,' Jacob said to Caractacus, 'you hired a French agent to do your blackmailing for you.'

'What? We never – I never – he's a refugee from the Terror!'

'Who appears to have made his peace with Emperor Napoleon. Percy, if you did not kill Brooking, then who did? I know you know.'

'*Putain*!' With a quick movement, Percy grabbed Fisher and held him, back to his chest, a familiar scalpel pressed against the man's jugular. 'Stay back.'

Jacob held up a hand to stop Caractacus tackling him. One jolt of a hand and there would be nothing they could do for Fisher.

'I fear I must take my leave early, gentlemen' said Percy with dry politeness. 'I don't want to harm anyone. But we aren't play-acting. I have a sacred mission to complete and you must not get in my way, *comprenez*?' he backed away, pulling Fisher with him.

'Sandys!' squeaked his friend.

'Keep calm,' said Jacob. He felt far from calm himself. This had all gone to the dogs. He hadn't expected Percy to be here of all places! 'Do what he says.'

'The doctor is correct, Monsieur Fisher. I have no desire to shed blood, but he will tell you I do so when I have to.' He pulled Fisher into the shadows of the wall. 'Do not follow us!'

Like hell they wouldn't!

The sound of a departing carriage released Jacob from his terror that one wrong move would spell the death of his friend.

'Smith!' he bellowed.

Alex shouted back from across the road. 'Coming.'

He arrived perched next to the driver on the hansom cab.

'Did you see which carriage they got in?'

'One pulled by a grey mare. That one!' He pointed to a carriage disappearing back in the direction of the West End.

'What can we do?' asked Caractacus, grabbing Jacob's sleeve. The Roman Knights milled around him in confusion, torches flaring, wine cups spilt on London grass.

'You can get out of my way!' Jacob shook him off and jumped aboard. 'Follow that carriage!'

'There they go.' Alex put away his spyglass. They'd followed Percy's carriage across London and ended up outside Lord Elgin's house.

The exhibition had long since closed for the night, but Percy forced Fisher to open the side gate. He had swapped the scalpel for a pistol.

'My money was on him making a run for it, so why come here?' Alex asked.

Jacob shook his head as mystified as his companion. What did

Percy want with the marbles? Sabotage? But would a connoisseur of ancient culture do anything to harm the very thing he loved? Was he acting in the spirit of 'if I cannot have them for France, then no one shall have them'? Dread grew in Jacob's stomach.

'Alex, we need back-up – and weapons. I'll follow him and stop him before he damages anything or harms Fisher. I want you to take the cab back to the office, fetch any weapons you can put your hands on and tell Dora and our team what's happening.'

Alex frowned. 'What the blazes is happening?'

'I think Percy has designs on the marbles.'

Chapter Thirty-Nine

Covent Garden Market

Dora studied the streetwalkers strolling under the porticoes of Covent Garden. There were so many of them, some decked out like Spanish galleons, others wearing tugboat rags. For any woman they were a reminder of what could be. Even those who felt themselves most secure might one day have nothing left to sell but this.

'Miss, I really think we should be getting back,' said her footman escort. 'Mr Yarton didn't mention anything about an excursion to the market.'

Stirring herself, she patted his arm. 'Neil, can you look out for a prostitute for me?'

His eyes widened.

'Not *for* me, obviously. I'm looking for a woman called Cathy Dean. She's tall, dark-haired, and usually wears a pink cloak.'

'Miss, ladies don't go looking for that kind of woman.'

Poor Neil. 'This lady does. I'm investigating a murder, remember. Those involved are not going to be nuns and saints.'

She turned down the passageway between market stalls. These were closed up for the day, the fruit and vegetables having been sold off in the morning. Her foot slipped on a bruised cabbage leaf.

'Perhaps the person you are seeking is over there,' Neil said glumly, his greater height giving him the advantage.

A dark-haired woman leaned by the door to Covent Garden Theatre. The play had already started but she was looking for latecomers, or those who decided it was not to their taste. Her low-cut bodice and pink cloak indicated her occupation, as did the assessing glance she gave to all the men who passed.

Dora was no stranger to the stage-door ladies. Be it London, Kendal or York, they were the same hardbitten, down-on-their-luck girls. She'd always rather admired their pluck for keeping on despite the horrible hand life had dealt them. She sallied straight up.

'Cathy Dean?'

'Who's asking?'

It looked like they had the right woman.

'If you want me to do both of you, it'll cost double.' She sauntered over to the footman and ran a hand down his side. 'I like the tall ones.'

Neil huffed and blushed.

'Stop teasing the poor man, Cathy. We aren't here to engage your services.'

Cathy deflated and went back to leaning against the wall. 'What are you here for then? Do you like to watch?'

'No, I like to ask questions.' Dora held out three shillings. 'You went with a man to Rose Street about ten days ago.'

All business, Cathy pocketed the shillings. 'What of it?'

'What do you remember about him?'

She shrugged. 'He had a funny accent – foreign, like.'

'French?'

'Yeah, French. He was a queer cove. Didn't want to prig. He wanted to sit and listen. He told me I could take a nap if I wished.'

'Did you?'

'With a bleeding stranger in the room? I'm not that stupid.'

'What did he do?'

'What he said. He listened. He left the room for a bit then came back. He washed his hands and said we should go.'

'Washed his hands?'

'Yeah, the water in the basin was red when he was done so he chucked it out of the window.'

'You're saying he washed blood off his hands?'

'I'm not saying nothing.'

'You know a man was murdered that night in that same house.'

'What of it?'

'Why didn't you come forward and tell the Runners?'

'You're joking, right? The Runners were looking for the whore that killed him. What's the betting they'd say it was me and I'd be hanged for just being there? And if you say anything to them, I don't remember a thing about it.' Her eyes slid past Dora and went to a gentleman who was slowing as he approached the theatre door. 'Oi, 'andsome, want some company?'

When he nodded, Cathy slid her arm through his and walked off without looking back.

Dora returned to the office with her disapproving guard. Saying farewell to Neil on the doorstep, she let herself in and found Kir already curled up on his bed in the corner.

'Busy day?' she asked. 'Have you eaten?'

He nodded and yawned.

'Any sign of Alex and Jacob?' Dora sat at the desk to update their case notes. Cathy's information confirmed what they already suspected. There was a second Frenchman in the mix, one who was shadowing Percy's steps – and theirs. What was he up to? Whose orders was he carrying out? He had money to back him. Hiring a man to kill Percy in the hospital and buying the wagon and gunpowder suggested as much. Travel wasn't cheap. He didn't have a boat at his beck and call, not like Percy, as he had arrived in London around the same time as they did. That suggested he had followed them by carriage, or on horseback.

'Monsieur Brown Coat, you are a mystery,' she murmured.

Footsteps approaching made her look up. Had Jacob and Fisher finished at the London Wall already? She couldn't wait to hear their impression of the Roman Knights.

No, the footsteps sounded wrong – too light. A single person.

With a glance at Kir, Dora searched the desk for a weapon. Jacob must've left his pistols at the hotel. She seized a pocketknife and held it against her side, concealing it in the folds of her skirt.

The door banged open.

'You bitch!' spat Dimitra. 'So this is where you crawled away to hide.'

Dora dropped the knife in her pocket. No need to raise the temperature any further with the fiery Greek woman. She motioned to Kir that all was well. 'No crawling was involved. This is where I work.'

'Doing your muckraking and your scandal-mongering? How much do the press pay you for your stories about Lord Byron?'

Dora blinked. 'What?'

'Oh, my cousin has seen it all – people trying to bribe him for stories. I have to commend you for working out my connection to his lordship and coming at him from an unexpected direction – that was clever.'

'You think this is aimed at Byron?' Dora almost laughed, but saw the Greek woman was deadly serious.

'He's a great man – a friend to the Greeks.'

'I've no doubt of that.'

'I won't have you attack him with false accusations.'

Now this was interesting. They'd moved into the threat part of the confrontation. 'Oh, really. What will you do?'

Dimitra curled her hands into fists. 'I'll … I'll tell everyone that you are Dr Sandys' whore.'

That familiar slur was losing its power over her. 'Who could possibly care about that?'

Dimitra looked uncertain. 'Your … family?'

'My brother was murdered six weeks ago. I have no other family.'

'Murdered?' That took the wind out of her sails.

'Yes. That's how I met Jacob. We solved the case and brought the murderer to justice.' And hadn't that felt good? She'd got more satisfaction bringing the Hellfire Club to their knees than any standing ovation on stage. Maybe Jacob was right? This could be a good profession for her.

'Well … good. I'm sorry about your brother, but you mustn't attack Lord Byron.'

Dora sat in the desk chair to signal she was not fighting. 'We've cleared him of any involvement. We were looking for people in his circle that might be wrongheadedly leaping to his defence and attacking Elgin.' She gave Dimitra a pointed look. 'They do exist, you know.'

Dimitra's lips twitched. 'Me?'

'Don't worry: we also cleared you and your cousin of any part in this.'

'What is "this"?' Dimitra asked.

'That's what we've been working to find out. It started with Lord Elgin's marbles—'

'The Parthenon marbles.'

'The *marbles*. And now seems to be leading us to Napoleon's war aims.'

A cab drew up outside the office and a man jumped out.

'Dora!' shouted Alex. He rushed into the room. 'Grab our weapons. Percy has Fisher and is going after the marbles.'

Chapter Forty

Kir lay still, eyes open, staring into the dark of the office where he lay. The noise of the retreating cab died away.

They'd left him again and Miss Dora was heading into danger. Dr Sandys had told him to look after her but how could he when she kept running off without him? Would they turn him out if something happened to her? It was no good saying, as Mrs Widgeon had, that he shouldn't worry and that he was safe in her kitchen, but that hadn't lasted long, had it? Miss Dora had been cast out quickly enough – and she was an adult.

Kir threw the covers off his legs and checked he had his little blade in his pocket. He knew where they were going. He'd gone there once with Miss Dora and Miss Dimitra. Having carried messages with some of the footmen around the West End, he knew how to find Lord Elgin's house again. It was near that park with all the fine horses and fancy people. He'd liked the horses. He pulled on his jacket and went to the door.

Miss Dora would want you to stay put, a voice struck up in his head, sounding like Mr Yarton. He was a great man. Kir would like to be as clever as him when he grew up, knowing exactly what everyone in the household was doing.

Perhaps he should go and find him, tell him what was bothering him. The butler had said he could at any time.

Kir thought what that would be like – creeping into the house, waking such an august person, seeing him in his nightgown, and blabbering about his worries for Miss Dora.

No, he couldn't do that. It was too scary.

What he could do, though, was follow and keep to the shadows, just in case he was needed.

Closing the door behind him, he set off for Park Lane. He took the route he knew best, through Grosvenor Square. He'd liked that house. Mrs Widgeon had been so lovely and cuddled him when he looked upset about Hattie.

Remembrance swept back. He'd shoved it away for an hour or two but now he couldn't get past the horrible fact. His kind, wonderful sister was gone. Kir wanted to scream, beat the earth, tear everything to pieces. It wasn't fair!

A hand caught his collar.

'*Et voilà!*' hissed the man who haunted his dreams – his sister's killer.

With a furious cry, Kir twisted and drove his knife into the murderer.

Chapter Forty-One

Park Lane

Jacob waited in the shadows across Park Lane from the earl's house. How was Percy going to leave with even one of the smallest of the marbles? Fisher was no Hercules and Percy only had one working arm, currently occupied with holding a gun. He must have had that stashed in his carriage. They could damage a piece by dropping it. Or maybe Percy simply planned to take a crowbar to them? Either way, the art lover in Jacob refused to let these beautiful survivors of antiquity suffer yet more damage in this war between nations.

He couldn't let it go so far.

Considering enough time had passed for them to have cleared the path, he crossed the road to follow Percy and Fisher. He glanced up at the windows of Elgin's house. His young family had been sent to the country for safety so the earl was alone. Only one window was lit at the front, possibly in his library. There was no time to alert him to the danger. Percy could come and go while Jacob was rousing the household.

The exhibition shed stood open. Percy walked the aisle of exhibits, Fisher a pace ahead with a pistol at his back. The hostage held a lantern out before him, turning it on the exhibits at Percy's instructions. The Frenchman had sangfroid, Jaco would allow him that.

Percy paused to consider a fragment of a torso.

'What do you think of this? Too big, no?'

'Look, sir, I don't know what you are trying to do,' said Fisher bravely, 'but you are highly unlikely to get away with it. You should be running for a ship, not sightseeing!'

Percy came to stop beside the horse's head.

'Put down the lantern and take out the sack I gave you.'

Fisher put down the lamp and shook out a sack that looked like it had recently held the oats of a hansom cab horse.

'Now put it over the head.'

That was enough of that.

'Stop right there!' said Jacob.

Percy turned. He didn't seem shocked to be interrupted. 'Excellent. You arrived at the right time. I am learning to predict you, Dr Sandys.'

'What the hell are you doing?'

Percy arched a brow. 'Taking what is ours naturally. If I could fit them all in my pocket, I would.'

'What if he drops it – what if it gets damaged?' asked Jacob.

Fisher looked desperately at Jacob. 'What should I do?'

'What I said,' said Percy, noting his hesitation. 'I would hate to kill one of you and I do have a second pistol in my jacket pocket already primed. By the time you'd covered half the distance, Sandys, you would be dead and your friend in the sights of another gun.'

'I'd have you on the floor before you could reach for it,' said Jacob.

'Then, please, have a go,' Percy said with a careless toss of his head. 'It is your life to throw away.'

Jacob had seen Percy's skills in action in the hospital. It would be foolish not to take him at his word.

'Why are you doing this?' he asked, because he wanted to know but mostly to delay him. Alex and Dora had to be on their way back by now.

Percy cocked his head to one side, considering. 'Lord Elgin has so many marbles, he won't miss one little one, surely?'

'Oh, I think he will, but that doesn't answer the question. What will you do with it?'

'I'll look after it, I promise. It certainly isn't worth spilling blood over. Never was.' Percy flicked the end of the pistol in a beckoning gesture. 'I was hoping you were following me – counting on it, in fact.'

Jacob had a sinking feeling that Percy had always been one step ahead of them. His years of service as a foreign agent made Jacob look like a beginner at espionage, which, in truth, he was. The only surprise he had managed to spring on Percy was the meeting with Fisher, and that had not been planned.

All he could think was to keep him talking.

'There's nothing you do that is an accident. You got Dora thrown out of the Fergusons' house on purpose, didn't you?'

Percy smiled. 'I did indeed. I couldn't have you sniffing around my business, and I needed to expedite the return of my book. I still need that by the way.'

'You're doing this for France?'

'*Bien sur*. Napoleon is the equal of any Roman Emperor. His collection is the one that will define European culture. So the marbles, Greece's finest artworks, should be part of that – not some ridiculous earl and his shed.'

'You can't take them all.'

'I do realise that, but this is a start, is it not? The blow to

English pride will be severe when this is exhibited in Paris, my position at the Louvre secure. I'll return when Napoleon invades and take the rest then. I promise you I will cherish them as they deserve.'

'You killed all those people for that?'

Percy tutted. 'I didn't kill anyone – or only a few who deserved it. I'm most disappointed you think that of me. Pick up the head, Sandys. I think you'll make a better pack mule than Fisher.'

Jacob glowered.

Percy sighed. 'Do you really want me to put a shot into your friend's leg? It might hit something vital.'

Jacob walked to the horse's head and lifted it. He staggered under its weight, then found his feet. 'This is madness.'

'Ah, but there is method to it. Fisher, pick up the lamp,' said Percy. 'As you can see, I don't have a free hand.'

Fisher scooped up the lamp by the ring at the top. 'Sandys?'

'Don't make any sudden moves,' warned Percy.

Jacob momentarily thought of throwing the marble at Percy's head but that might result in a discharge of the weapon and damage to the horse's head. The crisis where action was unavoidable had not yet come. He should continue to play for time.

'What now?' he asked.

'Kindly lead the way, Fisher, then Sandys second, and I will follow in the rear. What a procession we will make, worthy of our own frieze.'

'And who is the goddess that we are honouring?' asked Jacob sourly as they began walking.

'A god. Or emperor. I don't think even Napoleon considers himself a deity – not yet.'

'Did you kill Stokes?' Jacob asked.

'*Mon Dieu*, no! I told you already: I am a peaceable man.'

'Says the person who cut the throat of one in Berwick.'

'Ah yes, my finest hour. He was trying to kill me; I was merely restoring law and order. Hush now, we are near the house. I'd prefer none of Lord Elgin's servants to be injured if we can avoid it.'

Fisher pulled the gate open and Jacob cast a worried glance up and down Park Lane.

Damn it all! The cavalry was yet to arrive.

Percy whistled and his hansom cab drew up from where it had waited further down the street. The Frenchman moved swiftly to stand behind Jacob, the pistol sticking in his kidneys and hidden from the cab driver.

'Smile,' he murmured. Then to the jarvey. 'Thank you for waiting, my good man.' There was not a trace of a French accent now. He truly was as changeable as a barometer. 'Please put my package inside the cab.' He smiled affably at Jacob.

Jacob moved forward as ordered. He put the sack carefully on the seat, then stood back. Surely the odds were now in their favour with his hands free and the driver present as a witness?

'That man's a French agent,' Jacob told the jarvey. 'If you drive him anywhere, it should be to Newgate.'

The cab chuckled. 'Very droll, sir. He said you would say that. You can't get away with stealing another man's statue. You two should change your ways and earn an honest living.'

'I will be pressing charges,' said Percy, moving round so he was near the steps. 'Keep an eye on them, driver. They are more dangerous than they look.'

The jarvey prodded Fisher with his whip. 'Step back, young man.'

'You've got this all wrong,' said Jacob. 'Knock on the door here and ask Lord Elgin. That man has no right to the statue.'

The jarvey scratched his head, dislodging his hat. 'Lord Elgin? What's he got to do with it?'

Jacob pointed to the house. 'It's his exhibition of statues. We are working for him – your passenger is a French spy. You are aiding and abetting theft.'

A flicker of doubt crossed the man's face.

'You've heard of the Elgin marbles, haven't you?'

'I know a few fares have asked to be dropped near here to see some foreign nonsense.'

'Use your head, man,' growled Jacob. 'You're on the wrong side here. If you don't believe us, just take a moment and ask.'

'*Ça suffit.*' Percy pushed Fisher into Jacob with a shove of his shoulder and got up into the cab. 'Oh dear,' he said, now levelling his pistol at the driver. 'I believe we must curtail this most interesting discussion. Drive on or die. I'm quite capable to taking the reins myself should you fail to do your duty by your paying passenger.'

The jarvey turned to face his horse and clicked his tongue. 'Blimey, guv, none of this is worth a bullet.'

'My thoughts exactly.'

The cab rattled away at speed. Jacob ran after it but he had to give up when it turned the corner.

'Dammit!' They'd made a mess of that – or he had, delaying too long in hopes of Alex and company coming to their aid with weapons and numbers on their side. He looked up at the house, wondering if he should report the loss to Elgin. That would land them in very hot water.

With excruciating just-too-slow timing, Alex arrived with Dora and, perplexingly, Dimitra; Susan, Hugo and Ren peered out of a second cab.

'What's she doing here?' he asked, gesturing to Dimitra as he got in.

'She has as much right to protect the marbles as we do,' said Dora.

He couldn't stop to ask how that came about. 'You've missed

Percy. He's got away,' he said, he squeezed beside Dora. 'Fisher, climb in the second cab.'

'You're not hurt?' asked Dora, checking him for injury.

'Only my pride. I should've acted quicker, but he had a gun on us and that allowed him to control the situation. He stole one.'

'One of the marbles?' asked Alex.

'The horse's head.'

Dimitra gasped and cursed in Greek.

'He made me carry it while he held us at gunpoint. I would've made a move to stop him, but I thought you'd get here. And now he's escaped.'

Alex scowled. 'I apologise for my tardiness.'

'It wasn't your fault, Alex. I'd only just returned from Covent Garden and it took me a moment to retrieve the pistols,' said Dora.

'What were you doing in Covent Garden?' asked Jacob. 'No, let's scrap that discussion until after I've given the jarvey his orders.' He tapped on the roof. 'Head for Fleet Street.'

'Hadn't we better tell the earl?' Dora asked. 'He won't be pleased that we lost Percy.'

'My darling, we haven't lost him.' Jacob put his arm around her and hugged her to his side, his heart racing. Frightening though this was, he was enjoying the hunt. They still had a fighting chance. 'We know exactly where he is going.'

'We do?'

'Garlickhythe. Remember I checked his story about his passage from Scotland? His boat is waiting for him. What's the betting the crew is French and the destination Calais?'

Chapter Forty-Two

River Thames

The yacht was tied up at the bottom of the steps of Garlickhythe exactly as Jacob's messenger – one of Lady Tolworth's footmen – had reported. It was just small enough to fit beneath the arches of London Bridge. This was no pleasure craft but a hunter with its black paintwork and masts laid flat, like a hound with its ears back, growling. Once through the bridge, the masts would be mounted, sails rigged and, with a fair wind, Percy would slip over the Channel and beyond their reach. Fortunately, thought Jacob as he checked the state of the Thames, they had the tide in their favour. It had turned but the water level was still too high for a safe passage beneath the narrow arches. Only the most daring would attempt it like this. The captain would want to wait an hour or two to be sure.

'The pistols?' asked Jacob.

She opened the box on her lap. They had retrieved Alex's set from his room. Alex took one, and Dora took the other. Jacob had lost the coin toss.

'You're lucky I didn't pawn these,' said Alex, priming his gun. 'I was on the point of doing so when you met me.'

Dora took the powder and shot from him to prepare her own gun. 'We will try to keep you on the straight and narrow so you don't need to be so desperate again.'

Alex extended his arm and sighted his pistol. 'Is that what you call this?'

Jacob had a sword, another borrowing from Alex. 'I think we're ready.'

Dimitra produced a pocketknife – his pocketknife from the office. 'So am I.'

'I would really rather you stayed in the carriage, Miss Mitkou,' said Jacob.

'Not a chance,' she said.

Dora grinned at her.

'Where did you send the others?' asked Dora, tucking the gun in the pocket of her great coat.

'Hugo and Susan are watching from the bridge. Fisher is guarding the approach from St James's Church. Hopefully we shouldn't get any more nasty surprises.'

'Why do I feel that you've now cursed our endeavour?' Dora gave him an adorable scowl.

He brushed a kiss over her forehead. 'Because, my dear, you are falling for a baseless superstition. I've heard theatre folk were prey to such beliefs.'

'Humph!'

Ren returned from checking how many sailors were onboard. His smaller stature made him the perfect spy as he was able to walk the entire length of Garlickhythe hidden behind the barrels stacked along the mooring. His report had been encouraging – just two men visible on deck. They were preparing to sail.

'Thanks, Ren. Will you go and join Fisher. I think he's not made for battle.'

The little man chuckled. 'A real Sir Andrew Aguecheek, that one. I'll keep him out of trouble. Send for us if you need backup.' He hurried off into the dark.

'What are we going to do?' asked Dimitra.

'Let's try this by taking a leaf out of Percy's book,' said Jacob.

'Meaning?' asked Dora.

'Dora and I will pretend to be his friend. Dimitra, can you pretend to be our maid?'

She bobbed a mocking curtsey. 'Yes, sir.'

'Alex, stay back. If this goes well, we will separate the men on deck, and leave you to deal with the one left behind.'

Alex saluted. 'Sir.'

Dora and Jacob headed down the steps to the mooring.

'Once a soldier, always a soldier,' murmured Dora.

'Him or me?'

'Both.'

'How's your French?'

'*Pas mal.*'

'Dimitra?'

'*Magnifique.*'

'*Bon.* We are French agents whose cover is blown, needing a rapid passage to France. Our good friend Michel Percy told us to meet him here.'

'I think I'm pregnant. Dimitra, help me walk.'

'What?' His heart did a stutter and he had a marvellous but terrifying glimpse of Dora with a child at her breast. Their child.

'I mean that you should say I'm pregnant and in labour. They will panic – men do – and not search me.'

'That great coat does hide a multitude of sins,' he agreed, feeling a little sad as the vision vanished.

'You have no idea.' She grinned at him. She loved this, he realised, taking chances with outlandish stories, just another form of acting but with the highest of stakes – life or death. And maybe he did, too. He was more himself with her and her vagabond crew than he had ever been in a drawing room or an officers' mess.

They reached the yacht and Dora bent over, giving a little groan. *'Mon Dieu!'*

'Au secours, mes amis,' said Jacob, hurrying her up the gangplank, Dimitra supporting her under the other arm. Finding in himself the character of a harried husband, fearing for his wife in her first labour, he gabbled at how dangerous their predicament was and how their very good friend, Michel Percy, was their last hope. *'Réfléchissez: les Anglais laisseront-ils vivre un bébé français?'* He made it seem as if turning them away would be tantamount to child murder.

The captain came closer and demanded he surrender his sword, which Jacob did as if he trusted them fully, swearing he would give up anything they asked as long as his poor wife could lie down.

'We must check with Monsieur,' said the captain in French.

Dora cried out. *'O ciel!'*

'It's coming – the baby's coming!' announced Dimitra in excellent French.

The captain looked panicked. Give him a storm at sea and he would know what to do, but the mysteries of childbirth...! 'The lady may lie in my cabin.'

The captain rapidly led the way down to the little cabin in the stern. 'Monsieur, can you vouch for these people?' he asked, still thinking he had the upper hand.

'Imbecile!' spat Percy looking up from the hammock where he reclined. 'These are the very last people to welcome aboard!'

'Jeannieu!' shouted the captain. But no sailor answered his call, only Alex, pistol in one hand, Jacob's sword in another. Next the captain found a gun pointing at him drawn from the folds of Dora's great coat. He raised his hands. Dimitra held her knife to Percy's throat, which seemed poetic justice to Jacob.

'Very wise.' Jacob secured the captain with his cravat.

'How useful fashionable dress is for these situations,' said Dora. 'Every well-dressed man carries ties or bandages around their neck. Did you know, Mr Percy, your buttonholes gave you away?'

Percy smiled sourly. 'My mother always said my taste for a fashionable life would be my undoing.'

'An old lady recognised them – and you. You were with Brooking on the night he died.'

'But I didn't kill him.'

'No, you didn't.'

'I think we'd better keep this conversation between ourselves,' said Jacob.

With the promise that he'd keep watch for the return of other crew members, Alex bundled the captain out of the cabin.

Dora stood by the sack containing the horse's head and studied Percy with some amusement.

'You don't look well,' she said.

Percy moved Dimitra's hand away and swung his legs over the side of the hammock. 'My injury is not feigned.'

'That's far enough. Jacob, don't forget he has a pistol somewhere.'

Jacob found it on the captain's table – and another in Percy's coat pocket. Percy should have had a weapon in the hammock with him. He had been lured into feeling too comfortable being on a French vessel, his first mistake. His second was not to attempt the passage under the bridge immediately, trusting they would take longer to catch up with him.

'This is interesting. What now?' asked Percy, taking this turn in his fortunes better than Jacob expected.

'We return the marble horse head to Elgin.'

Dimitra huffed.

'But of course,' said Percy.

'And turn you into the authorities.'

Percy sighed and lay back in the hammock. 'Better them than my compatriots, I suppose.'

'What do you mean?' Jacob shifted to the end of the hammock so he could look down at their prisoner. Percy was very pale. He must've been running on nerves and determination as physically he was a wreck. What kind of opponent would he have made at full strength? Formidable, he guessed.

'Have you not worked it out yet? Perhaps you aren't as clever as I thought.'

But he was still just as annoying.

Jacob took a moment to consider – Brooking being killed by a second man – the wagon in Berwick and Percy's conviction he was the target – the book and Stokes – the mad plot to steal the horse's head – it had all to come together somehow.

'I had an interesting conversation with a Covent Garden lady this evening,' said Dora. 'She went with a man who spoke with, in her words, "a funny accent" to Rose Street on the night you were there. Is the man who killed Brooking and Stokes another French agent?'

Jacob drew his sketch from his breast pocket. 'Is it this man?'

Percy squinted at the picture. 'Not a bad likeness.'

'You know him?'

'Of course I know him. He's been dogging my steps for weeks – for years really.'

'His name?' asked Dora.

'That charming gentleman is known these days as Philippe Fleury. His real name is anyone's guess, so I am betraying no state secrets telling you that much.'

'He was sent to kill you?'

'I believe he considered he was under orders to wind up my operation due to my lack of results. He also bears me a grudge for a little misunderstanding in Portugal. In any case, he got to Stokes and poor Brooking. I was to be pruned too – they say I've gone rogue.' He curled his lip. 'I was merely being subtle and working a long game. But their patience ran out in Paris. His tactics were more in the nature of blowing up the orchard rather than pruning it.'

'One Frenchman killing another? Why?'

'There is a struggle for influence in certain departments of the French government. I am its victim.'

So were the poor people on the bridge at Berwick. Percy did not seem very concerned about them.

'Does he work for the French secret police? Is that who you are working for?' suggested Jacob.

'Him, yes. Me, not directly. My master is Director General Vivant Denon at the Louvre. You see, I am a man of culture like yourself, Sandys, and no assassin.'

Except when your back is to the wall, thought Jacob. 'I suppose your task for Denon started long ago in Athens?'

'How clever of you to dig up Fisher to confront me. I thought my role there had been forgotten.' He addressed that comment to the rafters as he lay gently swaying.

'You were to bring home the marbles?'

'Napoleon requires them for his collection. They dispatched me to Athens. I had plenty of money for bribes but not enough time to work my influence. Lord and Lady Elgin had got there first.'

How deep had his machinations reached? 'Did you sink the *Mentor*?'

'Please! Who do you think I am? Poseidon?'

'Then you came to England to try to get them from Elgin.'

'That wasn't my only goal, but it was one that was thought a desirable outcome.'

'No, you were here gathering information through your little blackmailing scheme, but that brought you to the attention of the Roman Knights.'

'That was a happy chance. It could have gone awry when they confronted me at Stonehenge. They were upset that I had hinted I would use a leading knight's predilection for erotic imagery against him in the college where he preaches.'

'You were blackmailing him,' said Dora.

Percy waved that away. 'Such a crude description of a delicate negotiation. However, they accepted my full confession and apology, then chose to turn my skills to their advantage. They share my goals, but for their own reasons. It turned out to be a gift as I could play reluctant schemer and team up with one of Elgin's own people. Brooking was already a knight. He loved the marbles but only in a private collection. He had become disillusioned with Elgin's plans to sell the marbles to the government.'

'Thus making them the centrepiece of British cultural identity,' said Jacob.

Percy nodded. 'He showed me the accounts. Elgin can no longer afford them. It is only a matter of months before he looks to someone to lift the burden from him.'

'It won't be the French that he sells them to.'

'He might not have asked too closely who was stumping up the money for him – the man can barely afford to keep oil in the lights of his house on Park Lane. He is washed up. I had buyers ready.'

'If that is so, why not wait until he is desperate – why steal the horse's head tonight?'

'All these questions – so fatiguing!' Percy closed his eyes and pressed his hand to his forehead. 'Because, because, because.'

'Because, Jacob, you'd exposed him as the French envoy in Athens,' said Dora, moving to stand beside him, 'because he had to leave and wasn't certain of his welcome in Paris, because taking such a prized piece as the head might've been enough to win back some favour from Denon.'

'Stolen from under the noses of the British – the emperor would like that,' agreed Percy. 'You are such a beautiful, intelligent woman, Dora. I wish we'd met in different circumstances.'

Dora smiled, her lips curved in a sharp line that should have been a warning. 'Think you would have stood a chance?'

'In my dreams I did.'

'The marbles don't belong to the French, either,' muttered Dimitra.

'Oh, you Greeks,' said Percy dismissively. 'The marbles are like pawns on the chessboard of power. Greece isn't even playing in this game.'

'We will do one day,' she countered.

'Let's not argue this now. Tell us about the book,' said Jacob.

'Ah, that damn book,' said Percy grimly. 'Smuggled in with brandy and lace, and out with Indian spices and newspapers, each time in new binding.'

'We guessed that the order of prints matches a key you hold.'

'Then you have guessed correctly – but don't ask for the key. That, my conscience will not allow me to divulge. They won't use that method again, so it is no matter you know.'

'And what were your last orders?'

'When the print *The Connoisseurs* is placed first, my time is up. I thought that meant I was required to return to France but the attack in Berwick told me that others in the French service had decided I was no longer required on Earth.'

'Making it all the more imperative that you had something to bargain with on your return.' Jacob nodded to the sack.

'But why kill you? Why not send you somewhere else to flatter the Tsar or an Austrian duke?' asked Dora.

'Because, my dear, I am not trusted in the Ministry of Security.

I really do have émigré parents. I have always been asked to prove myself. It is even worse now. Loyalties are continually changing in Paris. Look at Marshal Bernadotte, once the emperor's loyal general, now the Swedish king fighting against us. No one in Napoleon's regime is as secure as we would like to think.'

'And whom do you serve?' probed Jacob.

'Me?' Percy looked thoughtful. 'In truth, I think I serve history. *Temporis Vtrivsqve Vindex*. It was my misfortune to be born at a time of war. I would much prefer to be like your Mr Fisher, poking about old ruins making monographs only three people will read. Yes, that would've been the life for me. I'm sorry I gave him a scare tonight. He seems a decent sort.'

Jacob very much doubted Percy was sorry. A master of deception, Percy even deceived himself.

'Who shall we take him to?' asked Dora. 'This is beyond what the Bow Street Runners normally deal with. The magistrate?'

'I think we should—'

But his reply was cut off when Alex hurried into the cabin and thrust a note into Dora's hand.

'This just came,' said Alex. 'Kir has been taken hostage.'

Chapter Forty-Three

Dora's hand shook as she took the note. She had thought Kir was safe, left tucked up in the office with Lady Tolworth's staff within call. He'd been asleep when they'd left – or had that just been pretence? She should have checked, because she should know the boy better than that by now. If Kir thought she was going to be in danger – and the guns would've suggested as much – he would probably have tried to follow them. They hadn't hidden their destination when they had been talking in low voices.

They'd taken their eye off him and he'd wandered directly into trouble.

I have something that belongs to you, wrote Philippe Fleury.

> *France does not fight wars with children. Tell that to Kir's sister, thought Dora. I will return your lost item in exchange for Michel Percy and what he took this evening from Lord Elgin. Meet me in the Great Hall of the Egyptian Building on Piccadilly at midnight. Bring Percy and no one else. If you deviate from these instructions in any item, the boy will suffer.*

He signed the note with an F, which could have stood for France or his surname, or perhaps both. This secret war between the nations was ugly. She hated it so much she was quivering with rage. She refused to think of it as fear.

'They have little Kir?' asked Dimitra.

'Yes.' Dora thrust the note at Jacob. 'Fleury.'

'What does he want?' asked Percy.

'You – and that.' She toed the sack. 'We two are to go alone.'

'He'll kill us both and probably the boy, too, unless he is feeling sentimental and lets Kir go free.'

'I'm not stupid. Of course there is no simple exchange. He wouldn't get away, not without more hostages.' Dora looked down at the sack again, a misshapen vaguely round lump. 'He doesn't know what you took, does he?'

'What makes you say that?'

'You have one working arm and I can't carry that on my own. How are we supposed to bring it to him?'

'It doesn't matter. I'm not going so there will be no exchange.'

'You'll go,' said Dora.

'You, *mademoiselle*, cannot drag me there alone, and if others come with you, he will slit the boy's throat and flee.'

'What a coward,' said Dimitra.

'I am merely being prudent.'

Oh, no, Percy wasn't going to get away with responsibility for this. 'You'll go,' said Dora, 'because under your careless act, there is the ruins of a man of honour. We just need to dig it out of you.'

'Dora,' said Jacob softly, 'you can't go, either. We'll get footmen from Lady Tolworth's, surround the place and storm it.'

Percy scoffed. 'Fleury might be a sledgehammer when subtler tactics would have been better, but he is an experienced agent. He will have watchers. You won't get within yards of the place before he knows how many you are.'

They had underestimated the craft of these French agents

already tonight. She wasn't going to make that mistake again. It was time to get ahead of them and not trip along behind.

'Do you know what the Egyptian Hall is like inside?' asked Dora.

'He's probably been using it as a base. An empty but almost complete public building is a good place to hide,' said Percy. 'No servants to interfere. Tell the labourers you are meant to be there and they wouldn't question a gentleman.'

'I don't know if Bullock has moved in any exhibits yet,' added Jacob. 'It could be wide open, or with many places to hide. I'm sorry.'

'Sorry?' said Dora.

'Ironically, I could've gone earlier but turned Fisher down.'

'Will he know?'

Jacob's expression lightened. 'Yes, by George, he said he'd seen the plans.'

Elements of her rescue plan began to fall into place. 'Let's gather our people together at The Shakespeare's Head. That's close enough to plan this.'

Percy huffed. 'And yet, here I lie, a ruin, as unexcavated as a pharaoh in his hidden tomb.'

The weasel! 'Then let me crack open your pyramid. What are you, Michel?' asked Dora.

'Ooh, first names. I knew you would warm to me.'

She waved that away. If she was going to ask a man to risk his life, she could at least cede that ground to him. 'Are you not a scholar of classical culture? Is that not what you have dedicated your life to prize?'

'*Mais oui.*'

'Then why do you admire my ancestors?' asked Dimitra, standing beside Dora. 'Is it not for their ideals – the bravery of Hector and the cleverness of Athena?'

'I think that is what we called a loaded dice of a question. But do go on. This is most entertaining – two beautiful ladies pleading with me.'

'It takes bravery to work undercover in enemy territory, so I refuse to think you have no courage. Are you not on the side of an innocent child rather than the man sent to kill you?' Dora kept her tone calm though she itched to turf him out of his hammock.

'Indeed, notionally I am on your side, but sadly that isn't enough to overrule my desire to preserve my life.'

'He's hopeless,' said Dimitra turning away.

Dora wasn't about to give up.

'Fair enough, but this is the only way you can save your own skin. What is the penalty for being exposed as an enemy agent, Jacob?'

'Death,' said Jacob quietly.

'I was hoping for a prisoner exchange,' said Percy.

She had to cut off that hope. 'Is that likely if they hear you let a child die because you didn't lift a finger to save him – and believe me, I will testify very movingly to that effect. And I wouldn't even be acting.'

A flicker of worry passed across his face, but he regrouped. 'A street child.'

'The orphaned son of a British officer. Adopted by Dr Sandys, son of Viscount Sandys.'

Percy glanced at Jacob. 'You've adopted him?'

'It looks like it.' Jacob folded his arms, content to let Dora corner this slippery creature.

'So you likely face a death sentence and public anger,' said Dora. 'Dying at Newgate is not pleasant or heroic, particularly if the crowd is hostile. Trust me – I've witnessed it.'

'Then the anatomy men are allowed to carve you up so that you never get a decent burial,' added Jacob. 'I've seen many organs of murderers pickled in jars.'

Thank you for that lovely visual, thought Dora, feeling somewhat sickened.

Fortunately, it had a similar effect on Percy. His pallor took on a greenish tinge. 'Hence you are claiming that dying at Fleury's hands is preferable?'

'I said nothing about dying,' said Dora. 'We go. We fetch Kir. We kill Fleury. You then are a hero – that will count in your favour.'

'That's your plan?' Percy collapsed back on the hammock. 'For a moment I thought you had a real one.'

'Oh, I do. It just needs two elements to work.'

'And they are?'

'For Fleury to underestimate us, and for him to be curious about what you stole from Lord Elgin.'

Chapter Forty-Four

Shakespeare's Head Tavern

They were up against the clock but, fortunately, if there was one thing theatre people knew, it was how to be ready for curtain-up. Dora looked over their recruits in the backroom of the Shakespeare's Head tavern. Jacob was sketching a plan of the Egyptian Hall with Fisher's help. Susan and Dimitra were whipping up from spare cloth a hidden holster for her to wear under her skirts. Hugo and some scenery painters from Drury Lane, friends of Susan's husband, were putting the finishing touches to the little cart that Dora would use to transport the sack. Ren was keeping watch.

All they needed now was a lot of luck.

Percy sidled up to Dora. 'What about the book?'

Why was he so worried about that damn book?

'You promised I could have it back if I gave you the name of Stokes's killer. It was Philippe Fleury, as I told you.'

'Have you told us everything about that book that we need to know?' asked Dora.

'Do you expect me to answer that?'

'Here's another deal. If we survive this night, we'll get that book for you.' That wasn't exactly the same as handing it to him, but she wanted to keep him on side.

He gave her a long look then nodded. 'Can I trust you?'

'Let's find out.'

'Dora!' called Jacob.

She could tell with one glance at her lover that Jacob was not happy. He wanted to be the one to go in, but Dora had already told him that was impossible. Now the sketch plan was complete, he showed it to Dora.

'There's not much in the hall yet apart from a stone sarcophagus on an altar – Fisher says it is like an enormous trough. The mummy has been removed and will be displayed separately. Four large pillars down each side and a fanciful frieze all the way around but no balcony so I can't hide up there.' She brushed a kiss on his cheek in sympathy. That wouldn't have worked in any case as he would have risked being spotted. 'Thanks. I hate this. It should be me.'

'I know you hate it – and no, it shouldn't. Carry on.'

'Fleury is most likely to be waiting by the altar at the far end – it's the best vantage point, commanding a view of all the entrances, of which there are three, one on each wall, excluding the one behind the altar. That's a dead end.'

'Good – this is more information than I thought we'd get. I can visualise the stage.' Now she needed to plot the moves.

Jacob put his arm around her, telling her with the fierceness of his clasp what he couldn't express in words. 'As soon as you go in and we know he is distracted, we will close in, deal with any watchers he might have, and wait for your cue to enter. What is the signal? Have you decided?'

She pointed to the cart, loaded up with its lumpy sack. 'Trust me: you won't miss it.'

Percy paced beside her along Piccadilly, mumbling in French, nothing flattering this time, she was sure of that.

'Why am I doing this?' he exclaimed to the heavens as they approached the odd Egyptian façade of Bullock's new hall. 'Why am I following this insane woman into a trap?'

'Because it combines the two things you love most,' said Dora, again having to dampen down her desire to kick him.

'If that is bravery and selflessness then you are mistaken.'

'On the contrary, self-interest and the chance, if the cards fall right, to be a hero. Quiet now, we're almost there.'

The churches of the city began striking the midnight hour, each taking a different tone and slightly in disagreement as to when the last ding should sound. With the help of Percy's good arm, Dora bumped the cart up the shallow step. Thank goodness it hadn't been a steep flight or this would be over before they began.

'Be careful,' he said. 'You'll break it!'

'We couldn't have that, could we?' Dora was pleased she sounded calmer than she felt. There were so many parts of this plan that might go wrong and yet she had to proceed with confidence if she wanted to rescue Kir.

They entered the Great Hall. It was very like Jacob's sketch, but he had not caught the moonlight filtering through the glass dome. She would have to remember that. It felt like a stagey form of Egypt, something that might be put on during the pantomime. The illusion was not complete as the London night was too cold for Cairo, and the sounds outside of carriages and church bells too northern.

Someone uncovered a lantern at the far end of the room. Philippe Fleury stepped out of the shadows, Kir held in front of him, pistol to his temple. He made Kir put the lantern down several paces into the hall, then took the boy prisoner again. Kir looked unhurt. Fury rose in Dora, a dark tide that demanded blood in payment for the hurt done to the innocent. Oh, yes, Fleury had summoned the Eumenides. He just didn't know it yet.

'Miss Dora,' said Kir. 'I'm sorry.'

'Hush,' she said gently. 'This isn't your fault.'

'Your damn pup tried to stab me!' growled Fleury, showing a shallow cut on the back of one hand.

'Philippe, this is very bad of you,' said Percy in French, speaking in his way of making light of serious matters. 'Taking children hostage, threatening ladies. You will earn Frenchmen an ungallant reputation.'

Fleury ignored him. 'Miss Dora, take off that coat and turn in the lamp light where I can see you. You, too, Percy. Take your arm out of that sling and turn out your pockets.'

As expected, he was wanting to see that his potential hostages were unarmed. Dora slipped out of the great coat and spun as requested. Percy shook out the empty sling.

'See, we are quite defenceless,' said Percy. 'Now will you let the child go?'

Fleury deigned to look at him this time. 'What did you take from Lord Elgin's exhibition?'

'A fine horse's head. It is very heavy, so we had to improvise.' Percy waved at the cart.

'Good. That will be welcome in Paris. Push it nearer to me.'

'Only if you let go of Kir,' said Dora.

'I've a better idea,' snarled Fleury. 'You come to me and fetch him. Percy, you stay where I can see you.' Was he intending to kill Percy and take her and Kir with him? He probably thought he couldn't manage three, but believed a woman and a child would be easily cowed.

'Very well.' Dora gave Percy a look, warning him that they were almost at the point they'd discussed – the point where action could not be delayed. She pushed the cart under the dome where the light was strongest and carried on walking, hands up. Fleury shoved the boy to her. She gathered Kir into her skirts, feeling the little bird bones quivering with terror under her hands. Fleury gestured to her to move further back.

'Stand there while I check you haven't double-crossed me. Percy, open that sack.'

No, no, no, no – that couldn't happen. Percy had to stay put. Dora began to see her lovely scheme falling apart.

Percy moved to the cart. What was he doing? This wasn't the plan!

He fumbled and cursed. 'I do apologise, Philippe, but your attempt on my life has put one arm out of action as you see. I cannot undo the twine.'

Ah – clever!

Frustrated, Fleury stepped towards him, knife out in his left hand. 'I'll cut the damn thing myself. You will then draw back the sacking and show me the marble.'

Oh, hell, this was going to be close – for all of them. Dora met Percy's eyes. He seemed resigned, even amused.

'Very well, Philippe,' Percy said. 'You do that.'

Fleury was keeping one eye on Dora as he bent down to the cart, swinging the pistol between her and Percy. Just as he bent to cut the twine, Percy dived across the floor, aiming to slide behind one of the pillars. Dora threw Kir up into the sarcophagus and darted behind it.

Boom! The spring held back by the twine snapped. Cartridges used for stage pyro-techniques fired, exploding the small keg of gunpowder hidden in the sack. Fleury gave an inhuman scream as his face and hands were caught in the blast. The percussion wave from the explosion shattered the glass dome above. Fragments rained down in a deadly shower. That was something she hadn't bargained for.

Kir!

With the glass still tinkling to the floor, Dora leapt to her feet. Kir was curled in a ball at the end of the stone sarcophagus nearest her, so nearest the wall. That had protected him. Neither the fragments of glass nor the blast had reached him. She hadn't fared as well. Blood ran down her cheek from a cut.

'Stay there, Kir,' she said, retrieving the pistol from her thigh holster.

A breeze now blew in from the dome. As promised, her signal had been unmistakable. Jacob would be here with Alex and the others any moment now. Stepping onto the scarred floor of the hall, she looked down at Fleury. He had died hard, first feeling the pain of the explosion, but what had killed him was the shard of glass that had stabbed his neck and was still sticking into the wound. The blood seeped out, but sluggishly. No heart was beating in that mangled wreck. Her fury was somewhat satisfied.

She looked for Percy and found herself facing Fleury's gun.

Quelle surprise, she thought sardonically. She raised her own. Percy was sprinkled with glass fragments and tiny cuts, but he had reached a pillar to escape the blast in time. The man's instinct for survival was admirable.

'I believe we've been here before,' said Dora. 'But this time we both have a gun and you know that my friends will be here shortly.'

Percy gave her a slight bow. 'I do not wish to hurt you, *mademoiselle*, particularly after so fine a performance.'

'Then what do you wish?'

'That in payment for my heroism, both here and in the carriage at Berwick,' his mouth quirked in an ironic smile, 'you let me go. I do not trust the oh-so-upright doctor to be so flexible.'

No, Jacob would not want to let the man off.

'You believe I should let an enemy agent flee?'

'You should let me, a man of culture and not of war, return to the museums of Paris. I promise never to emerge to bother your nation again.'

'But you have no marble horse-head, no book – won't they punish you?'

'Mademoiselle Dora, if I cannot make this débâcle of Fleury's into my triumph, then I am no agent. It is not hard to explain. He was a loose cannon on a murderous spree, killing off useful contacts for us French when he murdered the printer. Stokes was an asset we all used and will be very hard to replace. I can justify this,' he gestured to the ruined hall, 'and emerge smelling of the proverbial roses.'

Take him into custody or let him go? Dora remembered Bellingham on the gallows. Did she really want to attend another hanging, particularly when this man's motives were admirable if seen by the lights of his own country's interests. He hadn't killed anyone as far as she knew who hadn't deserved it. She lowered her weapon.

'This is your lucky day, monsieur,' she said. 'Run!'

Chapter Forty-Five

Her friends entered shortly after Percy made his exit. With a searching glance at Dora to see she was on her feet and relatively unscathed, Jacob rushed to Fleury's side to check if there was any life remaining in their foe.

Fisher ran in, bypassed all the human victims, and went to the sarcophagus. He hugged it.

'Thank God you survived!' he exclaimed.

Dimitra gathered Kir up into her arms.

'This little one needs to be taken out of here before the Runner arrives,' she said, nodding to the mangled body of their foe. 'He's seen enough of such sights.'

'Thank you,' said Dora wearily, brushing the glass from her skirts. 'If you wouldn't mind taking him back to Lady Tolworth's. Ask for Yarton and tell him what's been going on.'

Alex arrived at her side. 'You've got glass in your hair.' He picked out a piece. 'Anthony would've been damned proud of you tonight.'

Dora looked up at her brother's best friend. He had come through for them both tonight – reliable and brave. Fate had taken her beloved Anthony away, but it had given her someone else in his place. She had been so busy being angry with Alex in her grief that she had forgotten to appreciate the gift he was to her. Someone who had loved her brother as much, if not more, than her. 'Will you give me a hug? I need one.'

With a delighted smile, he gently folded her to his chest and patted her back. 'So proud.'

'And I'm proud of you, too. I'm sorry I was unfair to you.'

'No, you weren't unfair. I should've made arrangements to send Kir back home that night. I should've thought more about the impact of my actions on you.'

'And I should not have lashed out. It was just that Anthony…'

'I know. Your brother could be an annoying prig sometimes.'

She gave a weepy chuckle. 'Yes, he could, couldn't he?'

'But we loved him.'

'Yes, we did.'

Jacob came over. 'Do you mind?'

Alex released her and turned her over to Jacob's embrace. 'I'll see to the mess we seem to have made.'

'And I must see to that cut,' Jacob murmured, tipping her chin. 'Is it bad?'

'No, just a scratch.'

She sighed and rested her head on his chest. 'Good.'

'What happened to Percy?'

'Oh, he must've fled in the confusion.'

Tensing, Jacob made to move away. 'We must alert all the ports.'

She clung on. 'Let someone else do that. I need you.'

He seemed to consider that for a moment, then hugged her tightly. 'All right. I'll stay for now.'

Chapter Forty-Six

Mount Street

Jacob was almost completely content. He was sitting in a fine salon after a good breakfast, Dora was beside him, and Kir was playing with Patch-demona on the hearth rug. The dog seemed to approve of the new name the boy had given him. William and Charlotte had listened with undisguised astonishment to the account of their night. The only shade on his mood was his recollection of hearing the explosion and not knowing if Dora and Kir had survived. That had been a difficult few minutes.

'When the dust settled, we sent for the Bow Street Runner Dora knows – Josiah Watkins – and he, at our suggestion, is now claiming credit for capturing Brooking and Stokes's killer,' said Jacob.

'Capturing? That's an odd way of putting it,' said Charlotte.

'Well, cornering. The explosion is being described as the desperate suicide of an enemy agent. I believe the government is going to give Bullock compensation for repairs and Watkins will likely get a promotion out of it.'

'I know you're a private man, Jacob, but don't you want the credit? You and Dora did such good work exposing what was going on.' Charlotte looked incredulous at their modesty.

'Working as a confidential agent, we are better keeping to the shadows. We already have too much notoriety thanks to the Hellfire Club investigation.'

'Such a shame that other Frenchman escaped,' said William.

'Oh yes, very unfortunate,' said Dora.

Jacob glanced at her. He had had his suspicions but...

'What about the book?' asked Charlotte. 'Do you think he'll come back for it?'

'Not if he wants to make good his escape. Besides I have it here.' Jacob got it out of his satchel. 'I apologise in advance for the contents, Charlotte. They are very shocking.'

'I'm a married woman, Jacob. If Miss Fitz-Pennington can look at them without an attack of the vapours, I'm sure I'll manage.'

She had been warned. 'Might I borrow your pocketknife, Will?'

William fetched what he asked for and the four adults moved to the table under the window.

Dora touched his arm. 'What are you doing with it now?'

'Percy's determination to get back this book must go beyond his fear that the message – one we can't read without the key – would be intercepted.'

'True, it was the last thing he gave up on before he fled.'

Or before Dora had let him go?

'And then I remembered that he said they rebound it each time they exchanged it across the channel. That's an awful lot of trouble to take to reorder the prints. Why not send a list of numbers so the recipient understands which print is first?'

'You're right,' agreed Dora. 'He had book-binding materials in his desk in Raith – I'd not thought anything of it at the time, assuming it was to do with his duties as librarian. Later, I got diverted from cutting into the book because I was so enamoured of my idea that it was a pattern. But did he have time to take out his instructions if they are in the binding?'

'Let's see.' With great care, Jacob slit the leather away from the marbled pages and peeled them back. It came away more easily than on a standard book, the glue not so permanent as was usually used by a binder. There, sandwiched between the board and the paper was a flat sheet of paper with tiny writing in Greek. The hand was unmistakeably Michel Percy's.

'Bloody Percy,' muttered Jacob. 'Pardon me, Charlotte. He not only took out his last set of instructions, but he's put his own inside.'

William handed him a magnifying glass and Jacob read off his translation. Dora grew ashen.

'He was a political agent after all, not just a museum man,' she said. 'This is my fault. Look, he'd been stirring up trouble here, pushing the influential men he knows to go to war with America – reporting on shipping in the Thames, reporting on the public mood after the assassination of Spencer Perceval.'

'I'm afraid so.'

'That … that scoundrel!'

William rubbed his chin. 'He does sound rather good at his job. He outwitted the pair of you.'

Dora growled – actually growled – at his brother.

Charlotte patted her arm. 'You can't do everything, my dear. Your boy is safe. That's the main thing.'

'And Elgin has his marble horsehead back,' added William. 'Excellent.'

'Much to Miss Mitkou's annoyance,' said Jacob. 'I had to stop her taking it home with her.'

'It's not fair – none of this is. I still think we should've given it to her,' said Dora.

Jacob smiled ruefully at his brother. 'Sorry, William. Dora is of the Greek party on this matter. However, I didn't even have to tell the earl it had briefly gone missing. No one will know that it went absent without leave. He was very pleased that we solved his case. He would pay us a bonus if he could afford it.'

Agitated, Dora stood up. 'I think I need some air. Can Kir stay here for the day, Charlotte? He's had a terrible fright.'

'Of course. Patch-demona will keep him company,' agreed Charlotte. 'I'll send him back with one of the nursery nurses after dinner.'

'Thank you.'

Jacob could tell that Dora was barely keeping her countenance. She strode out and he had to hurry to keep up. William gave him a look as if to wish him luck.

She was halfway down the street by the time he caught up.

'Dora!' he didn't know what to say about the marbles. They were never going to agree about that.

'I'm a fool – I let him go!' she exploded, her lovely brown eyes full of remorse.

Oh. This was about Michel Percy. 'I know.'

'I had him right in front of me and let him sweet talk me out of taking him prisoner.' She squeezed her hands into fists.

'I know.'

'I let you down—' She whirled round. 'What? You knew?'

He put his hands on her shoulders and brought her to a halt. 'Of course, I knew. You had your hands full, and he could've shot you if you'd tried to stop him, but that wasn't the real reason.'

'What was?'

'You liked him.'

Dora swallowed. 'Was that it? Not some high-minded reason but because I'd fallen for his charm?'

'I have to admit that I'm jealous of him.'

'Of Michel Percy?' she asked him incredulously.

'I heard the way you two talked. You were far more at ease with him in conversation than with me.' And it made him wonder if she would stay with him much longer. She suited him, but did he suit her?

She twirled her hand in the air. 'That was badinage – a nothing.'

'I can't talk like that to you, Dora.'

'I wouldn't ask you to. Lord, no. Look at the damage Percy did in London with his clever talk. Jacob, why do you think I want you to change?'

'Because I never feel as if I'm enough for you. You always speak of leaving.'

'I know – and I'm sorry.' She looked crestfallen. 'I'm a horrible person.'

'You are not!'

'I realised something talking to Miss Beamish – the old lady in Rose Street. You are already extraordinary, accepting me as I am and not demanding I change.'

'Why would I change the person I love?' There, he'd said it, and he refused to apologise for it.

Her eyes sparkled. 'And I love you for that. I was so busy asserting that I had to be independent that I'd forgotten how important it is to rely on others. But we all trusted each other when we went into the Egyptian Hall. Trusting isn't a bad thing – it's a strong and good thing.'

Jacob's heart soared. 'Yes, it is.'

'And you have changed, Jacob. The stuffy man I met in Kendal disdained the stage. Now you fit in with our crew of actors and cashiered officers, our bored dowagers and efficient butlers – just as I fit with you.'

She was right. He'd lost many of his prejudices against theatre people along the way – and become an actor himself on occasion. 'Does that mean you'll stay with me?'

She stopped and looked up at him, her earnest eyes searching his face. 'You don't hate me for my weakness in letting Percy go?'

He hugged her to him and rocked. 'My God, Dora: you went into that building on your own to save Kir knowing you might get blown up. There is no weakness in you. In fact, I'm mightily relieved to find out you do make mistakes. It makes my own more bearable.'

She gave a groan. 'But he outwitted us!'

'And we outwitted him. I'd say the scores are even.' He released her and offered his arm so they could take a more conventional promenade towards the park. 'In this conspiracy, we were tugging on just one thread in a vast web of spies and their machinations that stretches from Lisbon to Moscow. The masters in Paris are at odds with each other, fighting for influence with Napoleon. That pitted Fleury against Percy, and doubtless the same pattern is repeated throughout Europe with other men, other secret operations.'

'But why would they fight each other. Aren't there enough enemies outside France?'

'Of course. But if Napoleon wins the world, there will be spoils to divide between those who remain at the top. Get rid of the competition now and be promoted to minister, or general, or duke.'

'Or king?'

'Exactly. Knowing that, do you feel any better?'

She bent her head against his shoulder briefly then stood tall. 'Yes, I do. I'm sorry. I should not be surprised that we didn't defeat him in every skirmish. He is Napoleon's man after all, Europe's master tactician.'

'And we should celebrate solving our first official case for our agency, not thinking about our defeats. What would you like to do?'

She smiled up at him, mischief in her expression. Oh, he liked the way she was thinking. 'What do you have in mind, sir?'

They paused as they waited to cross Park Lane. Carriages rattled past, heading for a drive in the park where fashionable society wanted to see and be seen. That wasn't for them.

'I know. Let's visit some marvellous Greek marbles,' he teased.

'Let's not. This obsession for collecting is ruining nations. The bad blood it stirs up is going to be our curse in the future.'

He pressed her arm against his side in agreement. 'I've had my fill of collectors, too. But not of you.'

'What say we visit the new home that Yarton found for me further down the mews. I only saw it briefly, but I do believe it has a table that I can use as a desk.'

'Oh?' Desire warmed him. It would soon build into an inferno if they did not hurry. 'Now that is something we must definitely christen.'

'Who said he couldn't do badinage?' she teased.

Turning their backs on Lord Elgin's house, they headed home, laughing.

The author and One More Chapter would like to thank everyone who contributed to the publication of this story…

Analytics
James Brackin
Abigail Fryer
Maria Osa

Audio
Fionnuala Barrett
Ciara Briggs

Contracts
Sasha Duszynska Lewis

Design
Lucy Bennett
Fiona Greenway
Liane Payne
Dean Russell

Digital Sales
Lydia Grainge
Hannah Lismore
Emily Scorer

Editorial
Arsalan Isa
Charlotte Ledger
Bonnie Macleod
Jennie Rothwell
Caroline Scott-Bowden
Emily Thomas

Harper360
Emily Gerbner
Jean Marie Kelly
emma sullivan
Sophia Wilhelm

International Sales
Peter Borcsok
Bethan Moore

Marketing & Publicity
Chloe Cummings
Emma Petfield

Operations
Melissa Okusanya
Hannah Stamp

Production
Denis Manson
Simon Moore
Francesca Tuzzeo

Rights
Vasiliki Machaira
Rachel McCarron
Hany Sheikh Mohamed
Zoe Shine

The HarperCollins Distribution Team

The HarperCollins Finance & Royalties Team

The HarperCollins Legal Team

The HarperCollins Technology Team

Trade Marketing
Ben Hurd

UK Sales
Laura Carpenter
Isabel Coburn
Jay Cochrane
Sabina Lewis
Holly Martin
Erin White
Harriet Williams
Leah Woods

And every other essential link in the chain from delivery drivers to booksellers to librarians and beyond!

ONE MORE CHAPTER

One More Chapter is an award-winning global division of HarperCollins.

Sign up to our newsletter to get our latest eBook deals and stay up to date with our weekly Book Club!
<u>Subscribe here.</u>

Meet the team at
<u>www.onemorechapter.com</u>

Follow us!
 <u>@OneMoreChapter_</u>
 <u>@OneMoreChapter</u>
 <u>@onemorechapterhc</u>

Do you write unputdownable fiction?
We love to hear from new voices.
Find out how to submit your novel at
<u>www.onemorechapter.com/submissions</u>

Also by Julia Golding

The Persephone Code

Julia Golding is a multi-award winning writer for adults, young adults and children. She also writes under the pen names of Joss Stirling and Eve Edwards. Over a million and a half of her books have been sold around the world with best selling titles in a wide range of age categories, such as *The Diamond of Drury Lane* (children), *Finding Sky* (YA) and *Don't Trust Me* (adult). Her latest book is *The Persephone Code*, an adult puzzle thriller set in the Regency Period. She is also Director of the Oxford Centre for Fantasy which uses the inspiration of Oxford Fantasy writers such as Tolkien, C.S. Lewis and Lewis Carroll to inspire new creativity.

In 2019 she was writer-in-residence at the Royal Institution, the home of science. She can be found taking an early nineteenth century perspective on modern life in her Jane Austen podcast 'What Would Jane Do?'.

She is also a screenwriter, working on a number of feature and TV series concepts, featuring strong female leads.

Former British diplomat and Oxfam policy adviser, she has now published over sixty books in genres ranging from historical adventure to fantasy. Read carefully and you'll spot all sorts of material from her diplomatic and Oxfam careers popping up in unexpected places. She has a doctorate in English literature from Oxford.

www.goldinggateway.com

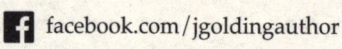